THE HUNDREDTH DOOR

CLIO GRAY

isbn: 978-1-914399-37-4

Printed and bound in by Ingram Spark

Cover Design © 2024 David McKinley Mercat Design. Images courtesy of Tate Images. All Rights Reserved

SPARSILE BOOKS LTD

The storm swept in, whipped the sea into a boiling fury, forcing the *Put Preko Mora* between Sweden and Sjelland towards the smaller Danish isles. Waves smashing into cliff and skerry, swirling about the ship's skirts, setting its strakes shrieking and shuddering, boards creaking and muttering, passengers panicking as crewmen lashed themselves with shroud-ropes as they pulled down the sails. Racing and ricocheting between Malmo and Amager before its captain steered it into calmer waters to wait out the night. Ship anchored, swung in optimal direction, when the storm strengthened, surged down upon them. Captain unworried, lamps of the lighthouses atop the Møns Klint glimpsing and winking to keep them right. Last of the sails secured, passengers commanded to their berths.

Only one disobeying, blessing the storm so fortuitously come. Donning his oil-skins, removing the plugs from the bore-holes he'd fashioned with bit and brace along one of the ship's sides deep in the cargo hold. Straightaway up top to where he'd secured his barrel. Quick sideways tug of the bowline-knot to free it, spare rope double-wrapped about his waist, and over the side to landward they went, decent length of line between the two. Shock of the cold extreme but barrel buoyant, tossed by the roiling waves towards shore, dragging him with it. And behind him his unplugged holes sucked in the sea, compromising the balance of the ship, fixed by its anchor. Weight of the incoming water pulling the ship onto its side, overwhelmed, inundated, irrevocably capsized by the wall of crashing waves falling like rocks. Ship pulled under within five minutes, subsumed by the storm-ravaged sea. Only external witness being one of the lighthouse keepers, who'd glanced outwards as he refuelled his light.

Went down like a stone, it did, as if God Himself had punched it from one existence into the next. People out there tossed about the surface like waterlilies. Nothing anyone could do to help them.

No hesitation nor remorse from the man who'd caused this disaster, hands crabbed as he pulled himself inch by inch along the rope tethering him to his barrel. Barrel and man cast up on the sands of Nyord Bay a half hour later, the only survivor.

Or so he believed.

Hadn't hung around to find out.

Divested himself of oil-skins, prised open the barrel, retrieved his booty, stuffed it into the empty flours sacks he'd stowed for easier carrying. Stole a few necessaries from a nearby lean-to, and was off. Long way home, and only one person who might offer help. Planning and preparing throughout the voyage, creeping down to the cargo hold at dead of night, cracking open the topmost crates, those from Kosovo. Smallest objects stowed in pockets, wrapped and deposited in his barrel. No worry of discovery. One cargo hold for provisions, another for the expedition's finds. No need for anyone to visit the latter since they'd got underway.

Couldn't take the lot, as he'd have liked, only those he could fit into his single barrel.

Leaving behind objects too heavy or fragile. Comfort, though, to know they would find another grave out there beyond the cliffs of the Møns Klint, never to be disturbed again.

1
New Places, New Pfiffmaklers
March 1852

Across the sea from Rügen came the Pfiffmaklers, Mergim newly christened Father of the Fair. Marvellous to Mergim how it had come about. Mergim released from Kragujevac Prison the previous spring; tracking the Pfiffmaklers to Rügen, where events more tragic than any of their plays had unravelled.

Mergim tasked to lead the rag-tags of the Pfiffmaklers into new territory, head forward instead of back, aghast to be given this duty of care. Mergim thinking hard on that duty as they were borne over the sea to the myriad islands comprising the Danish archipelago. Over four hundred of them, populated by folk who'd never attended a theatre performance in their lives.

Mergim looking over his small retinue as they prepared to land on the first.

Longhella and Diderik, as mismatched a couple as ever could be. Longhella contrary and vitriolic as a fulmar whose nest you are about to attack; Diderik, another ex-prisoner of Kragujevac, caught up in the events on Rügen where he had found Longhella. *A fate worse than death*, some might have opined. Not so Diderik, as overwhelmed by her as a snowstorm sweeping down a valley. Would love Longhella until he took his last breath.

Next were the boys, Lupercal and Jericho, Longhella's cousins. And Ortwin, a small misshapen lad they'd picked up on Rügen.

Last of all, and first of all, was Hulde.

The girl Mergim had travelled the length of Europe to find.

A girl, a young woman now, for whom Mergim would have swallowed the world piece by piece, rock by rock, if needed. Would have harrowed hell for her, walked the earth until his boots fell apart at the seams, and the next pair and the next. Would have carried on until he'd dropped.

And would do anything for her now she was found.

The one thing he couldn't do was summon back Heraldo, Hulde's putative parent since she was a child. Mergim wondering where Heraldo was. When and how he would return to them.

§

First couple of months spent finding their feet, gathering information, planning a long-term route, getting to grips with the language. Scraping by with puppet shows and sketches requiring minimal dialogue; storylines guided by visual theatre, the acrobatics Lupercal and Jericho were experts at, adapting local songs to include some of the weirder instruments Heraldo had left, of which Hulde was the undisputed aficionado.

All a bit boggling to Mergim, still learning what it was to be a Pfiffmakler, what was expected of him. As worried as the waves as the boat took them the short distance from Falster to the Island of Møns where their performances would change, move up a notch, become more relevant. Ortwin inadvertently providing their way after several weeks of barely passing muster. Ortwin suggesting the idea of performing Hans Christian Andersen tales, every Dane knowing the name of their national author, if not the specifics of his tales.

Hulde coming up beside Mergim as the boat hove to.

'I don't think I'm ready,' Mergim whispered. 'I don't know anything about this fairs' stuff. I don't even know why I'm here.'

Hulde smiling, taking his large rough hand in her own. A terribly tangled line tying the two of them together. Forgiveness so much more than Mergim believed he'd earned.

'You'll do grand,' she said. 'I'll make sure of it.'

Mergim's heart about to burst like a bud into its new florescence under the sun of Hulde's reassurance.

'You don't think our Comet tale is a bit cobbled together?'

Hulde laughing softly.

'Cobbling together is what we Pfiffmaklers do. You'll learn, as did I.'

As would Diderik and Ortwin, and Mergim too.

2
Hedgehogs In The Sky

Above the salt meadows of Nyord, a gibbous-moon hung hammocked in the night sky several days short of full, streaming a bright path across the placid sea. Jochen Steggle steadying the legs of his tripod into the short strip of sandy shingle below the dunes. Once secured, he lifted his telescope from his cart, slotted it into place. Adjusted lens and mirrors. Turned one knob and another, raising it to its calculated elevation.

Stars a riot above him. Milky Way curving over the Earth like a protecting hand.

A ritual he observed every dark clear night since he'd been on the island, hoping for a sight of the comet he'd witnessed thirty odd years before or, less likely, the small black dot of Venus travelling across the face of the coming morning's rising sun. The rarest of predictable astronomical events occurring every two-hundred and twenty, maybe thirty or forty, years. Last definitive sighting being 1639, so had to be a chance.

No transit of Venus or comet materialising during all his years of looking, yet Jochen was never disappointed. Gloried in meteor showers: the Perseids in August, Ursids at the end of year. Quadrantids the first of the new. Quadrantids this past January one of the best. Streaks of light dartling from the constellation of Gemini, too many to count, as if some cosmic hedgehog had chosen to eject its silvery spines.

Recalling a peddler he'd encountered years before.

'Purveyor of All Things Hedgehoggery,' the man had announced. 'Igel, Iritch, Arichi, to give it several of its many names.'

Dresden, that had been. Jochen learning how to create the wax models on which Leopold Blaschka based his intricate masterpieces of glass that graced the homes of the rich, populated the panoramas of museums across the whole of Europe. Medusae with trailing tentacles, translucent fish with all their inner chitterlings on view, sea-feathers, multi-hued corals and crinoids; deep-dwelling frog-fish, more vibrantly yellow than the glowing moon in this dark night, which took on shapes extraordinary—nobbles and protuberances, fins strong enough to walk upon, a skinny appendage it threw out like an angler's line already baited.

Natural curiosities unbelievable, unless you'd seen them for yourself. Like his recent meteoric nights. Hard to believe another would come so unpredictably on their tail and in so strange a guise, yet come it did, in the initial form of his neighbour—if half a mile down a rutted track could be called neighbourly—as night tipped into morning and Jochen began to pack up his gear, grinding his teeth as he heard Jansen approach.

Two cantankerous middle-aged men forced to find common ground by mutual need.

'Been looking for you for an age,' Jansen announced sourly, as if Jochen would be anywhere else, as Jansen well knew. Jochen grumbling internally as he carefully got his telescope wrapped and back in the cart, disinterred the tripod.

'Got back last night from the villages,' Jansen went on. 'Put your sack of flour in the outhouse, and you've a fair stack of mail. Near broke my back bringing it. Bloody letter writers. Never did understand them.'

'Why are you here then,' Jochen retorted, 'if you've done what needed doing?'

Ill-sorted men who didn't like company, settling on this neglected edge of Møns Island specifically to avoid it, if they couldn't completely avoid each other. Help needed, always given grudgingly, to haul up seaweed for their vegetable plots, looking after each other's livestock when one or another was forced to visit the villages, secure the supplies they couldn't procure for themselves.

Jansen newly returned from such a journey.

'Don't know why you bother with all that sky crap,' Jansen said, as Jochen began to pull his cart from beach to home. Jansen not offering help, merely adding an addenda to his previous complaint.

'No one in their right mind gives a curse about your little blobs of light up there in the night.'

Jochen gurning as he pulled his heavy cart, loose sand grinding beneath its wheels.

'It's knowledge,' he clipped, should have bided his tongue but couldn't help himself. Jansen was insufferable. 'No knowledge of the stars means no navigation, no ships. And therefore none of your rancorous tobacco.'

Jansen replying by stuffing his pipe full of his rancorous tobacco, getting it lit, blowing its smoke deliberately into Jochen's face.

'Know something you don't,' Jansen announced vindictively. 'Bet you can't guess what it is.'

Jochen didn't reply. Jansen wouldn't be able to button his lip, not when he thought he had advantage.

'Travelling theatre troupe's just landed on the island.' Jansen as predictable as ever. 'Saw two of their lads tumbling through the villages like human cartwheels.'

Jochen unimpressed. Had seen theatrics of many kinds in Dresden.

'Give us a bloody hand, will you,' Jochen panted, dragging the cart through a small break in the dunes.

Jansen smiling beneath his straggly beard.

'Sorry friend, can't oblige. Just dragged me own cart, if you mind, and me back's howling like a bitch. All that sodding paper.'

As if Jochen's mail could have weighed more than their sacks of flour.

Jansen rolling his shoulders, stretching his back to prove the point.

'Haven't told you the best part,' he said. 'They're going to do an Andersen tale, a moonlit performance.'

Jochen's interest piqued despite himself. A moonlit performance—he'd never heard the like.

'Knew that would get you going,' Jansen cackled, coughing and choking on his smoke. 'Bet you'll never guess which one.'

Not wanting to be beaten Jochen spooled various titles through his head, given the time of year. Most likely *The Snow Queen*, Andersen's most famous tale to date, begun in Dresden in the mid-1840s, a city he'd loved. Jochen by then long gone, but knew, like every respectable citizen of Dresden its opening lines.

All right then, we will start the story. And when we reach its end we will know so much more than we do now.

Gave his guess, irritated beyond measure when Jansen blew another stink of smoke his way, had the temerity to slap Jochen on the back whilst Jochen was bent almost double as he cleared the dunes and came out the other side.

'So predictable, our ever so intellectual Mr Steggle,' Jansen sighed, Jochen stumbling at the slight. 'And, as usual, our Mr Steggle couldn't be more wrong.'

Jochen dropping the handles of his cart, squaring up to his companion.

'No need to have a heart attack,' Jansen said, taking a few smart steps backwards, clamping his pipe-stem with his teeth, holding up his hands. 'It's *The Comet*. That's what they're doing. Got to be right up your street.'

And right up Jochen Steggle's street it was.

Had come right up his street and started hammering on his door.

All right then, we will start the story.

3

Prognostications

Desolate is this land in which we live. Snow glares all around us, black-shot scrub leaning wearily with the wind wondering who stole its leaves again this year, left their branches long-johned in ice.

Too poetic, Othmar Voort thought as the leeches lipped their way up the glass of his Tempest Prognosticator. A little further up and a hammer would fall upon the bell, meaning another storm was on its way, the third this year, and this year only a few months old. Nothing to look forward to but more of the same.

Days like this, he thinks of his rusty old gun locked inside his travelling chest lying at the bottom of the Baltic Sea. Another storm, another day, which stole from him the patchwork quilt his sister had laboured over for seven years, and the silver locket protecting the curl of hair he'd snipped from Irmgaard Prögen, the girl he'd loved and lost in his youth.

Loved and lost too were all the artefacts he'd assiduously collected on the expedition meant to make his name. All ruined now: quilt, locket, artefacts. And the rusty gun he knew he'd never have had the courage to use.

Everything gone, including his reputation, by the sinking of that ship.

Othmar Voort publicly shamed and humiliated because of it, he the sole survivor.

Sabotage mooted. The implication he'd been responsible for the wrecking in the first place. His Prussian parentage on his mother's side eclipsing his loyalty, assuming he'd destroyed his discoveries rather than hand them over to the Danish Crown.

As if Othmar Voort would ever do such a thing.

Hard days and nights Othmar's lot ever since. Sketching all the artefacts he could remember that no one would ever see. Writing obscure papers on their provenances no one would ever read.

Prussia and Denmark arguing over scraps, who owned this or that parcel of land.

Three battles fought in the little hamlet of Dybbøl on the south-eastern extremity of Jutland these past few years. None ending decisively. Danes making plans to build a line of fortifications across the land: ten redoubts connected by earthworks stretching from the headland of Als Sund, going north through Dybbøl and all the way to the sea.

Experts brought in to advise.

One of those experts come knocking on Othmar's door.

'My name is Grettir Wyssling. I only ask half an hour of your day.'

Half an hour of Othmar's day become a day entire after Othmar had brought the man in. Grettir explaining how, when the fortification plans went ahead, Othmar's home would be ploughed under. Recompense, naturally, from the Danish government to have him relocated. Grettir Wyssling apologetic, but advised Othmar to take full advantage to shift himself to a place he would rather be. Othmar's hands shaking as he took in the news. Could not contemplate going anywhere. This his home, his retreat, to where he'd returned after the sinking of the ship had sunk with it his scholarly life.

Leaving was unthinkable.

Had to excuse himself on the pretext of fetching a small bottle of schnapps to deal with the shock. Grettir Wyssling affecting not to notice how pale his host's face had become, how wet his eyes. Keeping his silence. Had visited many homesteads during the previous days. Without exception their inhabitants had perked up, enquired how much compensation would be due, where they might be rehomed and re-established, eager and excited by the prospect.

Grettir saddened this man did not feel the same.

Othmar Voort gone for a long time.

Grettir studying the room, so different to other homes he'd visited. No accoutrements or evidence of the clutter churned up by family life. Scholarly and spartan; desk stacked with several small towers of books precisely aligned, an un-lidded box filled with handwritten papers, several large folios of drawings—one of which Grettir flipped through carefully once it was clear Othmar Voort needed time to collect himself. And what Grettir saw was surprising. Laid out before him were excellent and very detailed sketches of numerous objects, each labelled with the places and times of their finding, along with a short interpretation of what they might be.

Othmar eventually returning with a bottle and two glasses.

'I apologise for my absence. Please, take a drink with me. Your news has come as somewhat of a shock.'

Grettir shaking his head.

'It's myself who should apologise. I'm so sorry for bringing such bad tidings. Can I ask,' he went on, indicating the folios, 'did you do all these?'

Othmar nodded, sat down, poured out the schnapps.

'I did,' he agreed. 'I was an archaeologist back in the day.'

No need to tell his visitor how that had all come crashing down about his ears.

'Then we're perhaps not so different, you and I,' Grettir replied affably. 'My main line of work is usually canals, brought in on this Danish project because of my familiarity with the area's geography and geology. And I've often uncovered the unexpected. Things like this, for example.' Turning back a couple of pages of the folio. 'I've seen one of these before. This small-scale model of an Islamic vertical windmill. Quite remarkable. Originated as far back as the ninth century, and are so much more advanced than anything we've seen in the West from that same era.'

And then they were off.

Othmar explaining where and when his own example had been discovered, which was Albania, and how he was convinced that if the local inhabitants hadn't been so pig-headed about Islamic science, about anything the incoming Ottomans had brought with them, they could have taken strides over their neighbours.

Foe become friend.

Grettir visiting Othmar on several occasions to discuss Othmar's theories, offer his own.

Friend finding his new companion of such worth he advised a correction to the planned fortifications specifically to spare Othmar's home.

The two corresponding frequently since Grettir had left the region, once it became plain those plans would not begin for several years, indeed did not get under way until 1861. Grettir Wyssling imbued with new direction since he'd met this man with his books and folios, inspired by the way he lived his life. Grettir Wyssling choosing to settle at the foot of the Dinaric Alps, begin his great retirement project. The Islamic windmill in Othmar's folio the first of many working models Grettir constructed for what would become his Museum of the Wind.

Othmar Voort allowed to stay on in his home undisturbed, immensely grateful for all Grettir Wyssling had done to make it so. Othmar taking a new interest in his old excavations, all brought back to the fore by his talking to Grettir and the correspondence which thereby ensued. And in one of those letters he'd felt steady and bold enough in this new friendship to tell Grettir the entirety of the calamity that had overtaken him.

How odd, Grettir had written back, *that you were the only survivor of the wreck. A blessing from God, one must consider, despite all that happened afterwards.*

It never occurring to Othmar precisely how odd it was.

The single reason being how low-laid by sea-sickness he'd been the entire journey from Trieste, spending most of his time wrapped in his oil-skins dry-retching over the rails instead of working on his papers as intended. Out on deck the night of the shipwreck, too ill and wretched to hear the captain's command for all to go below.

Othmar thrown clear over the railings as the ship lurched onto its side. Oil-skins saving him, as did his barrel-seat coming with him, the two pushed landwards as the bow-wave of the capsizing ship hit them, shoved them close together, made it possible for Othmar to grab hold of its staves. Othmar not as lucky as the actual saboteur with his own well-made plans. Othmar pushed and pummelled around the headland of the chalk cliffs into calmer waters. Othmar waiting out the night on his back, boots trailing, wrists threaded through the barrel's rope-handles, fingers frozen into place.

Traumatised by his ejection into stormy waters, exhausted by his days of constant retching, Othmar, incredibly, had gone to sleep. Might never have awoken had not the occupant of a fishing yawl spied his barrel bobbing and gone to investigate, hoping for salvage, some exotic haul of spirits or salted beef tipped from the side of a ship during the storm. Disappointed to find nothing more exciting than Othmar Voort, barely alive, revived by copious cups of warm water liberally laced with a harsh spirit that had Othmar's stomach chucking it all back up again, which had the advantage of jump-starting his heart.

§

As the leeches lipped their way up the glass of his Tempest Prognosticator and sent the hammer against the bell, Othmar thought again on the oddity of his survival, and the oddity of how the ship had sunk in the first place. For it hadn't exactly been wrecked, not as he remembered. Had gone down without any warning, as if a kraken had come up beneath its keel and ripped a hole through the boards. Only minutes from the first cry of alarm until it was under, everyone and everything.

Looked like it were being sucked under, the lighthouse man had told the Board of Enquiry. *Waves were high, as was the wind, for it were a bad storm. But it weren't so bad they shouldn't have been able to outride it, not when they were at anchor like they were, and couldn't see no reason it went down so much of a sudden. Weren't nowhere near the skerries on which they might've torn their boards and on which they afterwards ended up. But only afterwards, mind. Not at the time, sir, oh no. That ship dropped like the belly had bloody well been ripped out of it, excuse my language.*

Sabotage the obvious explanation.

Othmar Voort elected villain of the piece: the only person on board who had the merest whiff of a reason to cause it, and the only person anyone knew to have survived.

Odd, in old Scandinavian meaning a triangle or, more properly, the apex of that triangle when the rest has been taken away, its legs hacked from under it.

Othmar Voort's legs well and truly hacked.

Othmar Voort the apex left behind.

Knew it hadn't been him who'd caused that ship to sink. Which didn't mean another hadn't perpetrated it, nor that the other person hadn't survived. Merely that the other survivor hadn't deemed fit to declare himself—or selves—to have survived.

New world order descending on Othmar Voort in this early spring of 1852 as he hustled through his notes, following the receipt of Grettir's letter. Shuffled through his memories of various colleagues on the dig, of all the people he had met and discussed his work with. Listing every name he remembered, what he knew about them. Eyes travelling up and down his list, adding in details previously forgotten.

'Goddammit,' Othmar muttered. 'You've got to be in here somewhere. Who are you? Where are you? And what in God's name was the point?'

No ordinary person would have chosen to sink an entire ship and sacrifice everyone on it for no obvious reason. Conclusion being that he was looking for no ordinary person, although person and reason there had to be.

Grettir right.

Othmar's survival an oddity entirely unforeseen. A happy circumstance providing the real perpetrator a scapegoat on which to heap the blame without further scrutiny. Othmar utterly incensed to have given up, let this untruth go uncontended.

Would not allow it to lie any longer.

Time to fight his corner.

Time to start shaking the tree, long-johned in ice or no, to see what fell out.

4

Welcome, Phantoms

Warm wax soodled in its amphora, rims hardening about its edges like the ice collaring the pond beyond the steamed-up windows of Jochen Steggle's home. A harsh dark hulk of blackened timbers scavenged from a ship wrecked on the rocks of a nearby skerry in a fleet and vile storm. Crew, passengers and cargo tipped from its boards, swept away by the cunning currents winding between the islands, dispersing them along other shores many miles across the strait. The bulk of its keel overturned, stranded on the sand, too high and heavy for the sea to take it the same way. The keel dismantled plank by plank by Jochen Steggle, hauled limb by limb up the beach over weeks. Old divots, bolts and nails patiently removed, replaced with new as he fixed the boards against his constructed pilings and struts.

The resulting habitat taking on the gentle curves of the old keel, rising like a bee skep.

The whole edifice, bar the large light-giving windows and the single door, covered with living turf, grasses flattened now by winter, crackled over with frost. Gentle skirls of wind to be heard moving through the marram grass and trees around the walls of the *Put Preko Mora,* as he'd christened his home in honour of the ship inadvertently providing it. Words painted in high and precise letters on its stern, hoisted and fixed at the entrance gate marking the beginning of his little piece of land.

Jansen mocking him for this grandiose touch.

'Think you live in a bloody castle? You're nothing but a bloody nut-job eking out your life with all the rest.'

Yet the moniker proving invaluable for his commissions and correspondence. Letters frequently arriving on the island and swiftly put aside for him with nothing more on their address label than: *Steggle, Put Preko Mora, Møns.*

So let Jansen laugh. Jochen could live with it.

Jochen rubbed his hands over the wax pots, undisturbed by the cadaver glistening and growing day by day on the large timber bench at the centre of his single room. Shelves lining the walls containing ceraceous body-parts: heads divided along the sagittal plane; moulded hearts, kidneys, livers and spleens.

Jochen a creator of phantoms. Anatomically accurate models used by students of dissection; intricate replicas of faces with removable eyes, teeth, and tongues; foetuses curled inside wombs; lungs within their carapaces of ribs.

On the table, a whole cadaver. Waxen nerves, muscles and sinews carefully laid within their waxen flesh so surgeons could perfect their trade, study the inner workings of the human body, without the stench of blood, decomposition or formaldehyde. The finished articles indistinguishable from the real thing, until you put out your hand to touch them.

Apprenticeship with Leopold Blaschka well learned. Dextrous fingers dipping deftly into pots nestled in the holders about the edges of his bench containing brushes, colourings, solvents, hardeners, scalpels. The tools of his trade. He glanced at the clock on the mantle, eyes skimming over a small clay object beside it: an empty-bellied box, its front a yawning maw, a serpent arching above, presumably functioning as a handle. An object disinterred from the sand near the stranded keel, with striated lines dug into its sides like an off-kilter chess board, gouged-out dots incised inside each lozenge.

Plainly it had a use, which he'd never figured out.

Jochen waiting for Jansen's early morning call, for the trip to attend the moonlit performance of *The Comet*. Jochen disturbed, wishing he hadn't agreed to it. Hated to leave his homestead, hating even more to be travelling with Jansen, the two pulling the same cart. Might as well bring a few supplies back from the villages with them. Jochen worrying about the animals who would have to fare for themselves while they were gone, including the goat who had a character as malevolent as Jansen's since its dam succumbed a couple of years before, and was not above bashing head and horns against the paddock fence until he had it splintered into pieces.

Why he kept the damned animal he wasn't sure. No use for milk, and its meat would be stringy and tough as boot leather when he finally got it slaughtered. If he got it slaughtered. Something about the belligerence of the billy so far staying the knife. An obscure admiration for its obstinacy, its unwillingness to give in to any tenderness offered. Quite literally trying to bite the hand that fed it morning and night, a look in its angry amber eyes that said: *Go on, man. Just you try it. See how far you get.*

'Waste of bloody food, that animal,' Jansen would say whenever he came over. Jochen nodding his head in silent agreement.

'Might yet find him another dam,' he'd reply.

Not that he'd tried.

The touch of misrule in that bloody-minded animal somehow life-affirming.

Leaving off his pots and cadaver to go check one last time his livestock were as comfortable as he could make them before he left. The goat glaring through the bars at him as he thrust in one last handful of kale, lobbed a load of turnips over the palings.

'I'll miss you too,' he said, as the belligerent billy snorted in contempt, started digging at the cold ground with his hooves as if he couldn't care less that Jochen was giving him gifts entirely undeserved.

§

'How are we doing?' Mergim flustered, striding towards the stretch of grass demarcating their stage.

'Everything's ready,' Hulde said. 'Backdrops up and on their rollers, Diderik itching inside his beard, bubbles primed, and Long-hella has actually learned her lines.'

'I heard that, you little toad!' Longhella slapping Hulde about the head as she came alongside, if only lightly. Longhella previously so diffident towards Hulde, so vicious. Rügen finally drumming into her what Longhella had never truly appreciated: that family is family, no matter how it came about, needing to be valued and protected. And Hulde part of the small family Longhella had left to her.

'We're all on our best pins and toes, Mr New Father of the Fair,' Longhella went on sarcastically.

Hulde now accepted, Mergim not so much. Longhella wary of all the twists and turns that had bought him to the fore. Still an unknown quantity as far as she was concerned, one needing to be tried and tested. Had fumed and kicked her heels against it when told the news: Mergim to be put in charge instead of she. Had fumed and fulminated, blazed and cursed, until realising exactly what would be needed of her if she took on the role.

Which was a whole load of headaches, hard work and planning she could do without. Sticking instead to her well-worn script of foul-mouthed agitator, contrary diva, refusing to admit others were better placed to do what she could not do herself. Diderik weakly arguing her corner. So weakly he might have been a reed bending over in a shallow wind.

Yet garnering Diderik into her fold a boon so entirely unforeseen Longhella could hardly believe her luck: Diderik younger than she by several years, and handsome, fawning hand and knee to her every command. Diderik so besotted with her he was worth tenfold the mastery of the fair. Diderik her perfect partner, as it turned out, her pathetic Odysseus to her commanding Penelope. She might not be Father or Mother of the Fair, but knew herself to be its star, in Diderik's eyes, as she'd never been before.

Time to step up.

Time to prove herself to any doubters.

The Comet on track, lots of lines to give and she was going to sing her heart out.

'Very well then, Pfiffmaklers,' Mergim announced. 'Prime the fire-pits. Lupercal and Jericho, get yourselves into the villages to tell them we're about to begin.'

'Think they've beaten us to it,' Longhella observed, seeing a bobbing skein of lights coming up the track towards them, the quiet murmuration of conversation gaining strength with every step. Mergim's hand going to his throat, fingers wrapping about a small embroidered portrait of St Leonard given to him in Kragujevac by a man who had unravelled a multi-coloured pair of socks specifically to create it, and others like it. One of Mergim's most treasured possessions. One of his only possessions. Leonard, patron saint of prisoners, having apparently done his damndest to look out for Mergim ever since.

§

Jochen and Jansen were at the tail end of the snake of village folk coiling up the path towards where the fairs' people had set up their stage, right on the edge of the Møns Klint chalk cliffs, a couple of miles from the twin villages of Borre and Magleby.

Jochen reminded of the meteor showers as he spied sharp glints of lights clustered sporadically in the darkness of the sea, hints of all the tinier islands surrounding them. Møns itself nineteen miles long, five in girth, Borre and Magleby on its easterly point, and more easterly still had these Pfiffmaklers chosen to put on their play.

Excitement welling in each and every person as they wound their way onwards, lights below them on the islands, lights above them in the starry night, their own lanterns and brands flickering as they moved, smelling of smoking wax and burning wood. Scents too of chestnuts cooking gently in a charcoal brazier hauled aloft on a wad of sacking on an elderly woman's back. And, as they arrived, they saw a square demarcated in the dark dewy grass by glowing pits of silvery flames periodically spitting out sparkles of gold, crackles of crimson smoke.

No doubts for Jochen anymore about attending, no expectation of disappointment after the high theatre and operas he'd experienced in Dresden. Thinking instead: *This is real theatre in the real world, and under moonlight.* How no one had thought to do it before was a mystery, for this was true magic. Jochen swept up with the rest as they chattered and picked their spots, allowing Jansen to drag him to the front, laying out a tarpaulin on which they could sit, unspooling a blanket to wrap about their shoulders for it was wicked cold, although thankfully there was no wind.

But oh, the moon! Like a bright face of anticipation up above them, urging its players on. No need for tumbling boys to tumble through Borre and Magleby, for Borre and Magleby were already here. Everyone settling, taking out secreted bottles, uncorking them, sharing their bonhomie around. Jochen leaning forward eagerly as a lute began to flutter out a tune, and a sweet voice soon joined in. Jochen smiling as he recognised the words:

I look into the distance and see, as from nearby, the moon and the stars, the forest and the deer. I see the world's adornments and they delight me. Oh mine eyes, whatever you have seen, let all be as it may, for it has been beautiful!

Goethe's *Song from the Watch-Tower*.

Jochen having no time to wonder about it, for next came a medley of tunes performed by a young woman on the strangest instruments he'd ever seen. Then two young men back-flipping around the stage in dazzling sequinned costumes so they appeared as flowing streams of light against the darkness of the night and, from a huge plume of smoke, emerged a huge man clad in black, his whitened face like a physical manifestation of the moon itself.

'Welcome all!' Mergim shouts out. 'We thank you for coming. This is our very first visit to your island so forgive us if we mangle some of your words.'

A few of Jochen's neighbours tittering as the word *mangle* was truly mangled. But forgiveness the order of the night. Never had any travelling performers visited their shores before. All prepared to be magnanimous.

'Up top of your white cliffs,' the speaker went on, 'and beneath the light of your beautiful moon, we bring to you a tale...'

Mergim checking his speech, the words he'd been given. Not so quick to adapt to new languages as the actual Pfiffmaklers apparently did every day of the week.

To applaud your national author, Hulde prompted from the wings.

'To applaud your national author,' Mergim got back into his spiel. 'We give you *The Comet*, by your very own Hans Christian Andersen!'

More smoke wafting over the grass during which Mergim dematerialised and, in his stead, emerges the backdrop of a painted garden, flowerbeds arranged in an approximate map of Denmark, their own island edged with gilt that glittered and shone, as glittered and shone all the faces in the crowd who recognised it.

That's Møns, they cried out, *that's our very own island!*

Old man Diderik coming on stage in his itchy beard, several leaps of Bengal fire rising from the stage-pits as he creaks his way to a small lectern on which lies a heavy book.

'I am an old man now,' he declares, 'school master, astronomer and historian.'

A quick dig in Jochen's ribs as Jansen whispers loudly: *He's you, Jochen! He's just like you! Got to hope he gets the chop at the end of it.*

Jochen ignoring Jansen as the old man waves an arm about him to reveal a small tableau of a patently poverty-stricken woman and her child, lit by a single wavering candle.

'I was a boy back then, the wick curling like a wood shaving…'

'Oh my!' the woman crosses herself dramatically. 'That's a sign bad indeed, means my boy won't live to see another season.'

Longhella at her piteous best, tears rolling down her cheeks.

Diderik shaking his wise old head.

'My mother a woman as filled with superstitions as a bee-comb is with honey.'

The boy, unperturbed, begins blowing bubbles from a small clay pipe dipped into soapy water.

Big and small, Mergim, hidden in the shadows, intones, *changing from yellow to red, from purple to blue, or as green as a leaf in the forest when the sun shines through it.*

How the Pfiffmaklers have engineered it no one knows, those bubbles growing to the size of blown pig bladders, iridescent as rainbows, all the colours described in Andersen's tale floating away over the cliffs like magical lanterns into the night.

'Oh my child,' the woman sobs, 'if only you could have as many years as you are blowing bubbles.'

The boy laughing, unconcerned.

'But there are so many, Mother, so many! Surely no one could have as many years as there are my bubbles!'

But behold! What is this? Mergim calls.

The backdrop changes, a shining streak appearing to be in the sky itself, right above the edge of the cliff.

'It's a comet!' shouts a raggedy, hollow-chested boy as he runs across the stage. 'It's flashing across the sky!'

Mergim's voice booming from the edge of the stage.

Everybody looked: the rich from their balconies, the poor from their streets, the lonely traveller wandering across his pathless heath.

Cue Jericho, wandering across his pathless heath, gazing up in rapt amazement, disappearing into darkness as we hear a loud rapping on the door of the hovel encasing the mother and her bubble-blowing son.

'Come!' cry her neighbours. 'You must come and see!'

Some say the fiery tail of the comet was nine foot long, Mergim informs, *others, nine million. People see the same things so very differently.*

'Hurry out!' the unseen neighbours cry. 'Do not tarry!'

And out go mother and child.

'Another sign!' the woman gasps. 'This one worse than the last!'

Joined by the unnamed traveller released from his pathless heath.

Sounds of thunder, zithers of some instrument so exactly representing the vision of the comet that many of the audience are now in tears. Jochen included.

'It is a sign,' the traveller agrees. 'One having as many meanings as the people who see it. Do you know of your Danish hero Palnatoke?' the man asks of the boy, the crowd audibly gasping to hear this resonance of their own history being brought to the fore.

'I do not,' says the lad. 'Do tell me.'

As the traveller does.

'He was chieftain of an island just like this, who fought against foreign invaders, forced by those invaders to perform a terrible task…'

Backdrop changing: frightened pale-faced boy running down a hill that has the appearance of the Møns Klint, if not quite so sheer. His father, distraught on the ledge above, putting an arrow into his bow.

'...to shoot an apple off the head of his fleeing child or have the two of them put to death.'

'That's awful!' cries the boy.

'Why are you telling us this?' asks his mother.

'I'm telling you,' the wanderer replies, 'because this is what the comet means to me: the history of our land, our islands. Palnatoke courageous, faced with awful choices, and yet does the right thing. Lets fly his arrow and hits the apple. Saves his child. Tales forgotten that do not deserve to be forgotten. Tales disappearing until one day, one night—a night such as this—they are brought back to life. Exactly as comets do.'

Of a sudden all is change and smoke, and Diderik is standing alone at his lectern and dulcet tones are coming from the lute again, and they seem to be back at the beginning.

'I was a small boy back then,' Diderik calls out. 'I defied my mother's superstitions and lived longer than any of my bubbles of soap. Sixty years I have been waiting...'

Jochen's heart contracts. It was like they were telling him the story of his life.

'I have a clock that does not tick,' the old man goes on, 'a piano I never play. And then, and then...'

And then, oh my! The sky above the stage has come alive!

There's blues and golds, sparkling colours rippling through the air, and the lute is going strong and Diderik grips his lectern as if he would drop to his knees if he hadn't its support.

'Then came the night of the comet's return! But the night was cloudy,' he says hoarsely. 'I knew it was there, but I couldn't see it. Days and days I couldn't see it. I thought my heart would break! And then, oh and then, the clouds parted...'

Rapturous knocking on his door, as before.

'Come out! Come out!' call his unseen neighbours. 'You must come out!'

'And I saw it, friends!' Diderik laughs. 'Sixty years later I saw that same comet! And afterwards my hands flew across the keys of my ill-tuned piano as I played minuets and psalms and gay little songs I thought I had forgotten.'

Cue minuets, psalms and gay little songs from the wings. Longhella singing in accompaniment:

So many a rock and reef has the sea so wild,
So many tears of grief awaiting the innocent child.

'The comet came back!' the ancient schoolmaster declares, as it certainly does—backdrop swiftly returned. 'It flashed its tail of fire across the heavens! Was watched by the rich from their balconies, the poor from their streets, by the lonely traveller across his pathless heath!'

No need to mention how, in Andersen's tale, the schoolmaster is felled by the shock, drops dead after playing his minuets and gay songs.

Not at all what the Pfiffmaklers are aiming for.

Diderik instead rapturously holding up the heavy book from his lectern.

'And because of that comet I wrote tales! Tales of our history!'

He slaps at the book with his hand, riffles through its pages.

'Tales of Palnatoke! Of birds who move mountains, of leaves falling from heaven, of pearls born from sorrow.'

He speaks of hope, Mergim cries out.

He speaks of hope, Longhella sings, *reminds us how, on the darkest of nights, there are stars up above us and the moon there like a bubble blown by someone far greater than ourselves.*

'My name is Hans Christian Andersen!' Diderik is jubilant. 'It was I, the boy blowing bubbles! And my tales are my creations, sent out into the world, and this tale, my friends, has been but the first of many!'

More singing, more weird instruments, more firing up of strangely coloured smoke.

The company coming on and taking their bows to cacophonous clapping and cheering and the boys begin again their acrobatic light-show of tumbles, and pretty young women come amongst the crowd, still singing songs, holding out small pails in which to collect their coins.

Everyone eager for the next tale and the next, if more were to be had.

Which of course there were, for such was the Pfiffmakler way. And no better place than Møns to do a few practice runs before they head over to the larger island of Sjelland.

'We will perform for you again!' Mergim announces to rapturous applause. 'So be back here, friends, in two nights when we will have another tale to tell.'

Folk of Borre and Magleby unwilling to remove themselves immediately. So much to talk about! So much to celebrate! Chestnuts by now hot and cooked, cracked between the fingers of those quick enough to take them. More drink too, and more songs to be heard as the girls and the lute went on into the night as long as was needed. Moonlight above, village folk below having a grand time of it.

'Told you it would be worth it,' Jansen crowed. 'Can't wait to see what they do next.'

Jochen not so eager. Jochen thinking there was nothing could top this. Jochen having a strange thought as he looked up at the bright face of the moon.

Something he'd seen here, he knew. Something having significance. Couldn't put his finger on it. An echo of words he'd once read but couldn't quite recall.

Saw one of the young women returning with her bucket into which he, like others, had rightly put in a couple of coins. Saw her lift the flap of the tent into which she'd stowed her strange instruments.

Something there. It's something in there.

He couldn't shake the thought.

Headed back into the villages with the rest after another hour or more, Jansen getting raucous in the tavern.

Jochen sitting outside on a bench looking up at the moon, trying to figure why it fascinated him. Why it had fascinated so many minds greater than his. Thinking on comets and on pianos and clocks, and why *The Comet* tale had so energised and disturbed him.

Oh you Pfiffmaklers! You go to places you've never heard of. You shake them up, and then you leave. You put all sorts of ideas into their heads and then you're gone, without explaining any of it.

And Jochen couldn't stand that what was niggling at him would never be explained if they left without him speaking to them. Couldn't have articulated why or how, only that he would go back home with Jansen tomorrow morning—Jansen with a head as thick and tangled as a cocklebur with all the drink—and then would return to the Møns Klint for the Pfiffmaklers' next performance.

5

Suvid Calls From Afar

Quiet time that night for the Pfiffmaklers as they hunker themselves down after the rapturous reception of *The Comet.* Hulde and Diderik on cooking duties, Longhella having no interest in such mundane tasks. Longhella sticking to her own path, off earlier that day, armed and murderous, returning with several squirrels and an apronful of dormice whose communal hibernation in a mound of moss, between the outspread roots of an ancient oak, she'd tripped over. Their soft whistlings at her disturbance missed by most, not by her.

Not as fat as they would have been back in November; good enough for the Pfiffmaklers. Good enough for anyone on Møns, where fresh food was always in short supply over winter months. Sizzled in oil and honey, sprinkled over with salt and pepper, a delicious adjunct to their evening meal, and their slim bones, shucked of flesh and life, making excellent toothpicks and needles.

'Well done, Hulde and Diderik,' Mergim said once sated, 'for a most delicious meal. And well done Longhella,' he added quickly, seeing the petulant lift to her lips about to set forth a barb, 'for providing the necessaries. We could never eat so well if not for you.'

No need for Mergim to lie or embellish. A vibrancy to this particular type of cooking, relying entirely on whatever had been caught, skinned and gutted in the morning, cooked later the same day. Another advantage of the peripatetic life of the Pfiffmaklers he appreciated more with every passing day.

'And a very special thank you to Ortwin,' Mergim said, 'without whom our success here on Møns would not have gone as well as it did.'

'Pish and tottle,' Longhella admonished. 'We'd have managed fine well,' although threw the lad a smile that had him melting from the inside out. Ortwin never meeting anyone as magnificent as Longhella, nor believed he would again.

'Fact remains,' Lupercal put in, 'we've still to perfect our other tales. We haven't really thought them through properly, let alone got the backdrops ready.'

Mergim held up his hands.

'I know, lad. But we had to see how this performance went before we invested time in others.'

Mergim previously of the opinion this performance would have gone about as well as a goat tumbling off a cliff. Should have known better. Hulde's idea its making, to enact it beneath the moon, capitalise on the comet backdrop with the pyrotechnics seen against the night sky. Should never have doubted her. Had no place to doubt her.

Fine bright life replacing the old since he'd found Hulde, the world opened up to him as if the shutters had been flung back from a window. Hells bells, more like the entire wall had disintegrated, been blown into dust, revealing previously hidden vistas of paths wending away in every direction, new discoveries and joys to be found around every corner.

He could hardly believe his luck.

Heraldo, the missing Pfiffmakler wandering the pathless heath of his self-dictated pilgrimage, at that very moment believing the same.

One single month, after leaving Rügen and his family, he was back on Serbian soil.

Over one thousand miles he'd come: on foot, horse-back, a vast part by water. Far longer for the Pfiffmaklers to have travelled the opposite route the previous year with carts to drag, performances to give, money to be earned.

He'd none of those obstacles. Had youth and purpose on his side and was in his stride, having the easy ability to live from the land, his mandolin and his voice to earn a few coins when needed. And he'd luck too: the last days of January warm and wet, followed by a cold dry February, leaving the majority of central waterways open to traffic.

Only one aim in mind: to reach the strongholds of the cult of St Vid—or Vidovdan, Svetovid, St Vitus, however you wanted to call him—ancient God of the Slavs and of Rügen, and of Serbia and Croatia too.

The people he'd met on his travels, or rather those few to whom he'd revealed his purpose, had doubted his ability to get there.

'You're insane! That's a ridiculously long journey.'

'Not when your break it down,' Heraldo had argued. 'Twenty-five walking-miles per day means one thousand miles covered in forty, even if I have to walk it all the way, which I don't.'

Outlining the route sketched out before he'd left, putting to use the knowledge he had of all the circuits fairs' folk had travelled over the years, a route honed the further he went, taking the advice people gave him of where to go, where to avoid, the quickest ways from A to B.

Heraldo following the Oder River all the way from Stettin on the Baltic down through Silesia and Moravia, the Vltava River through Prague and into Cesky Krumlov. Short hop from there to

Linz on foot, back on the Danube to Vienna, and from Vienna to the Tisza bringing him directly into Belgrade.

Thinking, as he travelled, on the Knights Teutonic and Livonian who must have come a similar way to join the crusades. An entire army on the move, from every edge of Europe. An army coalesced, disembarked across the Mediterranean, getting to the Holy Land fit enough to put up a fight.

Not that Heraldo was looking for a fight.

What he wanted, what he craved and needed, was understanding and direction.

What had befallen his family on Rügen shaking out of Heraldo every belief he'd had about the certainty of life going on as it always had. For patently such was not the case.

The hardest part of his journey being the beginning, when he'd left Rügen, battling his way on foot, ploughing along dismal unfrequented tracks infilled with snow, pushing his way onwards through thigh-deep drifts. Remembered telling Hulde about snow years ago when she was young.

It's always new, every time it falls. It's never the same. Every snowflake is unique, has never been before, and never will be again.

How utterly joyful the two had always been on opening their tent flaps to find the world white and aglow after a silent recreation during the night. As white and aglow as Heraldo hoped he might be after completing his sojourn to the Dinaric Alps.

Reminded himself frequently, as he went, of Mergim's last words to him on Rügen:

What we did will always be there. It doesn't have to be our undoing. Look at me—the new Father of the Fair! I could never have foreseen it, not in a hundred years of guessing. No one knows what's around the next corner, so please Heraldo, don't let this be your last corner. Don't be the man who goes out into the wind and snow just so everything will stop. Leave it long enough and it will stop all by itself. It will stop and change, and it will get better.

Hulde a quiet prayer by Mergim's side.

'Come back,' she'd whispered, as she'd hugged Heraldo.

'I will, my darling,' Heraldo had whispered in return. 'Don't do anything bad.'

As if Hulde ever would.

'And look after Longhella,' he'd added, Hulde tutting exactly as Longhella might have done.

'You know I will, as she will me. This is a new age, Heraldo. A new dawn. All that's passed is done. Nothing to do but go on.'

He'd hugged his putative daughter once, and again.

And then they were off from him and he, not so very long afterwards, off from them in the opposite direction. Scratchy guilt to be deserting in their hour of need, same scratch of guilt pushing him onwards and away. Remorse and self-recrimination bad bedfellows.

Had regained some equanimity, some peace, as he went on his way alone—first time he'd ever travelled alone in all his life—and in the people he'd met, the places he'd happened by. The last, and most impressive, stumbled across when he was almost at his goal, wandering the foothills of the Dinaric Alps uncertain how to proceed.

Found a museum dedicated to wind-power of every stripe, shown about it proudly by its curator. Heraldo studying the miniature constructs of windmills. Cutaways, so you could see the inner workings.

'These here are the three main European types,' the curator informed Heraldo, 'starting with the medieval post-mill, where the entire body of the mill pivots around a single massive wooden post. Until, in the fourteenth century, we get the tower-mill, where it's only the cap on top that has to be turned; and next the smock-mill which superseded it, although works on similar principles.'

Laid out next to the mills were a hundred different types of caps and their attendant sails and sail-frames, all in miniature, able to be studied side by side, picked up and attached to towers and mills, small labels alongside describing ogees, stagings, fantails, fly-tackles.

On another shelf, a display of kites of all designs.

On yet another, various kinds of Slovenian *klopotecs*. Wind-powered machines going *klop-klop-klop* to frighten birds from the crops.

'Did you make all these yourself?' Heraldo asked, although obviously the man had for there were several more examples in progress on a work-bench at the end of the long room.

'Every single one,' the man answered, as expected. 'And don't believe that all mills do is process flour. They grind bark for the tannery dyes, flint for the production of chinaware; then there's sulphur, cement, clinker and chalk, sawing and splitting timber. Not to mention paper. But look at this, young man.' He called Heraldo over. 'This here's when I really became fascinated by all these mills can do.'

Heraldo following him, the man pointing to a small wooden type of mill Heraldo had seen only once before.

'Goes back to the ninth century,' he was informed. 'Friend of mine found a working model in Albania,' meaning Othmar Voort, still sitting in his lonely house on its lonely Danish isle. 'It's from the East. Entirely different to our Western versions. Has the sails set inside the tower instead of on the out. Wind brought in by ducts. Could have revolutionised wind-power if only we Westerners hadn't been too blinkered to realise its potential. And look at this!'

Taking Heraldo to a diorama encaptured in its glass case: a watery landscape of bog and mire, a windmill at one side, a crank handle protruding that the man began to turn when, right before Heraldo's eyes, the landscape changed into a habitable, hospitable place as the water gurgled away into some hidden reservoir and, at the press of an unseen lever or button, tiny houses emerged onto the newly drained polders, alongside even tinier figures of men and women who began to dip and work at the land.

'My masterpiece!' Heraldo's host exclaimed. 'I saw first-hand all you are seeing now. Travelled the length and breadth of Europe in my capacity as a canal engineer, saw all they were doing in the Low Countries and the fenlands of England.'

'It's marvellous,' Heraldo sighed, face pressed against the glass, trying to work out how this diorama had been engineered. Started talking cams and gears, spindles and flywheels, analysing the mechanics.

The two soon ensconced about Grettir Wyssling's workbench.

A chance meeting that would turn out to be the start of Heraldo's healing.

Grettir inviting his young student for a meal during which they carried on discussing mechanics and engineering. Grettir showing Heraldo his blueprints for an Atmospheric Turbine he considered might revolutionise the harnessing of wind-power to produce electricity by means of linking his turbine up to Leyden jars.

Grettir explaining how almost the entire country of Holland had been created by the wind powering mills to drain the land. Telling him too of the strange urn-field he'd come across in the countryside near Brabant during a canal excavation: burial mounds ploughed over hundreds of years before nevertheless retaining their urns in neat lines and rows over a vast distance, each mound containing a single huge urn in which the cremated remains of the dead still resided.

Grettir Wyssling seeing the dark shadow flitting across his young visitor's face at this mention of the dead, recognising the grief of loss when he saw it. Grettir winkling out of Heraldo the purpose of his visit.

'I'm not here by chance,' Heraldo admitted. 'I've come to visit Suvid mountain. I've come all the way from Rügen Island in Mecklenburg specifically for the purpose.'

Grettir Wyssling startled.

He'd never been to Rügen, but had visited Denmark a little further north. He leant forward, poured out more wine. Grettir knowing far more than mere canals and windmills. A travelled man who'd not stopped travelling once he'd retired and settled here to set up his museum; had climbed the mountains, knew them as intimately as he might have known his wife and children had he had any, which he had not.

'Well, well,' said he, 'then I might be of some help. The mountain you're looking for we call Zvijezda in these parts. On a clear day, as was the day when I climbed it a while back, you can see all the way to Kragujevac.'

Heraldo choking on the sip of wine he'd imbibed moments before.

'You know Suvid?' he asked unnecessarily. *And you know of Kragujevac,* he didn't quite get out.

'I do, my fine young man,' Grettir affirmed. 'I'd be very glad to take you up there, if you would consent to me being your guide. And you will need a guide. It has several peaks and is not the most accessible of mountains. But tell me, what is it about Suvid that has you in such a spin?'

And in a spin was Heraldo, so much was obvious. Heraldo blessing the chance happening of spying the windmill sails erected above this otherwise normal dwelling and had thought to investigate.

'Is there a chapel up there? Somewhere on Suvid?'

Heraldo's voice a strangulated whisper, his fingers gripping the stem of his glass, terrified the answer would be *No.* Grettir pausing, unsettled by the intensity bleeding out of this young man like resin from a wounded pine. Casting a line through his memory of the last time he'd been up there. Retrieving the requisite information.

'There is,' he said. 'It's boarded up. Not so many pilgrims, I gather, as there used to be in the old days.'

'But it's there?' Heraldo looked up, fixed his dark bright eyes on his interlocutor. 'And you can take me?'

Grettir not in his first flush of youth, but fit as a butcher's dog from all his climbing. Suvid formidable, a challenge to be relished. Visitors to his museum few and far between, and never anyone as engaging as this young stranger who'd landed on his doorstep. Grettir mighty curious.

'I will,' he therefore said. 'We'll set off first thing in the morning.'

All right then, we will start the story, and when we come to its end we will know far more than we do now.

6
Howling Into The Wind

Mergim spent the next day with Ortwin, ferreting through Ortwin's books, filleting the lad on everything he knew about Hans Christian Andersen, which was a fair bit. Ortwin taking out several letters from his grandfather, who had emigrated from Rügen to Denmark in his youth, carefully folded and placed within the pages of those books given him by that same grandfather.

'Andersen wrote loads more than fairy tales,' Ortwin informed Mergim. 'Lots of poems and some novels. One of them is about an abandoned girl who is adopted by travelling musicians.'

Quick smile at Mergim, quick smile back. *Hulde would love that,* both were thinking.

'Unfortunately I don't have any of the novels,' Ortwin went on, with a slight drop of his head, for he would have liked to have given that particular one to Hulde. 'But there are several of his poems in the letters. *The Dying Child* was always a favourite. Maybe we could turn them into songs?'

A grand idea, had Heraldo been with them. Heraldo able to compose a song out of several minutes of thin air.

'It sounds a bit gloomy,' Mergim responded. Children adopted by travelling musicians one thing, dying children quite another.

'Yet well known,' Ortwin put in. 'And if we coupled it with... well, *The Ancient Tree?* That's all about travelling, and the joys of returning home afterwards.'

Mergim pulled at his beard.

'I think Hulde could do it,' Ortwin said. 'She's good with the music and I could help. I know I wasn't allowed to sing in the choir.' His voice like the scritch-scratch of a night-jar, so the choirmaster had informed him. 'But I know plenty of tunes. I'm sure we could find something to fit.'

Mergim thinking it might just work. Mergim saying so. Ortwin up like a stoat shooting out of its grassy hole.

'Just give us tonight! If we can't get anything proper by tomorrow I'll never mention it again.'

Mergim amused, watching Ortwin skipping away with the levity and lightness of a hare.

Hulde and Ortwin not disappointing, presenting their two pieces on the morrow.

Hulde nervous, looking to Longhella for guidance.

'It's only a start,' she excused. 'We really, really need your to help with the descant.'

Longhella brushing down her skirts as she sat for the recital, irritated she'd not been invited to the first little meeting of skulduggery between these two waifs, yet straightening her back, recognising that with Heraldo no longer here she was in charge as far as their singing went, her adjudication carrying far more weight than Mergim's. Mergim acknowledging he'd cloth ears, hardly able to tell one tune from another.

'Begin,' she commanded, Hulde prevaricating.

'It'll only be a small part of the set. The opening, we thought, before we move on to...'

Longhella sighing theatrically, interrupting.

'Just get on with it, Hulde. We'll decide if it's worth a place once we've heard your blasted songs.'

'First one's *The Dying Child*,' Ortwin stepping heroically into the line of fire, 'followed by *The Ancient Tree*. The two kind of go together.'

Longhella raised her eyebrows, scratched delicately at her cheek. No need to speak.

Hulde getting her fingers ready on the lute, setting the first string strumming to provide her right pitch.

Mother, I'm tired, Hulde sang a little shakily, to the tune Ortwin had given her.

I need to sleep.
I know you too are sick and weak,
But please don't weep.

Another few verses until the child dies. Longhella grimacing throughout.

Hulde moving swiftly on to the next more optimistic song, expectant of Longhella ripping her to pieces like a rabid boar.

It's for the travelling roads I yearn,
Yet in truth one travels only to return.
For home is heart and heart is home,
No matter where one's heart has roamed.

Hulde's eyes downcast as she sang, seeing plain as day the objections pushing about for priority on Longhella's lips as she wondered which to let loose and which to let lie; and yet, by lowering her eyes, Hulde saw Longhella's foot tapping out the metre of the tune as she reached the last few lines:

And when I see that tree blossom-tall
I'll know that home I've come after all.
So do not let fall that ancient tree,
For that ancient tree is me.

Hulde stopped, blinked, closed her eyes. Heraldo in every breath of that last verse, that ancient tree, that wandering minstrel. Unable to raise her face to the inevitability of Longhella's critical onslaught. The onslaught not long in coming.

'That, my fine young intruders into our fair,' Longhella never shy with her opinions, 'was absolutely ghastly.'

Ortwin's face going scarlet. Hulde keeping her eyes downcast, the lute held loosely by her side. Mergim and Diderik about to argue when Longhella held up a hand.

'But, Pfiffmaklers all,' she went on magnanimously, 'it can be rescued. A descant here, a descant there. A little more instrumentation, some dramatic phrasing. And with me taking the main singing role I think we've a real shot at squeezing these islanders dry of every last tear and coin they've got left.'

'Hear hear!' Diderik agreed enthusiastically.

'It's decided then,' Mergim put in. 'The boys and Hulde to work on the changes under Longhella's supervision; myself and Ortwin back to the books to find another suitable tale to finish off with.'

Thank you, Hulde mouthed at Longhella, Longhella giving the merest dip of her chin in acknowledgement. The import of the Tree song and its parallels to Heraldo not passing her by, nor that Heraldo would have done an entirely better job than she. A slight frisson to the challenge therefore, knowing she would be judged by Heraldo's ferociously high standards. Might even be found wanting. But, by hell's teeth, Longhella would not bow down to that threat. Had always had an innate belief in her superiority and this not the time to be doubting it.

'I say we need two backdrops for each song,' she demanded, daring Mergim to deny her. Mergim, infuriatingly, twitching his mouth in his beard exactly as Heraldo's father used to do.

'I agree,' he agreed. 'Me and Diderik will see to it. If you've any specifics let us know, unless you trust us to get on with it on our own?'

Longhella momentarily nonplussed by his easy acquiescence.

'I'll give you bloody specifics,' she countered, with a menacing hiss. 'First do some sketches. I'll tell Diderik what I'm wanting, and you better make damn sure they're right or you'll have me to answer to.'

Mergim smiling outright.

'I expected nothing less, my dear.'

A mistake on his part, those last two words. Longhella taking a few strides towards him and poking her finger at his chest.

'Don't you ever *my dear* me again, Mr Newcomer. The second Heraldo gets back, and he'll be back, don't you fear,' *for home is heart and heart is home,* 'you'll be out on your cloth ears as Fair's Father, and don't you ever forget it. You can boss me around now,' not that Mergim had done much bossing, 'soon enough it'll be me and Heraldo bossing you, and oh my! What a joy that will be.'

Longhella stomping off to join Lupercal, Jericho and Hulde, who were already discussing how they could beef up the musical accompaniments to the songs, create layers and depth where previously there'd been only the lilting of Hulde's lute.

A timely reminder for Mergim, bringing to mind the unseen but definitive lines of hierarchy in Kragujevac. Top of the roost he'd been back then. An anomaly, a murderer who would be set free. A man who could deliver letters to family members of all the other murderers come his release, at least to those the inmates hadn't despatched. Stark years spent inside those walls. Stark years he wouldn't have missed for anything. Stark years making him what he was today, brought about the changes needed, introduced him to men who kept moths, made talismans from the threads of socks, and the mathematician who had explained the Birthday Paradox that had so confounded and astounded him.

The trajectory of Mergim's life, both before and after Kragujevac, more confounding and astounding to him than even the mathematician could have guessed. Birthday Paradox as anomalous as Mergim himself. The mathematician going to great lengths to explain to Mergim the nature of coincidence and randomness, how out of the twenty-three murderers in Kragujevac it was no surprise a couple of them had the same birthdates.

You've to tip the conundrum on its head. Think instead how extraordinary it would be if we all had completely different birthdates. Think in exponents, not linear lines.

A turning point for Mergim, teaching him to see the world from angles he could never previously have imagined.

Randomness is just that, Mergim. It's random. It has no care whatsoever about our human obsession with making connections, seeing meaning where none is to be had.

Like what had happened to the Pfiffmaklers. A series of connections and coincidences none of them could have foreseen, nor could have predicted where they would lead.

End result being Mergim pontificating over songs and performances of folk tales he'd never heard of, in places he'd never known existed.

End result being Mergim happier than he'd ever thought possible.

End result being Mergim harangued by Longhella Pfiffmakler on a daily basis, but goddammit, as Longhella might have said, the Birthday Paradox proving its worth. For here was Mergim, living the best of all possible lives against all logical and contrary predictions.

Time to get to the task in hand.

No real need to speak to Diderik, knowing well enough by now how Longhella would see her role, how she would choose the backdrops to her songs to keep her centre stage at all times during the recital.

And such glory in that simple task.

Such joy to be here in the world and have a second chance at it, with people like these.

Wouldn't begrudge for a second Heraldo taking over when Heraldo returned.

Mergim become his own tree, blossom-tall, and couldn't have done it without the Pfiffmaklers, or Kragujevac come to that.

§

Heraldo and Grettir were on their way, Grettir's backpack stuffed with food enough to fuel them for the two days it would take them to reach and ascend the mountain, and the two more days back again.

On the first leg they talked generalities, Grettir educating Heraldo about the outlay of the land.

'Our Dinaric Alps stretch four hundred miles unbroken, echoing the coastline of the Adriatic all the way from Slovenia through Croatia and Serbia, right through to Kosovo and Albania, where lie the worst of the peaks.'

'I know something of those,' Heraldo stated.

Hard black mountains, called Accursed. Cold dark peaks.

'Indeed?' Grettir enquired. Got no answer, didn't push. 'They're composed of sedimentary rocks for the most part. Dolomite, limestone, sandy conglomerates. Formed by the seas and lakes that once covered the entire area. Now, of course—who knows how many millions of years later—we're no longer under water and ice and have become a different land entirely.'

'Like your diorama,' Heraldo commented. 'You really are a geologist and geographer as well as an investigator of wind power.'

Grettir smiling, easing the weight of his pack, envying the way the younger man toted his own as if it had no weight at all.

'Canal engineering goes hand in hand with geography and geology. Detecting what rocks lie where and how they came about, what their nature is, in order to direct a canal working in the easiest of directions. That's why canals so often mimic the passage of natural rivers, for where a river runs so too can a canal, which is only a straighter more navigable version of the same.'

Heraldo nodding, Grettir's words making sense.

'Because of this geography,' Grettir went on, 'there's a tremendous and very specific wind pushing periodically through these mountains, called the Bora. It's dry and frigid, builds up under certain climatic conditions against the other side of the mountains until the air pressure is so high there's nowhere for it to go but down towards the Adriatic. Punches its way through various passes with tremendous force. Enough to knock down trees, blow over cattle grazing in their fields and drag them several hundred yards, rip the roofs off houses. Suck fish out of the sea, scattering them many miles distant; topple ships, covers everything in its wake with ice. It's a fearful thing to most locals, although we get many travellers coming to these parts specifically to experience it for themselves.'

Grettir pausing as he navigated several boulders strewn across the rutted track.

'Is that why you came here?' Heraldo asked, putting out a hand to steady Grettir who was rocking with the weight of his knapsack, having jumped from one of the rounded rocks.

Grettir smiling, straightening himself, regaining an even pace by Heraldo's side.

'You're very perspicacious,' he said, 'and yes, you're right. Wind has always fascinated me. It's so much more than the movement of air. Certain types of geography produce very local climates. There's one I experienced in England affecting a mere dozen villages in the Vale of Eden, coming from their own set of mountains called the Pennines. Again the wind builds up, not dramatically but steadily and, in certain conditions, when the air up above the mountains is paradoxically warmer than the air down below, it suddenly rushes down the steep incline below Cross Fell like a wave. And oh my! The sounds it makes! Sends shivers right through you. Mutters, moans and hisses, sometimes roars like a waterfall or rolls like thunder. When I heard it, I thought a dog must be being strangled around the next corner.'

Grettir laughing softly at the memory.

Heraldo adding to his thoughts.

'Lots of folk tales recount demons taking flight on the wind. Mythic beings for whom it's their natural habitat, suspended between heaven and earth.'

Heraldo sympathising. Feeling suspended himself. The Pfiff-makler life going on elsewhere without him.

Grettir regarding his companion with interest.

'You're knowledgeable about folk tales, then?' he asked.

Heraldo nodding, volunteering nothing more. Supposed he might at some point divulge his past, the history behind this journey. That point not yet reached.

'Then let me tell you one of my own,' Grettir went on undeterred. 'It has to do with the Bora and the creation of the Karst, which is at this end of the Dinaric Alps. A mean and harsh place,' he explained, 'scatters of rubble and stone above, riddled with sink-holes and caves beneath. Barely a plant able to grow more than an inch from the soil.'

He took a sip from his flask of watered wine, handed it to Heraldo who did the same.

'Virgil tells us of the god Aeolus and his land of Aeolia where the storm-clouds have their home. In a huge cave he has captured the brawling winds, fettered them within his prison, has them raging from door to door, buried deep within the mountain. They're furious and arrogant. They roar and batter, would have snatched up the land had they been released, caught the sky in their fists, swept everything from earth up into the heavens. Aeolus has a daughter. Her name is Bora. And, because this is a tale, she is more beautiful than any flower.'

Heraldo involuntarily slowing his step, cocking his ear towards Grettir, for here indeed was a teller of tales, saying it exactly as the Pfiffmaklers might have done. Thinking, for the first time since he'd left, on his return. And that he would return, and this needed storing up.

'She falls in love with a mortal,' Grettir explained, 'with the brave Tergesteo, an Argonaut returned successful from the seemingly impossible quest for the Golden Fleece. She loves Tergesteo far more than she loves her life of luxury and privilege, leaves the caves to join him. The Karst at that time a place of wonder, of pretty waterfalls, meandering streams, water so pure and sweet you could drink it all the days of your life and never tire of it. Flowers of such radiance and splendour they surpass the most glorious sunsets you've ever seen. Trees girded with leaves as green and translucent as emeralds. And they were in bliss those two, Bora and Tergesteo, for seven days and seven nights, in the most blissful place the earth had to offer. Her father not so enamoured. Her father in a blinding rage.'

Grettir lifting his voice, shouting out the words of Aeolus, brandishing his fist in the air, getting into the part.

'How dare a human lure away the daughter of a god. Brave warrior he might be, and handsome, but he has no right! No right at all!'

A sputter of sparrows hie-ing up from a nearby bush, twittering in alarm.

'I am the Keeper of Winds!' Grettir hollers into the empty morning. 'This mortal underling must pay for what he's done. I shall strike him dead, lay him at my daughter's feet! She shall weep and cry in her sorrow, and this land on which they trod shall become dust and rubble!'

Grettir stopped speaking abruptly, aware how loud he'd become. Heraldo twitching at his side, speaking into the silence.

'And so the Bora.' Making his own deductions.

'And so the Bora,' Grettir agreed. 'Her unceasing tears eat away the stone in which the winds are imprisoned so every now and then they can escape.' Grettir smiling weakly. 'I got a bit carried away there. Apologies if I alarmed you.'

Heraldo not so much alarmed as heart-struck, holding Grettir's gaze for a moment before lowering his head, loosened by Grettir's tale and how it had been told.

'There's something I need to tell you,' Heraldo said.

'I thought there might be,' Grettir replied. 'And it's to do with St Vid?'

'Sort of,' Heraldo agreed. 'It seemed to start with him and I'm hoping, now I'm here, this is where it ends.'

7

Spires And Speakers

Lupercal and Jericho were on an exploratory mission.

Ostensibly they'd been sent off to scour outlying homesteads and hamlets whose inhabitants may not have heard of their upcoming performance. Going inland to Stege Nor lagoon, cut to the coast, gone along the bay of Hjelm Bugt all the way to the lighthouse on the edge of the chalk cliffs. Giving to everyone they met their news, ratcheting up the excitement, doing a few free-for-all acrobatic turns in which they'd encouraged the younger children to take a minimal part: spacing them out, back-flipping over them in im-pressive arcs, leaping and pirouetting, pretending on occasion to fall and groan, arising a moment later to laughter and applause.

All part of the act.

First mission successfully completed. Nagging children making parents sigh and give in, promising they would attend the proper performance of these astonishing Pfiffmaklers. Promised in return by these astonishing Pfiffmaklers they would not regret it, would not be swizzled out of a single coin if they couldn't afford it or felt the performance unworthy of the cost.

Second mission now on track: to explore the headland of the Møns Klint, from where they could see all the way to the tip of Sweden in the north-east and, thirty-five miles south-east, to the island of Rügen from where they'd departed a couple of months before. The children they'd met on this brief journey falling over themselves to inform Lupercal and Jericho what they absolutely had to do was follow the thin pebbled shore-line beneath the beech-topped cliffs. Told they could get down by a set of tortuous steps carved into one of the verdant gullies spilling down the chalk-face like dry green streams.

'You'll get the best view of the cliffs from down there,' a girl piped up, 'and you'll get to see all the different parts of it.'

'That's right,' agreed her brother. 'There's the *Sækkepiben*, which sounds like a bagpipe when the sea strikes it just so.'

'And the *Taleren*,' another child intervened. 'The Speaker, we call it, because it echoes when you shout into it.'

'Don't forget the Hammers and the Queen's Seat,' another added.

'And you can't miss the Summer Spire, which looks like it's been carved out of ice,' said the girl, not to be outdone.

The gaggle of children surrounding Lupercal and Jericho effusive, eager to please, to be able to lay claim their acquaintance during the following night's performance. The entire lot would have accompanied Lupercal and Jericho on their peregrinations had not their parents shouted them back to work.

'Are you really going to dance under the light of the moon?' asked the girl, unable to tear herself away.

Lupercal smiling graciously.

'We'll be singing and dancing, and performing a little play too,' he explained.

'And there'll be light shows and fireworks, and instruments you've never heard the like of.' Jericho adding a touch of mystery.

'What's the play about?' asked the girl's brother.

'Ah now,' Lupercal put his fingers to his lips, 'that would be telling.'

'It's a secret,' Jericho whispered, 'one you'll only find out when you attend.'

§

Once there lived a prince who had a library far greater than anyone else has ever had, either before or since, in which he could learn about everything that had happened in the entire world.

Mergim practising his introductory lines.

Cleared his throat, coughed, got on with it.

But of the Garden of Eden they told him nothing, which saddened him, for it was Paradise that interested him most.

'How are you doing?'

Hulde come to check on him, knowing this particular tale Ortwin and Longhella had designed between them worried Mergim. Longhella obviously taking the main roles, the mother of her four recalcitrant sons— the four winds of the world —as well as the beautiful princess later on. Hulde solo music maker, Mergim narrator and back-drop shifter.

Mergim concerned by the many quick changes between his speaking and shifting roles.

'I'm getting in a bit of muddle,' he admitted.

'It is quite complicated,' Hulde agreed, sitting down beside him. 'But I'll be right behind you and will prompt you if need be.'

'I don't deserve you,' Mergim said quietly, 'any of you.'

'And you think I do?' Hulde replied. 'And do any of us deserve Longhella?'

Quick chuckle from Mergim and Hulde alike.

'We've all our places, Mergim,' Hulde went on, 'and at the moment this is yours and mine.'

Mergim took Hulde's hand in his own.

'You should have been the princess in this story. I've never met anyone so young and yet so wise.'

Hulde sniffed, squeezed Mergim's fingers.

'It's only how I've been brought up,' she said. 'Could have ended up as someone else entirely, as crotchety and curmudgeonly as Longhella's wind-mother, sewing her sons up in bags.'

Mergim smiling, shaking his head.

'Don't think you could ever have turned out like that.'

This tale reminding him of himself, for in it a prince has been condemned to wander the earth atoning for his sins, becoming good if he can, before he finally reaches his princess in the Garden of Eden. Her job to judge if he's succeeded, become kind and generous enough to ascend to the stars. The alternative being her plunging him and his black heart into the earth in his coffin.

Hulde's job to tend the same service to Mergim. Hulde, unlike the princess, always choosing for him the stars.

'He must be a strange man, that Hans Christian Andersen,' Mergim went on, when Hulde remained silent. 'All those stories he comes up with, knowing so much about so many things.'

Hulde shifting beside him.

'I think he's like Heraldo,' she offered. 'Takes things apart, puts them back together in ways no one else would think to do.'

'You're missing him,' Mergim stated.

Hulde quiet beside him, leaning her head against his shoulder.

'I can't tell you how much.'

Mergim hugging Hulde to him, eyes a little wet.

'I know, my dear. And I know I'm no substitute, no prince who can whistle up bad things, tie their feet together and shove them into sacks. But I'm here whenever you need me.'

Hulde subsiding into him.

'You know you really mangled that metaphor?' she got out.

Mergim smiling, hugging her one more time, seeing the threatening form of Longhella bearing down on them, order them through their starting paces.

'He'll be back,' he whispered, stroking Hulde's hair. 'Heraldo will be back.'

§

Lupercal and Jericho shouldn't be dallying, but after what the children had told them it didn't seem a heinous crime to return to camp along the shore-line instead of up above. Directions simple: down the steps by the first lighthouse, along the beach below the cliffs around the headland to the second lighthouse, up another set of steps, and only a short walk from there back to their performance area outside of Borre and Magleby.

'Let's do it,' Lupercal decided. No need for Jericho to reply. The two off and down the uneven eroded steps descending through the green gully. Off across the shingle, oohing and aahing as they picked up one rock after another in which appeared to be imprisoned tiny whorls and swirls of crustaceans. Appreciative of the sculpted chalk cliffs dipping down to their level in some places, towering above them in others. Top-heavy bulges here and there, with straggling beech trees straddling their over-burdened ledges.

The boys arguing about what might be the Hammers, the Queen's Seat. No doubt about the Summer Spire, rising in a pinnacle high above the rest. And heard for themselves the Bagpipe, wading through thigh-deep water as they rounded it, the sea flinging itself against the white cliffs and into hidden caves. Completing the four mile walk along the shore from one lighthouse to the other, from one set of steps to the next, up which they began to trudge.

§

Their brother Heraldo, trudging too, if not up steps nor vertiginous cliffs.

Heraldo halting his trudging, sitting, introducing Grettir to his past, the reason he'd come all this way to visit the chapel of St Vid on this obscure mountain in the midst of the Dinaric Alps.

'I lost my wife,' Heraldo explained quietly. 'Someone took her and I didn't find her until it was too late.'

Grettir taking a deep breath. So here it was. He'd understood heartbreak to be the centre of Heraldo's story, hadn't expected such tragedy.

'We were on Rügen,' Heraldo said. 'It was Advent, and they had a church there built on the remnants of a temple dedicated to Svetovid. Had a statue of him, and a fire burning by his feet day and night.'

Heraldo shivering at the memory, how the flames in the pit had leapt and burned, giving Svetovid the appearance of being alive, shifting with shadows, malevolent, not yet done.

'And your Svetovid is our St Vid?' Grettir asked. No great leap of understanding needed on his part, given the congruence of their names. Heraldo nodding assent.

'He is. From pagan god to Christian Saint. And this next part is going to sound...' Shrugging his shoulders, taking his time. 'Well. Perhaps strange to you, if not to me.'

Grettir saying nothing. He'd settled here because of the winds and the mountains, had a small pension on which he could scrape by, his innate curiosity liberated by his new circumstance. All his expeditions through mountains and karst mapped and charted, as was his first trip up this particular mountain. The boarded-up chapel of St Vid catching his attention, requiring research duly followed up.

St Vid a local variant of St Vitus, whose saint day was Vidovdan. Svetovid, Slav God of War, become Sveti Vid, become Vid, become Vitus, invoked since medieval times in the constant fight against illness and demonic possession. The saint still a God of War, if of a different kind.

'I couldn't leave Rügen,' Heraldo explained, 'until my wife was found. My family left. I didn't. Spent my days with a kindly old soul whose husband had been swayed by the old ways, by Svetovid. And in one of his books I came across the fact of this chapel of St Vid.'

'And you felt the need to come here,' Grettir finished for him.

'I did,' agreed Heraldo. 'We came to this part of the world years ago, got tangled up in fights for independence by the Serbs and Croats...'

Heraldo finding it hard to keep steady. History in these parts sweeping his family along in its undercurrents, new branches caught up in the twisted arms of the old as the river flowed on regardless.

Grettir following the river back to source. Points of origin stacking up in his head. Wanting to tread lightly. Remembering his talks with Othmar Voort.

'Do you know of the Battle of Kosovo?' he asked.

Heraldo seeing the old book spread out before him on the worn table. Some mention of it, he seemed to recall. Grettir filling in the blanks.

'Source of inspiration for Serbian Independence. Took place on St Vitus's Day 1389. June fifteenth in the old calendar, twenty-eighth in the new. Prince Lazar going up against the Turks on the Plains of Kosovo. Lazar and Sultan Emir Murad both losing their lives. No real winning for either side.'

Extraordinary for Grettir to contemplate how a battle fought half a millennia previously could still be dragging folk along in its wake. Legends and songs created back then still at the heart of this young man's life. Lazar turned by those songs into a saint; his son-in-law Milos, who had slain the Sultan, feted as the hero knight. Turks creating their own legends and songs. Murad as much a martyr to his faith as Lazar. Contemporaneous chronicles focusing on the cult of St Vitus, linking Lazar to it because of the coincidental dates of Battle and Feast Day.

Perhaps, therefore, no wonder Heraldo had turned up here, carrying his grief like a tombstone on his back.

Battle of Kosovo always a heavy load, never yet laid to rest. Hammering on down the centuries as a pivotal point no one was permitted to forget. Symbol of hope for some, of nationalistic fights for others, absorbed into them like fish taking oxygen from the rivers in which they swam.

Grettir recalling the letter in which Othmar Voort had laid out the ruination of his life, which had been his excavations on that same Plain of Battle.

Desolate is this land in which we live. Snow glares all around, folding us into the blue shadow of the hills.

Grettir's task to take this young Pfiffmakler into the blue shadows of the hills, to his Svetovid, to the chapel of St Vid, in hope he could lay down the tombstone of his grief, leave behind his wife, return to his family, start his life anew.

'Come along,' Grettir said, getting to his feet. 'If we hurry we'll be at the chapel by nightfall.'

8

Starlings Come Home To Roost

Jochen and Jansen were returning to the Møns Klint for the Pfiffmaklers' latest, and last, performance. Jansen casting an eye at the sky.

'Gonna get bloody drouked this time around. There's rain a-coming. Can feel it in me bones.'

'You and your blasted bones,' Jochen muttered. 'Haven't you heard of barometers?'

Jansen shrugging for yes he had, since Jochen had washed up on these shores. And a buggering mystery how Jochen managed to predict the weather with such accuracy. A constant source of contention between the two: Jansen relying on his not very reliable bones, Jochen on his meticulous notes of the previous days' cloud cover, wind speed and the pressure readings on his blasted barometer. Extremely annoying to Jansen how Jochen was usually more right than he. Jansen secretly hoping the next performance would be a wash-out, given how Jochen had predicted a fine clear night and a moon still bright enough to illuminate another remarkable performance.

Jochen carrying more with him than his weather predictions. Jochen carrying with him the small trophy he'd dug out of the sand and placed on his mantlepiece of which, so far, he'd been unable to wring any sensible interpretation.

Jochen and Jansen arriving with the gaggle of village folk gathering on the cliff edge, as they'd done before, along with visitors from Stege Nor. All listening to the whoosh of waves drawing up and down the shingle scattered below the cliffs, the sounds of night-birds waking, of the many other birds floating in congregations on the surface of the sea, or huddling in the branches of the beeches lining the cliffs of the Møns Klint. Every last person expectant as they gathered about the Pfiffmaklers' stage, awaiting the entertainments about to begin.

A night cold and frigid. The moon low and bright. A creeping mist swathing them all. The populace holding their collective breaths as they sat, blankets about and beneath, upon their hill.

Mergim announcing the start of the show as he'd done before, this time without apology, steady with his words.

'We will begin, Ladies and Gents, with one short act, with which we hope you will be familiar,' he announced, 'followed by our main entertainment of the evening.'

And so their theatre begins.

Jochen leaning forward, eager for all to be revealed. Expected to be disappointed, Pfiffmaklers unable to exceed what they'd had done before. Curious, nonetheless, as to what would come.

Which was a lone woman emerging from the resting mist, cowled, wringing her hands as she walked slow and stately across the stage. And the eerie sound of a tremendous wind, despite the air about them being still. The woman folding herself down on her knees beside a narrow bed.

Mother, I am tired, came Hulde's tremulous voice from her narrow bed. *I need to sleep. I know you too are sick and weak but please, Mother, please don't weep.*

Jochen—and several close neighbours—blowing air through their teeth, preparing to be bored, to live through yet another recitation of the most famous and well-promulgated poem penned by Denmark's most famous and well-promulgated author: Andersen's *Dying Child.* And a more sentimental load of tripe would be hard to find if, like Jochen, you'd never had children. Jochen mildly surprised the words were being sung instead of spoken. Jochen more surprised by the manner in which the Pfiffmaklers went on to depict the poem, their singing lifting the flat grey words from the page in three dimensional enactment, an exchanged dialogue between mother and child he was entirely unfamiliar with.

A thunderclap jars Jochen, makes him jump it's so loud and ominous.

I'm so cold, Mother. This storm is eating away my bones.

The wind gearing up, seems to be screaming around hedges, into eaves; Jochen having to look about him to reassure himself it is not so. There's a small movement as the wind lifts the bedcovers from the girl's cot, revealing how thin and pale she is; the girl wailing and shivering to an undercurrent of what sounds like a saw going through bone. Jochen's teeth set on edge, for he's heard such sounds before—usually accompanied by god-awful howls of agony and the unpleasant stench of blood. Recalls amputations and dissections. The reason he'd come up with his phantom business in the first place, so other young men wouldn't have to go through the same.

I hear your moans, my darling, the mother cries out into the wind, *and cannot bear them.*

The daughter comforting her mother as the mother should have been doing for her child.

And yet my dreams are wondrous bright. I see the angel children living in the light.

It's heart-wrenching. And uncannily it *is* suddenly wondrous bright, and there are her dreams, on a backdrop whose edges cannot be distinguished from the night. Scintillations of silver and gold swirling with the glories of her angel children.

I'm so near I could touch them, the daughter whispers, clearly heard, the wind having suddenly dropped away. Jochen frowning to see the girl's lips and fingertips visibly blue. It has to be paint but looks real so deftly has it been applied, and Jochen knows how hard that is to do.

Mother: *They look upon you gladly and oh, now one descends! And I hear...what do I hear?*

There's a shimmering golden haze materialising at the foot of the child's bed, seeming to have stepped right out of the girls dreams, and into the night comes an unearthly utterance, the hairs going up on the back of Jochen's neck as a bow is drawn back and forth across the sounding board of a nail fiddle.

Your angel child for you sings, the mother exclaims.

And see, the daughter exhorts, lifting herself on one elbow as if she might revive at any moment, *how beautifully glisten its wings.*

It's a greeting from our Lord, is the mother's interpretation, as the daughter leans forward.

As does Jochen. He'd never expected this.

I see greens, Mother, golds and reds all about us.

She's not alone. The very air is glowing. The Pfiffmaklers' pyrotechnics enhanced by the low-lying mist which has become an integral part of their play, floating here and there in ethereal wisps throughout the entire scene.

They are flowers, my darling, the mother informs, *gifted to you by your angel child.*

Jochen enrapt, as are his neighbours. Jochen not quite understanding what has him so taken. The singing, maybe, or because the mist is making everything appear like one of the child's dreams. He sees the daughter holding out her hands as if to grasp the flowers that cannot possibly be there. Sees the daughter shaking her head sadly to find her fingers empty, subsides back onto her bed as the mother draws closer to hear the words her daughter sings next.

I know I can't have wings while this life bounds both you and I,
But surely they'll be gifted to me when I die.

Oh Longhella! Time to pull on those heart-strings as if they were stretched upon Heraldo's lute! She weeps, she puts out her arms and draws her child to her—a miracle Hulde can get out her next verse.

I will be flowers and wings where I'm going, and knowing...

Longhella appropriating the next lines as her own. They had sounded melodramatic at rehearsal, but in this atmospheric setting they sit exactly right.

We've both done our best, my dear. Time to lay yourself down to rest.

Longhella's vibrating timbre just the ticket, her voice breaking, her fingers wiping none too gently at her putative daughter's cheeks. Hulde easing herself from Longhella's grasp. Longhella moving to one side, allowing the audience to see the child who is about to pop her mortal clogs. Tolling of a distant church bell sounding as if from the vast darkness of the sea to signal the end is nigh.

More glories of lights, more hints of an angel child out there in the vicissitudes of the wreathing mist. And a melancholic, slightly discordant, wordless chorus tingling through the air.

Your angel child is calling, Longhella opens her arms wide, *and soon you will be soaring*— audience taking an involuntary breath to see the child apparently rising in a column of intensely bright white light—*like a blessed dove to Paradise.*

And as suddenly as that light appeared, it is ended. Entirely extinguished. A few last whispered words rippling out of the darkness.

God's speed, my love. God's speed.

We did our best. Time to rest.

Silence atop the chalk cliffs of Møns for three seconds, four, five.

And then rapturous applause. People getting to their feet, wiping their cheeks, clapping loudly. Not a dry eye in the house. Including Jochen's. Jochen unable to figure out quite why he's been so affected. Tried to rationalise it: the singing, the music, the mist, the tolling bell, the inexplicable manipulation of light.

Sat through the main performance, hardly registering it was taking place.

Did not join in when *The Ancient Tree* came to jolly everyone up. Folk joining in, with Mergim's exuberant encouragement. Some even dancing as the melody was repeated, including Jansen, cavorting with the children from Stege Nor who were claiming their previous acquaintance with the Pfiffmaklers by doing their own leaps and pirouettes on stage as Lupercal and Jericho took them by their eager hands to guide them on.

Jochen taking himself away, needing space and silence. Wanting to clear away the images of *The Dying Child,* which had so unexpectedly moved him. How vividly they'd invoked the lurid stories Jansen had told him of how the ship from which he'd built his home had been wrecked.

Went down like a bloody stone, it did, like the belly had been ripped out of it.

Saw it all, friend, from my lighthouse. Saw all them citizens on board scrambling like rats, clinging to the railings and the masts. But it weren't no good, not for any of `em. That ship went down like it had nowhere else to go. Poof! Just like that. Here one minute, gone the next.

Jansen proud of his part in the disaster and the following enquiry. No ordinary shipwreck this, the valuable artefacts of a state-sponsored expedition possibly crammed into its holds going down with it.

Floating like bits of weed they were. You should've seen them! Some face up, some face down, some of `em scrabbling in the water like they could be saved. But waves were big, mind, tossing them here and there like they was pieces of rotten straw. Here one minute, gone the next, poor buggers.

Not that Jansen sounded like he was sorry.

Saw them hauled off by the current, I did. Lines of pale little faces getting littler and paler by the second. Like water-lilies they were, until the lot of them was gone. So think on that, Mr Weather Prognosticator, when you're tucked up cosy and warm in your bed. You're living in the hulk of the thing what made them dead. Gotta think they'll come after you, those lost souls. Find their way back to the ship what did them in and the person what's decided to put the cause of their death to better use. So sleep tight, friend, don't let the bed-bugs bite.

Words meant to frighten and discombobulate.

Words that hadn't been anything other than words until Jochen witnessed the Pfiffmaklers' performance of *The Dying Child,* seen that pale face becoming paler, small hands grasping for flowers not there to grasp, as there'd been nothing to grasp for all those desperate people in the freezing waters beyond Nyord Bay.

Jochen become as frightened and discombobulated as Jansen had intended.

Went down like a stone it did, like the belly had been ripped out of it.

And the belly had been ripped out of it, Jochen realised.

Couldn't understand how he'd not seen it before, for it had been right there in front of him. He'd dismantled that stranded hulk board by board, plank by plank, discarding those deemed of no use. Chopped them up for firewood. Piles and piles of it seeing him through many winters, and Jansen's winters too. His mind putting all those boards back together, seeing what he'd not registered back then, which was that in not a few of those discarded pieces had been finely augured holes. As if someone had deliberately set to with bit and brace.

A hard task to carry out such maladministration.

Wooden sailing ships having deep and well-hewn keels.

Yet wooden ships merely wood, when it came down to it. And where there was wood there were bits and braces able to undo the work of any boat-builder, competent or otherwise. Send a few well-aimed holes through the lower sides, plug them up, and anyone who knew what they were doing could remove those plugs and sink a ship in seconds.

And down it could go, like a stone.

And down, apparently, it had gone, as had everyone and everything on and in it.

Irmgaard Prögen's snippet of hair.

Othmar Voort's old rifle.

The collection of artefacts that should have made Othmar's name instead of ruining it.

Jochen Steggle, sitting on the very edge of the Møns Klint, trying to ascertain why anyone would do such a thing. Jochen, not having the nerve to approach the Pfiffmaklers with his paltry artefact, soon taking his way home, dragging his cart behind him.

Moonlight good enough for that. Jochen caught up by Jansen not far into the walking.

'Thought you'd got rid?' Jansen slurred, taking out his bottle, taking a slug. Not offering it to Jansen. 'You an' me, we'se joined, is you an' me.'

Jochen too disgusted to respond. Disgusted by Jansen, more disgusted by himself for not having the nerve to approach the Pfiff-maklers. Tramped all the way home and, despite the tramping, did not sleep easy.

9

Jochen's Holes Enter The Plot

The trees thinned as they gained height up the mountain; the snow getting deeper, more compacted, making their going easier. Grettir's map keeping them to their path which appeared, mysteriously, to have been tracked by other people not long before. Grettir could think of no reason why, but blessed them for it and for the way-posts they'd erected when the path became difficult to detect. The afternoon murmuring with soft wind, while up above haphazard eagles and honey buzzards wheeled, the air divided by the occa-sional blue-grey streak of a peregrine plummeting into a crevasse to latch onto a bunting mid-flight with their yellow eyes and yel-low claws. Softer snow covering low-growing crowberry and ling patterned with wide-spaced staccatos of mountain hares on the run, tracks criss-crossed here and there by those of fox and lynx following the delicate scents meaning here was a meal to be had, if only they could catch it up.

Gloaming shifting the afternoon into crepuscular shadow as Grettir and Heraldo reached the base of the short peak into which the chapel's base was hewn right into the rock. The two men paus-ing a few moments, rolling their shoulders beneath their pack-straps, readying themselves for the final scramble up the steep slope to gain their goal. The strengthening wind soughing and sighing between the frosted branches of the sturdy twisted pines up top, hiding the chapel from view. Deep moaning calls of long-eared owls somewhere in the vicinity, waking into the night.

And then something entirely unexpected: human singing. A dirgeful lament, maybe a hymn, a two-part descant given by bass and tenor with the slight mournful clash of minor keys that had your heart contracting and your eyes weeping without conscious thought.

'Do you hear that?' Heraldo asked softly.

'I do,' Grettir answered quietly.

'What does it mean?'

Grettir shaking his head, had no answer. Grettir thinking back to the other footprints that had gone before theirs, and the way-markers. Grettir seeing thin tracks going not up the steep slope where he'd been about to take them, instead to the right. Through a copse of skinny trees, seemingly in the opposite direction. Taking Heraldo's elbow, leading him into the trees and, when they came out the other side, was astonished for there, right in front of them, was a well-worn track going from copse to chapel.

Signs of wood-working and carpentry, low stacks of planks; axes and two-man saws, a firkin of flat-headed nails diminished to its final layer. A foot-powered lathe, a mess of curlicued shavings and sawdust fresh on the snow. And, a mere few yards up a short incline from the trees, was the chapel of St Vid, apparently reborn: no longer derelict and denied, its windows streaming illumination into the night. The scrachety worm-eaten boards torn away, replaced by firm shutters that were not shut, the newly installed glass glimmering and glancing as the light from inside spilled and spooled out onto the snow. The chapel, ill-tended and crumbling, left to die alone in the hills when Grettir had previously visited, resurrected. No Dying Child this.

'They're singing in there!' Heraldo exclaimed, shrugging off his back-pack, abandoning it to the snow, leaping off up the path.

Grettir unable to fathom how this small chapel had been rejuvenated so fortuitously, exactly when Heraldo had most need of it. Finding the moment extraordinary. Heraldo's life on a cusp from which it could skew one way or another. His proverbial fork in the road. Grettir having the sudden revelation it was not Heraldo's fork alone, his own future never so clear to him as it was now.

His life a happy one. Predictable and sure.

No wife, no children, and no regrets for either. Had the libido of a mollusc, if molluscs had libido.

Always a yearning in him to trip across the new and the strange. The creation of his Wind Museum an unconscious plea for it yet to be so. He'd thought himself content, thought he'd found the perfect place to live, thought he would never crave more. Yet since he'd met Heraldo, and they'd come to this mountain, to this inexplicably rebuilt chapel, it felt to Grettir as if the trim tidy world he'd inhabited thus far had been holed through, had a ringing in his ears as its dismantled pieces rat-tat-tatted about him, settling into new and different patterns, creating a map other than the ones he'd made since he'd settled here.

A map beginning and ending with Heraldo Pfiffmakler. And up he was and off after his young protégé, running up the incline, arriving as Heraldo put his hand to the door of the chapel he'd crossed a continent to find.

§

The seeds of accusation Jansen had put in Jochen's head would not stay inert and buried, emerged and swarmed like locusts blocking out the daylight. All those lost souls Jansen had spoken about, all those swept-away faces, bubbling back to the surface of Jochen's mind as he lay awake on his bed. A terrible thought that if they chose to anchor themselves to the place of their death they would be clinging with their broken nails to the boards of his house, maybe even burrowing inside his walls.

Stupid thoughts. A nonsense.

He was going to throw Jansen in with the belligerent billy-goat first chance he got for putting such idiocies into his head. Except the deed was done, couldn't shake the notion of the dead being inside his *Put Preko Mora*. Could hardly contemplate what they would make of his phantoms, his wax corpses growing hour by hour upon his table. Ten or more of them by his reckoning, without recourse to his accounts book, created to specification, packed in straw and shipped away, every one lingering in his preparatory drawings and models, exactly as Blaschka had taught him to do. He knew he was being ridiculous, behaving like the children Jansen had cavorted with who would believe anything their elders told them. Chastised himself, tried to clear his head. Wondered if he should dismantle his wood-heap plank by plank, log by log, find any others with holes bored through them. Get down to the last layer where the very first of the wrecked boards of that wrecked boat had resided these last years through.

Which had been what, eleven? Plus the year it had taken him to complete the building of his home. So twelve, maybe thirteen years since a man had brought down a ship and everyone with it, and no one any the wiser. Time to ask a few of the locals, find out all he could about that ship. Recalled something else about the morning immediately after the shipwreck, not that he'd known of the shipwreck at the time. Jochen newly arrived back then, living in an old herring-smoking barn. How he'd found an empty barrel on the sands attached to a long length of rope, and a set of oil-skins. Had assumed they'd been mere flotsam washed up on the shore. Remembered cursing Jansen, for there'd been a few supplies missing from his store the same morning, and one of his hand-carts going astray. Hadn't confronted Jansen about it, for Jansen had already started pilfering this or that and always flatly denied it. Jansen sauntering off gaily on his way, no more conscience than a stone. Jochen boiling from the inside out at the injustice of it.

But if Jansen hadn't been the culprit it stood to reason it had to have been someone else, and certainly not the only known survivor, infamous as he was, who'd been washed up on some other bay a couple of miles down shore.

After spending half the night wrestling with these disturbing notions, Jochen took a decision. A few hours later, in the early shift of dawn, he was back up the track to Borre and Magleby, walking fast, fluttering nightmares of locusts dispersed, allowing him a weak glimpse of the sun.

10
Webs That Catch And Bind

Heraldo put his hand to the chapel door and pushed it open. Pulse quickening to see a flaming pit before the altar, several young men kneeling about it, eyes closed, chanting softly, hands held up in abeyance. Between them an imposing wooden totem seeming to expand and grow, the four faces of Svetovid flickering in the eaves, as if holding up the entire edifice of the chapel.

Grettir, coming on behind Heraldo, similarly affected. Might have stepped back a thousand years into a pagan world as he came in. No one acknowledging their entry, so intent were these young men in their communal rite. Grettir pushing Heraldo down onto one of the sparse pews to their left, hidden in darkness, unreached by the licks of flames exuding from the pit, the sole source of light.

Almost the moment they sat, subsumed by the shadows, one of the young men by the fire loosed himself from his fellows and stood up, flung out his arms and spoke.

'Welcome, brothers, to our old chapel which we have renovated and put to new purpose. St Vid returned to his roots, to Svetovid—God of War, Fertility and Divination—from whom our movement shall regrow, become strong—' he took a step backwards, placed his hand upon the wood of the totem, '—fed as it is by the blood spilled on the Plains of Kosovo.'

He raised his head, closed his eyes once more, spoke in a rhythmic monotone taken up by his peers, all speaking as one their predetermined script.

'Our forefather in that great battle, Prince Lazar, become our Christ; Miloš Obilić our Beloved Disciple; Vuk Branković our Judas. As is written in the Holy Chronicle of Peć and the Field of Battle.'

Three times they recited their own peculiar trinity.

Grettir raising his eyebrows, lips twitching; what had previously seemed surreal and eerie fading into farce. The basic facts subsumed by ill-informed rhetoric lifted with imprecision from the pages of a book Grettir knew well. *The Story of the Battle of Kosovo*, a cleverly wrought manifesto by an anonymous Kosovan patriot drawn from original accounts of the Battle. His own copy sent to him by Othmar Voort; marginalia, in Othmar's neat handwriting, directing Grettir to a salient point or its source material.

Motifs of heroism and betrayal, Othmar had written.

The slain warrior-prince equated with Christ, as in the medieval poetic epics of the English and the French;

Vuk B the traitor, accusing the hero MO of the treachery he himself is guilty of;

The women's involvement—both MO and VB married to daughters of Lazar—VB concocting quarrels between the daughters to provoke discord between MO and Lazar;

MO the loyal vassal, even in his hour of death, as Christ is to The Father, as too is Lazar who willingly lays down his life for his citizens and friends.

Grettir considering how these motifs related to Heraldo's past.

Heraldo the hero-knight who would have lain down his life in a moment for the recovery of his wife, if he'd been given the chance. Which he had not. Heraldo betrayed and broken; setting off, family abandoned, on his knightly quest.

Heraldo a mute witness at Grettir's side. Grettir snatching a glance at him, seeing Heraldo leaning forward, fingers gripped about the pew before him.

'How can this be?' Heraldo asked of no one. Had Grettir not been looking he would not have caught the words. A question to which Othmar Voort could have supplied the answer.

Kosovo always a touch-point for Nationalism. That's what I was researching when I carried out my excavations, lines going from Istanbul to Bulgaria, Albania and Montenegro, and from those latter into Serbia, Bosnia and Croatia, right up the Adriatic coast.

Lines, he'd told Grettir, of battles and invasions, science and languages, meld and mix, once Mehmet II stormed the great Christian stronghold of Constantinople, renamed it Istanbul. Populace, bizarrely, mostly consisting of Jews, Greek and Armenian Christians, when not enough Turks could be persuaded to the task.

Became a city of artisans and learning, Othmar had enthused. *The fortifications and walls defending Constantinople for a thousand years broached and destroyed by Mehmet or, more precisely, by a huge cannon constructed by Orban, an itinerant foundry worker from Hungary, after Constantine had declined his services. Think of it, Grettir! One man from Transylvania changing the course of history, causing the entire empire of Byzantium—and its founder Constantine—to fall.*

Drawing for Grettir his detailed depictions of Orban's process for making the cannon.

Bronze made from easily sourced copper and less easily sourced tin; more found ready-made, filched from bells stripped from Christian churches.

Two bricked furnaces constructed, lined with fired clay inside and out, reinforced with large rocks.

Furnaces filled with wood, set alight, heaped over with charcoal. Their two gaping maws tended by founders and stokers stripped almost naked because of the heat: nothing but slippers for their feet, eye-holed caps pulled over their faces, thick sleeves drawn up their arms as they fed the fires with wood. A full twenty-four hours until they were deemed of sufficient temperature to place into their furnaces' cauldrons the copper and tin needed to make the bronze.

January 1453, after three months' work, Orban created for Mehmet a cannon twenty-seven feet long with a barrel diameter of two and half feet reinforced with eight inches of solid metal. The whole capable of firing a stone projectile of fifteen hundred pounds.

I've studied the fortifications of Constantinople, Orban assured, *and with this gun we will shatter those walls unto dust.*

Orban not wrong in his boasting.

The giant cannon, along with many smaller more mobile guns, dragged from Adrianople to Constantinople by sixty of the strongest oxen and two thousand men.

Mehmet ordering seventy small ships to be hauled overland from the Bosporus to the Golden Horn to aid the attack, force the defenders to divide their defence.

Friday, 6th of April 1453, the siege begins. Thank you, historians, for being so precise.

Fifty-three days the city held out until, on Tuesday 29th of May, the one-thousand-year-old walls were irrevocably breached and Byzantium fell to the Ottomans.

Think of it, Othmar had repeated. *If Constantine had chosen to employ Orban, how different would be that part of the world! No Ottoman strongholds striding down the centuries along the shores of the Mediterranean and the Adriatic from Bulgaria almost to Trieste.*

And no need, Grettir was thinking, if Orban had never existed, or for the Serbo-Croatian fights for independence from Ottoman rule to have existed either. Which meant, by existential deduction, given what Heraldo had told him, that Heraldo's wife might never have died, and the Battle of Kosovo Othmar had been investigating might never have happened. And this chapel never built upon this hill.

How can this be? Heraldo had asked the universe.

The universe about to give answer in a manner Grettir Wyssling would never have guessed had he lived to be as old as Methuselah. A woman, stepping from the tiny sacristy to the right of the fire-pit, taking centre stage beside the totem of Svetovid, her back as straight as Svetovid's, her condemnation as forceful as any he might have given.

'This is a travesty! An absolute travesty! Everything is wrong, from beginning to end. Didn't any of you heed my instructions? Have you forgotten everything I told you about what needed doing? This is about as half-baked as anything that is half-baked can be, and that means it is inedible, indigestible. Fit only for the midden. And if you don't believe me,' she finished, 'let's ask our spectators.'

The woman striding down the nave, landing a few moments later by Heraldo and Grettir, both compelled to stand as she pointed them out.

'You can be honest,' she said. 'Does this look like a dramatic rendition of our history or a chunter of boys peddling rhetorical rubbish?'

She fixed her eyes on Grettir, who gave a brief bow, saw her as she was: long necked, strong featured. Not a woman to be brooked with.

'Speaking truthfully,' he began.

'Which is what we need,' she interrupted. 'Truth is where learning starts.'

A small hint of humour detected in the lift of her lips, the glint in her eyes which were remarkable in the intensity with which they pinned Grettir to the spot.

'It was a little over-done, in my opinion,' Grettir went on.

'So, over-done and half-baked. Did you hear that, boys?'

Definite amusement there now, as Grettir continued his critique.

'The history needs correcting.'

'Exactly!' the woman agreed. 'And what of you, our younger visitor?'

Heraldo, having subsided to his seat, quickly standing up again.

'I'm not sure,' he said quietly, head lowered. 'I've met Svetovid before, but it wasn't anything like this, although the earlier singing was impressive.'

The woman looking at Heraldo with narrowed eyes.

'You've met Svetovid? What do you mean?'

'On Rügen Island,' Heraldo expanded. 'A Christian church built on pagan roots.'

Unable to say more. Heart-sore for all that had happened there.

Jitters of annoyance coming from the young men, who had swept after the woman and were now clustered about her and the strangers.

'We've worked on this for weeks and demand to know what the hell is wrong with it!'

The woman turning her attention to her little class of ingrates, her profile throwing Grettir into a stir for he'd seen that profile before. Couldn't put his finger on where or when, but knew he'd seen it. An uncommon woman, early fifties he'd guess, if no stooping of shoulders or back, no jowls to mar her neck nor that strong chin. Everything about her seeming animated, long and lean, as if youth had never left her.

'What was needed from you,' she turned on her heel, facing her band of unmerry men, 'was explication and clear direction, letting loose the bolt of circumstance from past into present to rejuvenate interest in what might be all our futures.'

'You said drama,' one of the youths sullenly replied. 'You said mystery and revelation.'

'That's right,' another added. 'And that's what we've done. And we've spent...'

'Weeks, I know,' the woman butted in. 'And for your efforts you should be applauded, if not the results.'

Speaking as a teacher to her pupils, encouraging and chastising all in the same breath. An odd position of authority for a woman, thought Grettir, not that Grettir knew a great deal about women—libido of a mollusc and all that—but a man greatly given to observational detail. Revelation falling on him like Summer rain, completely out of the blue.

The young woman Othmar had drawn repeatedly, several portraits of her framed on his walls, several in profile, looking like this woman. Older, but those core features remaining the same.

Webs in life that catch and bind.

No immediate explanation why they'd done so.

No earthly reason for Grettir to be right.

11

Profiles, And Un-Pfiffmakler Performances

Irmgaard turned to Grettir and Heraldo having quelled her wayward wards.

'Maybe you can help,' she said, 'seeing as you both apparently know so much about Svetovid which is fortuitous.'

Rumbles and grumbles coming from her taciturn young men.

'Never discount coincidence,' she cut them short. 'History thrives on it, as should we. So have at it, strangers. Why are you here? And why now?'

'Spies!' the leader of her pack concluded. 'Sent by one of our competitors.'

His fellows bunching in, the woman pushing them away with her arms.

'That's ridiculous,' she reprimanded. 'Spies would spy, not walk in the door and sit themselves down for all to see.'

The lead youth colouring, falling back.

'Maybe a double bluff,' he mumbled in his defence, knowing it was weak and deserved no answer. The woman's loud sigh her only reply.

'Can I ask something?' Grettir held up his hand. 'It might seem a little odd...'

'And you think prancing around an obscure chapel on the top of a mountains isn't?'

The woman as quick with her words as she was with her wit.

Grettir admiring her for it. Heraldo taking a step forward.

'If it's theatrics you want, and putting history in ways you can present to others, I can help.'

The woman, who might or might not be who Grettir Wyssling suspected her to be, fixed her dark eyes on Heraldo.

'And how might that be, young man?'

'Because,' Heraldo stated, 'I believe I know what you're trying to do and that I'm not here by chance. That I was sent. Not because I'm a spy, instead to further your cause.'

Grettir gritting his teeth. So like the young to assume they had a purpose when they had nothing of the sort. The young men in the chapel grasping at the straw of Heraldo, taking him off, sweeping him away.

'So you're a man of entertainment?' Grettir heard one say, as Heraldo proffered his wares. 'This is exactly what we need!'

Leaving Grettir and the woman standing in their own small circle of doubt.

'He's from a theatre troupe,' Grettir explained, the woman nodding her head.

'So I gather. Which explains one part of the equation if not the rest, nor the sum it is meant to express.'

Grettir's opinion of the woman elevated further.

'An interesting analogy,' he commented, 'and unusual for one of your sex, if you'll forgive me for saying so.'

'I will not,' she replied shortly, nevertheless gesturing Grettir to sit, which he did, as did she. 'To make such an assumption is ignorant at best, profoundly dangerous at worst, and precisely the opposite of what I have been trying to demonstrate to my pupils these past thirty years.'

Grettir smiling, feeling comfortable and companionable with this woman, in this chapel, as the evening outside swivelled unnoticed into a night that had begun to swirl with snow thick and earnest, intent on covering tracks and paths, closing them in.

'Can I ask what it is you're doing here?' he proffered.

'Only if you will answer in kind,' came the swift reply. 'But, in the interest of mutual co-operation, let me begin. This is the inaugural year of a regional competition sponsored by the Serbian Senate, for which schools, amongst others, have been tasked with performing some aspect of history to bolster unity in the area.'

'Laudable,' Grettir commented.

'Your turn,' she pushed him on. Grettir acceding.

'I'm a retired engineer and canal worker. Presently engaged in running my Museum of the Wind.'

'Interesting,' she said, sounding truly interested. 'Have to admit I've never heard of it.'

'Not many have.' Grettir sanguine. 'More of a hobby than a going concern. Got the idea from a friend of mine.'

Wondering if he should say more. Throw Othmar Voort's name into the mix.

Given no chance, the youths up top of the chapel clapping and shouting as Heraldo threw they knew not what into the flames at Svetovid's feet bringing up a towering cascade of red and golden sparkles.

'He's an uncommon young man, your friend,' she said.

'He is,' Grettir agreed.

'And you'll tell me no more of him?'

Grettir shaking his head.

'He's his own tale. One he has to tell you himself, if he chooses. Another question, if I may?' Looking at her straight on, before averting his eyes. 'It might be rather delicate.'

Here I go, he thought.

'Ask,' commanded the woman. Grettir straightening himself on his uncomfortable pew, weighing up the evidence as he'd done his entire life.

'Is it possible you've ever met a man named Othmar Voort?'

The woman taking in a sharp breath.

'Good gracious,' she said quietly. 'I've not heard that name in years.'

'But you know him? Or did know him?'

'I did,' she answered.

'Are you by any chance Irmgaard Prögen?'

A slight hesitation, a creasing of her smooth forehead.

'I was. Irmgaard Simiĉ during my marriage. Now widowed, so I suppose I am Irmgaard Prögen once again. How could you possibly know this?'

How indeed.

Grettir having trouble getting to grips with it himself.

Never dismiss coincidence, she had said, and he did not.

'I met Othmar a few years ago,' he said, 'not long before I retired.'

Neglecting to mention it was primarily Othmar Voort who had prompted his retirement.

'I'd been consulted about fortifications to be built on the Danish island of Sundeved, which is where he lives.'

'Denmark,' Irmgaard murmured. 'I'm rather surprised he ended up there.'

'He'd been working for the Danish government,' Grettir explained. 'A two-year archaeological expedition taking him from Bulgaria all the way up the Adriatic to, well. To this area as it happens, on the coast if not the mountains.'

Irmgaard smiled sourly.

'Of course he did. That was always his great thesis, the comingling and confluence of the east with the west. He never did see a division, not as others did.'

The lads about Svetovid's pit began singing under Heraldo's tutelage, shifting a descant here, a bass note there, Heraldo sorting high from low. Grettir and Irmgaard quiet as Heraldo directed their voices to their best pitch, put them back together, harmonious and discordant to the very best effect.

'If he can do that in ten minutes,' Irmgaard commented, 'imagine what he could do in in ten days.'

'Which is when you give your performance?' Grettir asked.

Irmgaard smoothing her skirts with her fingers.

'It is. And why we've renovated this chapel, which is the perfect place for it. How odd, though, now you've mentioned Othmar, because I'd not have come up with any of this if not for him.'

'How so?' Grettir was curious.

Irmgaard taking her time, sorting through skeins of memories.

'We grew up together, Othmar and me. A village on the edge of the Baltic. A place of shifting borders from one year to the next. Pomeranian, Polish, Prussian.'

'And he had a Danish father and a Prussian mother, I gather,' Grettir put in.

'Quite so,' agreed Irmgaard. 'He found it all so arbitrary, people clinging to one strand of their history, ignoring another equally valid. And worried greatly about war, how one can blow up out of nowhere.'

Grettir thinking him not wrong.

'A concomitant fascination with languages and religion,' Irmgaard continued. 'How they could change in accordance with those arbitrary borders. A fascination bolstered after our families spent a few summer weeks on Rügen Island, a short boat trip across the water.'

Thus Svetovid puts in his appearance.

'And it was there,' she went on, 'when Othmar first heard of the old religion and went at it like a fox after a hare.'

Irmgaard sighed, cupped thumb and forefinger about her chin.

'We'd seemed a good match until then, approved on either side. Irmgaard and Othmar,' she added, a little wistfully. 'Othmar and Irmgaard. But Othmar simply couldn't let things go. Buried himself in the university library in the city, researching the provenance and peregrinations of this old religion he'd never heard of before as if he'd found his way through the trees. Which I suppose he has, from what you've told me. But the plain fact was he followed his own path. Left the rest of us behind without a second thought.'

She stopped speaking, for the singing was now pervading the small chapel from eave to eave as Heraldo led his young choir into uncharted and wholly beautiful melodies.

'He asked me to go with him,' Irmgaard said softly, 'once he'd begged and bartered an unpaid internship at the university library and a part-time job with the bookbinders. Which would have been no life at all.'

Penury the path he was offering her, and no help to either of their families, first-born children as they both were and which duty should have been foremost. No hope of advancement for Othmar, with no formal education, no money, not for many years to come.

'And yet he became an archaeologist and you a teacher,' Grettir observed, 'so perhaps the right decision for you both.'

A sudden silence descending as the singing ceased. This conversation too intimate to be witnessed other than by the walls of the chapel and the snow falling outside, unseen and unheard.

'I've something in my backpack might aid us,' Heraldo's voice bright, urgent with his heaven-sent task, or from wherever Svetovid saw fit to inhabit. Heraldo rushing past Grettir and Irmgaard, flinging open the door to the chapel, coming to a swift stop.

'Oh my,' he whispered. 'Will you look at this.'

The night outside flurrying and scurrying with shifting screens of snow, a rising wind leading them in a dance of its own making. Footprints obliterated; backpacks, curlicues of wood, stacks of planks, all interred beneath several inches of snow.

'It's a sign,' Heraldo sighed, taking a step outside, holding up his face to greet the most gentle of onslaughts.

'It's a blasted nuisance,' corrected Irmgaard at his back. 'Means we'll not get back down the mountain until morning.' The brands and lanterns meant to light their way already buried. 'No moonlit procession for us, not tonight.'

Should have been one of the Big Moments she had planned to evoke the curiosity of the people in the villages at Mount Suvid's feet. A line of lights wib-wobbling down paths very few had taken since they were children. A moonlit procession intended to provoke wonder and interest in the competition, garner support and a good audience when it was their time to shine.

Irmgaard not easily thwarted, a woman who twisted herself about to suit circumstance as does a blackthorn when faced with the constant batter of the wind. Irmgaard battling such winds for years and years. Irmgaard planning for such an eventuality.

'You know what to do,' she commanded her troops, her boys coming down from their stage to join her. 'Survival plan now in place. And fetch our visitors' backpacks while you're at it. They might be strangers, but they are also our guests.'

Not that she felt them strangers anymore. A whiff of Heraldo's conviction they'd been sent clinging to her like smoke from the fire-pit.

Boys pushing out the door past Heraldo to fetch the necessaries secreted beneath a tarpaulin in case of this very situation. Grettir believing he knew these mountains well, Irmgaard knowing them better. How swiftly weather and winds could change, and how unexpectedly one's life could shift from one circumstance to another.

Othmar Voort the unlikely source of her resilience. No overwhelment by grief after he'd effectively rejected her. Irmgaard buckling down, going at life like she was racing for the finishing line. Irmgaard not about to let the blinkered selfishness of the man she'd believed she'd loved hold her back. Irmgaard marrying Gregor Simiĉ several years after he'd taken up residence in their Baltic village as the local school teacher. Gregor Simiĉ tall and imposing, stern and fair to his pupils, gentle and jocose with Irmgaard, brimming over for both with an endless storehouse of fascinating facts.

Loligo is the name of the genus embracing the common squid, and is my favourite word;

If you get a splinter while you're gathering driftwood, use mussel-shells as tweezers;

The great French inventor and chemist Lavoisier constructed a contraption of dual lenses to harness the heat and light of the sun to such an extent he could melt diamonds. Diamonds, my young pupils! The hardest mineral on earth!

Chinese Shadow Theatres use silhouettes cut from donkey skins, lacquered and brightly painted, for their puppets.

This last enacted upon after the demise of one of the village donkeys. Gregor acquiring its hide, initiating a practical project resulting in a grand end-of-term Shadow Theatre performance of their own.

Gregor teaching Irmgaard, almost by osmosis, to become a teacher too.

Gregor later taking her to a new life here, in his homeland, at the foot of Mount Suvid, after his parents died; their farm, house and lives needing sorting and sifting. Including the many trunks in the barn in which they'd amassed years of accounts, of crops planted, tended, harvested, which portions kept and which sold; detailed notes of their livestock's lineages going back forty years; weather diaries the same. And all they had of Gregor since he'd been born. A late child, an only child, everything about him precious: his school work, the wooden toys made by his godfather, bundles of letters sent them as he made his way abroad; his books, the only things he had desired since he was six, and given at every turn they could be afforded. Mounds of baby and children's clothes knitted or sewn by his mother, all smelling of the camphor they'd practically been soaked in, yet serviceable after a wash and a good airing on the laundry green, distributed throughout the village. Little echoes of Gregor wandering about the streets, making Gregor laugh.

A sudden thought assailing her. Irmgaard turning back from the door and looking at Grettir Wyssling, who had left his pew in order to take a closer look at the totem of Svetovid, wondering how such an ancient god could still wield influence over people as enlightened as Othmar and Heraldo.

'How did you know it was me?' she asked, the two of them alone in the chapel, Heraldo having set off after the boys. 'You must have had reason.'

Grettir turning to face her, shrugging his shoulders.

'Because you're not so much changed,' he said simply. 'Othmar spoke to me about you, and I saw the portraits he'd drawn of you in his house. His way of saying he never forgot you.'

'Nor my incredibly square chin,' Irmgaard laughed. Grettir shaking his head.

'I don't think that's it at all. I think he always regretted your loss. Found no one else, not after you.'

'Oh for the Lord's sake.' Irmgaard put a halt to the gush. 'That's so like Othmar. He never could pull his boots out of the mire of the past.'

And yet she smiled, could not deny she found it immensely gratifying she'd been his one and only. Othmar the pig condemned to hanker after the one trough he couldn't feed from.

'Don't be too harsh on him,' Grettir said, observing that sardonic smile, the way Irmgaard straightened her back at his words. He might be a mollusc of a man when it came to women but he knew men like Othmar, being not so unlike himself. 'He believed he had a higher purpose, felt impelled to follow wherever it led.'

And so much Irmgaard might have said in reply.

How dare you take the moral high ground? What gave him—or you, come to that—the authority to decide what was best for him at the expense of his family and of me? Did he consider us for an instant? No he did not, is the answer to that.

The diatribe she might have made interrupted by Heraldo and the boys re-entering the chapel with noisy garrulity, garnishing their sparse accommodations with food and drink, blankets and bed-rolls, a large canister of water, a small grill, several wax-papered packages of food. And Heraldo's backpack, from which he withdrew a miniature mandolin made by his own hand. He might have left the Pfiffmaklers, much as Othmar had left Irmgaard, but music he could never leave behind. Music with him wherever he went: in his head, in his fingers, on his lips. Heraldo beginning to tune his instrument as the boys went about their duties, laid out bed-rolls by the side of the fire-pit, throwing in several armfuls of branches followed by five or six large boles to keep them warm while they ate, talked, and planned.

All tucked up tight within the chapel of St Vid.

Svetovid gazing down imperiously upon the small congregation held fast within his fiefdom, small as that fiefdom might be this night, although not so small it hadn't stretched from Rügen to this mountain a thousand miles distant and left tendrils of his influence all the way from there to here.

12

Fiefdoms And Folios

Othmar Voort was tucked tight within his own small fiefdom, looking through the drawings he'd made of the objects lost when the ship went down.

A hollowed-out cow's horn stuffed with twenty-two gold coins, dating back to the reign of Mehmet II.

Several knife handles from late Roman times, decorated with depictions of fighting men.

A plate inscribed with the early hijâzî form of the Arabic script.

A wine chalice incised with a later version, dug up from the Plains of Kosovo, so grand it might have belonged to the Sultan Emir Murad himself.

Numerous scraps of knives, swords and armour, also from Kosovo.

Othmar, getting to the end of this first folio, coming to rest on one of the smallest objects. His personal favourite, and a terrible regret he'd not kept it in his pocket instead of with all the other finds: a minuscule copper alloy trinket in the form of an open book, probably Venetian. Engravings on one side made to look like leather bindings, the spine and covers intricate. On the other, two apparently open pages divided by the central binding and, on those pages, seven hand-stamped words: *Pax Tibi Sanctus Vitus, Semitam Meam Subibant*

Peace to you, Saint Vitus, my path and my way forward.

Might have been written of himself.

Othmar hauling himself out of the meagre village he'd been born into, educating himself, getting a job and a purpose. Irmgaard falling by the wayside his first sacrifice. Long years of scrimping and saving, slaving at dead end jobs until, at the age of thirty-nine, he had money enough to buy his way onto his first proper archaeological dig. Excavating one of the northernmost outposts of Roman occupation when Othmar unearthed, with trowel and brush, a figurine, cowled and cloaked, which had the lead archaeologist rubbing his hands in delight.

'This is Cautopates!' he'd exclaimed. 'Do you know what this means?'

Othmar did not. The man excitedly explaining.

'It means we've very likely stumbled on a temple dedicated to Mithras. Very popular with Roman soldiers. A secretive religion. Always built their temples underground to replicate Mithras's cave. Mithras born out of rock, so the legend goes. Dig! Dig! Abandon all else and dig!'

And abandon all else they had, digging over six foot down until they found the outlines of tumbled walls, ancient Roman masonry.

'They do that, small artefacts,' the archaeologist informed Othmar, 'get wriggled out of the earth, brought up by the push of groundwater, or rain soaking down and loosening the soil, and by worms. Never discount the power of worms, Othmar, who eat soil for breakfast!'

He couldn't have been more pleased, so pleased he named Othmar Voort as the discoverer of the figurine in the very influential paper he published on his excavation of an indisputable temple of Mithras, confirmed further the more they dug.

The discovery of the figurine of Cautopates was the key to our work. Cautopates, usually shown with his companion Cautes. The first representing sunset, darkness and death, always shown with his torch held downwards. Cautes, by comparison, with his torch held upright to demonstrate sunrise, light and life. The very essence of the cult of Mithras…'

'This will be my making,' the archaeologist had told Othmar, 'and yours too.'

And he'd been right. Letters of recommendation and invitation showering down upon them, furthering Othmar's career by leaps and bounds. Financed his own excavations and expeditions, all yielding yet more important finds. Othmar Voort at last on the up. Othmar presenting to the Danish government a proposal to prove his Grand Thesis, that early motifs of civilisations had moved east to west, north to south. The Slavic god Svetovid— still extant, if barely—on Rügen, not so dissimilar to the Mithras of Persians and Roman soldiers alike.

Light and dark. Night and day. Death and life.

No difference in their essentials.

Mithras had Cautopates and Cautes.

Svetovid, his four opposing faces.

Othmar turned to the next folio, studied his drawings, forefinger following their outlines, running along the words written below each one.

Metal bowl, highly coloured, three of the five pieces severely corroded.

Saxon brooch in the form of the cross studded with amber from the Baltic, garnets from India.

Several Bronze Age horns, side-blown, which demonstrably could still make music, producing a deep sonorous sound.

Seventy-seven shards of bone, including one intact femur showing definite signs of sword-strike, dug up from the Plains of Kosovo. Probable indication of mass burial of the casualties of that battle, given how the skeletons were laid side by side, heads and feet aligned.

Lips twitching as he read the next words, mouthed them silently: the deductions made, jotted down, reconstructed from the one surviving journal he'd had on his person at the time of the shipwreck. This last journal documenting the final few months of excavation before winter brought an end to their travels and they forged on to Trieste to board their ship home to Denmark.

Seventy-seven shards of bone, including one intact femur showing definite signs of sword-strike.

A fraction of the amount they'd actually uncovered. A whole load more in that same patch of earth, most so friable they'd crumbled into dust at the merest touch. And skulls too. Hard to forget the skulls. All in pieces, some showing signs of a violent end to life and far too fragile to be lifted. And another memory, sudden in its intensity: one of the local men brought in to do the heavy lifting, the worst of the digging, before Othmar and his team of proto-archaeologists got on with the real work of excavating whatever had been left on the Plains of Kosovo for them to find.

Skeletons laid side by side.

Discovered feet first.

A man who'd been hovering at the edge of the pit as they brought out the bones able to be lifted, working along the ancient bodies from foot to pelvis, from pelvis to clavicle, very little left of the rib cages, bones too thin and insubstantial to have survived, until they'd reached the skulls. None of them intact, most extant being jawbones cradling teeth. Othmar and his fellows gently lifting and scrutinizing the skull pieces scattered about those jawbones, at which point the man had shouted out at them, animated and adamant.

'Those you should not touch! They might be archaeological specimens to you, but to me they are my ancestors and need to be left to their rest.'

And let them rest Othmar had. Not because of the man's outburst—whose head he had verbally ripped off for attempting to interfere—merely because he'd not the time nor the means to excavate and treat them properly. His storage capacity already at the questionable end of full, given the berth capacity he'd been allocated in Trieste for the end of their expedition, pre-planned and pre-paid for. He'd certainly had the intention of returning and excavating every last one of them at a future date, along with Murad's tomb—for which he'd not been given permission back then to explore—once he'd garnered more finance on the back of what they'd already discovered.

Which hadn't happened.

The shipwreck intervening. Wrecking not only the ship and all their expedition had uncovered, but Othmar's life in the process.

A life, Othmar was realising, he'd been meant to lose.

Back then to his list of names of everyone he'd worked with and encountered on that trip. Couldn't for the life of him conjure up that angry man's name, either with or without his list, but by God he remembered exactly what he'd looked like as he'd glowered over the grave-site shaking his large workman's fists.

Those you should not touch!

His previous conclusion being that no ordinary person would have caused the ship to sink, nor for any ordinary reason. Othmar now having an inkling of what such a reason might have been. Othmar's fingers picking up pencil and charcoal, turning to the last untouched page of the last folio, beginning to sketch, bringing that workman's face back to life. He might not have a name, but if he conjured up the face it might yet come to him. And, if it did, he swore he would chase him down.

'For us,' he murmured, glancing up at the several portraits of Irmgaard Prögen he had fixed and framed on his walls, 'so it won't all have been for nothing.'

13

An Explanation, In Part

Marko Poploviĉ packed away his tools, putting chisels, axes, mallets into their allotted spaces as he'd been taught. Thinking, as always when he'd cause to construct a coffin, of the larger-than-usual wooden overcoat made many years ago. Outsized coffin for an outsized man. Six feet four inches in life, less in death; strong hands calloused, cupped with scars like the older bark of the sycamore maples he liked to work with.

Best kind for carving, clean and white, best for textile rollers because it don't stain any. Better still for fiddles and the like, for sides, back and stock. Never the belly, mind, nor the front 'cos it ain't got no resonance which ain't no good for them instruments. Spruce for that, and you've to watch on the number of growth rings per inch for that's what governs the tone. We're perfect for it here, slow-grown trees best for both and there ain't no slower growing trees than them up in them mountains at our back.

An outsized man with an outsized knowledge of everything dendrological. The uncle who'd brought him up after Marko's father had perished at sea. Taught him his trade of carpentry, beginning with the basics.

Felling a tree is an art. You've to control the direction of fall if you don't want your napper or legs crushed to a pulp. Needs two main cuts. Kerfs, we calls them. First one at waist height and absolutely level. Remember that, lad. Absolutely level. If you don't make it so then the tree will twist, direction of fall lost. As might you be. Second kerf must have its bottom plane two or three inches above the level one, and must penetrate just above it. Got to look at everything in the round before making a decision. Like life itself. How you chooses will determine what you gets.

A man as placid and simple as the wood he found fellowship with, only three interests in his life: his family, his work, and a tattered old book of the Norse Atlantic Sagas he'd been given as a child.

Them Norsemen, he'd chuckle, *them ones what first left their own lands in their oak boats, although no oak oars. They knew that well enough. Pine for oars, and only pine. And sails made of wool. Know how they found their first havens? They followed trails of drifting wood, is what. Let them lead them to shore. Wood following wood. They'd chuck overboard their high seat-posts, enormous boles they used for sitting about their fires. Most precious possessions they had, carved with the faces of their gods and on which they told their stories. Chucked 'em over, followed 'em in. And when Kvelduff knew he was about to croak on his way over, guess what he said?*

Marko didn't need to guess. Had heard those old tales over and over.

Make me a coffin and put me overboard, Marko whispered, as he often did at the end of the working day in memory of his uncle. *Put me overboard and let me find my own way home.*

And, thinking on people finding their own way home, he glanced up at the mountains bearing his uncle's trees, growing them slow and quiet, just like Marko had grown under his uncle's tutelage. Marko's son up there in the chapel he and his friends had restored under Marko's directing hand. Marko's son completely imbued by the competition introduced by his teacher, begging his father's help. Pleas Marko could not ignore, given the help Irmgaard's husband had once given him. Gregor's idea what should be done with Marko's spoils once Marko got back home.

'Leave it a good few years, choose your time, then take it to the Senate,' he'd advised. 'It mustn't be lost to our people for a second time, no matter how long it takes.'

Sage advice, Marko biding his time.

Until Vuk Karadžić, intellectual philosopher and politiciser, came into Kragujevac with his polemic.

The core of our people are entirely peasants and farm-hands!

We need to think Serbian. The people in the towns have forgotten this, not so those who work the land!

Vuk strengthening the notion of national identity.

Vuk pushing for *Vidovdan,* a day of National Celebration, provoking interest in all it stood for.

St Vitus's Day, and its own commemoration of the Battle of Kosovo, on everyone's lips.

Several fact-finding missions to Kragujevac. Marko shivering as he walked the length of the river, seeing the walls of the prison growing with every step, the stink of its foetid moat getting stronger in his nostrils. A real possibility he might end up in there if people knew what he'd done. Recalled the furore a while back when one of the inmates escaped. First time ever that had happened, and never would again. Inner moat rimmed round by a new wall high enough that one tall man on another tall man's shoulders couldn't get over.

This far, and no further.

No hope for Marko if he found himself on the inside, even if there was someone as tall as his uncle already there, and no one taller he'd ever met. Time to tread warily, according to Gregor's advice.

Kragujevac fired up by Vuk's words more than most, being so close to the Plains of Kosovo. And the low-down Kragujevac town officials he'd met with very keen, after a while, to hear what he had to say. Marko evasive with the details of how he'd come by what he had. Marko having a trump card: the earlier journals of the man who had led the Danish expedition. Marko met at first with har-rumphing disbelief, for why on earth would any Dane be interested in what had happened in Serbia hundreds of years before?

Marko eager to enlighten them.

'He's a theory,' he explained, not once but many times as he moved up the echelons of the Kragujevac men who mattered. 'He believes the Slav god Svetovid is linked to our own St Vid. Thinks Svetovid's followers travelled from Rügen Island in the northern lands, down through Bulgaria and along the Adriatic coast up our way. Wanted to take our past and make it his own, got permission to dig up the Plains of Kosovo.'

Outrage then, more so when Marko handed over Othmar Voort's journals. They couldn't understand a word, yet could see well enough the number of artefacts he'd uncovered and claimed as his own.

'He stole them,' Marko supplied quietly. 'Was taking them back to Denmark.'

Marko sweating badly, wishing Gregor was here to say his words more eloquently. Marko a mere carpenter; Gregor Simiĉ a teacher, a man of learning who'd travelled the continent, ended up settling not far from Rügen Island where he'd been astounded to learn that the island's Svetovid—their own Serbian St Vid—was still held in some regard.

'And you came by these artefacts, how precisely?'

The question Marko was keenest to avoid. For how to explain that in its entirety? Opting for simplicity, with no added details. Had the wit to not give his proper name throughout this whole process. Intent being to hand everything over, leave the rest of the mess to the Senate.

'I stole them back,' he said baldly. 'At least what I could. And if it's all the same to you I'd rather not have my name linked to any of it.'

Eyebrows raised amongst the Grand Men of Standing who exchanged glances, for that was all right with them. Theirs to be the glory. Lowly worker, by his own insistence, to be dismissed; repatriation of all that was holy to Serbian history theirs alone to crow about and do with as they would. And great political capital it would make in this age of newly animated nationalism. Vuk Karadžić doing most of the hard work for them.

Marko returning to his village after a last visit to Kragujevac relieved of his booty, and his guilt, for it was obvious—given how he'd been received by the Grand Men—that he'd done right back in 1839 when he'd been as foolhardy as his son was now. Not much older than Yanni when he'd seethed and boiled himself into that most hot-headed and reckless of schemes involving oilskins, bored holes and barrels.

It hadn't seemed so at the time, taking his uncle's mantra as unshakeable truth.

Wood follows wood. Throw the coffin overboard and it will find land.

And so it had, as had Marko.

Where the rest of the coffin had ended up he'd no care, not back then, and no notion how risky had been his plan, how many variables might have scuppered it. Marko and his barrel brought in exactly as he had surmised. Marko believing himself blessed by old gods and new to have been landed on the sands of a bay with only one tiny habitation visible, a barely thrown-together shack nevertheless having an outside shed with provisions he'd thought nothing of taking, and—more fortuitously still—a hand-cart obligingly left outside onto which he'd loaded his sacks and scarpered off with into the vicious night, plunging into a dark forest, feet pressing on until he came out the other side. Rain pelting him from every direction, wind pushing him off course this way and that as he traipsed a tiny track, the miracle of a bright moon studding periodically through the storm-raddled clouds telling him he was on his right path.

This way, she'd encouraged, *only one path to follow.*

And she'd been right. That single path threading him through several villages to the small port of Stege, straddled precariously astride the mouth of its lagoon. Arriving minutes before dawn. No one abroad because of the storm. Enough light to see him along the winding main street with no one to observe his going, no witness to him being there at all.

Battling on through the next day and the next, until he was exhausted. Had to find out where he was, asked a few stumbled questions with his hands. Møns Island. A spit away from the bigger island of Falster, from where he'd boarded a boat over the Mecklenburger Bucht to Stralsund, nearby Gregor Simić's new domicile.

Everyone back home knowing its name.

A letter from Gregor a village occasion, everyone gathering to hear his latest news. His letters so entertaining they were not to be missed. The chosen reader holding the letter up, pointing at the strange place names they'd been sent from. Until he'd met Irmgaard Prögen.

I've met the woman I intend to marry, the place I therefore intend to settle down!

Had drawn a map, marked it with an X.

A small impromptu celebration for Gregor at this news, despite everyone being a little disappointed his travels were apparently at an end. All assuming the succeeding letters would contain the trivialities of domesticity, of children—how treasured they were, or how diseased and then dead. Which hadn't happened at all. Instead the next fifteen years of Gregor's missives were studded through with snapshots of his new life in which they all back home partook of, came to feel they had another family out there in the great beyond, became invested in those other people's lives.

Little Theobald only went and fell down the well when he was fetching water...

Oh Lord! Was he all right?

A broken wrist is all, and Gregor's wife had it splinted and on the mend in moments.

He did well, marrying that Irmgaard, although I know it didn't seem so at the time.

And that hound, the one the Bogens found so hard to train...

Not the one who kept pissing under young Fritzl's bed?

The exact same. Well, he found someone lost in the marshlands. They was looking for days and days it seems, until Fritzl's hound sniffed him out. Right up to his armpits in mud, he was. Come from Rostock to net ducks for market.

What an idiot! Them townspeople know absolutely nothing.

Their reply a communal affair: every family adding a few sentences to the ever-growing letter so Gregor would never forget his roots. Last words always appended by Gregor's family, by his mother and father, his several cousins and their children. Never any word about Irmgaard and Gregor having any of their own. A topic at first asked about excitedly in every message. A topic soon dropped once it became apparent that miscarriages were the order of the day and never one child brought to term.

A sad day when the villagers had to inform Gregor his mother had died.

Another sad day when his father followed her a few months later.

1841 that had been, seventeen years after Gregor had stepped into his new shoes with his back then new wife in his new village on the very edge of Germany a few miles from Stralsund, a place all these Serbian villagers by then felt they knew family by family, stone by stone, farmhouse by farmhouse.

So no wonder the back-then Marko chose to stage his sabotage where he did, in the waters of the Kattegat.

Family, in the shape of Gregor, not far distant.

Marko knowing every inch of Gregor's life and opinions from his letters, certain that if he pulled off his spectacular rescue of the Kosovo Finds he would have a safe place to go, find succour, the help he needed to get back home.

Remembering Gregor's final letter after the news of his father's passing:

The decision is made, friends, Irmgaard in entire agreement. Our place is with you. Once we've found replacement teacher for the school and sold up we shall begin our journey. If you can care for father's farm until we return we shall never ask more. We'll be coming by sea, from Denmark to Holland, and from there around Spain into the Mediterranean.

The same way Gregor had provided for Marko, paying for his passage.

My last big adventure, and Irmgaard's first. We're expecting visits to exotic ports where we'll eat foods we don't know the names of, see buildings we've never seen the like of, hear languages we've never heard before. We're anticipating storms that will have us biting our tongues with trepidation, hardy captains and sailors who will see us through the worst. Maybe even pirates! But never fear. One way or another we will soon be with you.

14

Enter The Murdering Thieves

Irmgaard watched the boys about their fire, saw the bright scatter of sparks as the fat on the meat began to melt and sizzle, reminded of a morning soon after she'd arrived here with Gregor. She'd been walking through a field close-cropped by sheep who'd recently been led up the mountain to summer grazing, leaving behind only tufts of unpalatable spiky grass and their grey droppings, on one of which she'd spied a perfect circlet of red. Curious she'd leant down, discovered it to be a tiny ladybird and, looking closer, saw it was merely one of a multitude about her. Hundreds, thousands, of them on bare patches of earth, on the droppings, on the short-clipped sward, and didn't know what to do, where to put her feet without stamping them into the ground. Her hand going to her throat, did not want to crush these newly nascent ladybirds.

Horrible grief-stricken memories of the puddles of blood that were all that became of what should have been her and Gregor's children.

'Jump on the clumps!' A high merry voice coming from the morning.

Irmgaard looking towards the rickety fence dividing this field from its neighbour, smudged at the edges by soft balls of wool left by the rubbing of sheep, the girl straddled there in a corn-flower-blue smock. Irmgaard doing as told, taking long leaps and bounds from one spiky clump to the next, soon clearing the sea of scarlet ladybirds which seemed remarkably localised now she'd time to take a breath.

All concentrated in the barest part of the field where the earth had warmed under the sun, which in turn had warmed the clipped grass stems where the eggs had been glued to their bases, and now were releasing their progeny into the world in a swift scarlet burst.

Irmgaard reaching the girl, who was laughing at her ungainly progress, Irmgaard's skirts hitched up so she could get better pur-chase for her leaps and bounds. Irmgaard laughing too as the girl cleared the fence, ripping part of her smock in the process which seemed to amuse rather than annoy.

'You're Gregor's wife,' the girl stated, studying her with undis-guised curiosity.

'I am,' Irmgaard replied. 'I'm very pleased to meet you.'

The girl cocked her head to one side.

'We've already met,' she said, 'at your welcoming party.'

Irmgaard nodded, a blush of pleasure on her cheeks for that had been some night.

Arriving at Gregor's family farm and settling in without anyone to see them, it being on a farther edge of the village. Gregor taking her hand, formally introducing her to his homestead as if it were a person instead of a collection of ramshackle buildings leaning at rather hazardous angles.

'This the barn in which we over-winter the animals; this the shed in which my mother carded wool; this the well and next to it, for convenience, the butchering block; this the feeder stream coming all the way down from the mountains and in which we catch our fish; this where we made our butter and cheese. And this, my dear,' coming to rest outside a surprisingly large two storied cottage, 'is where we shall live.'

Ramshackle on the outside, everything on the in neat and tidy. A fine dust settled over the furniture, over the large kitchen table pocked and scarred by years of jars and pots into which boiling jam had been poured, by innumerable pans of coffee or pine needle tea, straight jags of knives that had missed the chopping boards filled with vegetables from the allotment.

Irmgaard had imagined all would seem out of joint, as if she was stepping into someone else's old boots. Had felt instead familiar: the large iron range exactly where she would have put it, the pans hanging on the wall exactly as she might have done, the chairs about the table neatly tucked in at their waists as if waiting for her to pull them out and sit.

'It's wonderful, Gregor. Thank you for bringing me.'

Gregor laughing. Grasping her hands, putting them to his lips.

'It's I who should be thanking you,' Gregor blinking quickly as several tears escaped his eyes. 'I never believed I would return. Never imagined that if I did I would have the joy of bringing the cleverest, most beautiful woman in the world with me.'

Irmgaard about to remonstrate. Clever, certainly. Beautiful, certainly not.

The moment broken by a god-awful clattering, as if a metal feed barrel was being battered about the yard by a hammer. The two going to the grimy window and looking out, seeing people lining the fence about the yard, clamouring at the gate, all banging metal trenchers with ladles and spoons. Wouldn't do to approach without some warning, which simply wouldn't be polite.

'It's the villagers come to welcome us,' Gregor announced. 'I'd no idea they'd come in such numbers.'

His face as alive and alert as when the donkey-pelt Shadow Play had been performed, as when he'd stood before his class ready to impart some new and interesting experiment. As when he'd first clapped eyes on Irmgaard Prögen, straightening his shoulders, his tie and collars all at the same time.

'I should have warned you about this,' he said, squeezing her hand. 'I hope you're ready.'

Irmgaard ready. Irmgaard never more proud, nor so overwhelmed, as when Gregor opened their new front door and the villagers took it as the sign it was and pushed back the gate, some ignoring the bottleneck, stepping over the fence, just as the girl in the ladybird field had been trying to do. Everyone flooding into the yard, one way or another, bringing food, drink, *Halloos* and *Welcomes!*

A celebration going on into the night, introductions taking forever. Irmgaard forgetting people's names the moment she'd been introduced. Nobody forgetting hers. Everyone knowing everything about their life back where they'd used to live, peppering Irmgaard with questions about the various people Gregor had talked about in his letters.

How's Fritzl? Did his wrist heal well? I hope it didn't dint his blacksmithing career.

What happened to the piss-beneath-the-bed hound after he rescued that bird-netter from the marshes?

How's Frau Meckler doing? I pray the twins are well. That Scarlet Fever can be a bitch!

Scarlet Fever.

Scarlet ladybirds.

Scarlet jumps of sparks from the fire.

Irmgaard jolted from her thoughts as Grettir Wyssling sat down beside her.

'Your boys seem to be adapting to circumstance, even enjoying themselves,' he commented, watching them tend the food on their brazier, clustering about Heraldo and his miniature mandolin.

'I've taught them curiosity,' Irmgaard answered abstractedly. 'How to use the tools they've got to best advantage.'

Grettir raised his eyebrows.

'Very admirable,' he said. 'Perhaps the same tenets held by your husband?'

Grettir grimacing as he saw Irmgaard plucking the skin of her neck in irritation.

'Why do people always assume any good idea a wife has had to have come from her husband? Do women's intellects count for nothing? Aren't these the traits every teacher the whole world over should be instigating in their pupils?'

Slight chagrin in her that Grettir was right, for it had been Gregor who had allowed her to put such premises into action. Not that Gregor would ever have laid claim to it. Gregor leading her by the intellectual hand to make the deduction all by herself. Gregor, who had taught her so much. Gregor four years dead, and his death an ache in her every day she woke without him by her side. Othmar doing her a favour, for a better man than Gregor she could not have met. Gregor a travelling man back then, moving from place to place, soaking up whatever he could in whatever new place he found himself, conjuring a living as a private tutor, an itinerant school teacher, filling in wherever gaps were found. Moving on after permanent staff were sourced.

No knowledge of this when she'd first met him. Gregor only divulging this information once they'd properly met, or rather when he'd engineered a meeting at the Sunday School she taught. Sunday School teaching the only job, naturally unpaid, women were deemed worthy of. Not so Gregor, who had straightaway taken an interest in her, sought her out, diffidently asking if he could sit in on her classes. She'd been so angry when he'd first suggested it she'd refused, assumed he thought her methods shoddy, her interpretations of the bible stories insipid at best, inane at worst. Which hadn't been the case at all. Turned out he'd admired her from the off, had been listening outside her classes specifically to hear what she had to say. And what she'd had to say was momentous to him, if not to the catchment of children newly come to her that particular year.

'I want you to consider,' she'd told them, 'how what appears to be consistent truth might be nothing of the kind. We're here to learn about the Bible, and the first truth the Bible teaches us is that it expects us to take contradiction as its first premise.' Hefty stuff for seven and eight year olds. Extraordinary stuff to Gregor, listening outside.

'Let's consider this. The Israelites spent forty years in the wilderness. Everyone knows it. What they don't consider is why. It's only sixty-five miles from the Red Sea to the Promised Land, a distance easily covered within a week.'

Nothing from the children. Irmgaard trying another tack.

'Let's begin at the beginning,' she says. 'In the first few pages of Genesis, at the very start of the Bible, we have two distinct versions of creation. We're told in one place, in verse 1:27, *God created man in his own image, in the image of God he created them; male and female he created them.* And this is on the sixth day of creation, before God chose to take a breather and a well-earned day off. At the start of the very next chapter we're told all is done. Creation finished. Except now Adam is alone, and woman apparently no longer exists. Woman instead created from a rib God takes from Adam in his sleep. So what's wrong with this picture?'

Bored silence as Irmgaard's students chew their lips, unable to grasp the nuances. Not so Gregor. Gregor coming in and sitting himself on one of the child-sized seats ranked about Irmgaard Prögen. The chair listing with the unaccustomed weight and splintering into pieces, landing him on the floor, arms and legs flailing as all the children laugh and point.

'It tells us exactly what you surmised,' Gregor managed to get out as he attempted to right himself, failed dismally, rolling himself on the floor until he finally got himself upright. 'That the first rule of reading any text is to do so with a critical eye. Never take it as it is presented. I'm Gregor Simić, by the way,' he told the children. 'Your new teacher.'

The children enchanted by this man who thought nothing of splintering seats to pieces and rolling about the floor like a beetle on a dung-heap. Irmgaard enchanted also. Othmar would never have done such a thing. Far too stuffy to allow himself to be made a fool of. Although a fool he'd been to have left Irmgaard, and satisfaction for Irmgaard that he apparently understood it to be so and far too late to do anything about it. For which she was immensely grateful. Wouldn't have swapped the life she'd had for anything. Her grief at losing Gregor surging through her, as it did at other unaccountable moments for no apparent reason.

Grettir misinterpreting her stillness, the bright shine to her eyes, attributing it to his clumsy attempt at conversation.

'I'm sorry. I didn't mean to offend.'

Unaware of the memories set off in Irmgaard's mind by those few bright sparks thrown up by a touch of fat upon the flames.

'Think nothing of it,' Irmgaard said quietly, touching a fingertip to the corner of her left eye. 'It's only what most people believe. And not just men. Most women hamper themselves by believing it too.'

A rather tragic sentence it seemed to Grettir because it was, now he thought about it, at the very least superficially true. Recalled Heraldo talking about his old grandma who had ruled the Pfiffmaklers with an iron rod, tongue sharp as a scalpel.

'It isn't always the way,' he said. 'You should talk to Heraldo about his family. I told you before they're travelling folk, theatre people. What I didn't say is that they don't work the way the rest of us do. In their family, women often take the upper hand.'

Irmgaard looking at Grettir with narrowed eyes.

'Explain,' she commanded.

Grettir quailing. Not his job to pass on Heraldo's secrets, much as he'd have liked to do to aid this woman who, he realised, he rather liked.

'Talk to him,' he said again. 'Ask him about his great grandmother, about his wife. You might be surprised.'

Irmgaard taking a deep breath, went on as if this conversation had not happened.

'My Gregor travelled too. Left these mountains, left that village down below years ago. Brought me back years later, after his parents died.'

Grettir quiet, watching the boys turning the meat on their make-shift fire and grill, sparks flying.

'Gregor was your husband?' he surmised.

Irmgaard quiet at his side, watching as he was watching, their eyes latching instinctively onto the only source of warmth in this bare chapel, in this bare night, on this bare mountain.

'He was,' she said shortly. 'And he was the most wonderful of men.'

A sudden catch in Irmgaard's throat as she spoke aloud what she'd never confessed to anyone, although everyone in the village knew it must be so. Nothing clearer in Gregor's letters than how much he had adored her, how much she had adored him in return.

'And I miss him,' Irmgaard whispered. 'I can't tell you how much. Every night and every day. I wake up having dreamt of him, and every morning I wake expecting him to be there. But he isn't. And so it goes on.'

Grettir could find no words adequate to the moment. Stayed silent, gazed instead on Heraldo, thinking how much these two disparate people had in common.

'I hoped this experiment, this contest,' Irmgaard went on, 'would somehow bring my grieving to an end. Set me on another course. Rebuilding St Vid's always something Gregor talked about once we were home. Hating how it had been abandoned, its original purpose forgotten. Allowed to sink slowly back into the earth from which it had been born.'

Which hadn't been at all what Irmgaard had said before, when she'd said the seed of inspiration had come from Othmar Voort. Grettir thinking back to Heraldo's words when he'd discovered what was going on here.

It's like I've been sent. Like I was meant to be here.

Perhaps not his exact words. Grettir couldn't be sure, but sure he was that Irmgaard Prögen and Heraldo Pfiffmakler had more in common than either knew. Grettir getting to his feet.

'Wait here,' he said, no command in his words. Merely a suggestion. Irmgaard not reacting. Too much going on inside her.

Being trapped in a snow-bound chapel newly built on the side of a mountain will do that to a person: make them see what they haven't seen for years, make them say what they hadn't expected they would say. The wind building up outside, most of it getting caught up on the other side of the peaks, trapped and livid, stymied and strictured, starting to boil and churn.

§

Down below, Marko noted the shift in the wind as he stepped out of his workshop onto the snow-sparkled grass. White Bora the gentler kind of blow doing little damage, half-hearted in intent. Ruffles the waters of the Adriatic, maybe does some mischief to the fishermen, little more. Black Bora a different species altogether, intent on destruction, seeming to swerve the world off its axis, wanting only to hie down from the mountains and wreak havoc, remind people the world is not theirs alone. The kind of wind that could rip off roofs, tear up bridges, blow cattle from one field into another, hairs of their pelts flattened widdershins. All the easier to freeze them to death when the snow came on its heels, as it was doing now.

All Marko could think of was of his son up there in the mountains. No more musings on Othmar Voort, nor the Kosovo Finds, nor the gnawing guilt of how it had come about. A guilt felt only latterly, once Gregor and his wife had returned to the village, when he'd finally confessed to Gregor how he'd come to possess them.

'You sunk an entire shipful of people? My God, Marko! How could you have done that?'

Marko unrepentant back then. Belligerent, fighting his corner.

'What would you have had me do? Let that hell-bitten man take all our heritage to the Danish Government? There were bones, Gregor. The bones of our ancestors. I could not let it lie, and I will not apologise.'

Gregor acquiescent, seeing Marko's point of view, despite abhorring his methods.

'You murdered people,' Gregor stated starkly. 'And not only your Othmar fellow. Think on them, Marko. Think of all the others who were blameless.'

Marko would not yield.

'All those folk on that ship had to do with the dig one way or another. All equally guilty.'

'Were they?' Gregor had asked. 'What about the crew? Extra passengers shoved aboard at the last minute? Did you think about them?'

Marko able to set Gregor right on that score, for there'd been no other passengers. Only the people from the dig. Ship booked a few years previously to take them and their hoard and no one else. The crew, though. He could see Gregor's objection to that. But time had been of the essence. The ship almost to Denmark. Almost, but not quite. Marko taking his time, calculating the odds. Sacrificing what needed sacrificing in order to save what was dear to him and his. To him and Gregor. Gregor not as fervid as Marko had been, but Gregor hadn't seen all those skeletons. Gregor helping him nonetheless. Getting Marko home. And never speaking a word of it bar that single time after he'd returned with his wife.

Returned with Irmgaard, the thought suddenly in Marko.

Irmgaard up there now in the chapel with Marko's son. No one to tell them the Black Bora was on its way. No one up there ever knew. You had to be down to see the signs. And no one in the swiftly rebuilt chapel of St Vid knowing it would not be able to withstand the onslaught. The whole project done on a shoestring. Quick job, quick result. Serviceable chapel of St Vid for the up-coming competition.

Providential his son was up there with Irmgaard Simić, knowing how capable she was, quick to judge circumstance, make right decisions. Irmgaard a vital addition to the village, who inspired as no other teacher had ever done.

Marko looking up at the mountain, gauging their chances.

Could see the highest trees, far above the crag on which the chapel was built, already bending. Weak trees, young trees, parents torn up by previous storms and discarded. Hard bare rock behind them, spirals and ginnels, where the karst was at its worst, through which the wind would funnel when enough force had built up. Image in his head of a gang of marauding thieves clutching broken window frames with raggedy fingernails as they hauled themselves into the house of a sleeping unsuspecting family.

Could not sit here somnolently, waiting for the murderers to come crashing down the mountain. Ran to the shed where he kept his dogs, hitched them to the sled and hied them up to fever pitch. Got them going up the hill and the tracks that would—God willing—get him to the chapel before the worst of the Black Bora was upon them. Whipping the dogs mercilessly, pushing them on as White Bora threatened to turn into Black.

Cautes to Cautopates.

A swivel through Svetovid's four faces to the worst.

It doesn't always go that way. Marko hanging onto the hope. Bora a bully; bullies sometimes finding threat was thrill enough without carrying through. Horrible twist in his gut. *Maybe this isn't providence, maybe this is vengeance.* Murdering thieves piling through the broken windows of his conscience, marauding ghosts snarling in his face as the salt-tipped breakers had done back in `39.

You're the murderer, screamed the wind in his ears.

You saved bones by making more, accused the snow, *and now is the time for retribution.*

Badly reconstructed chapel their target, wanting to rip out its heart, its altar, its pagan totem, take Marko's son and Irmgaard right along with them when they went.

15

All Roads Lead To Serbia

The Pfiffmaklers were breaking down their tents and sets, packing them onto carts, preparing to move on from Borre and Magleby. Moonlit performances over for the while, although would feature strongly in other places whenever they could. One last thing to do, at Lupercal and Jericho's insistence.

'You've got to see the chalk cliffs from down below,' they'd chirruped. Badgered, if Mergim was honest. Longhella predictably complaining.

'I'm not going down a load of slippery steps to march along a beach only to crawl up another set of slippery steps on the other side. Not likely.'

And just as predictably she had not, which had been her loss. Mergim appreciative of this enormous example of natural sculpture, these white cliffs. The boys pointing out its various features.

Summer's Spire, Queen's Seat, Castle Gables. Bagpipe and *Speaker* living up to their monikers as the waves boomed into their crevasses and out again.

Forchhammer's Point. Named for the Danish mineralogist who'd surveyed these cliffs in the eighteen thirties. A man the islanders were keen to claim. A man who'd invented his *Principle On The Salt Content of Sea Water*, maintaining it remained geographically constant. Give him a sample of sea water from anywhere in the world and, given enough sample sets, he'd tell you were it came from. Mergim supposed there must be some practical purpose to it, although couldn't think what it might be. Wondered what that particular feature had been called before Forchhammer came along. Everything changing when one person pops up out of nowhere, the old name subsumed and forgotten.

Back to camp, last of their gear being packed up, when another individual popped up out of nowhere.

'There's someone coming,' Diderik informed.

Mergim straightening his back, looking in the direction Diderik was pointing.

'It'll be nothing,' he said. 'Some village boy come to ask if he can join us.'

Quick glance at Ortwin, who had been such a boy. Ortwin too invested in his task of tying down a cart to take notice.

'He's older than that,' Diderik supplied, having better eyesight than most. 'Maybe in his forties or fifties?'

Mergim's heart jolting, couldn't help it. Their old enemy dead, they all knew it, yet the jitteriness from that episode had left none of them. All of it too raw, too recent. Mergim therefore calling everyone together, just in case. Everyone feeling likewise as they saw the stranger approach, everyone standing defensively behind their carts, except Longhella. The arrow to their collective bow.

'You know the drill,' she commanded. 'Stay behind and stay low. I'll handle this.'

Had Irmgaard been there at that moment she would have understood entirely what Grettir meant about Heraldo's family.

'Declare yourself!' Longhella shouted out. 'You'll come no further until I know who you are and what are your intentions.'

The man stuttering to a stop.

'State your purpose,' Longhella demanded. 'Tell me who you are and why you are here. And don't think for a moment I won't put an arrow through your heart if you tell me what I don't want to hear.'

Putting action to the words, taking up her bow, fitting an arrow expertly in place, pulling the string taut.

Jochen Steggle completely discombobulated. They'd seemed calm and accommodating, these Fairs Folk. Couldn't understand how his appearance had so riled them. Held up his hands, tried to shout, wasn't up to the task. Jochen too much on his own. Never any call to shout out anything, unless it was to curse Jansen. Jochen reminding himself why he was here, gingerly swinging the pack from his back to his front.

'I'm no danger,' he said, loud as he was able. 'I only wanted to ask you about this,' moving his hand to the pack, about to lift something from it.

'Oh no you don't, friend,' Longhella said, sounding anything but friendly. 'You'll lay it down where you stand and take a few paces back.'

Jochen doing as bid. Couldn't comprehend this adversity and mistrust. Longhella inching forward, removing another arrow from the flitch, using it to ease open the eye of Jochen's sack.

'Oh for pity's sake,' she said, biting her lip, annoyed to have been so panicked. 'It's just a load of nothing.'

Stepping back, reflitching her arrows. Querulous to have, even for a minute, thought it might have been otherwise.

'Pfiffmaklers, stand down,' she said, turning away in disgust. No more interest in Jochen and his beggaring sack any more than she'd had interest in the white cliffs of Møns. Mergim coming forward, feeling foolish and a little faint as the fear flooded away from him following Longhella's pronouncement, motioning Jochen to approach. Jochen picking up his pack, stepping forward.

'I didn't mean to alarm,' Jochen apologised. 'It's just, well, I have this object I can't make head nor tail of, and with you being so travelled I thought…'

Petered out. Felt like an idiot, cowed by these people who were so different from himself. By a young woman who'd been ready to send an arrow into his chest .

'I shouldn't have come,' he apologised, would have turned swiftly on his heel had not Mergim by then reached him, Mergim forcing a smile to mask his erstwhile panic.

'Yet come you did,' Mergim said, 'and you've done nothing wrong. It's merely that we're vulnerable on the road, and have recently come from…difficulties.' Mergim did not elaborate. 'What have you brought? We may as well have a look now you're here.'

Jochen taking from his pack the object that had been puzzling him for years. Handing it to Mergim. Mergim cupping its flat base in the palm of his large hand.

'Some kind of box?' he asked, which much Jochen had already assumed.

'Can I see?' Hulde, having come up beside Mergim, plucking it up, turning it one way and another, studying the squares incised across one side. Hulde letting out a small *ah*, which had Jochen and Mergim swapping glances.

'You don't see it?' she asked. Hulde holding the object out to them. 'It's all in the angle. Look,' holding it at forty five degrees, the open end of the box upwards, the closed end down. 'There's fifty squares here, now on the level,' she pointed out, 'twenty are blank. The others filled with varying numbers of dots and swiggles.'

Mergim scratching at his beard.

'I see that. Can't see what it means.'

Neither more could Jochen.

'Such blockheads,' Hulde opined, shaking her head as Longhella might have said and done. 'Think,' she prompted. 'What have we just performed here on Møns?'

'The Comet?' Jochen asked.

'The Dying Child?' Mergim's contribution. Jochen shivering to hear those words after all they'd engendered in him.

Hulde patient, leading them on.

'Both of those. But in what circumstances?'

Mergim rubbing at his nose, Jochen moving a tentative way forward.

'In moonlight?'

Sudden revelation.

'Oh but yes! In moonlight!'

Hulde was right, he'd been a blockhead. All those hundreds of nights he'd set out his telescope studying the stars, the moon, and it took this stripling of a girl to point it out to him.

'It's a moon calendar!' Jochen laughed. 'Marking its waxing and waning, when it's full or fallen.'

'That's how I see it,' Hulde said. 'Can't be sure I'm right.'

Mergim looking down on Hulde, who was always so right it hurt him.

'It makes perfect sense!' Jochen Steggle exclaimed. All so simple, those dots and squiggles, tracing his fingers over them.

'You're a miracle,' Mergim said fondly, putting his hand on Hulde's shoulder.

'She really is.' Jochen quick to endorse the sentiment. 'I've been trying to figure it out for ten years, and you!' Looking over at Hulde. 'You had it in less than a minute. How did you do that?'

'Because she's a lick-spittling toad who doesn't know when to keep her nose out,' Longhella intruding. Grabbing the object from Hulde.

'It's no mystery,' she stated pejoratively. 'I've seen a hundred of these in Serbia,' which was a massive exaggeration, for in fact there'd been only one. 'Heraldo said it was old. Sacred to whoever the blazes made them about a million years ago. It's a kiln, serpent guarding the entrance. Telling us low-down folk we're too dull-witted to notice what the moon does. Well, more fool them.'

Longhella stalking away, point made, dropping the clay calendar into the waiting hands of the lick-spittling toad who handed it carefully back to Jochen.

'And there you have it,' Hulde concluded. 'I didn't see the one from before but I remember Heraldo talking about it, said around five or six thousand years old. Three hundred times of how long I've been alive.'

Jochen stirring as he stowed the figurine back into his pack, looking at Mergim.

'That can't be right,' he murmured, Jochen always good with numbers. Jochen guessing the miracle girl had to be about twenty. Maybe a little less.

Mergim shrugging.

'She does that,' he said. 'Has a way of bringing the past back to the present, and the present to the past.'

Hulde excusing herself. Going off to help with the packing now the drama was done.

Jochen fascinated, working out the equation in his head: three hundred multiplied by twenty. It didn't seem possible, but Hulde was right. The sum total was indeed six thousand. Which meant in Jochen years, given Jochen was forty six, that number dwindled to around one hundred and thirty lifetimes since a lump of clay was dug out of a river bank in the environs of Serbia, was fashioned and incised with the cycles of the moon, fired in a kiln exactly like the one it depicted.

He shook his head in wonderment. In fewer than one hundred and fifty of his lifetimes preliterate societies had produced objects like this; gone on to create writing, compile ancient texts, become able to predict astonishingly rare astronomical events such as the regular return of comets or of the Transit of Venus.

'Anything else we can do for you?' Mergim asked, Jochen brought back to the moment, swiftly arranging several thoughts in his head.

The Pfiffmaklers had seen an object like this in Serbia.

This object very likely to have been cast up from the same shipwreck he'd built his house from.

Which meant that ship might have been sailing from Serbia to Denmark.

'Your young lady,' he said, meaning Longhella, 'said she'd seen one of these in Serbia?'

'That's what she said,' Mergim agreed.

'Does that mean you travel there a lot?' Jochen fumbling towards the root of his questions. Mergim clearing his throat, trying to shift things on.

'Travelling is rather what we do.' A little thrilled to be including himself in Pfiffmakler ways.

'Then maybe you can help me further,' Jochen said. 'If I give you a few words, could you tell me what language they're in?'

Mergim nodding.

'I don't see why not.'

'*Put Preko Mora*,' Jochen said simply, the name of the ship that had been wrecked.

Mergim unconsciously leaning forward an inch or two.

'It's Serbian,' he informed. '*The Road Over The Sea.* Why would you ask?'

Lots of Serbian ships named in their own language, especially if they were dependent on Venice or Trieste for the majority of their trade. The old spectre of Nationalism clinging on however it could.

'Because,' Jochen answered, 'this might sound a little odd.'

Mergim raising his eyebrows. Oddity daily fare for the Pfiff-maklers, as he was coming to realise. Mergim inviting Jochen into the camp. Almost packed, if not quite. Kettle still hanging over the embers of the fire to provide one last swallow of something hot prior to their departure.

'It's like this,' Jochen started…

16

The Quest Becomes Questionable

'I'm sorry about your husband.'

'And I about your wife.'

Heraldo and Irmgaard talking quietly, Grettir having briefed both about their similar circumstances.

'Much worse for you,' Irmgaard said, 'your wife being so young.'

Incredible relief for Heraldo to speak to someone about it who hadn't known Ludmilla, nor was suffering her loss.

'It's like I've been trapped in a tunnel underground,' Heraldo admitted. 'It's dark and lonely, and so hard to breathe.'

Irmgaard sighing, understanding.

'I'd look out of the cottage window. See the yard, the animals, the track leading off to the village. All insubstantial, unreal, shadows and echoes of what they were before. And I was immeasurably tired, yet couldn't sleep.'

Taking a deep breath.

'But I carried on. Had duties, children to teach. Didn't want to let anyone down.'

'Going through the motions,' Heraldo agreed. 'Dirty water swirling around a drain with nowhere to go but down.'

Irmgaard frowning, taking his hand. Here a pupil in need. Her own grief side-lined.

'We're not dirty water, nor are we yet down that drain. We're both here for a purpose.'

Heraldo raising half a smile.

'Are we?'

Plucking at his trousers with his fingers, his earlier certainty gone. Seeing his journey not as predetermined fate, instead selfish from first to last.

'Why did you come here?' Irmgaard asked gently.

Heraldo hanging his head to realise the truth.

'Because I'm a coward. Couldn't bear anyone's pity any longer, so invented a reason to leave.'

His mind manufacturing a mechanism of escape from the people who loved him most at the time they had most need of him.

'I should never have left Hulde,' he sighed. 'How could I ever have thought that the right thing to do? What must she think of me?'

'She'll not think badly,' Irmgaard tried. Although to leave a daughter, even an adopted one, should have been unthinkable. Both shaken from their self-absorption by Grettir coming in, fighting to get the chapel door back into its jamb.

'That wind is strong,' he announced, jitter of excitement to his words. 'Think it might be a real Bora coming on!'

Heraldo lifting his head, standing up, Grettir's excitement contagious.

'That wind you told me about?' he asked.

Furious and arrogant, roaring and battering.

And seeming so very apt after this revelatory conversation with Irmgaard. A purging needed, a heart-jolting happening to bring an end to his selfish and self-aggrandising quest. Time to go back home to the Pfiffmaklers and face the music. Make new music.

Make new music with Hulde. Give her the comfort he should have done, instead of deserting her.

Moment broken by Irmgaard getting up beside him.

'I hope to God you're wrong, because if it really is the Bora we're in serious trouble.'

Grettir untroubled by the troubled expression on Irmgaard's face.

'Not at all! We're in a stone chapel. There's nothing can do us harm. And this will be my very first Bora. Imagine that!'

Irmgaard shaking her head.

'You're wrong,' she repeated. 'Yes, we're in the chapel, but this chapel has been out of use for years.' Quick glance at the boys about their brazier. 'Our rebuilding has been superficial, a few additions of planks and nails.'

'My dear lady,' Grettir began, cut off by Irmgaard.

'I'm telling you, it isn't safe. Boys!' Irmgaard yelled. 'Get yourselves here. Right now.'

Boys on the run, alarmed by the urgency in Irmgaard's voice.

'Two of you, get that pit below Svetovid raked. Push everything hot and burning to one side. Use the water canisters to make the other half of it tolerably habitable.'

Boys about to argue. Irmgaard not finished.

'The rest of you, outside. Bring in every unused plank you can find.'

Grettir shuffling from one foot to another.

'I don't understand.'

Irmgaard spelling it out for him.

'If the Bora really is coming we need to get down, get hid, else the whole glorious lot of St Vid is going to come crashing down about our ears.'

'But the fire-pit?' Grettir queried. 'Wouldn't we be better outside?'

Irmgaard looking at him as if he was a dullard.

'You want to be outside when some of those trees up above get pulled from their roots and are sent hurtling right into our midst?

Send us rolling with all the rocks down slip and slide with snow and scree?'

Grettir alarmed. Seeing the situation for what it was. Fine to be talking Boras when he was safe and snug within the walls of his Wind Museum.

Different now he was possibly about to experience the real thing for himself.

Furious and arrogant, roaring and battering, no one and nothing standing in its way.

And nothing standing in its way as it roared and battered down the mountain towards the sea, except this chapel.

§

Marko cleared the lower slopes with relative ease. His dogs, Slovensky Kuvacs, bred for guarding livestock, equally adept at pulling a sled up any mountain. The snow, compacted by the boys' many trips through the previous weeks, aiding their going. Irmgaard's posts keeping them straight and true.

Weather already deteriorating. Skies blown over with harsh dark clouds, wind increasingly strong. Gusts and buffets swirling up near-impenetrable screeds of snow from the top of the drifts either side of the track. Dogs not so blinded, following their noses, scenting patches of urine and faeces deposited on previous journeys. Marko's face smarting despite the thick scarf secured over nose and mouth. Hands crabbed about the hand-rail of the sled, fingers frozen inside their gloves. Spine aching from the swift sways and lurches dictated by the dogs' going, but the dogs going on doggedly, as dogs do.

One hour in and he was over two thirds up.

Another half hour and the dogs, dogged as they were, beginning to flag.

'Get on!' Marko yelled, commands muffled by his scarf, by the screeching of sled-runners bouncing over the snow, by the wind that had flattened their ears. Marko hitting the nearest dogs with his switch until the switch slipped from fingers numbed by the cold. Marko cursing, bashing impotently at the sled rail. The scarf had ridden up almost to his eyes. Marko tore it furiously away.

Goddamn, goddamn...

Scarf catching beneath the sled-rails, making it bump and swerve.

Go on! Go on!

Dogs at the tail end of their stamina, slowing as they moved towards the tree line. Stopping. Dropping down. Panting, licking at the snow. Marko unhitching the dogs, slapping at their thick-hided sides. Two running on ahead the moment they were released, the other pair not to be moved until they got their breath back, when they turned their noses, turned their bodies, hurtled themselves back down the track with as much mad strength as they'd come up it.

Marko forging upwards after the first pair. Taking a swerve in the track, making out the dark rise of the chapel on its little mound of rock, his lips blue as the smock of the girl Irmgaard had seen on her day of ladybirds.

'Thank God,' Marko whispered, hauling himself onwards, dragged up one of Irmgaard's markers and stabbed it into the snow before him, used it to drag himself a further yard, and another and another, going on hands and knees, wind too strong to allow him to stand.

Almost there.

Up the curve and there, beneath the trees, were his two remaining dogs, whining and whimpering, laying themselves down, snuggling together against the woodpile as if they knew.

And they knew.

Terrible crash of thunder all around them having numerous birds squawking and chittering as they lifted themselves from nests and roosts; black cloud of bats joining the birds' frenzied flight, all circling above the chapel and the trees near about, then gone in a moment, blown away, dispersed and scattered, many wing-snapped as the Bora broke through all those ginnels in the spiky karst above.

The Keeper of Winds shall not hold us!

Marko hammering his way-marker hard as he could into the compacted snow, ripping off one glove with his teeth, forcing numbed fingers to unbuckle his belt, re-buckle it about the way-marker, wrapping the rest of it around his wrist.

Thundersnow all about him, booming like some ogre-sized bittern in hideous mountain marshes.

Lightning spiking down to left and right and up above.

And, in one of those frightening jagged spears of light, Marko saw the worst was about to happen. The slim trees above the chapel not built for this, their roots splayed wide instead of deep, and out they came. Plucked up one after another like an old woman pulling hairs from a troublesome wart upon her chin. Up and out, and inevitably down, and the snow coming too, loosed from between trunk and branch, slipping and sliding. An entire tranche creaking and groaning as it broke free, hundreds of tons of it sliding down the hill-side carrying the uprooted trees with it, Black Bora at its back.

Black Bora in the worst of moods.

We will turn this land to dust and rubble!

Destroy you earthlings, who tried to steal the daughter of a God!

Snow booming down the slope, sweeping up several large boulders and carrying them on its back for the ride.

§

Inside the chapel, they heard it coming.

'Into the pit,' Irmgaard commanded.

Marko's son leading the way, his friends lowering him down. Eight feet deep, like other Svetovid fire-pits from here to Rügen. Yanni helping the others as they came after him.

'You too,' she told Grettir and Heraldo, Grettir's face pale as the ghost moths shivering up from the grass in warmer months as he descended.

Heraldo shaking his head.

'It'll need two of us to pull the planks over.'

No argument from Irmgaard, both swift to the pile, lifting up one and then another, placing them rapidly over the pit, one's lip slightly overlapping its neighbour for maximum strength. Next few over, and the next. Last two to go, last two almost down when the chapel's unsteady walls began to shake. Heraldo glancing at Svetovid, but no help coming from that quarter. Svetovid already quaking in his boots. Heraldo quick about the pit and taking hold of Irmgaard, shoving her through the small gap left by the planks and over the brink.

'Catch her!' Heraldo yelled, and catch her they did, a little unceremoniously. Irmgaard winded and breathless once she'd landed, impotent to stop Heraldo sliding home the last two planks into their allotted places.

'Don't be a fool!' she got out, hammering her fists onto the base of the pit as she righted herself, stood herself on tiptoe, ordering her boys to lift her up so she could shift back the planks enough to allow Heraldo in. Heraldo having no intention of doing so. Heraldo standing square-shouldered in the chapel he'd come so far to find, staring at Svetovid. Heraldo seeing that if Svetovid fell, when Svetovid fell, he was going to crash right across the middle of the planks he and Irmgaard had erected and turn them into splinters. Heraldo having a better plan, moving about the uppermost end of the fire-pit, grabbing a crowbar as he went.

'Heraldo! For pity's sake! What are you doing?'

Irmgaard's voice quavering up from the pit.

'Keep to the farthest end!' Heraldo shouted back, shoving the crowbar beneath Svetovid's base, hefting and heaving, aided by the tremor beneath both their feet. Heraldo, at the last moment, putting his arms about the ancient god as it tipped, forcing the direction in which it went. The two hitting the ground as one, Heraldo not quite quick enough, tips of his music-making fingers crushed by the fall. He felt no pain, only glee to have succeeded, put his foot to the fallen god and, with the help of the crowbar, shoved him a yard or two into position, rolling him over the top of the pit, side coming to rest against the planks, head over one edge of the pit, scorched feet the other, able to take the weight of the back wall behind the altar if it collapsed.

Which it did.

Three minutes later.

Snow, with boulders on its back and trees in its midst, clearing the rise above the chapel. Nowhere to go but down.

17

Back To Phantoms Of Varying Kinds

'In 1839,' Jochen started, settling about the remnants of the Pfiff-maklers' fire, Hulde and the boys come to join them. 'Not long after I'd moved here from Dresden...'

"Great big city like Dresden to a nowhere place like this?' Jericho immediately interrupted. 'Why would you do that?'

'Not everyone likes cities,' Hulde put in, 'being surrounded by hundreds of people they don't know.'

Quick smile at Mergim, who knew it more than most. A prison like Kragujevac able to drum such a lesson right into your skull and out the other side.

'Hulde's right,' Jochen said, glad to know the girl's name. 'I was there for my apprenticeship in glass and wax-working, lessons in dissection and anatomy.'

'Ugh,' Jericho said. 'Last bit doesn't sound much fun.'

Ortwin disagreeing. 'Fascinating, surely, seeing how a body goes together.'

Ortwin suffering a scoliosis that curved his spine, hollowed out his chest.

'Oh it is fascinating!' Jochen was animated. He didn't like company as a rule, but the Pfiffmaklers were no ordinary company. 'And because of it, and because of my apprenticeship, I became a maker of phantoms.'

No one understanding.

'What's a phantom when it's at home?' Lupercal asked. 'Surely you don't mean ghosts?'

'How could anyone make ghosts?' Jericho jeered, digging an elbow into his brother's side.

'Isn't that partly what we do?' Mergim asked mildly. Lupercal swift to back him up.

'He's got you there, brother!'

Jericho grumbling, having no quick riposte.

'Not those kind of phantoms,' Jochen explained.

'Told you,' Jericho couldn't resist.

'My phantoms are wax models,' Jochen explained, 'for medical students and dentists to practise on. I make heads with removable eyes, teeth and tongues and, at this very moment, I have almost an entire corpse laid out upon my work-bench.'

The boys' eyes widened.

'An entire corpse?' Ortwin was staggered.

Jochen nodded.

'Complete with excisable muscle mass, arteries and nerves, from the top of his skull to the bottom of his toes.'

'Amazing!' Ortwin breathed. 'I wish I could see it. Could I maybe see it?'

Looking at Mergim for answer.

Lupercal and Jericho of the same opinion.

'We can't miss out on something like this.'

'Not a sight someone sees every day.'

Mergim himself looking to Hulde for guidance, although could see no real objection. A couple of days here or there having no bearing on their long term plans.

'Heraldo would have loved it,' Hulde said quietly, eyes fixed on the fire. Enough for Mergim, squaring his shoulders, straightening his back as Ortwin could never do.

'I agree,' he said, holding up his hands to stem the rising excitement, 'but it is not my decision to make. That decision belongs to our guest and I apologise,' he added, looking over at Jochen. 'I don't know your name.'

'Jochen,' Jochen said, 'Jochen Steggle. And you would all be most welcome. In fact it would be an honour for I am in your debt, in Hulde's debt.'

Small smile at Hulde, small shy smile back.

'It will take a day's travelling, given you have your carts,' Jochen added. 'But there's plenty space once there to set up your tents and I will happily provide food and drink, tell you my tale when you're settled in.'

Surprising himself to realise he was looking forward to having actual guests, and Pfiffmakler guests at that. Not to mention it would be a right royal slap in the face for Jansen who had never valued his work, had called it a load of useless crap on more occasions than he could remember.

'Very well then, Pfiffmaklers,' Mergim announced, slapping his hands on his thighs, standing up. 'It's decided. Thank you, Mr Steggle.'

'Jochen, please,' Jochen put in.

'All right, thank you Jochen. Boys! Let's get moving!'

Younger Pfiffmaklers swiftly up, kicking the fire over with enthusiasm, stowing kettle and cups.

'Longhella's going to raise a fit,' Hulde observed.

'Doesn't she always?' Mergim replied easily. 'A day without a fit from Longhella is the day we should all hang up our coats and be done with it.'

Hulde smiling.

For yes, a day without Longhella throwing a tantrum here or there was an unusual day, not that anyone would have it any other way. Longhella seeming to hold the base energy of life itself in her every movement, in every syllable of everything she said. Longhella standing up against the universe that had done her wrong as neither Mergim nor Hulde could do. Longhella sometimes discovered to be missing from their ranks on one night or another, having crept from the tent she shared with Diderik. Diderik always a lesser person on his own than when he was with her. Diderik always coming to Hulde or Mergim on those occasions.

'She's gone again,' he would whisper, and up would Hulde or Mergim go, slim candles held in sleep-ridden fingers.

'I know I should go myself...' Diderik would say, but Diderik never would. Diderik knowing it wasn't him Longhella had need of at such times. Longhella never far. Mergim or Hulde finding her weeping on a nearby boulder or bole. This night-time Longhella so different from the one they knew during the harsh light of day.

'It should never have happened,' she'd whisper.

Reciting the names of those she'd lost, most particularly her sister.

'It's done, darling,' Hulde would whisper back, if it were her. 'And now we're all we've got.'

'There's nothing could have changed it,' if it were Mergim.

Would put their arms about her shoulders, hold her close. Sit witness through dark nights swinging towards the washed-out watercolours of an on-coming dawn when they would deliver her back to Diderik, who would curl himself about her, warm her with his body. No need to tell anyone else about this other Longhella who had a loss in her too great and deep to leave behind.

18

Cometh The Wind

Marko felt made of thunder. Everything booming and crashing, bones thrumming with their reverberations. Might have been trapped inside a giant kettle drum, a delirious percussionist hammering at it with mallets.

Fleet vision of when he'd been caught in the Stone Gate of Zagreb, more a tunnel than a gate, when an earthquake hit. Legs going out from under him, breath pushed out with the shock of the fall. Edifices above him trembling and groaning, Marko sure his last moment had come.

Marko having the same conviction now as the snow surged over him in a moment.

Covering him. Smothering him.

Granite-hard jag catching his shoulder, ripping away coat, shirt, a fistful of flesh.

Might have thought it due retribution had he been able to think, which he could not.

Instinct keeping that belt-strap about his wrist, the pole to which he was anchored bent at its neck, its waist, its knees, right down to the ground, an inch from Marko's forehead. Fear resurgent when the dogs who'd been snuffling by the woodpile hurtled past him in a maelstrom of terrification, splinters of wood sharded into their bodies, tongues hanging out, blur of red blood on white fur. A split second before they were over the lip of the crevasse below the chapel with the snow-spill. Marko almost gone too.

Strong leather belt-strap and stout brass buckle all that tethered him.

Wind still bashing about him.

And then more snow smacking at his head with the force of a sledgehammer.

Marko overwhelmed.

Buried beneath three feet of snow.

Alive for the moment, if not for long.

§

In the fire-pit, Irmgaard, Grettir and the boys cowered, arms held over heads, hearing the thunder approaching them. Awful impression of deliberation in its direction, as if the avalanche had transmogrified into a hundred trolls stampeding and rampaging, intent on trampling them beneath their feet. Snow over them in a heart-withering, ear-splitting whoosh, walls and joists shuddering and juddering, window glass splintering, roof-planks screaming as they were ripped from their new nails.

Horrendous crash and batter as one of those errant boulders bowled into the back wall of the chapel. The highest courses of the extant gable-end wobbling and toppling as the boulder came to rest, its precipitate journey over. Its fellows and the rest of the trolls going on without it, leaving calling cards of spillage through the broken windows, filling the foremost part of the chapel with snow, pushing out the door, ripped it from its hinges, took it on a wild ride over the chasm into the forest below where it carried on with exhilarating speed over tree tops, caught in the mad wings of the wind. Was finally hurled into a cattle shed in the down-below village, partially decapitating the herd's prize bull. The avalanche by then spent, sighing and soughing, spreading itself between the trees it had bent but not broken, coming to an uneasy rest.

§

Irmgaard, Grettir and the boys pressed themselves against the very back of the pit. Their quickly erected roof of planks had held so far, but the smashing of the boulder into the back wall sent the boles in the fire juddering and rolling towards them, the rest of it seeming to creep along behind, intent on devouring them. The heat tremendous as Irmgaard inched forward and kicked at one of the boles with the sole of her boot, the boys gaining courage from her and doing the same. The embers gaining new life by their sudden forward momentum, which pushed air back into their fiery lungs, made them glow and spit, buffet out smoke. No care for the humans who had been tending them, those humans now beginning to cough, holding shirts and skirts across their faces, shuffling their feet away from the onward tide of fire.

Irmgaard didn't think the situation could get worse. They'd survived the onslaught of the avalanche, but now the back half of the chapel roof, weakened by the tumbling of the topmost gable-stones when the boulder hit, was stressed and strained, groaning with the weight of snow it was finding hard to bear. A terrible screeching of wood wrenching against its nails all the worse for being long and drawn out; everyone hearing its excruciation as it sawed through their coughing, sound of talons being scraped slowly down a blackboard, maybe gouging out their names, totting up their scores of rights and wrongs, weeding the sheep from the goats.

Irmgaard not beaten yet, not with these boys under her care. Put her hand on Marko's son's shoulder, removed her skirts from her face.

'Yanni,' Yanni coughing, looking into his teacher's calm grey eyes. 'You're the tallest, so get two...' stopping briefly to clear her throat, cough, wipe eyes dripping with tears from the acrid smoke... 'two of the others to shove you up, push away the planking at the edge so...'

More coughing, Yanni understanding, fetching the strongest of his friends, getting their hands cupped about his feet to push him up. Yanni hardly able to see, the smoke up top so thick, but pushed his hands high, got his fingertips under one of the planks and shoved.

'Higher!' he tried to say, started to choke.

'Higher!' he heard Irmgaard repeat from down below, and higher his friends pushed him, Yanni bracing one hand against the pit wall to steady himself, get enough purchase to haul that first plank out of the way, the sudden influx of fresh air a godsend, giving him strength to pull away another and another. Sudden wobble at his feet as his friends fought the smoke curling, thick and writhing, towards the outlet Yanni had created.

'We've got to get out,' Irmgaard croaked, as Yanni was shakily lowered back down. 'What did you see? Any rope? Anything we can use?'

The air more breathable now the smoke had somewhere else to go.

Yanni shaking his head, glancing upwards as the chapel's roof carried on crying out for help.

'Couldn't see. Not high enough up to get my head out.'

'What are we going to do?' Grettir bleated.

'They've to get me back up, give me a boost,' Yanni replied. 'If I can get myself over the lip I can get some of them out...'

Some, but not all. Always two needed below to shove the next one up, even with Yanni up top to pull them on. Irmgaard stoic, Grettir quailing by her side. Youth before age the obvious conclusion, never mind the older might be of more worth.

'Got to get as many out as we can,' Irmgaard decided. 'More up top, more hope of finding rope, more hope of...'

Everything stopped by that ominous creaking gaining voice, getting ready for its big finale.

'Oh heavens,' Irmgaard breathed, as the back half of the roof decided it had had enough, let go plank after plank, tile after tile, all shrieks and splinters as it crashed down from the rafters, broke-backed by the snow it could no longer support, coming down on them with horrendous certainty.

Everyone in the fire-pit holding their breath, clutching each other's hands.

I'm sorry, boys, if this is it.

Words in Irmgaard's mind, no time to speak them out loud.

Everything in those few moments crack and splinter, thump and thud, jolt and judder.

Small thought in Irmgaard about Heraldo, what had become of him.

If he'd already been buried alive, as it seemed the rest of them were about to be.

Yanni next to her, curling into her side, ready to embrace the worst.

Yanni more scared than he'd been in his life.

A line flitting through his head from his father's Norse Atlantic Sagas, read to him as often as his father's uncle had read them to Marko.

It is not a good thing you have done, yet some will say there is excuse of a kind.

Yanni, in the role of school secretary, who'd brought news of the competition into Irmgaard's ken, urged her on when she'd mentioned St Vid, cajoled his father into rebuilding the chapel.

A lot of trouble is heading our way, and it will cost him his head.

Or all their heads, as it might turn out.

'I'm sorry,' he whispered, clutching at Irmgaard's hand. Irmgaard turning to him, putting her free hand below his chin, staring at him with those oddly serene sea-grey eyes.

'You're not at fault. This is what it is, and nothing you or I could have done to prevent it.'

And what it was, was what it was.

Roof collapsing, coming down, the great mass of snow upon its fragile shoulders crashing through the planks at the farther end of the fire-pit, putting out the flames with hiss and holler. Svetovid, rolled over the pit by Heraldo, taking the brunt of fallen roof-struts, lengths of which piled against his back, teetered upon the pit's edges but did not come in, could not bolster the fire that crackled and spat and then expired, defeated.

Irmgaard, Grettir and her boys saved, by the slimmest of chances.

By Svetovid.

By Heraldo.

Boys quick to exploit the enabling snow to leap over the buried fire, get up the recesses carved into the fire-pit's wall, emerging with hollering whoops into the chapel above.

§

Marko scrabbled and scraped, pushed away enough snow to make a small space to left and right of him. Was breathing too hard and fast he knew, tried to slow it, tried not to gulp, not to cry. Not to think on those people he had drowned in the Kattegat who had to have been as feared as he was now. Weird thought in him that it could be so dark when snow was such an epitome of light. Having an atavistic urge to see the sky again, if only for a moment. Started hollowing out his hole, brushing snow first from the sides and then the top, or what he assumed was the top, given his wrist was still attached to the leather belt when he woke from however long it was he'd been unconscious.

Nowhere for that snow to go, of course, so he pushed it down below his feet, made of it a compacted platform as he grew from homunculus to a person crouched, to one who could wriggle this way and that, gradually uncurl his spine, found the tip of the marker stick, when he went at the snow above him with both hands, the un-gloved as well as the gloved. Couldn't feel either of them, which was advantageous, allowed him to go at it without thinking of frostbite or concomitant injury. The snow he dislodged by doing so coffining the rest of him, but finally got his head out, took a breath, gloried in the air, the dim light. Craned his neck, looked towards the chapel.

Which was so much worse than he'd feared.

The back end of St Vid stoved in by a massive boulder.

The front half overtaken and immured in snow.

And the Bora not yet spent, still guffawing with undisguised glee as the buffoon who had attempted to get out from under it tried and failed to haul himself from his hole, knocked him this way and that. Marko caught fast from the chest down as the snow capitulated to its master, shuddered and trembled, slid and poured itself into the grave he'd dug for himself.

§

'It's a proper shambles up here,' the escaping boys called merrily down, exhilarated by how close to death they'd come: first by avalanche, then by smoke and fire, and next by the tumbling down of the roof that had—by glorious circumstance—liberated instead of condemned them. The Svetovid totem—no idea how this had happened—acting as a prop bridging the fire-pit, along with the few remaining planks, shielding them from the worst. Just enough space for the snow from the roof to empty itself down onto the fire, just enough strength in Svetovid to support the collapsing eaves, prevent them smashing through their paltry pit-hiding planks onto those below.

A surmise proved correct when, a few minutes after they'd all got out, Svetovid, lying on his side, seemed to let out an audible sigh as the rafter beams he'd been supporting rolled him on an inch or two, and then another and another, until his base-end swerved over the pit's edge. Irmgaard, Yanni and the others watching awestruck as he went, thumping into the snow that had extinguished his fires, followed by the rafter beams he'd been supporting, which in turn took with them the planks. A creaking splintering orchestration of ruin and collapse, as they went into the snowy pit.

And a surreal scene once all was done: Svetovid landing on his feet, standing upright, back braced against the pit-wall; his four faces staring out implacably at the four-cornered wreckage of the chapel, his wooden head regarded with awe by his creators.

'Talk about a fall from grace,' Yanni murmured.

'And yet still standing,' Irmgaard noted. 'As are we.'

Except Heraldo.

For of him there was no sign at all.

19

Try Not To Crack The Egg

Jansen groaned, leant his pitchfork against the fence, his back giving out after several hours of half-heartedly digging seaweed into one of his small fields. Keeping at it because he was so very curious about his neighbour. This plot closest to the track, in the outer ditch of which he'd spent the night, not quite making it home after their return the previous night.

Not unusual, given the amount he'd drunk. More unusual to be woken by footsteps, Jochen sneaking off along the track just past dawn without giving Jansen tedious pleas to keep an eye on his livestock, no rants about how well he'd itemised his stores, *to the ounce, Jansen, to the ounce.* So plainly Jochen intended to return the very same day and, when he did, Jansen meant to pounce.

This trip entirely out of character. Fine when they'd gone to see the Pfiffmaklers, and a hoot they'd been. Jansen still laughing about

The Comet, for that had been Jochen Steggle to a tee. Bemused to see Jochen shedding a tear for *The Dying Child*, for what the hell was that about? Dying children hardly news, in anyone's book. Had none himself, and wouldn't have been so bloody melodramatic about it if he had. Children prone to fits and diseases. No point getting too attached when the inevitable could come calling at any moment.

But wait a minute…

Who was calling now?

Jansen holding a hand above his eyes to block out the sun, which was dying as inevitably and slowly as had that ghastly child.

Who's this on the track, then?

That's Jochen, and that's the bloody Pfiffmaklers!

Jochen leading the way like he was Christ Almighty coming into… well, Jansen couldn't exactly remember where. A donkey involved, palm fronds too, if he wasn't mistaken. And wasn't mistaken about the Pfiffmaklers. He'd recognise that woman in the orange skirts anywhere, the rest pulling their carts down the track after her.

The world, for Jansen, going seriously out of kilter. Jochen Steggle bringing people as prestigious as Fair's Folk to the deserted shores of Møns! Jochen bloody Steggle, of all people, who could hardly hold a conversation with his own blasted animals, let alone actual human beings. You could have knocked Jansen down with a feather.

'Almost there,' Jochen called over his shoulder. 'Another quarter mile and we'll be at the shore. Well hello neighbour.' Jochen waved, lifting his hat as he saw Jansen gawping like a beached fish as he watched the procession approach. Jansen too surprised to answer Jansen hurriedly reeling in his neck, pretending to tie up his boot laces. Wasn't going to be seen by the likes of Jochen Steggle to hold even the merest flicker of interest about his goings on. Annoyed he'd ducked down so obviously and hadn't thought to do so the moment he'd seen them coming. Certain he heard a couple of the younger boys of the retinue tittering.

Couldn't decide whether to stand up or not. In the end remaining crouched below the threadbare hedge through which he could see legs and wheels passing him by.

'Visitors,' he heard Jochen crow. 'I wonder what my neighbour will think of that? And where did he go so suddenly?'

Jansen so incensed he stood up.

'You fucking bast....'

Words dying on his lips as he came face to face with the woman in the orange skirts.

'I'm sorry,' Longhella said politely. 'Were you speaking to me?'

Jansen not particularly averse to swearing at women, but this one had the look of an executioner in her eyes. Jansen stuttering out an ill-thought answer, trying to make those words other than they had been.

'You've forgotten the bast...the baskets. That's it! You've forgotten the baskets, you idiot!' Jansen shaking his fist, shouting at thin air, the crew having already moved on. The executioner nonetheless relaying his message, very loudly.

'Jochen!' Ludmilla called out for all to hear. 'Your neighbour tells me you've forgotten the fucking baskets!'

Jansen's face resembling the un-lanced boil he had at that very moment beneath his left armpit: very red, ready to explode at any moment.

'Bloody fucking Jochen,' he muttered beneath his breath as he turned away. 'And bloody fucking women.'

The two things he most despised in this world, yet a creeping admiration for a woman who could let such expletives fly from her lips. Glancing back down the track only to see that woman looking right back at him, cocking her best snook.

Jansen grasping the pitchfork tightly about its neck, exactly as he'd have liked to do to Jochen Steggle. And damned if he was going to let Jochen keep his secrets. Jansen knowing his crowing enemy through and through. Not a chance Jochen wouldn't bring out his blasted telescope come nightfall and start crowing about that too.

Time to change the habits of a lifetime, maybe take a moonlit stroll along the sands.

Always a first time for everything.

§

Always a first time for everything, those in the chapel were thinking.

My very first Bora! for Grettir Wyssling. Surviving by the skin of his teeth. All he'd heard about it, perhaps not quite believed, proved beyond doubt. Queue of questions about previous visitations. How to display it in his museum. Interrupted by Irmgaard and the boys' calls. Grettir arrested, shame in every pore.

'Heraldo!' they were yelling. 'Heraldo!'

All of them going at the snow-filled front of the chapel with their hands. More concerned with finding the man Grettir had brought to their doors than himself. Grettir mortified, joining in, soon redirecting their search.

'That totem didn't move by itself,' he pointed out. 'Someone brought it down, rolled it over the pit.'

Irmgaard looking past him, regarding the heap of rubble at the back of the chapel where the gable-end had fallen. Irmgaard dismayed. No one could have survived that, unless…

'Boys!' she ordered. 'Over there. Take those stones away one by one. And be careful, take only from the top.'

Boys obeying, Yanni at the helm, Yanni imbued with the impetus of rescue because he saw the entire disaster as his fault.

Pile of stones growing from one place to another.

Pile in front of them diminishing, that at their backs accrescent.

'There's the altar's edge!' Yanni shouted. This Yanni's personal contribution to the project. His idea to restore it, re-erect its collapsed pieces. Cursed hard work to tie ropes about the two hefty monoliths of its side-plinths and haul them into place within their sockets. The larger dolmen of the altar slab harder still to manipulate, pulleys needed, and all their strength to get it raised and in place. His father saying he could make a serviceable replica from wood, yet admiring the finished article.

'That's grand, that is,' Marko had commented, glad Yanni had not been moved from his plan.

As had not been moved this altar. The top shoved forward a few inches by the boulder hit. All else intact.

Grettir at Yanni's shoulder as the last few rocks were pulled away. Heraldo there, curled like a dormouse in a nest of dust, hands held over his head as they'd done in the pit when they'd feared the worst.

Boys standing back, rolling their shoulders. Irmgaard coming forward, crouching down, putting out a gentle hand, placing fingers to his neck, trying to find a pulse.

'Heraldo,' she called softly. 'Can you hear me? Are you hurt?'

Silence.

Wind moving on, fading away down to the sea.

'Heraldo?' Irmgaard asked again.

Here the man who'd done everything he could to save people he didn't know; who'd shoved her down the pit to stop her doing the same to him; who'd pushed the last planks over their heads and somehow manoeuvred Svetovid so he was in exactly the right place to stop the falling rafter beams crushing the lot of them to death. Terrifying down there, but with a modicum of protection. How much worse for him up top.

Grettir beside her.

'Remind him of Hulde,' he whispered. Irmgaard bobbing her head.

'Come out, Heraldo. Hulde's waiting for you.'

A slight movement beneath her fingers.

'Take it slow,' Irmgaard warned. 'If you're hurt at all we can help.'

'And don't lift your head up too suddenly,' Yanni advised, 'or you'll crack it like an egg.'

A drift of dust ploofing upwards as their words wheedled through the ringing in Heraldo's ears and he moved his hands. Unsure if he was actually alive. After his grappling with Svetovid he'd stood, fighting for breath, fingertips throbbing, snow blowing out all the windows, pouring in with the lubricity of quicksilver. And then the boulder hit and the stones of the gable wall began tottering, wind screaming and laughing, roof groaning and sighing. Threw himself beneath the stone altar, rocks tumbling down, cutting him off from the outside world.

Thoughts of Ludmilla, so alone when she'd died. The words she might have spoken as she'd waited for her end.

Come soon, my love, or I'll spend my last day without you.

Heraldo back in the dark forests of Jasmund calling out her name. And in his black hole hearing her voice, as if she was beside him. *I'm here, my love. You're not alone. You'll never be alone.* Heraldo unable to answer. Throat and nose clogged with dust, lungs raggedly pulling in what little air was available. So little time left as the rocks of St Vid were pulled away from the altar one by one, crack of light coming in at him, small wisp of air a-tingle with the scent of snow. Heraldo convinced it wasn't real, was his mind's way of coping with dying. Ludmilla there to ease his guilt by allowing him go the same path into oblivion she had done.

Hulde.

He heard the name distinctly.

Hulde's waiting for you.

And don't lift your head too suddenly, or you'll crack it like an egg.

It seeming such a joke he would have laughed if he'd been able.

Settled for moving his hands from his head, creaking out several words as he saw Irmgaard's face leaning solicitously towards his own.

'Everyone all right?' he croaked.

Felt her hand upon his cheek, couldn't hear her words but could read them on her lips.

'Everyone all right, thanks to you, my boy.'

My boy.

Ludmilla used to call him that when they were young.

He'd always hated it back then, but now they seemed the best of words in the best of worlds.

Everyone all right, including him.

Nothing like nearly dying to make you realise you'd far rather be alive.

20

Come up, Yanni, Come Up.

Jochen led the Pfiffmaklers to the place he'd deemed best for their camp.

Mergim shrugging off his harness, seeing salt marshes stretching away to his left, long sandy bay and dunes to the right.

'Nyord Bay,' Jochen said. 'No one here but us.'

Exactly as he liked it. Would have preferred it to be emptied of Jansen. Smirking to think on Longhella shouting out those words.

Your neighbour tells me you've forgotten the fucking baskets!

Shocking to hear her swearing like that, a little exhilarating too.

'Any prevailing winds?' Mergim asked, as if he were a real Pfiff-makler. His untrained eye regarding the way the reeds lay at a slant, the neatly woven cups of buntings' nests one side and not the other; a staggered line of small burly trees, branches crabbed over in the same direction. The distinctive hump of an ant nest grown up between the outer trees of the larger wood beyond the reed beds.

They eat more flesh, do ants, in Africa, Heraldo had told him, *than all the large carnivores put together.*

How Heraldo knew it Mergim had no notion.

'Best to pitch midway between forest and reed beds,' Jochen advised. 'Firm ground, access to fresh water, not too much wind.'

Pfiffmaklers setting to. Tasks carried out efficiently. The boys eager to get pitched, the sooner to be off to Jochen's home.

'That's it there,' Jochen had pointed out, having led the Pfiff-maklers to this place which, only by the by, could be seen from the tiny windows of Jansen's poky little hut.

'Wow!' Jericho had enthused. 'And that's where you keep your ghosts?'

'Phantoms,' Lupercal corrected his brother. 'It's a peculiar shape. And what's that on top? Is that grass?'

Jochen bemused, looking at Mergim who shrugged his shoulders as if to say *they're boys. What did you expect?*

'I built it from the wreckage of a ship thirteen years ago,' Jochen explained.

Swift arpeggio of voices putting in their bit.

'A real wreck? Did you see it go down?' from Jericho.

'Looks enormous,' from Lupercal.

'How long did it take to build?' Ortwin more practical.

Hulde's voice a moment after the others, who had spoken simultaneously.

'Does it ever bother you, what happened to the people on it?'

Jochen chewing his lip because it truly never had, not until Jansen had put all those bad images inside his head.

'It has troubled me lately,' he admitted. *Real ghosts, inside my house.*

Hulde nodding her head sagely.

'They're probably glad you've given them somewhere to go,' she said. 'That should give you comfort.'

Jochen taken aback. He'd not looked at it that way before. Just as he'd not looked at his moon calendar the way she had, nor the thousands of years of history it represented. Hulde seeming to come at everything from a different angle. Jochen wondering if she'd been born that way or if life had somehow skewed her onto a different path, going the same direction as everyone else but parallel in some odd way.

'Can we go now?' Jericho asked Mergim with undisguised impatience.

Mergim regarding the sea, the sky, the lateness of the afternoon.

'Best take a lamp,' he advised. 'It'll be dark when you get back.'

'You're not coming too?' Jochen asked. Mergim give a small shrug.

'Not sure I want to see any more dead bodies,' Mergim answered, 'even if they're only made of wax.'

Strong implication being that Mergim had seen more dead bodies than he cared to remember. Jochen storing away this snippet. Odd people, these Pfiffmaklers. Supposed they had to be in their peripatetic line of work, although Mergim and Hulde seemed odder than might have been expected, carved from a knottier, more complex kind of wood. Jochen thinking on all the storm-felled trees hauled out from the forest by chains and Jansen's scrawny donkey. The concentric circles revealed, after being split with adze and axe, denoting the course of its life. Some thin, some thick, others neither perfect nor round: indications of abnormal weather, or a cataclysmic volcano happening on the other side of the world.

'I'd like to go,' said Hulde.

Jochen casting a glance at the older woman, who'd shouted out Jansen's words so blithely. She seemed uninterested, otherwise engaged sharpening arrows and knives.

'Very well,' he announced. 'Let's go.'

Lupercal and Jericho eager in the lead, Ortwin keeping up as best he could. Hulde and Jochen taking a more leisurely pace behind.

'And the night is clear,' Mergim could hear Jochen saying. 'A few planets will be visible using my telescope. Venus, Mars and Jupiter. And we're cusping from winter constellations into spring,' Jochen added happily, 'so Auriga the charioteer will be moving to the right, dragging the chariot of Ursa Major behind him.'

Which kind of made sense to Mergim, to whom the stars meant nothing except for always being up there. And what he knew about planets you could have scratched on the side of an acorn. *Wanderers,* the sum total of it, as Hulde had told him. *They're called wanderers, just like us.*

§

Heraldo was eased from beneath the altar. Irmgaard solicitous, worried at the state of his fingertips, swiftly fetching a bowl of snow, burying them in it.

'It should arrest the bruising,' she told him. Heraldo too shaken to do anything but comply.

Your beautiful fingers, Ludmilla's voice again, a comfort, not an alarm. With him when he'd believed he was dying, still with him now. He knew it was all in his head, which was a comfort too. Able to think of her, conjure up her voice, her words, without that black wall of guilt keeping her out. Wall of his guilt crumbling like the gable end of St Vid.

'I'll be back soon,' Irmgaard assured him. 'Get those fingers splinted.'

Leaving him snow-gloved and shivering as she set about ordering her troops.

'Yanni,' she called. 'Get that fire going again. Start shovelling, see if you can find any embers. If you do, shore them up and get them fed. Everyone else, check the pulleys. And start lifting off our planks, get them broken up for the fire.'

'What can I do?' Grettir asked. Irmgaard, having forgotten all about him, quick to add him back into the equation. She cast a quick look about the chapel, which was a wreck. Worse than when they'd first encountered it.

'Door's completely blocked,' she diagnosed, 'if not that one window on the left. Take one of the boys. Heave him out. Got to know what everything's like outside.'

Grettir nodding curtly, glad for a task he could follow. Picking the lithest looking lad and pitching him through the window, craning his neck out after him.

Darkness out there, although a faint luminosity from the snow.

'See anything?' he called, the lad answering back.

'It's a bit weird!' the lad yelled. 'All the trees below the chasm have been bent double by the avalanche.'

Grettir pedantic, about to say it wasn't the avalanche had caused the damage but the tremendous push of air an avalanche causes to go before it. Grettir not getting it said.

'Hold up!' the lad called out. 'The woodpile's gone, and I think I see something moving just down the…think there might be…

no, I'm sure. Irmgaard! Tell Irmgaard I think there's someone out here in the snow!'

Grettir's throat tightening, for how could that be? Maybe a bear, trapped in the snow, caught in the sudden down-rush, but the lad already away, caught up in the excitement. Grettir calling to Irmgaard, telling her what was going on. Irmgaard similarly vexed. Grettir telling her to push him out of the window so he could go check. Irmgaard not about to argue. A farcical moment when Grettir was halfway in, halfway out, hands scrabbling at the air, legs kicking as he fought for balance, catching Irmgaard on the chin before she had her arms about his ankles and shoved him out.

Grettir going headfirst into the snow, breaking his fall with his hands, the rest of him tumbling on in abandon behind. Taking a few moments to right himself, brush himself down.

The lad reappearing on the scene.

'It's Marko,' he said. 'It's Yanni's father. And he don't look good.'

No time to ask Irmgaard for direction, time to get doing. Grettir the adult. He the one to take charge.

'Is he conscious?'

The boy looking worried, shaking his head.

'Not sure he is. Buried right up to his chest.'

Grettir not knowing much about avalanches, but knew a lot about mining and the accidents concomitant with it. Snow surely not unlike soil when it was trying to swallow you whole.

'We're going to need a rope and boards, a shovel or a rake.'

'Can get you rope, mister,' the boy moving off to fetch it, calling over his shoulder. 'Latrine-hole lid's gone, but the shovel is still inside!'

Grettir sticking his head back through the window.

'Irmgaard! Need several lengths of planks, four or five feet long if you can manage it.'

Irmgaard responding quickly, the boys already breaking up the planks that had covered the pit. And about the right length. Sending several out the window, and another boy with them. Irmgaard's face appearing in the empty space.

'Do we know who it is?'

'It's Yanni's father, the lad says,' Grettir told her, seeing Irmgaard rubbing her fingers against her temples.

Irmgaard not surprised. Marko always having one eye on the mountains, gauging the forests, the weather, especially since she'd brought his son up here. Would surely have worried when their moonlight procession never materialised, realised why. Would have hooked his dogs to his sled and come up to try to rescue them. Marko always a carer since she'd known him.

'Do what you can,' she told Grettir. 'Bring him here if possible. Stay with him if not. He's been a good friend to me and mine.'

'Got a bit of fire going down here!' Yanni called, Irmgaard and Grettir locking eyes.

'I have to tell him,' Irmgaard said. Grettir nodding grimly, no time to waste, hauling the plank lengths up below his arm and setting off, the young lads bouncing at his back with rope and shovel.

Marko, as previously diagnosed, not looking good, head lolling on his chest, no hat, no scarf, only one glove. Arms splayed out around him which made getting the rope about his body easy. Not so easy to pull him out, snow packed so tightly about him he maybe couldn't breathe, was maybe already dead. Grettir putting his fingers beneath Marko's chin, bringing up his face. Marko's skin pale and clammy as mayweed after rain. Faintest push of breath from his lips.

'He's alive,' Grettir said quietly. 'Let's get going. Hang on to the rope. I'm going to dig a circle around him, get in those boards, start loosening the snow inside, see if we can't get him out.'

§

Down in Svetovid's pit, Yanni was triumphant. Had scraped some of the snow away to the right of the totem where it was thinnest, discovered a thick layer of embers beneath. Almost burned his fingertips off raking away the damp top layer to get to the fire still alive beneath. Breathing a sigh of relief. No point surviving an avalanche if you went on to freeze to death. Yanni already making stories up in his head about this most momentous of nights, how he could work it into their pageant; the old god not exactly rising up in their moment of need, more like lying down, yet enough to save them from the worst. Yanni standing on the snow, pushing away more and more like a dog going at sand, soon had a sizeable patch of living breathing embers he could coax back to life. Started gently kicking the edge of it with his boot, introducing a little air, small judder of excitement as he saw the embers brighten, small flames begin to lick up and out.

'Need some tinder down here!' he called. 'Hey!' he yelled again, when no one immediately answered. Moments later, Irmgaard's voice.

'Yanni, come up for a moment will you.'

Yanni puzzled by her tone. No command in it, yet a kind of urgency all the same.

'What is it? I've got to get this fire…'

Irmgaard's face appearing over the lip of the pit, right next to Svetovid's. His so hard and crude, hers so entirely opposite Yanni involuntarily swallowed.

'It's your father,' she said, shaking the world away from Yanni and Yanni from the world. Yanni biting his bottom lip, tears coming of their own accord as he saw all unfold as Irmgaard had done before him: his father worrying, always worrying about his only son; checking out the mountain every few minutes when Yanni was up here. Wind coming, Bora coming, dogs, sled, snow…

'Is he alive?' Yanni whispered.

Irmgaard shaking her head, saying *I don't know. Come up, Yanni, come up.*

21

How To Construct A Cofferdam

'Welcome to the *Put Preko Mora*,' Jochen said, pushing open the door, his visitors awed by this vast hulk of a ship he'd engineered into a home. Jericho whistling as he gazed into the eaves, at the unmistakeable curvilinear outline of a keel, albeit one turned upside down.

'Look at that,' he said. 'Heard it takes a hundred oak trees to make a ship as big as this one must have been.'

'There's the body!' Lupercal exclaimed, he and Ortwin heading for Jochen's work-bench.

'Careful, boys,' Jochen warned, as Lupercal put out his fingers for a touch. 'It's real delicate, and not quite finished.'

Ortwin running his eyes over the ceraceous corpse, seeing the human condition laid bare before him. Shivering to think that all he could see—those white worms of nerves, this yellowed fat, those blood-red layers of muscles and glistening intestines—must be like for like bagged up inside his own skin.

'Can you show me the intermaxillary bone?' Ortwin asked, as Jochen came up beside him. 'The one Goethe discovered?'

Jochen raising his eyebrows. Pfiffmaklers getting odder every moment.

'Something about the... the vertebral...'

'The vertebral theory of the skull,' Jochen finished for him. 'A theory held by the philosophical anatomists, those looking—like Goethe—for an Ideal Plan amongst the multiplicity of physical structures in the world.'

'Homology,' Ortwin nodded, small face scrunching as he dredged up his grandfather's preface to one of Goethe's books. *The leaf is the base-mark of all plants, other parts mere variations of that single unit of growth.*

Jochen smiling broadly. This lad something of a revelation.

'Precisely right, young Ortwin,' he agreed. 'And Goethe positing that the bones of the skull were likewise mere adaptions from the bones of the spine. Hence the…'

'The vertebral theory of the skull,' Ortwin finished for him, shyly looking up at Jochen for approval. Would have puffed out his small chest if he'd been able. Jochen, master anatomist as he was, not missing the hints of scoliosis Ortwin carried: the lowering of one shoulder, the hollowing out of the chest as his spine took a curve to one side taking his sternum with it.

'Disproven theories, I'm afraid,' Jochen went on, 'despite being admirable in their time. Might do us all well to seek out an Ideal Plan, of one sort or another.'

Jericho a sudden burst of energy on his other side.

'What's this bit called? What's that? And ugh, what are those?'

'Stomach, liver, entrails,' Jochen informed, following Jericho's pointing finger. 'Once finished, they'll be hidden. Have the correct layers of skin, muscle and fat laid down over them so it will look like a real person.'

'A real live dead person,' Ortwin said with some reverence.

'A real live dead person,' Jochen agreed, amused by the oxymoron. 'Which means when it's delivered to the Copenhagen Medical School the students there can learn the rudimentaries of anatomy and dissection before they…' Had been about to say butcher. Bit back the word, it seeming too visceral for ones so young. 'Move on to an actual human corpse.'

'And they do that? Where do they get all the bodies?' Lupercal asked, keen to get specifics.

'Executed prisoners,' Jochen told him, 'or those who die in gaol, or who've done themselves in for one reason or another. People not allowed to be buried within the confines of church law.'

'And the drowned?' Hulde asked, Jochen surprised by her all over again.

'Well, yes. If they can't be identified or claimed by kin.'

'Like the people from your shipwreck?'

Jochen distinctly uncomfortable to once again be found wanting.

'I suppose. I really don't know where any of them ended up.'

Wincing at the words, such callousness on his part to not have cared enough to find out.

'There was one documented survivor,' he added, mostly for his own ease.

Hulde nodding, apparently satisfied.

'At least you've given them a second road across the sea,' she said, 'by building your home. And it's a marvellous home. You've done them proud.'

Jochen frowning. She said such unsettling things, this young woman. Jochen leading the boys away from his work-bench so they wouldn't start poking and prodding, showing them instead his other phantoms placed upon shelves too high for them to reach, bringing down one or another to demonstrate how a person's older teeth were already stacked up in their jaws when they were young, ready to erupt, take the place of milk teeth the moment they were shed. How the tongue was so much longer than people assumed, how the larynx worked, where tonsils and soft palates were situated. Soon enough getting them back out into the night with the promise of his telescope being set up on the sands.

The boys eager to help, pulling his cart for him, setting up his tripod sure and steady.

Jochen pointing out one constellation after another, directing them to the places in the sky where the ascensions and transits of Jupiter, Mars and Venus might be found, how to look properly at the moon, see its craters, the darkness creeping in as it shifted from full to waning gibbous.

Hulde sitting a little way distant, gazing at the sea. Happy to be apart, knowing she'd get her own look once the scrimmage of boys were done. Jochen leaving them to it, sitting beside her.

'Can I ask,' he asked, 'why you worry so much about those people from the wreck? It was over for them many years ago.'

Hulde shrugging.

'I'm not sure thirteen years is long,' she answered, untroubled by his asking.

Jochen having to agree. His six-thousand-year-old moon calendar reduced to being a mere one hundred and thirty of his own life spans, in Hulde's unique timeline of history.

'And I suppose,' Hulde added, 'it's because I've lost so many people of my own.' Could have ticked them off on her fingers but did not. 'And can't bear to think they're all alone out there in the universe. Or to have simply ceased to exist. My head knows that's most likely to be the case. Sparrows flying in from darkness through the window. Brief life in the light, before flying out the opposite window and once more into darkness.'

Looking at the darkness all about her. Jochen doing the same.

'So I choose to believe otherwise,' Hulde went on, 'as irrational as that belief might be.'

Jochen quiet, wondering how someone as young as Hulde could be harbouring such deeply metaphysical thoughts when almost the entire population of the world believed in a God Almighty, or many gods. All assuming some sort of life hereafter. Existence on this earth a mere hiatus, a stepping stone into an eternal that might be good or bad, yet undoubtedly went on. He'd long ago abandoned the bland narratives of religion. Cutting people open and studying their innards a sure and certain antidote to such notions. Humans on the inside the same as all the other myriad animals you'd cut up.

Horrified that a great thinker like Descartes could have believed animals had no souls and therefore could not suffer pain. An illogical deduction from an otherwise logical mind. Cruel and abhorrent.

As cruel and abhorrent as the person who'd bored the holes in the Put Preko Mora without caring for the suffering of those who'd drowned because of his actions.

One documented survivor, he'd told Hulde.

Surmising now there had to have been another, undocumented. Realising he needed to track that first survivor down, hear what he had to say. Realising also, in this dark night on the sands, there was someone close at hand who might possess such information, who'd taken gleeful interest in the wreck having seen it at first hand. And much as he would have enjoyed putting his hands around Jansen's scrawny neck and squeezing the information out of him, it occurred to him there might be a more efficacious way.

'Hulde,' speaking as much to the night as to her. 'There's things I'd like to tell you about that shipwreck, things I've never told anyone. And when I'm done, and if you agree, will you do something for me?'

§

Grettir had dug his circle around Yanni's father and slotted in his planks.

Same principle as erecting a cofferdam: temporary structure holding back soil or water. Snow in this case. Had overseen the building of many during his career. Building them up, draining them of water or disburdening them of soil, so the proper work of civil engineering could begin. Pilings and starlings for a bridge; redirection of a river so it didn't flood a new canal. Grettir once holding back the sea to facilitate a lighthouse being built upon a rock.

Planks put in to hold back the worst, Grettir beginning to bash at the snow within his circle, Marko at its centre. Yanni arriving, taking the strain of the rope wrapped about his father, yelling at his friends to help Grettir with the digging.

Friends going at it under Grettir's direction. Not enough planking to make a complete necklace of wood, more a clock-face marking out the hours. Frustratingly slow, snow tipping in from every side, but soon down deep enough for Grettir to start at the base, loosen the snow with his shovel, bring it up from the top of Marko's thighs, to his waist, to his chest.

'Start pulling, boys,' Grettir commanded.

Boys doing as bid. Marko their hero, Yanni their friend. Nothing going to stop them.

'Haul away!' Grettir encouraged, shovelling out snow as quick as he could. Marko slowly emerging inch by inch as the boys hauled and Grettir shovelled. One last tug, and Marko was freed. Laid on his back on the snow, knees cricked over the edge of the cofferdam. Grettir still down below, perspiration shining on his forehead despite the cold. Oddest thing for Grettir being that he'd no idea of the time. Only that it was dark and frigid, skies cleared of clouds. Stars strewn across the heavens like corn.

The trees that hadn't been uprooted springing towards upright as snow sprinkled and tipped from them into the calmness of this newly relaxed night. Branches sloughing off the weight, reclaiming their rightful places. Birds tippering and chattering as they winged in from the dark sky, taking once more to their nests, tucking heads beneath wings. The entire forest on top of the mountain of St Vid breathing a sigh of relief that all was over.

Morning due to resume as normal.

And if Marko was going to be anywhere near normal they needed to get him to the chapel. Marko frigid and sallow. Grettir throwing out several of his cofferdam planks, directing they be bound into a serviceable pallet. Marko laid upon it. Hauling ropes secured.

Yanni and his friends pulling Marko on. A hundred yards to where the woodpile had been, a few more to the chapel. Two of the boys going in through the window, Yanni and Grettir lifting Marko's pallet from below until they could slide him horizontally between the splintered jambs, the boys inside lowering him down. Met by the welcome sight of flames leaping once more in the firepit, Svetovid having been pulleyed away, leaning at an ungracious angle against the stone altar, grimacing up into what was left of the chapel roof.

'Keep him on his boards,' Irmgaard came over with swift strides. 'Lower him into the pit. We've left one half clear so we can all bunk down for the night.'

Grettir brushing himself free of snow, stomach grumbling as he detected sizzles of cooking food.

'You rescued the brazier?' he asked.

'We did,' Irmgaard agreed. 'Bent and lopsided but will do. Scraped up what food we could. Hope you're not too particular.'

Grettir smiling broadly.

'Would eat right through a sheep's wool to get at a chop,' he said.

Irmgaard smiling to recognize the local idiom.

'No wool in the offing, and no chops. But got the finest carbonated sausages and beef steaks you're ever likely to eat. Might not taste too good,' she said, before adding the last line of the proverb, 'but will fill our stomachs and make our teeth shine with its fat.'

'And who could ask for more?'

Grettir and Irmgaard lowering themselves down by hand and foot, utilising the niches dug into the pit's walls designed for the purpose. Grettir wondering how long those niches had been there, how long this pit and this chapel had been on this site. How many other wind-shrieking, wall-shaking, heart-juddering Boras it had lived through. If any had been as bad, better or worse, than this last.

22

Don't Move A Muscle, Mergim

Jansen itched with annoyance. Having skulked away from his field once the Fair's Folk had passed, he returned to his home. Kettle on, looking out his tiny grimy window to see blasted Jochen leading the Pfiffmaklers onto the bay. So annoyed he'd knocked the kettle over. Fire extinguished in a sighing sizzle, needing to be raked out, started all over again. To hell with it. Grabbed a bottle of the moonshine he was adept at making. He couldn't build houses out of ships, nor corpses out of wax, but he could better Jochen at stilling.

He'd his father's equipment in his ramshackle little barn. It was old, maybe needed a repair here or there, but it damn well did its business. Jochen a bloody upstart in these parts, unlike Jansen's family. Jansen pulling the cork from the bottle with his teeth, quick smart in his eyes as the fumes hit. Jansen used to it, blinking them away, pouring a generous glugful into his cup. Pouring a dribble of it onto a dirty rag and rubbing it against the window. Clear view of

Jochen directing the Pfiffmaklers where they'd no right to be. Few more mouthfuls from his cup and he decided he'd bloody well go down there, demand they pay him rent or else they could clear off. Pitch their camp on the sands belonging to anyone and no one.

A few more mouthfuls and he was revising this course of action, for even he could see how petty it was, given the entertainments they'd provided free of charge. Or free of charge for Jansen, who'd not parted with a penny until he'd got to the tavern. Plenty others handing over their coins, so why should he? Jansen missing the entire premise of how the Pfiffmaklers earned their living. Every penny adding up, every penny counting.

Jansen thinking it likely travelling folk like these would be continually lapping up the strong stuff whenever they came across it. Jansen the man to provide it, opening a warped cupboard whose only merit lay in having been custom-made to take the height and weight of his liquor bottles. Dithering over which to part with. No point handing over the best. Pfiffmaklers unlikely to be fussy, would no doubt grab anything they could get their hands on. Jansen selecting two jars of sloe brandy never properly cleared, despite being racked off several times. Not exactly cloudy, except at the very bottom. Racked it off one last time to make it as presentable as possible.

Took a quick look out of his window, and sure enough could see a couple pinpricks of light on the sands of the bay. Jochen, predictable as always, having taken out his telescope to impress his guests.

Moonlit strolls across the sand never Jansen's thing, despite his earlier thinking.

Jansen going a different direction entirely.

§

Mergim brought out his folding table, shifted several toggles to release the legs, secured them with the built-in struts. Laid upon its planed surface the map Heraldo had sent before he'd departed Rügen; extrapolated, so Heraldo's note had explained, from Clark's Chart of the World.

Who Clark was, Mergim had no knowledge. Of only interest was the wiggly line indicating where Heraldo had made up his mind to go. And from where he would eventually return. Had also included this part of the world to the north of Rügen, Mergim tracing a finger from Rügen to Falster to Møns, coming to rest on the tiny peninsula they were now camped on.

'Ulvshale it's called. Means Wolf's Tail,' Jochen had told him, 'on account of its shape.'

It didn't look much like a wolf's tail on this map, which admittedly was a little sketchy. Mergim concentrating not on Møns, instead studied the way they would soon be going, which was over the water to the larger island of Sjelland. This sojourn on the sands of Nyord a welcome hiatus. Practice rounds on Møns going better than expected. Sjelland where they might make proper money, if all went to plan.

Decisions to be made thereafter about whether to go further up into Sweden and Norway, or retreat back to Germany. All unknown territories for Mergim. All equally terrifying. Mergim fearing how it would play out, twisting his fingers together on his lap. Pfiffmaklers intent on going north, as they had told Heraldo before they'd left him. Mergim figuring, given how large it appeared on this map, they could comfortably spend a few months on Sjelland, fervently hoping Heraldo would be back to take over, make the final decision Mergim felt ill-equipped to dictate.

Mergim interrupted by Longhella.

'Someone's coming,' she said, jutting her head. Indicating not the bay, nor Jochen's home, so not Hulde and the boys.

But no possible threat. No one knowing they were here. Yet still. Wolf's Tail.

Not too long since they'd had their own wolf to contend with on Rügen.

As a child, he'd been aware of packs of wolves roaming the mountains. No threat to people, nor livestock, except in bad years. One year particularly bad. A rogue male taking a real interest in his village. Folk glimpsing him in their peripheral vision when dusk shadowed the world into shades of grey; caught it slinking around the corners of outhouses, snuffling at a midden, at the wattled fences penning in sheep and goats. No one entirely certain it was real, nevertheless cautioning young children against going into their yards at night, the men having any guns loaded and ready at their doors.

Mergim's father the one to voice what all were thinking:

If he's really out there we've to find him. We can't stay hidden for ever, nor protect the livestock if he chooses to attack. Tonight will be clear and moonlit, so we take the offensive to the enemy.

Always enmity back then, in one form or another. This phantom wolf merely the last in a long line. Every man and boy worth his salt taking their allotted places in the late afternoon, keeping statue-still for an hour and more, weapons resting on their knees. Wolves wily, would never approach if human adults were moving abroad. Women and children indoors. All lamps extinguished. Young Mergim sitting on a barrel at one corner of the goat enclosure.

Don't move a muscle, Mergim. Don't cough, don't sneeze. Don't fiddle with the billhook.

Billhook Mergim's only weapon, sharp as any of Longhella's knives.

If you sees it, don't quicken your breath. Don't make no noise. Stay exactly as you are. If it's close enough you'll only get one chance. If it ain't close enough, let it be. Let one of the others take it.

Mergim seeing it all again in his head as he sat at his table.

Afternoon darkening into evening, everything going into grey monotones with the gloaming, eyes accustoming themselves to the growing darkness, picking out what was familiar and what was not. And that wolf was not. It was huge and grey and shaggy, slung low at the waist, paws padding over the snow, eyes aglint with the light of the rising moon and seemingly staring right at him.

Don't quicken your breath.

Don't make a noise.

Young Mergim letting out one long breath which spooled up about him as the wolf nosed along the bottom of the wattles, held up its enormous head and sniffed the air, maybe sniffed him, it was so close. Only five yards away, only four, only three…

Mergim's fingers tightening about the handle of his billhook, muscles tensing.

Two yards, one yard, and then only inches between himself and the wolf as it went to go by his barrel. Mergim springing up and whooshing down his billhook, catching the animal on the side of its neck, and my God the noise that came from it had Mergim chilled from top to toe. Mergim lifting the billhook for a second strike, staring into that wolf's yellow eyes for a second, which proved to be one second too long. Wolf up and at him, claws ripping into his shoulders, bared teeth going for his neck, the two of them down in the snow, no idea whose blood was whose. Mergim large and strong but only eleven years old and this animal larger and stronger, maybe older too, maybe not.

Life in wolf-world a hard game. This one not leaving it without a fight. Mergim, winded by his fall, pushing fingers into the wolf's fur as it bore down on him. Mergim so frightened he peed himself, yet found an odd comfort in the depth of that fur, the denseness of it, how it was rough and soft all at the same time.

A deafening blast in his ears and the full weight of the wolf fell on his chest, the other look-outs congregating towards that unworldly sound engendered by Mergim's first strike. Several men lifting the dead wolf off him, whooping and hollering at their victory, lights going on in the windows, women streaming out into the snow.

'Well done, lad. Couldn't have done better myself.'

His father kneeling at his side, levering him up, packing snow into his wounds.

That wolf's tail attached to Mergim's hat by a leather thong, hanging from it and successive hats for years. Its pelt made into a coat for him, best coat he'd had from that day to this. A sadness to have outgrown it within a few years. Would have liked to have hung onto it, push his fingers through the coarse outer growth into the softer layer beneath. But no, too good to hang upon a peg when it could do someone better. Passed on to a small-boned cousin, who in due course handed it to his younger brother and that brother to another.

Wolf's tail a different matter. His and his alone, swinging from his hat, marking him out.

There goes Mergim, the one who almost killed the wolf.

Mergim proud. Mergim wondering what those villagers would think of him now, not that there'd be many left. Most of the men, including his grandfather, cut down in a stand-off against the Turks who were demanding increasingly higher taxes the villagers couldn't afford to pay.

Mergim shaking his head. Pointless to speculate about such things.

Old life gone, new one begun.

Pfiffmaklers his family now.

Mergim fixing his eyes on the person approaching their camp, or rather on the small bob of light heralding whoever was coming.

Mergim standing up, ready for confrontation if it was needed.

Mergim beaten to the punch by Longhella as the man shambled into their circle.

'Well, if it isn't Jochen's neighbour,' she announced. 'Run out of baskets?'

Jansen, lit by the several lamps hooked on poles to light their camp, colouring profusely.

'No, Miss, thank you,' he got out between his crooked teeth. 'Have brought you something.'

Bringing out his gifts. No doubt in him they were gifts, would be getting no remuneration, since he'd locked eyes with that wretched woman again.

'Two bottles of sloe brandy,' he announced. 'Thought a few nips might be welcome.'

'Because it's not like we do this every day,' Longhella quipped.

Mergim's lips twitching beneath his beard. Longhella might be a troublesome cuss-tongued woman, but you couldn't help admiring her wit.

'It's very thoughtful. Thank you,' he intervened. 'I think you were at one of our performances?'

Remembering the man who'd been dancing with the children, the mutters of disapproval from his fellows. Mergim not thinking it disgraceful. If a man wants to dance, let him dance. Quick throwback to Kragujevac where men had done the same for some paltry celebration, when out would come the rudimentary instruments they'd fashioned inside the prison walls from whatever was available. A fiddle made from a piece of wood, several nails and lengths of string; a carillon of sorts, scraps of suspended metal struck lightly with sticks; a piece of guttering hammered into a cylinder, pierced through with holes, making a screeching kind of trumpet. Enough for them back then. Men dancing with men, murderers with murderers, pretending they were dancing with murdered wives, lost sweethearts, dead children. Stumbled steps, trodden-upon toes, a fair bit of weeping.

No one minding. All you had in a place like Kragujevac.

And perhaps these less than limpid bottles all that were to be had in a place like Ulvshale. Mergim sitting their visitor down, offering Jansen the last scrapings of their hare stew, which Jansen took with gratitude.

'That's mighty fine of you,' Jansen said, a little perturbed to be so welcomed. 'Suppose the rest of your lot are over with Jochen,' he added, between spoonfuls of what was the best meal he'd tasted in years. His own culinary skills limited to eggs in scrambles and omelettes, potatoes boiled and roughly mashed with watery kale and butter.

Mergim nodding, taking out cups, getting a couple of inches of Jansen's offerings into them, handing them around. Longhella taking one sniff before handing hers off to Diderik.

'Smells like rat's piss,' she dismissed. Diderik taking a sip.

'Actually,' he said, 'it's not half bad, once you've got past the smell.'

Jansen having the grace to look up from his bowl.

'Aye well. Can't say it's the best I've ever made, but it's service-able. Didn't think you lot would be too fussy.'

Could have bitten out his tongue as Longhella narrowed her eyes.

'Just meant that with you lot being on the road and that…'

Father of the Fair coming to the fore.

'It's very good of you. Thank you.'

No coat of wolf fur needed to make Mergim feel prouder than he was now. Someone who'd been to their performances come to fête them, offer them gifts, while another had invited them to his home, to this campsite. Mergim beginning to get into the Pfiff-makler way. Beginning to understand its benefits, work himself into the weft of his new life.

23

To Sleep, Perchance To Dream

In the pit, the situation was less decisive. The two casualties propped against the walls, stone still warm from the previously roaring fires now revived, stabilised and contained.

'How's my father doing?' Yanni asked. Irmgaard on her knees, inspecting her first patient of the night. Marko more of a worry than Heraldo. Marko unconscious. No frostbite nor broken bones that she could detect. A ragged wound in his shoulder. But not awake was not good. Marko limp, clothing sodden by the snow in which he'd been encoffined, his blood moving slow and sluggish.

'We should strip him of his outer layers,' she advised, 'position him closer to the flames.'

He's troublingly cold, she might have added. Recalling a song she'd heard when ice-cream was all the rage in the cities, about a man who'd eaten so much he'd frozen himself from the inside out. *Shivery Shakey, oh ho ho, criminy crikey isn't he cold. Ooh-wee-ooh, oh do behold, the man who couldn't get warm.*

Yanni undoing his father's coat, peeling away clothes and boots. Leaving only socks, vest and underpants. His skin pale and clammy, like a chicken newly plucked.

'Don't look too good,' Yanni said, tears filling his eyes. His father looking horribly naked. Friends huddling around, taking off their coats, slinging them over Marko; taking hold of his shoulders and ankles, laying him as close to the edge of the fire as they dared, curling his body about a small heap of embers they'd pulled from the main burning.

Friends saying *He'll be fine. Just got to get him warmed through.*

That song continuing to unspool in Irmgaard's head.

Close to a blazing fire he got, and took to drinking brandy hot;

He sent for doctors such a lot, the man who couldn't get warm.

Doctors' fees chilling their blood near twelve degrees.

And doing no good for Shivery Shaky.

In a hot bath he was found, the water frozen all around.

The jury proved it in a thrice, he'd died from indigested ice.

Foreman advising eating ice-cream warm, which rather did away the point of it, if not the snow-baths into which Heraldo's fingers had been immersed. Time to inspect her second patient.

'Any pain?' she asked, squeezing a fingertip. 'If so, how much?' as she moved from one to the next. Which proved surprisingly little. Only significant discomfort coming from his middle and index fingers on both hands.

'We've to strap those two together,' Irmgaard told him. 'Keep them immobile until they heal. They'll be crush breaks,' she deduced, given how Heraldo had gone down with Svetovid, 'so will be lying in their right places. Need to give them time to join themselves back up.'

The broken fingers strapped together, leaving the others free. Heraldo adamant about that.

'Means I'll still be able to pluck a tune from my mandolin,' he explained. 'Keep your boys right for their performance.'

'Surely you're not going ahead with it?' Grettir butted in.

'Of course!' Heraldo replied. 'All this,' holding up his hands, wiggling the fingers he could still wiggle, 'has to be worth something.'

'Hear hear!' someone shouted.

'And look above you,' Heraldo added. 'Look at that multiplicity of stars! Why do you need a roof? It's like looking through a window onto the universe. All you need do is pick your time.'

'And clear out all the snow,' Grettir commented, unconvinced. 'And the rubble.'

Heraldo shrugging.

'It won't detract at all. In fact I think, in the long run, it will do you well. Your attempted rebuild is admirable, and if you go on despite disaster it can only strengthen your corner. This is your theatre. You've to make of it the best you can. And I'm here to help you.'

Irmgaard frowning. This young man indefatigable. In their ken a mere few hours, during which he'd managed to corral her boys into getting out a serviceable tune, saved them from being crushed and suffocated, and now encouraging them to believe they could carry on despite the renovations to St Vid had literally collapsed about their ears. That destruction seen not as waste but as betterment to their cause. And continuing to offer his help for no earthly reason she could think of.

All looking over sharply when Shivery Shaky miraculously revived, Marko coughing like his throat was filled with stones.

'Where am I? What's been going on?'

Astonished to see the face of his boy right in front of him. Flabbergasted when Yanni cupped his hands about Marko's face, kissed him on one cheek and then the other, heard words whispered into his ears.

Thank God you're all right.

Yanni never an effusive boy; no more affectionate towards his father than his father had been to him. Emotional needs met by mother and wife, until she'd been taken by the mountain. No Bora needed. She at home, Yanni suffering a fever, while the other women shepherded their sheep and goats up to spring pastures. Women already back when she set off alone with her family's herds. No one worried during the several days she was expected to be away.

Yanni and Marko going up when she didn't return. Going higher and higher, misled by the sheep and goats who'd scattered far and wide. Yanni and Marko finding no trace of her the first day, nor the second, nor the third. The two distraught. Marko thinking to go back down, gather up a proper search party. Yanni arguing, digging in his heels.

'I'll not leave until I find her.'

Bunching his small ten year old fists, standing his ground.

Marko exasperated, trying to be reasonable.

'We know something's happened. We can be down and back within the day, bring up the whole village.'

Yanni not to be moved, squaring his shoulders, obdurate heels digging into the dirt of Suvid.

'I'm not leaving. And neither should you.'

Marko throwing up his hands in anger.

'It's not your place to tell your father what to do!' he'd shouted. 'Certainly not where your mother is concerned. Do you think I'd not be doing what I think best?'

Marko stomping away, leaving Yanni to it.

You arrogant idiot, you pompous self-righteous…

Accusatory words looping through his head as he'd sped down from the top peaks of Suvid towards the chapel. Seething with rage at his son, and worry for his wife. Having St Vid in view when a wailing leaked down to him from the hills.

'Fa …ther! Fa…ther!'

Such clear air up there on bright spring days, winds barrelled up within their caverns. So far a voice can carry. Couldn't make out the words, but recognised the urgent register of his son's voice. Turned on his own obdurate heels and began back up the path.

'Fa …ther! Fa…ther!'

The word repeated quick and oft the higher he went.

Other words soon distinguished.

'She's here! She's found!'

Marko cursing himself for cursing his son, for leaving when he should have stayed. Cursed himself ever after when he'd reached them. She slumped against one of those huge boulders scattered about the top of Suvid; Yanni leaning over her, holding her hands in his own. Her ankle blue, puffed to the size of a melon; scattered remnants of provisions at her side: a few crumbs of bread, the skin of a salami, a partially eaten cake of peas-pudding. The imprints of her teeth in it breaking Marko's heart.

Deduction being she must have tripped, stumbled or tumbled not long after she'd got up here, six days previously. Broken an ankle. Food enough for the three days she'd planned to be up here, far longer if she'd access to water. Hands torn and scabbed, dress ripped through at the knees as she'd crawled and dragged herself over the sharp stony karst to one of those sparse skinny streams threading through its bleakness. Tried and failed. Propped herself up against the boulder when she could go no further. Jammed a cup into the ground beside her. A cup bone dry.

There'd been rain two nights after her ascent and again the following morning.

Enough to keep her alive for the while, until son and husband arrived.

Would have survived, had they found her on their first day, or their second.

But not the third.

Three days without water all it took.

Marko's wife soft as sun-warmed butter where Marko and Yanni were concerned. Contrary as the karst when she'd made up her mind how this or that had to be done in this or that particular way. And like a tick when it suited her, would have clung on as long as she could.

Obdurate, just like Yanni.

Marko seeing himself taking up that bone dry cup, made by himself, placing it on his bedside cabinet to remind himself how fragile and easily broken is the line between life and death.

§

'You got caught in the Bora,' Marko heard Yanni saying. 'In the snow.'

Vaguely remembering seeing two of his dogs hurtling by in a maelstrom of splinters and blood; his own sudden immobility, the dread creeping through him as it must have crept through his wife. Spring for her, snow for him.

'It's a miracle he's alive.' A deep voice Marko didn't recognise. Hearing the shrug the stranger must be making by the intonation of his voice. 'Met a man a few years ago who survived a shipwreck against the odds.'

Marko not really listening. Marko levered up, propped against the wall which was warm against his back and very comforting, as was the presence of his son. Yanni's arm about his shoulders holding him close. Marko resting his head upon Yanni's, happiness and relief making him somnolent, closing his eyes as he breathed deeply, about to slip into sleep.

'I never told you about that part, Irmgaard,' the man went on. 'But while we're holed up here I see no reason to dissemble.'

Irmgaard saying something in reply Marko couldn't make out, only one ear open to the conversation, the other nestled in Yanni's hair.

'You and your husband may have left by then,' the man went on. 'Othmar's letter said it was 1839.'

Marko's breathing suddenly arrested.

Shipwreck.

Othmar.

1839.

He couldn't be hearing right. How could he be hearing right? He began to shiver uncontrollably. Yanni shifting beside him, whispering to his father.

'It's all right, papa. You're here with me, in the chapel. We'll soon get you warm, and come morning we'll get you home.'

The unknown man carrying on regardless.

'He was on his way back to Denmark from an archaeological expedition,' Grettir explained. 'He'd been digging in this neck of the woods, as it happens. Or not far.'

Marko taking an audible gulp of air, like a fish swallowing an unexpected fly.

Irmgaard turning her head in consternation.

'He'll be thirsty.' Jutting her head at Yanni's friends. 'Get him some water.'

Pannikin of melted snow handed over, Yanni putting it to Marko's lips, Marko lapping at the melt-water like his dogs used to do .

Marko picking out the relevant words he'd not long heard:

Archaeological expedition.

Denmark.

This neck of the woods.

It didn't seem possible.

Gregor would never have told anyone here about that shipwreck. Had made that absolutely clear more than once. *It's your guilt, and mine, Marko, and ours alone. Irmgaard must never know of it. Swear to me, Marko. You must swear to me.* Gregor abhorring Marko's methods, if understanding the import and value of what had been salvaged because of it.

Marko putting shaky fingers to his chest, seeking the one part of the hoard he'd repatriated to himself. A reminder of what he'd done and why. The single most important deed of his entire life, far above the duties of hewing down trees, creating the wooden accoutrements people needed to carry on with their lives. The tiny trinket strung on a thong about his neck. Miniature words on miniature pages.

Pax Tibi Sanctus Vitus, Semitam Meam Subibant .

Peace to you, Saint Vitus, my path and my way forward.

Words and pages hidden beneath his vest.

'Something from your expedition?' his wife had asked, his first night back, as he'd taken it from his neck, stowed it in the drawer of the bedside cabinet. Wife yawning broadly behind an outstretched hand, Marko saved from answering by three year old Yanni wailing in his crib and she'd pushed away the bedcovers to see to him. Never mentioning the trinket again.

Marko closing his fingers about the *Pax Tibi*. So tired he could no longer keep himself awake, despite the awful implications of what he'd heard. Soft drifts of words winding their way like somnolent sheep through his dreams.

It ruined him, I'm sad to say.

Never got over it.

Talk of sabotage.

Marko's limbs twitching, dreams saturated with vivid images: the dark and freezing waters of the Kattegat, ropes and barrels, sandy bay, forest, buffeting wind and rain. Occasional glimpse of a white and winsome moon in which he could see his own face reflected. Boat journey over the Mecklenburger Bucht to Stralsund, fear he would be apprehended at any moment. Gregor Simič, tall and gangling as a puppet whose operator has taken a fit when Marko stepped into his path. Marko laughing hysterically in his dream-world as Gregor stammered and spluttered some verse about doppelgangers. Marko putting him right, explaining he was here to save the world, or rather a few shards of their old shared past.

Images out of order, like he was whooshing down a river, turning without warning into rapids through which he raced and swam, got knocked about by boulders as he swung them by. Marko sweating in his sleep despite the chill at his core, mumbling and muttering now and then. Yanni leaning in to catch words he could make no sense of.

Pax Tibi Pax Tibi

Soft as butter

The road over the water

There were bones

Yanni undisturbed, glad his father was recovered enough to sleep and dream.

Yanni wondering vaguely what it was about his father's neck his fingers gripped so hard. Probably a memento of his mother. A lock of hair, perhaps.

Yanni yawning loudly, grinning sheepishly at his fellows in apology. Needn't have. A long hard day, a harder night, and all now leaning against the warm walls, heads back, eyes closed. Only Irmgaard keeping watch. Yanni breathing deeply as she cast a quick smile at him and nodded. Giving him grace to sleep.

All well in Yanni's world. All well.

24

Different Directions

'I said before there was only one survivor,' Jochen explained to Hulde. 'But I think that's wrong.'

Hulde continuing to stare up into the stars.

'One documented survivor is what you actually said.' Shifting her gaze, looking at Jochen. 'You think there was another?'

Jochen cleared his throat.

'I do,' he agreed. 'After I saw your *Dying Child*…'

Trailing off, trying to order his thoughts, saw Hulde raising her eyebrows in the faint light of the lamp. Felt suddenly foolish, about to brush everything off when Hulde spoke again.

'That's the power of theatre for you. I experienced something similar when I was very young. Saw a face, a profile… dislodged a load of stones from my path. Cleared my way.'

A shiver going through Jochen to recognise the experience.

'I believe another person was cast up on this beach,' he said quietly. 'The ship was washed up later, when it had broken apart, so current and tides were right.' *And brought me my little moon calendar.* 'I noticed in the morning some supplies missing, and a handcart.'

'Which didn't ring alarm bells?' Hulde asked. Jochen shaking his head.

'I assumed it was my neighbour. He's always taking things that don't belong to him.'

'And a stormy night, presumably,' Hulde added for him. 'The perfect time for a little neighbourly pilfering.'

Jochen smiling at her perspicuity.

'Thing is,' he said, 'after I'd seen your play I remembered how when I built my home from that ship's boards, some of them had holes bored in them. Saw nothing in it back then. Holes for ropes, maybe. Who knew? I'm not a shipbuilder.'

'Just a builder of homes,' Hulde commented, turning her head, regarding the dark skep of the *Put Preko Mora* in which lay phantoms and ghosts nestling together side by side. Jochen letting out a long breath which wisped, wraith-like, in the air before dissolving.

'I think,' Jochen continued, 'the ship had help going down, and I believe I've the proof.'

If Hulde was shocked she didn't show it. Merely twitched her face back towards him, fixed her dark eyes on his.

'How can I help?'

Jochen pinching his brows together.

'I'd like you to talk to Jansen,' he said.

'Ascertain if he stole what you now think he didn't?'

Jochen relaxing.

'That's it,' he agreed, although wasn't about to let Jansen off entirely. 'He's done it plenty other times, but maybe not then.' And the more he thought on it the more he realised the truth. Hated to admit it, but had to get it said.

'He was manning one of the lights that night,' he told Hulde, 'on top of the cliffs. I don't know when he got back home. What I do know is that the food and cart were missing when I got up early, not long past dawn, because of the storm. To see to the animals. Check for any damage.'

Hulde nodding.

'He'll not tell you whether he pinched the stuff,' Jochen said. 'But he saw the ship go down. Ask him about it and he won't shut up. Can't stop bragging about it.'

Bragging. An odd word to use. Hulde getting it immediately.

'His moment in the limelight,' she interpreted. 'I get him to tell me all about it, find out when he left the lighthouse and when he got home. Whether he had time to commit the crime.'

Jochen couldn't have put it better himself.

'And if he didn't, then we've proof someone else was in the bay that night. Or at least that morning. I saw oilskins and a barrel on the sands.'

'Which would put your holes in a very different light,' Hulde finished for him. 'And you'll begin the path of detection until you reach its end.'

Jochen frowned, hadn't thought that far ahead nor how to go about it; to whom he should take his evidence, if evidence it was assumed to be. The enquiry into the shipwreck closed long ago, lid nailed down. No one likely to want to prise it open.

Went down like a bloody stone it did, like the belly had been ripped out of it.

Jansen's evidence compelling, yet ultimately inconsequential. His account, the lone independent eye witness, tallying with that supplied by the documented survivor; neither of their reports given much import. Everyone knowing ships go down in storms for any number of reasons. Bad lading, too many passengers, flawed navigation, underwater skerries.

If he took Hulde's suggested course of action Jochen would need to find out the name and whereabouts of the documented survivor, get his rendition of the accident. No notion how to go about it. Hulde already on the trail he was baulking to pursue.

'We'll need to get your Mr Jansen to tell us who he spoke to about it all,' she advised. 'It'll be written down somewhere, filed safely away, in case the sea shucks up one of the passengers who've not been seen from that day to this.'

Staring at the dark waters of the bay.

'Your lost ghosts won't have been forgotten,' she stated quietly. 'There'll be folk out there who'll not have given up on finding them.'

Such certainty, as if she were one of those waiting, sitting here on the sands of Nyord in expectation of the sea-wolf returning one of her own.

'When Jansen gave his statement,' Hulde asked, 'was it in person or by written statement?'

Jochen could have laughed. Jansen barely able to compose a shopping list in his illegible scrawl, let alone a coherent document.

'I think someone met him at the lighthouse,' he said, rubbing his fingers against his thumbs. 'No. I'm sure of it. They wanted to check he had line of sight, wasn't lying like he so often does.'

Hulde pushing her boots into the sand, giving a small shake of her head.

'It's obvious you don't think highly of your neighbour.' Quiet words, Jochen wondering if she was thinking less of him because of it. 'But no matter how bad a person, he surely wouldn't lie about such a thing, not when so many people died.'

Hulde right. Not even Jansen would lie about such a thing. Not when he'd conjured up the scene so vividly: those pale faces floating away on the waves like waterlilies. Jansen didn't have the imagination to make that up. Only surprise for Jochen being Jansen knowing what waterlilies were.

And so they decided.

Hulde would talk to Jansen, listen to his version of events. Prompt him for details, to whom he'd given them. After which Jochen would contact whomever that had been, offer up his own witness statement, no matter it was so long after the fact.

Jochen admiring the way Hulde removed the stones, cleared his way forward. Put Jochen's nose to the trail. And it seemed the trail was coming directly at them. No mistaking Jansen's voice.

'He's like a monkey showing off his tricks. Hey Jochen! Jochen!'

Jansen's words slurred, his gait shambling.

Jansen drunk again. Jochen gritting his teeth.

'Nose to the trail,' Hulde reminded him, laying a restraining hand upon his arm as Jansen came into view, Diderik holding a lantern to light their way. Diderik grimacing at Hulde as if to say *I tried to stop him, but what could I do?*

Hulde smiling back at him, standing up, brushing her skirts free of sand, coming to meet them, holding out her hand.

'Mr Jansen! It's a pleasure. I've heard so much about you.'

Jansen disarmed, the wind taken out of his sails so unexpectedly he had no choice but to take her small hand in his own.

'Is that so, little Miss? Not all bad I hope?'

Glaring at Jochen, who was scrambling up beside Hulde. Alarmed when Jochen bared his teeth in an apparent smile so unsuited to his habitual enmity. Jochen sauntering off towards his telescope and the boys clustered about it who, annoyingly, appeared to find it as fascinating as Jansen had assumed they would have found it dull.

'I gather you witnessed a shipwreck,' the young woman was saying. 'I'd love to hear about it. Jochen says you're quite the storyteller.'

Hulde reposing back onto the sand, giving Diderik a glance, a quick lift of her chin. Diderik sitting, gathering something was on the go, a pot put onto flames and not long before the water boiled.

This the essence of being a Pfiffmakler, knowing when to stay and when to go.

Diderik staying.

Bad times behind him, better ones to come.

New adventures around every corner.

And here, he understood, was another.

'I think it was 1839,' Hulde was saying to Jansen, the squirrely man who'd crashed into their camp with his offer of free drink. Partaking of it far more freely than either Diderik or Mergim, then insisting Diderik bring him down onto the sands.

'Got to see the monkey jumping,' Jansen had said mysteriously, and here was the mystery unfolding.

Went down like a bloody stone it did, Jansen began, settling into the well-worn ruts of his tale now Hulde had dressed the stage, got him primed and going. *Like God Himself had ripped it from one existence into another...*

Morning rose over the chapel like a benediction, the sun shining thinly behind crenellated crags gaping black and crooked against its light.

A peaceful night spent by those in the pit.

All hustle and bustle now the day was upon them.

First task to excavate the snow from the doorless doorway.

Second to send a lad down the mountain with Grettir. Supplies needed, and strong men to wield Marko down if he couldn't manage it himself. Marko shivering despite the warmth of his redonned clothes. Hot food what was needed, in Irmgaard's opinion. Grettir arguing he'd be more use in the chapel, now it was decided—despite his previous remonstrations—that it be cleared as best it could, the performance to go ahead as scheduled.

'I can't send anyone down on their own,' Irmgaard had argued back, pitting her formidable logic against his. 'We've no idea how the avalanche has changed the course of the path, or if the path still exists. If we're lucky our way-markers won't have been ripped up or buried over their necks and might see you right. If not, there needs to be two in case one gets into trouble.'

Grettir acquiescing, her argument making perfect sense. One to go on ahead, another behind to place new markers in the form of stout sticks bundled into a faggot bound to his back.

The rest left behind to carry on the clear-up. Heraldo, with splinted fingers, unable to help. Feeling useless. Irmgaard sympathetic.

'You can see to the fire,' she told him. 'Got to keep it burning, just in case.'

Just in case the weather changes.

In case no one can get back up to reach us.

In case Grettir and the boy never manage down.

Mountains unpredictable places on the best of days, switching from skittish and exhilarating to dark and desperate with no warning. Suvid, mid-morning, seeming benign and nonchalant, a band of mist collaring its waist even when the sun had shouldered its way a few inches above its topmost peaks. Suvid telling them plain as day to watch their step, might not yet be done with them.

§

Early afternoon.

Chapel's interior cleared of snow, all shovelled out the doorless doorway into heaps. Its remnant slicks of water on the floor beginning to skitter over with ice as the light began to fail.

No one back yet from the village.

Irmgaard totting up the options in her head: spend a further night up here with grumbling stomachs, nothing but pine-needle tea to sustain them. Fire-pit warm, fire burning steadily, sustained the day through.

Easy to survive another night, if uncomfortable.

The other option was to order a mass exodus. A fervent, fast descent down Suvid in the hope Grettir had managed to spike in more way-markers. Assuming Grettir had made it, about which she couldn't be certain. Might still be on his way down, the descent always taking longer than going up, even in normal conditions. Suvid contradictory that way. So many times she'd been up here with Gregor.

'This chapel is the heart of us Serbs,' he'd say, 'reminds us who we are, how we got to where we are now.'

A warm spring morning that first visit, her hand firmly clasped in his. An easy climb, no snow nor ice. Gregor pointing out one bird or another.

'There's a griffin vulture! And a red-footed falcon!'

Gregor breathless with excitement to show her all he could, pausing their progress as the next surprise unveiled itself, and the next and the next.

'That hissing comes from a female lynx in her lair. She's usually burrowed beneath a large rock or a hollowed-out tree bole.'

Pointing out plants and flowers, some Irmgaard recognised, others she didn't. The trees on the lower slopes scarred by villagers tapping for sap; lower branches stripped of new Spring needles made into syrups, added to bread, pies and marinades. A whole new world of learning for her and Gregor to explore. Whole new world cut short a few years later when Gregor's bouts of bronchitis worsened.

Their last trip occurring in autumn, 1845, both knowing he'd be unlikely to last the winter through, chronic bronchitis by then bleeding into recurrent pneumonia. Marko harnessing his dogs, folding Gregor into the trap, smothering him in furs, tying him in.

One last visit to his beloved chapel of St Vid all Gregor wanted.

One last visit made. She and Gregor sitting outside the ruins looking down on the waters of the Adriatic which had, that afternoon, been smooth and green as malachite. Glittering, threaded through with turquoise wakes of fishing boats plying their lines. A beautiful day, a wondrous time together. Gregor pulling the mountain air into his ruined lungs as if it might heal him. Irmgaard by his side knowing it would not, no matter how much both wished it. Hands clasped as he remained in his sled, the weight of the furs keeping him warm and immobile, Irmgaard parked on a log beside him. Gregor starting to push aside the furs.

'I need to go,' he'd said, an awful worry shrouding his face. 'I don't think I can wait.'

The stopping up of his bowels an after-effect of the treatment advised by the local doctor.

Lots of compresses, keep him warm, feed him meat. No vegetables, under any circumstances.

A regimen Irmgaard had disputed, been overruled. And here was the consequence. Days of constipation, followed by Gregor being unable to control himself, soiling his trousers before she'd got him halfway out the sled.

Gregor weeping with humiliation. Irmgaard weeping too, knowing it could have been avoided it if she'd stood up to the blasted doctor or surreptitiously disobeyed him.

A breaking point for both.

'I can't go on like this,' Gregor had whispered, Irmgaard having removed his trousers, cleaned him up, settled him back in the sled. Taken away the ruined underclothes and trousers, shoved them in a hole beneath a boulder that was maybe the lair of a lynx for all she knew. Irmgaard not caring. Let that lynx do with Gregor's leftovers as it saw fit.

Irmgaard and Gregor making a pact, up there at Saint Vid.

No more suffering, no long drawn-out death.

Going back down the mountain deciding what must be done.

'It can't be too quick,' Gregor had advised, Irmgaard swiping tears from her eyes. 'But I don't want it to be too slow.'

Gregor telling her how it should be done.

Gregor always so knowledgeable about the plants growing up the forbidding slopes of Suvid.

Irmgaard telling Grettir that by putting on this performance she'd hoped to stem the grief that had come of Gregor's dying.

Never had she told anyone she'd been the one to precipitate it, at his insistence.

That all she really wanted was for the guilt to go away. For someone to tell her she'd done right.

Tears incipient, when she heard shouting.

'Someone's coming! Hoy there! Hoy!'

As the rescue party rounded the bend it became apparent why it had taken them so long. Grettir urging the villagers into action, the men pulling up with them sleds loaded with gear: rolls of waxed cloth to stretch over the damaged roof, and the ropes needed to fix them; more boards and planks; the several extra sheets of white glass wrapped in blankets that Marko had ordered for the windows assuming his helpers would break the first ones as they practised fitting them; pots of putty and gum, more nails, saws, hammers and shovels, bits and braces, nuts and bolts.

The last sled laden with food and drink.

Everyone clapping as rescue party and rescuees were reunited, all the boys' fathers eager for the ascent, for all had been terrified what might have happened to their boys during the Bora. They'd already assembled early morning to see to the immediate damage, to the random door that had inexplicably been rammed into the head of the best bull-sire anyone had known for years. A bad loss for the entire village, this particular bull being strong-shouldered, easy tempered, easily mated, offspring quick to thicken and put on weight.

After which duties they'd trained their eyes on the mountain, wondering how best to tackle it. Paths obliterated by the snow. Putting hands to brows to keep out the sun-glare, seeing two figures making a downward descent with great difficulty: slipping and sliding, up to their waists in drifts one minute, the next skittering and skating for ten or more yards before being sunk down into drifts again, hauling themselves out, starting once more to skitter and skate.

Men quickly up to aid them with ropes and stout walking canes, guiding them down the lower slopes. Grettir shaking hands, introducing himself, giving a quick precis of the night's occurrences, assuring them their boys were well. And that Irmgaard was adamant the chapel performance would go ahead as planned, despite the utter destruction of their erstwhile handiwork.

'She's bloody mad, that woman, to even be thinking about it,' one opined, spitting out a wad of chewing tobacco, staining the snow an unpleasant brown. Another quick to argue, stamping the spent tobacco under his boot to make his point.

'I disagree. They've been planning this for weeks. All my boy could talk about. Never seen him so enlivened.'

'Quite right,' added another. 'And if they win it'll make us all look good. Put us on the map.'

'Mustn't forget there's a cash prize,' came a further voice. 'And us could really do with that, especially now the bull's been snuffed. Gonna need a replacement if none of last year's sirelings aren't up to scratch.'

All having a good think about that.

'Can we not take up more supplies?' Grettir suggested, the men shuffling and shallying, unsure what to do. 'What your boys did was grand, but surely with all of you we can do a better job. Give them a proper chance at the competition.'

'Best get to Marko's, then,' the first man said.

'Ah,' Grettir adding his postscript. 'He's up at the chapel, and not in great shape. Got caught in the avalanche.'

One of the village men rolling his eyes, shaking his head.

'Of course he bally well was. Him and his beggaring dogs. Got stuck, did he?' Shaking his head again. 'That's so like Marko. Why the beggaring hell didn't he say anything last night?'

'That's not fair,' the tobacco-spitter put in his tuppence worth. 'We all know the only person he's got in the world is Yanni, and them dogs of his. Always regretted not taking a brace of them last time they pupped.'

Grettir putting a stop to the havering.

'We've not much time. Took us ages to get down and won't take much less to get back up.'

Nods all around. Decisions made. Sleds loaded and they were off. No dogs to aid them, only strong shoulders at the fore, strong arms behind, and the markers left by Grettir to give them direction.

25

A Bowl Scattered Over With Wheat

Hulde listened as Jansen rabbited on, and Jansen could rabbit with the best. He'd told his tale many times, always glad to give it another airing.

I was at my light, I was, getting it refuelled. Good job, earning good coin, especially in winter. Have had to give it up since, more's the pity. Young man's game that is, going up and down them stairs. Got to have good knees, and me knees ain't so good as they were. Anywise, there I was…

'Refuelling your light,' Hulde prompted.

That's right, young Miss. Refuelling it because it was a wicked night, and those wicked nights is when ships needs us lights the most. You don't want to know how many dangers there are out there in the water...

Hulde interrupting, because apparently she did. Jansen explaining about currents, skerries, promontories, sandbanks, onto any one of which a boat could be skewered, splintered to pieces by strong waves; boats bashing into one another because their sails were down, lights extinguished by the wind. Hulde asking how the particular ship she was interested in could have navigated all that.

Well, gist is this, told me by the enquirer 'cos I was so involved. The ship was s'posed to be coming down the left side of the Kattegat, go up the canal to Odense. But storm was pushing them the wrong direction. Big winds will do that. Waters between the small islands so choppy it's not safe to go there. Went instead down the strait between Sjelland and the end of Sweden into our bit, where water would be calmer and they'd be safe. Ride out the night, head back around Falster and Lolland come morning, arrive in Odense as planned...

Hulde noting all those names in her head.

Falster, Kattegat, Sjelland, Odense.

Jansen going on with his recital about stones and lily-pale faces.

Hulde posing a question once he'd reached his end.

'But they weren't safe? Why was that?'

Jansen unstoppered the second bottle with his teeth, took a glug, waggled it at Hulde who politely refused.

'Well that there's the mystery, right enough,' he got out. 'Cos they should have been. Sails were lowered, anchor down. Could see that with me own eyes.'

'What did the enquirer reckon?' Hulde asked, Jansen shrugging his shoulders.

'Told me all the usual bollocks, excuse my language. Said it couldn't have been laded right, must have been bad kept, captain giving bad orders.'

Jansen making a snorting sound at the back of his throat, took another swig to clear the obstruction.

'You don't agree?' Hulde interpreted. Jansen sniffing, scratching at his badly shaved chin.

'Course I bloody don't,' he said. 'Told them at the time. Went down like a stone, it did, like God Almighty had punched a hole in its side...'

Might have repeated the entire episode had not Hulde gently curtailed it.

'Excuse me, Mr Jansen,' and Mr Jansen liked that. Jansen feeling important. Hulde pleasant and polite. 'Forgive my interruption, but I'm curious. Did folk go out looking in the morning for anyone who might have been washed up? You had to have been the best person to direct such operations, seeing as how you saw the whole disaster.'

Everyone liking flattery and Jansen, as Hulde had divined, liking it more than most.

Jansen preening, and then became peeved because she was right, goddammit. He should have been the person to direct such operations, yet not a damn one of the islanders had asked for his help. Then again, the islanders hadn't known anything had occurred. He'd not bothered raising hue and cry, not in the middle of the night. Had to see to the light in case other ships were abroad, and anyway what would have been the point?

I seen it with my own eyes. Not a one of them got out of that alive.

Fact was that come dawn he'd extinguished his light, put his head down for a much needed kip. Slept like the dead for a few hours, before heading home. Filled his gullet with fried bread and bacon. And by the time he'd got to the villages news had already reached them of someone being picked up beyond the lighthouse on the other side of the cliffs, which had to be some kind of miracle in Jansen's view.

'He was a gibbering wreck, by all accounts. Stayed with the fishermen, bundled up in blankets, till he was well enough to move.'

'And the enquirer,' Hulde pushed gently on. 'Did this man meet with him?'

Jansen swirling more liquor about his mouth, swallowing, grimacing.

'Dunno. Asked me about him, how likely it was he'd got picked up alive, given all I'd said. And I'm telling you like I told him. He must've had the luck of the gods. Got swirled from the wreck, sucked into the shore-side current going from here to the cliffs and Hjelm Bugt beyond.'

Shaking his head.

'Luckiest man in the world,' was his opinion. 'If the tide had been wrong when he went round the headland he'd've been in the Baltic proper. Could've had a thousand boats out looking for him and he'd never have been found.'

Clearing his throat, explaining how fortuitous it had been.

'Only a few yards between those two currents, between land-wise and shallows, sea-wise and deep. And if he'd been pushed from the inner to the outer he'd've been a goner, right enough. Nibbled down to the bones by fish and crabs, no matter his oilskins and bashed-in barrel.'

Hulde impressed with Jansen's telling, Jansen becoming more loquacious the more he drank. Impressed too by the details, the expert information about currents and tides, the mention of both barrel and oilskins. One set saving the life of the man who'd been found in the sea, the other side of the chalk cliffs; second set abandoned on Nyord Bay. Meaning two separate people washed up that night from the same wreck, barring a huge coincidence. One extraordinarily lucky to have been found, the other well enough in head and body to divest himself of oilskins and barrel, pilfer provisions and a handcart, make his stealthy way off into the storm-battered night without informing anyone the ship had gone down, raise the alarm.

Last questions put to her informer.

'This enquirer, the one you spoke with, when and where did he come from?'

Jansen taking another swallow, scouring his memory, not wanting to disappoint.

'Came to see me a few days later.' Puckering his lips, 'Met him at the lighthouse. Had me take him up, point out where the ship went down.'

Jansen staring out into the bay to that very place, as close as he could pinpoint it.

'Christian something. Schumann, maybe.'

Couldn't get any closer to the name, but gave this polite young woman his final flourish, waggling a finger to emphasise the importance of its telling.

'Knows he was a government man. Didn't tell me as much, of course. Them folk never do.' A brief angry outburst requiring a quick glug before he went on, raising a skewed smile, tapping his finger to the side of his nose.

'Shall I tell you how?'

'I wish you would,' Hulde replied, with a correspondingly conspiratorial smile.

'By his paper, of course.' Jansen stated dramatically. 'Wrote down everything I said, word for word, which took an age. And all the while he took dipping his pen into his blasted ink I took a good gander at the heading.'

'You read it upside down?' Hulde letting out a breath of fabricated admiration.

Jansen puffing out his chest, straightening his back.

'I did, young Miss. Saw it and read it. *The Municipality of Odense. Enquiry into the sinking of the* Put Preko Mora...' Surprising himself with the detail. Could recall it with exactitude. Saw the headed note-paper as if it was as real and close to him as Hulde was now.

'*On behest of the Government of Denmark,*' Jansen recited, recalling how excited he'd been to be a part of it, no matter he didn't hold much with governance of any kind. '*And the Archaeological Expedition of the Royal Geographical Society.* There,' he said proudly, 'that's exactly what it said.'

Letting out a couple of burps, so pleased with himself he didn't see the need for apology. Hulde smiling graciously, thanking him profusely. Hulde seeing Jansen metaphorically swelling up like a frog in the rain. Remembering Heraldo reading from a book about the human voice-box.

The first proper voices on earth, as opposed to sounds mechanically produced by the percussive tappings, scratchings and scrapings of crustaceans and fish underwater, must have come from some ancestral amphibian.

Fish and crabs again, and now amphibians too.

Hulde looking out across the water where all three species waited in darkness for what must fall upon them from above: the carcasses of whales and dolphins come to their natural end, the corpses of men and women spilled from ailing ships, sinking into the depths.

Hulde seeing too a vast opalescent bank of fog out there, upper edge silvered by moonlight as it hovered uncertainly on the horizon for a few moments before rolling in with great speed towards the sands like some huge breaker sweeping over the surface of the sea.

Jansen levering himself up, shuggling down the last of his brandy, discarding the bottle.

'Best get ourselves off,' he advised. 'We calls it the Running Wolf hereabouts. Be on us in ten minutes, and when it gets here you'll not be able to see your own hand in front of your face.'

Jansen not wrong.

Jochen already packing up his telescope, getting it on his cart, setting off over the dunes. The boys sent to fetch Hulde. Lupercal snatching up Diderik's lantern, holding it high as Jansen led them rather wobblily back to their camp before setting off for his home. The bank of fog rolling over them a minute later. Settling, cleaving to the land as it had previously cleaved to the sea. Taller than the tallest man, wider than the widest ship, stealing in as insidious as a thief. Takes nothing, instead leaves his calling card. Letting you know he can come into your domicile unbidden whenever he wants and for as long as he chooses. Soaks everything and everyone so slowly and with such cunning it's hard to know he's really there at all.

§

A different kind of thief had crept into the home of Othmar Voort, stealing away his peace of mind, disrupting the rhythm of his days, the unruly sleep cycles of his nights. Dark circles growing beneath restless eyes, emphasising the pallor of his skin. Sketches scattered about his table of all the men who'd accompanied him on his expedition. Othmar suspecting everybody until he could narrow it down. Five times he'd gone through the sketches putting names to faces as far as he could remember, sorting them into piles: those he trusted more than not, others he wasn't sure about, those he couldn't decide upon either way.

For a long time the topmost sketch on the latter pile had been the nameless workman who'd shouted out *Those you should not touch!* Yet surely he couldn't have been on the ship. A local man, along with all the other labourers. The only people on board being those returning to Odense, and from there to wherever they had initially come from: the three Royal Geographical Society men who were his direct assistants, one of whom was a lecturer at Copenhagen University hoping to gain a professorship from the trip; the second a relation of the great historian Niels Petersen whose *Guide to Northern Archaeology* Othmar had greatly admired; the third a wealthy Odense merchant who'd contributed funds for the expedition and had a tendency for grandstanding Othmar had thoroughly disapproved of. Then there were the gaggles of students from Danish universities and others as far flung as Jena in Germany and Paris in France, all eager for the practical experience.

He'd consorted for the most part with the Society men, not that he'd been exactly friendly. The purpose of the expedition—to prove his central thesis of the transmigration of civilisations from the north to the east and south— all-consuming. Othmar spending his days directing the digs, his evenings cataloguing and packing their finds, making his notes, totting up how each separate discovery fitted with the others, tracing evidentiary paths, linking artefacts through time and space, through history and geography.

Othmar having no inclination to socialise, irritated by the others frittering away their off-duty hours drinking and chatting, laughing, playing cards, even mixing with the many casual labourers the expedition employed as they snaked their way from Varna, on the edge of the Black Sea, into Montenegro and Albania, up the Adriatic coast towards their endpoint at Trieste.

Two long years during which Othmar Voort might have been expected to get to know his Society colleagues intimately, if not the disparate bands of students the next level down. Not how it had gone. Othmar withdrawing from their company the longer and further they'd travelled, realising how little the Society men cared for scholarship, were treating this trip as a couple of years on the hoof, a jaunt. Two of whom, Othmar was certain, had begun to compile their own little notebooks, nothing like Othmar's. Merchant and lecturer conspiring together to produce a travelogue for publication of the popular sort, designed to sell and make money, chattering about where they'd been, the natives they'd met, the adventures they'd had.

Othmar convinced the Danish Geological Society had set him up. Their intention not to highlight his thesis, instead to preen themselves within their nests, draw in more wealthy merchants and thereby their donations. It had rankled and riled him, made him redouble his efforts, re-brace his belief in his thesis, shutting out the rattlers the rest of his expeditionary companions had become.

He knew that in return they found him irksome and aloof, a dictatorial nit-picker who hovered over them to make sure they had no chance to pilfer anything that caught their eye. Othmar meticulous in keeping dig spaces tight and close, thoroughly excavating one section of the grid before filling it in, covering it over, moving on to the next. Had heard them talking about him on occasion when they'd had a few glasses, perhaps forgetting how close by he was in his tent, perhaps not. Perhaps meaning him to hear.

He's such a bore, they'd say. *Doesn't he ever loosen up?*
He'd have made a great prison guard in another life.
Grumbles and agreements all round.

Don't think he has a life, except for this expedition.

About that they'd been right. The expedition everything to Othmar and, as he sat here in his study, he was beginning to work up a theory. For how exciting would the merchant and lecturer's book be if they could end it with a dramatic shipwreck. An idea maybe mooted during the voyage, and the storm—as they'd rounded Schleswig Holstein into the Kattegat—maybe precipitating idea into action.

'God damn them,' he muttered, slamming his fist onto the wealthy merchant's face, his smile wide and nonchalant. Plastered there so often it appeared to be his natural demeanour. A smile insincere, meant to indicate bonhomie and honesty in his many business dealings which, in Othmar's experience and assuming the man was as wealthy as he boasted, had to be nefarious and underhand at best, downright crooked at worst.

The kind of man who might think it a grand wheeze to take down a ship to further his own ends, safeguard the sales of his upcoming travelogue. The final chapter: *How we almost drowned, how our ship capsized in a storm, how brave and resourceful we were to come out of it alive...*

A course of action not undertaken if he hadn't believed rescue was assured.

The captain maybe inadvertently bolstering that belief.

'We'll be making anchor in the Fakse Bugt where the waters will be calmer, ride out the night in sight of both land and the Møns lighthouses to keep us right.'

A statement given to all the passengers after he'd taken the decision to slide down the other side of Sjelland Island instead of to Odense.

'A simple task to tack back up the other side in the morning when the storm has blown itself out.'

Othmar hearing the captain's assurances along with the rest. And the captain had been assured, Othmar realised. It never occurring to him for a moment they might go down. Othmar hadn't spent much time with the man, the captain obliged to invite the

Society men, including Othmar, to his dinner table, given how illustrious they were. Students foddering with the crew. The captain not a talker. Table conversations carried on by merchant, lecturer and historian gabbling on companionably while Othmar pushed his food about his plate, too sea-sick to eat too much. Captain shovelling his rations down the hatch before excusing himself, needing to check charts, fill out logs, but please, gentlemen, stay as long as you like. Here the port, here the cigars.

Othmar and the captain men alike, who'd chosen their own paths, fought to get on them and stuck to them rigidly. Unlike lecturer, merchant and historian who'd started in good places, expected therefore more betterment must come. Theirs by right, no need to fight for it, not as Othmar had done, neither more the captain given the one unguarded statement he'd given the first night after they'd left Trieste.

'I'll not pretend to be your class,' he'd said, 'but while you're on board I've been instructed by your Society you're to be kept special and entertained. Eat at my table, sleep in the best berths, have a portion of the deck allocated you where the other passengers, bar your invitation, will not be allowed. And so will I do. What I'll not brook is interference in how I run my ship or my crew.'

The way he'd managed his ship and crew impeccable.

Othmar having absolute confidence in him, especially after the storm had struck.

Joviality and exhilaration the main reactions in the three Society men as the ship swept down the Kattegat, setting their faces to the wind, whistling up the rain, hollering into the night. Students gathering a little nervously at their backs before contagion set in and they too were leaning over the rails, putting out hands to catch the reins thrown up by white-horses in spume and spray. Until they'd reached the relative calm of the Fakse Bugt, well past midnight, and the captain ordered all to their berths, having had as much of their frivolities as he could stand.

Only Othmar left on board, stomach churning, knowing he wouldn't sleep, wouldn't be able to keep to his cot, would be retching and spewing. Preferred to be where he could breathe clean air.

Othmar recalling something he'd stumbled across in Varna before the others had convened there and the expedition had got properly underway. Using the time burrowing through book stores, garnering histories of the area, pottering in antiquity shops, fascinated by the language. Uncovering a tattered philological text in German providing an overview of it: associating Bulgarian with old Slav, giving cogent examples of how it belonged to a dialectical continuum that included Macedonian—with which it was near identical—and the closely related strands of Serbian, Croatian and Slovenian. Exactly as Othmar's thesis of transmigrating civilisations had predicted. Him and the author sharing the belief in an ancient Proto-Indo-European language and civilisation spawning all others, from Slavic, Germanic, Celtic, Italic and Anatolian, to the languages and civilisations of the present day which were as varied as the day was long.

The author providing numerous examples and confluences tracing individual words through time and space, as Othmar would later do with his artefacts. One line sticking with him, for it was so apt and so beautiful.

The night is a dark bowl in which the stars are scattered like wheat, exactly as languages are scattered across the world as if spilled from a single point from which all must have come.

He drummed his fingers over the merchant's smiling face, soon placed next to it that of the lecturer and, for good measure, the historian's too. Wondering if all three had been in it together.

Sigismund Griffen
Malachi Juel
Theobald Petersen
Merchant, lecturer, historian.
Men who had possibly conspired to sink the *Put Preko Mora*.

Othmar leaning back in his chair, trying to guess how they might have done it. Othmar supposing that if you knew what you were doing it mightn't be so very difficult.

The puzzle then being why it had gone so catastrophically wrong.

Perhaps they'd underestimated the strength of the storm, the distance to the land.

Except it hadn't been so distant. Well remembered that ribbon-thin stretch of sand as he'd been swept past it and away having tried and failed to kick towards it. But he'd been weak, exhausted, hadn't been strong and resilient like the corpulent merchant, the well-fattened lecturer, the pot-bellied historian. Not to mention the crew. Hard-muscled, strong-limbed, well used to turn and tide. Shake a few money-bags in their faces…

Tried to fasten his mind onto the last few minutes before he'd been swept over the side, before terror had so utterly overtaken him; whether the wind had violently increased, whipped the waves up in sudden fury. If perhaps they'd been in the eye of the storm, the saboteurs lulled into a false sense that all was calm and therefore perfect for their purpose before realising they'd been misled. Eye passing so swiftly from one dark side to the next they lost their window, and nothing any of them could do to halt it.

Othmar closed his eyes, pressed his fingers hard against them to stop the sensation tumbling through his head. Vicious cold. Vicious wind. Vicious water.

Othmar the single ear of wheat scattered across the bowl of the ocean, certain that night would be his last.

26

Shove Over, You Running Wolf

'The show begins,' Grettir shouts from the stage at the back of St Vid where the round-shouldered boulder was halfway in, halfway out, holding up the remaining courses of the gable wall. Chapel packed, rammed with chairs and benches. Competition judges given front row seats, villagers taking the rest, more folk crowding in behind, jammed against the walls.

Up above, waxed canvases sighed and soughed in a gentle breeze, sleet pattering haphazardly upon their shifting surfaces. The chapel eerily atmospheric, illuminated by the flames soodling in the fire-pit, soft wafts of smoke sending scents of forest into the air in a quivering haze, furthering the sense of mystery and anticipation.

'Behold!' Grettir calls, a great crackling coming up from the fire-pit, a furious fountain of crimson-gold sparklets exploding from its depths, leaping and twisting far into the eaves and, once subsided, the audience let out a collective sigh as, right in front of them, rises the totem of Svetovid as if awaking from sleep. Audience oblivious to the pulleys and wires which have roused him. Audience seeing only what they are meant to see, as was the Pfiffmakler way. Heraldo *de facto* director of this performance, Irmgaard ceding to his authority in the putting on of plays.

Judges already enthralled, brought up the side of Suvid in sleds, a new pathway scoped out, well-marked, well-trodden. Marko's dogs gone if not their progeny, who abounded in nearby villages and outlying farmsteads, and were readily loaned. Sleds and judges taken up by panting hounds, plenty of willing lads and men to keep them right. Judges landed at St Vid early afternoon, shuffling their feet outside as Grettir recites the prologue to the tale.

'This chapel has been ruined for many years, Lady and Gents.' One woman amongst their number, who'd once sung arias in startling soprano vibrato in the opera houses of Vienna. 'And ruined not once but twice. Rebuilt by the brave lads of the village before the brawling winds imprisoned inside the caves of Aeolus broke free once more,' Grettir waving his arms dramatically, raising his voice, 'and the Bora hurled avalanche and boulders down upon us, reduced our hard work to rubble, smashed the new roof with its fists, broke all the windows, filled the chapel with snow, trapped our builders and their teacher. Almost killed them all.'

Judges regarding the chapel with new respect. A sorry place it had seemed when they'd arrived, a wretched hulk topped by canvases, ropes thrown over the remaining strakes of eaves, ends tied off about rocks at the chapel's base.

'But we did not give up!' Grettir shouts triumphantly. 'Once we'd decided this place would be the arena for our performance, we built it up. It may have been torn down by the Bora, Lady and Gents, but we built it up again. And would have built it up once more if we'd needed to. We did this for you, and for St Vid. And we have much to show you.'

Bowing low and deep, sweeping down a hand, bringing it back up in a broad arc inviting them into the chapel. Judges glancing at one another as the door to the chapel appears to open of its own accord and they step towards the threshold, hoping it will not be as filled with snow as it had erstwhile been. It is not. Filled instead by a low humming chant reverberating against the walls, enveloping them, welcoming them in. Irmgaard there, draped in white robes, to guide them to their allotted seats. Villagers a reverential throng behind them. A soft scrum as everyone settles in their pews like rooks to their roost, the humming growing louder, more insistent, scents of pine and myrrh rising from the open grave of the pit leading them on.

Then Grettir on stage, the humungous crackles and sparks, the resurrection of Svetovid. This so unlike what the judges have seen previously they are already totting up marks and possible scores in their heads. A great honour to have been invited to preside over this inaugural regional competition, sponsored by the Senate, to promote a shared pride in Serbia's history, no matter the ethnic origins of its citizens; to promulgate unity, establish themselves as a nation state to be reckoned with.

They'd listened to choirs and orchestras from more schools than they could count, and ramshackle folk groups in all the many villages they'd passed through. Never, until now, had they been ferried up a mountain by dog-sleds to a semi-ruined chapel. And never would they witness another performance like this.

'Our god has arisen,' Grettir intones. Svetovid a huge wooden deity before them, recast by Marko on Heraldo's instruction. Features deeper, harsher. Lips snarling, flashes of white in the eyes, licks of gold to catch the light. Base untouched, blackened and charred by his sojourn in the fire. A god reborn, as had been this chapel, witnesses in no doubt of it.

'Four faces has our ancient god,' Grettir goes on, 'representing the four points of the compass, the four seasons of the year, the stages of our human lives.'

A soft chanting as the boys sing the words Heraldo has provided them:

We are your holding and your salvation.

Our four faces to be feared, respected and accepted.

We symbolize the eternal and the mortal in equal measure. We are Heaven and we are Earth. We come to you from the High Places. Thus has Svetovid spoken.

Yanni appearing on stage with three of his brethren, garbed from cowled heads to feet in their relevant colours.

Green for East, for Spring, for birth, announces the first.

A soft rustling as of new leaves opening. Boys scrumpling up paper in the wings.

Black for South and Summer, for growing and maturing under the scorching heat of the sun.

A brittle sound, handfuls of straws being broken in small strong fists.

Red for West and Autumn, for your harvests, your fecundity, your children.

Softer noises, hands drawn through pails of dried pine needles as of someone striding through piles of dying leaves.

White for North, a faint undertone of rumbling, *and Winter, the approach of death, the passage into the afterlife. This Winter we are sharing with you, which almost destroyed St Vid,* the rumbling crescendos, *and ourselves,* getting so loud and ominous Yanni has to shout out his last words: *who are nevertheless standing here on this stage before you, ready to provide our tetralogy of plays!*

The threat of a tetralogy of plays might, in any other place than this, have struck alarm in the hearts of the visiting judges. One play bad enough in most cases, but not here, not now. Not when the fires in the pit below Svetovid's feet have begun of a sudden to leap, to audibly groan, coughing up high silvery-green sparkles as if the ancient god is clearing his throat, ready to begin.

§

The Running Wolf has ceased its running, yawed a hovering pall over the sands of Nyord, laid its head upon its paws and settled for the night. Would not be moved until the sun rose a quarter way up the sky the following morning when it would draw itself back to the sea.

Jochen had stowed his telescope, delivered it safely home, dithered on his doorstep, then pulled his coat about his shoulders, started back towards the dunes. Knew the Running Wolf as well as anyone, took his steps accordingly, keeping the dunes to his left, the sounds of the lapping sea to his right. No need of a lantern, whose pauce light would only obfuscate, be reflected back by the shifting screeds of mist, leave him blind to the markers in the landscape leading to the Pfiffmaklers' encampment. Softly stepping into their purview, seeing the shadows of their tents before him, calling out into the mist.

'Hulde. It's me. It's Jochen Steggle. Hello?'

Brief waft through the breath of the Running Wolf as Hulde lifted the flap of her tent to guide him in. Jochen ducking, feeling large and intrusive, tent not quite high enough for him to raise his head. Hulde not alone. The boys sitting either side of the small fire. And Mergim, hunkered down at the back, a big man all the bigger in this tight place, all muscle and moustache, arms bulging about the sides of his knees.

'Told you he'd come,' said Jericho.

Jochen alarmed, hearing accusation, seeing the situation as they must do: Running Wolf hiding him as he crept across the sands to seek out young Hulde. A lonely middle-aged man presuming to find her alone, isolated by mist and night. Blood hot in his cheeks to be so misconstrued, about to stammer out his explanation, expecting to be set upon at any moment. Saved by the crooked boy, Ortwin, steering him down. Jochen subsiding into an uncomfortable squat that had his joints screaming, legs trying to get themselves into the easy cross-legged position the boys were in.

'We're as eager to hear what Jansen told Hulde as you are,' Ortwin said, a little wheezily, patting his chest to ease in more air. Jochen sympathising. Wolf's breath damp and heavy, unwilling to share itself around. All part of the nature of the Wolf, he supposed, unwilling—unlike its ancestors—to pat itself into a dog.

Hulde smiling at Jochen.

'Ortwin's right. Thought we'd wait a while, see if you'd come back.'

'That's very gracious of you,' Jochen got out. 'I confess I'm curious.'

'As you've a right to be,' Hulde said, as gracious as Jochen had supposed her to be. 'It was very illuminating.'

Taking a deep breath, looking over at Mergim who gave a quick shrug of his shoulders. *This is your show. Do as you will.*

Hulde about to give a summary when they were interrupted, the tent flap roughly lifted. Longhella's face looming and flickering in the light of the fire, her mouth already on the move.

'So what have we got here?' she asked. Had she been a viper she'd have flicked out a menacingly forked tongue. 'Diderik told me something was up.'

Diderik coming in at her back, stupid grin on his face as everyone scrunched up to give the newcomers room. Longhella giving Hulde a shove and a venomous look as she parked herself down beside her.

'Always got to have your own little mysteries, keep me out of the loop. You're like a spider, Hulde,' Longhella said, poking a stick at the fire, 'spinning your little webs. So what's going on?'

Hulde unflustered neither by Longhella's appearance nor her words.

'Jochen asked me to find out about something that happened here a long time ago.'

Longhella pluffed out a breath from her lips.

'Not that silly little calendar again.'

Jochen feeling compelled to speak. Hated being jammed in with all these people, was already uncomfortable, calf and thigh muscles starting to cramp with the unaccustomed manner of sitting.

'It was a shipwreck,' he said. 'Certain aspects of which have never been fully explained.'

Shifting his legs, getting his heels on the ground, crooking up his knees, wincing with the pain.

'A shipwreck, is it?' Longhella asked. 'Well, I suppose there's a certain amount of drama in that. Anything we can use?'

Once a Pfiffmakler, always a Pfiffmakler.

Hulde seizing the opportunity given her.

'We're not sure yet,' she said quickly, 'although there are certain intriguing aspects. Like how everyone assumed at the time there was only one survivor, although we believe now there were two. Also because the evidence suggests…'

'Stop, ' Longhella commanded. 'Why do you always have to start in the middle instead of the beginning?'

Exactly as spiders began their webs. Longhella sounding angry and aggrieved, annoyed she'd not been in at the start of the tale. Diderik telling her some of it, if not all. So like Diderik. Longhella, before Diderik had returned, compelled to venture from their tent into the eerie mist that swam and swirled, thickened and thinned, devious in its patterning, making you see what wasn't there. Longhella detecting her sister's ghostly outline within its writhings, always on its edges, a few yards out of reach. Longhella catching her breath as the Running Wolf rolled in, Longhella holding out her hand.

Ludmilla? Is that you?

Which of course it wasn't. How could it be? Would never be.

'They're talking shipwrecks and survivors!' Diderik had announced as he'd come to her, clasping Longhella's hand in his own, finding in it the solidity he'd been seeking since the Running Wolf had overtaken them, mistaking the tears spilling from Longhella's eyes as mere droplets condensed from the mist.

'I'm sorry,' Hulde apologised. 'It was 1839 when it happened, and a lot of the wrecked ship's timbers got washed up on this beach.'

'Jochen built his house from them,' Lupercal interrupted.

'And a grand fine house it is,' Jericho averred. 'You should see it.'

'That's neither here nor there,' Hulde got back on track. 'What matters is that Jochen recently realised some of the ship's timbers had holes bored into them, and…'

'It's taken you thirteen years?' Longhella quick with condemnation. 'How in blazes has it taken you so long? Are your eyeballs screwed in backwards?'

Jochen coloured, got in his defence.

'They were in the ones that were always underwater, the wood not best for building. Burned many of them. The rest on the woodpile, ended up underneath.'

'Hmm,' Longhella said. 'Must have been a mighty big woodpile if you've only just got to the bottom of it.'

Hulde taking over again.

'Getting to the bottom of it is precisely what we've been trying to do. Why I spoke to Jansen, who actually saw the ship go down.'

Longhella prodding and prickling until the rest came out.

Holes bored in wood.

Oilskins and barrel abandoned on the beach.

The stealing of provisions and handcart.

Jochen suspecting Jansen until Jansen freely volunteered to Hulde he'd not returned home until much later in the day.

The coincidence of wreck and stealing, the unignorable fact that the thief had to be presumed to have come from the sea—given the abandoned oilskins—and therefore from the wreck, and yet alerted no one. Hadn't straightaway gone banging on Jochen's door begging for help, get everyone in the vicinity looking for stricken comrades or crew.

'You have to admit it's a little peculiar,' Hulde tacked on, watching Longhella's face, seeing the cogs turn as Longhella came to her own conclusions.

'Jansen told me more,' Hulde went on, after a few seconds. 'There was an official enquiry. Someone sent here to talk to Jansen about what he'd seen, who also talked to the survivor dragged up by the fishermen on the other side of the Møns Klint.'

'Ooh, that's news,' Lupercal perked himself up. 'Does that happen often? Enquiries, I mean?'

Jochen too taking note. A lot of shipwrecks in these parts, as in anywhere there was sea and storm. No enquiries necessary. Storms came up, ships went down.

'It isn't,' he offered. 'I mean I knew there was one. Jansen talked about it often enough back then.'

Blew himself up like a blasted toad with all his talking. Boasting and gloating.

'This is where it gets interesting,' Hulde held up a finger, 'for several reasons.'

'Keep it short, Hulde,' Longhella sighed, despite being as intrigued as the rest.

Hulde obliging.

'Jansen told me it was on behalf of the Danish government, when the ship didn't arrive as expected in Funen, one of the bigger islands just up north. Everyone aware of the storm, of course. The oddity is the speed with which the enquirer got from there to here.'

Short silence, until Mergim spoke up from the back of the tent.

'More odd is the why.'

Mergim living in Zadar for years. Ships going down in the Adriatic all the time for any number of reasons. No point trying to figure out how they went. And certainly never any enquiries, official or otherwise.

Hulde's face shining back at him like a rising sun.

'I think because of its cargo. I don't believe the *Put Preko Mora* was any old ship,' Hulde taking a bit of a leap into the dark. 'The enquirer wasn't only government, but came on behalf of the Royal Geographical Society of Denmark.'

'My silly little moon calendar,' Jochen murmured. 'You said you'd seen similar in Serbia, and that the name *Put Preko Mora* is Serbian for...'

'The Road Over The Sea,' Mergim finished for him.

'Add in the fact of the Royal Geographical Society,' Hulde said, coming to a conclusion, 'and you've got to wonder if the ship wasn't carrying back to Denmark the finds of an expedition they financed. Maybe archaeological.'

Longhella tapped her foot on the ground.

'I think you've been a Pfiffmakler too long,' she announced, spiky words puncturing Hulde's balloon. 'You're so used to telling stories you're seeing things that aren't there.'

Just like she'd seen out in the mist.

'But if Hulde's right,' young Ortwin piped up, 'there might be far more than your moon calendar buried in the sand of the bay. Have you never found anything else?'

Directing his question at Jochen, who shook his head.

'I'm sorry.' Quick glance at Hulde, hating to appear to be in disagreement with her theory which, up to this point, had seemed remarkably cogent. 'Not in all this time.'

'Oh well,' Longhella straightened her back, shrugging everything off, bringing the conversation to a close. 'It was good while it lasted, but I for one am looking forward to my bed. If I can find my blasted way back to my blasted tent in all this blasted mist.'

The boys sighing and shuffling. It had seemed such an adventure, a mystery unravelling before their eyes. Getting ready to head for their own beds until Mergim stirred, held up a hand.

'Wait,' he counselled. 'Aren't we forgetting the most important aspect of the tale?'

'Like what?' Longhella countered, splaying a hand over her crumpled orange skirts to indicate her disinterest. 'If it was a ship stuffed top to bottom with valuable collectables then why haven't they been discovered by now? Why weren't they scattered over the dunes like sand-flies? And why, come to that, didn't the Danish Geographical whoever they were have men out here digging everything up looking for them? Come on, Diderik. I've had enough.'

Diderik rising obediently at her back, although Longhella did not make it to her feet.

'Because it went down like a stone,' Hulde said quietly. 'That's exactly how Jansen put it. It went down like a stone, lurched to one side and then went over. And he said the same to the enquirer.'

'And if it went down like he said,' Mergim added, 'then it didn't do it all by itself. Ships simply don't go down like that, not even in the worst of storms.'

'And it wasn't the worst of storms,' Jochen put in, 'it really wasn't. It was bad, but not that bad. Blows were hard, waves big, but the ship already at anchor in the bay, sails down and stowed.'

'No point looking for what can't be found,' Jericho stated grimly. 'Down it went and down it stayed.'

'Except it didn't,' Lupercal disagreed. 'Half the hull came up onto the sands where Jochen found it. So why didn't everything else? Assuming there was anything else.'

Jochen thinking on what Hulde had said about a possible expedition.

'Because the cargo would have been stored in sea-chests,' he said slowly. 'Whatever they'd collected—botanicals, fauna and flora, skins or hides—would have been dried or pressed, or kept in alcohol. All needing to be kept safe.'

Like he transported all his phantoms. Parcelled up, carefully packaged.

'That's right!' Hulde agreed, her theory not completely shredded by Longhella's scepticism. 'And if the ship went down top first, like Jansen said, then maybe the deck smashed to pieces on the sea bed, stayed down there with the chests, the other half of the hull lying on top of them while the rest separated, got hauled away by the current, some of it ending up here on the sands. Isn't that possible?'

'Anything's possible,' Mergim agreed, 'particularly in storm conditions. And I'm guessing the waters out there conceal rocks of some sort, given the two lighthouses on top of the cliff.'

Treachery at every turn.

Mergim knowing about treachery, had been treading on its coat-tails for years.

'There are certainly rocks out there,' Jochen broke in, 'and if the ship got partially caught on an edge…well yes. That could explain a lot.'

'Like how the ship broke up as it did?' Hulde asked, leaning forward.

'Like that,' Jochen agreed. 'If it hit one of the underwater skerries going down, got partially lodged, it's not unlikely the impact could split the whole in two, current strong enough to take the uppermost part—which paradoxically was the lower, the keel—and left the rest to eventually topple over and sink. And if one of the chests was damaged in the falling…'

'Your moon calendar could have been light enough to be snatched up by the same current and brought to the exact same shore,' Jericho finished for him.

'Buried by new sand brought in with the storm,' Mergim added, knowing how that went. Several feet of sand dredged up and deposited by one storm, taken away with the next, depending on the shift of the tide when the storm was at its height. Gave with one hand, took away with another. Not overnight, sometimes weeks, sometimes months later. Sometimes never.

'So there might be more out there?' Lupercal added, ready at that moment to snatch up a shovel and start digging away at the bay. 'More moon calendars, or small things like it?'

Jochen tapping his cheek with his finger. For more than a decade he'd brought seaweed up and carted it away, taken regular strolls over the sands. Eyes up and ahead, looking out to sea more often than not. Only coming across the moon calendar because he'd been digging to steady the tripod for his telescope. At least nine inches down, going into damp sand to keep the legs steady.

'I don't see why not,' he said. 'If one of the chests did break open, then it stands to reason anything lifted by the sea might end up hereabouts.'

Fingered out by the water, bobbing along in the currents before coming ashore.

'This is complete supposition,' Longhella this time managing to her feet, feeling heavy and a little queasy. All this talk of sea and storms had her stomach in a churn. 'Feel free to go off digging miles and miles of sand for what quite obviously isn't there. Have at it. Be your own little Geographical Expedition, why don't you.'

Stomping back out into the mist, clinging to Diderik's arm because she really didn't feel well, and she really, really, didn't want to see the shadow of her dead sister out there in the maw of the Running Wolf.

The two swallowed up as they headed towards their tent.

'You won't ever leave me, will you Diderik?' she whispered, as if Diderik ever would. Longhella stumbling, Diderik righting her. Diderik pulling her close.

'Never,' he assured, his lips a whisper from her ear. 'You're the rising of my sun and the setting of it.' A line from one of their plays. 'You go into the darkness and I'll be an inch behind.'

No havering. Absolute conviction. Diderik's devotion as solid and steadfast as this mist was flit and fickle.

'If I ever catch a real Running Wolf,' Longhella replied, smiling grimly, 'I'm going to skin the blasted thing alive.'

Diderik wrapping an arm about her shoulder.

'And a fine coat we'll make of it. Best you've ever had.'

No nightmares for Diderik about such a bloody scenario.

Diderik too happy in this new life, sleeping every night fast and secure as a turnip bedded into its right ground, as long as Longhella was by his side.

27

Flow Fast, Oh River Sava, Flow Quick And Fast

'Svetovid swept from the north, across the barren wastes and frozen seas of the Slavs,' Grettir announces, 'with wings of snow, face of fire.'

He waves an arm, from which appears a flowing band of smoke and, when it clears, there is Svetovid, vast and terrifying; broad arcs of colour across the back-cloth, swirls of white impasto behind. A titanic tintinnabulation of tolling hand-bells filling the air as comes a shout from one side of the stage, *God of War!* and from the other, *God of Creation!*

'He holds fast within his fist peoples and nations,' Grettir booms, 'has dominion over the demons of the air, over wind and rain; can draw up wheat and corn to the height of men, plump their ears so they hang and sway like olives. Or crush the crops beneath his feet, as he sees fit.'

Swift change of backdrop, a solemn tattoo heralding its reveal, wooden sticks beating on a metal drum.

'To the Red Island of Rügen Svetovid next passes.'

Heraldo adapting the battle scenes the Pfiffmaklers had put on for the people of that island, pared down of necessity, making do with lengths of canvas left over after securing the roof, bottles of pigments from Marko's workshop and the village potter, various solvents and oils.

'The Christians come,' Grettir intones, 'intent on stamping out the old religion. Bloody battles and slaughter bleeding out across the sea before they reach the land.'

Heraldo cannot depict naturalism, his mind filled with music and imagery, creating by intuition and abstraction: here the scene is black and dark, streaked through with slashes of carnelian, lashes of silver and gold-yellow ochre, evoking feelings not actualities. Heraldo's backdrop spangling and jangling in the glittering light of the fire-pit.

Two boys coming on stage at its feet dressed in black, bearing silver-glinting swords whittled from birch boughs. They tussle and curse in high dudgeon, clashing and dashing at one another, rolling and reeling, sharp sounds of metal against metal, the boards apparently slithered with blood as they slide and collide, separate and re-square up. All carefully choreographed by Heraldo.

Brief hiatus behind the scenes as everyone else readies themselves for the next scene.

'I think it's going well,' Grettir says, *sotto voce.*

'I'm nervous,' Yanni whispers back.

'Don't be,' Irmgaard encouraged, putting a steady hand upon his shoulder. Yanni nervous, nonetheless.

'Going to fall and rest on this last part,' he jittered. 'What if they don't get it?'

Irmgaard stoic, resolute. Thinking of wings of snow, how far they can go, how swift and silent.

The boys on stage finishing their theatre of war, one prostrate, the other with the tip of his opponent's sword to his throat.

'You can kill me,' the fallen one cries out, 'but you cannot kill Svetovid. He is red as Rügen, his soil drinking in my blood will only make him stronger!'

The victor raises his sword, both hands about its wooden hilt; holds it aloft for one second, two, until down it goes, piercing his enemy's neck, the howl of anguish and anger coming from his victim's lips raising the hairs on everyone's arms. No time to further react for the hammering has started up again, constant and deafening, filling the air with thunder.

'I will not be stopped!' Svetovid booms, Grettir putting his lips to the cone of metal Heraldo has made for him. His words reverberating, melding with the manufactured thunder. Audience awestruck, billows of smoke roaring from the pit, green and sulphurous.

Yanni appearing from the dissipating clouds, short stilts strapped to his legs, moving with slow gait, green clouds sinking, hovering at his feet so he appears to float. Tall mask resting on his shoulders, rectangular wooden frame covered with a hood of canvas. Red face of Svetovid. Painted flames burning upwards from his cheeks coalescing in scarlet-orange hues upon his brow, licks of fire rising into the darkness of the chapel.

From the aspect of the audience he seems eight feet tall.

Yanni trembling inside his prosthetic architecture, fearing he will stumble, or let loose the mask. Through the eye-slits he sees rows of seats teetering into gloom, tiers of upturned faces, all rapt and somewhat anxious.

Breathe, he tells himself. *All you've to do is stand still, stand tall.*

To those below he is imperious, imposing and vital, risen from the bloodied soil of Rügen stronger than ever.

'He cannot be stopped,' Grettir's lips put once more to the metal cone. So simple an instrument, so dramatic the results. 'He passes from his northern strongholds to the east, sets his feet on the shores of the Black Sea.'

Sudden change of back-drop: more of Heraldo's artistry. Hints of pale buildings, a brooding landscape of marshes, streaks of birds gliding through stormy skies above stormy seas, crenellations of breaking waves out there in the darkness.

'He goes to Varna, city of salt, city of gold...'

This Grettir's personal contribution, for he's been to Varna— the most ancient of Europe's prehistoric towns. Has seen the tiny pendants and earrings said to be the oldest worked gold in the world. Has visited the walled settlement of Solnitsata, touched his fingers to the salt-bricks baked from Black Sea brine. Wealth coming initially from this salt. Nobody on earth able to live without salt. Everyone able to live without gold.

'And from Varna, from Bulgaria,' Grettir booms, 'on Svetovid treads to our southern coasts. Comes, in 1389, to our Field of Blackbirds...'

Yanni sweating, for here it comes. The lynchpin of the performance, of Serbian history: the Battle of Kosovo, during which Svetovid becomes St Vitus, becomes St Vid.

At the back of the chapel, on the last tier of seats, Marko sits and shivers. Ten days since his rescue, and he's still cold, feels the stricture of snow about his chest, fears the pneumonia might get him as it got Gregor. Still misses his dogs. Goes to their shed every morning. Opens the door, looks into emptiness. Caught by Yanni that very morning as Marko stood there, tears coursing down his cheeks. Yanni hanging uncertain on the threshold for a few moments, as Marko's shoulders heaved with sobs. Yanni running forward.

'Oh Papa,' he'd whispered.

Taking Marko's hands in his own, wiping away his father's tears.

How does this happen? Marko had thought. *How does the father becomes the son and the son the father?*

Marko fixing his eyes on Yanni now, steadfast on his makeshift stage, recognisable to Marko only because he knows of Yanni's part, helped him construct the mask from green willow boughs, canvas and paint.

He's been moved by the entire performance. What has been done in the ten days Marko has been shivering in his bed is more than remarkable. It's been astounding. And now here is Yanni, embodiment of Svetovid, and the timbre of the booming voice has changed, is reciting the events of the Battle of Kosovo on the Field of Blackbirds where Marko had taken his stance, allied himself with those ancient heroes and ancestors, made his mark.

Those you should not touch.

The backdrop behind Yanni changes, and Marko is right back there again. The painted scene filling his head with vivid images: a maelstrom of colours, a whirling dervish of greens and whites, reds and blacks, and there, to the far right, is the unmistakeable outline of this very mountain rising high and gaunt and, on one of its several pinnacles, is this chapel.

Marko cannot stop himself. He stands, feels tall as Yanni's Svetovid up there on the stage. Opens his mouth, opens his chill lungs, begins to sing *My Beautiful Homeland*. A patriotic anthem doing the rounds since 1846. Words penned by a Croat, set to music by a Serb. By Antun Mihanovic and Josip Runjanin, neither of whom will ever know that forty years hence their anthem will become a song of revolution. The only anthem in the world to which a monument will be built and dedicated.

What is the fog hiding within its reams? It hides our people's dreadful screams.

Marko belts out into the short silence following Yanni's appearance.

Who prays for death's decree? The downtrodden or the free?

Yanni unnerved. Recognises his father's distinctive baritone. High notes strong, lower ones tremulous and weak. Gazing through the eye-slits he sees his father standing, fist of his right hand clenched over his heart.

It is war, brothers and heroes.

Saddle your horses, take your weapons, join the throe.

And extraordinarily Yanni sees others getting to their feet, hands across their own hearts, beginning to join in.

Infantrymen, let's enter the story, for wherever we are there will be glory!

Basses booming like bitterns in the marshes, high tenors adding to the top notes.

Everyone in the wings wondering what to do. Grettir and Irmgaard exchanging glances.

Grieving mothers, be joyful.

The singing goes on, gets louder. More men standing, including the judges.

Awful for your brave sons to have fallen,
Adding their blood to our homeland's soil.
But heroes, mothers! Heroes all!

Heraldo pulls the boys back, motions to Irmgaard and Grettir, puts a finger to his lips, shakes his head. *Let them go on.*

And go on they do, because now the opera singer has swept her skirts from her seat, straightened her back, stretched her neck, cleared her throat. Pours into the chapel's twilight the voice that once filled the opera houses of Vienna.

Flow fast, oh river Sava, flow quick and fast,
And Danube, never lose the power of your voice.

Murmur on wherever you take your waters.
Tell the world we love our homeland.

A beautiful vibrative soprano rising from the milieu of men, pure and sure as a blackbird in the dawn.

We will love it when the sun warms our fields,
When the winds lash our forests.

The lower voices falling away as she reaches the last lines of Antun's anthem, all feeling deeply, some weeping freely, including Marko.

Graves have swallowed our fallen heroes, our honoured elite.
And still we love our homeland.
Every man, every woman, will love our homeland
While we have hearts that beat.

Absolute silence in the chapel of St Vid as the opera singer's last notes die away.

A few faint crackles coming from the fire-pit.

The fainter pittering of new snow upon the canvas roof as the wind moves up a notch.

On stage Yanni is petrified, daren't move a muscle.

Obvious to him his part is done. Their entire play done, no matter it never reached its planned end. Saved by Heraldo who has caught the melody of this song he's never heard before, is plucking it out with his few working fingers upon his mandolin.

'Get out there,' he whispers urgently to Grettir. 'Wrap it up.'

Grettir flummoxed. Heraldo might be used to plays going off-script into unforeseen directions, but not he. Irmgaard taking to the fore, stepping onto the stage, putting a steadying hand on Yanni who is beginning to wobble.

'Thank you,' she says to her audience to Heraldo's sweet playing. 'We couldn't have imagined a more wonderful ending to our performance. You might expect us to take a bow, your applause. Not this afternoon.'

She motions to the boys who come on dutifully, wide eyed, adrift, looking to Irmgaard for their cue. Irmgaard not failing them.

'But this afternoon,' Irmgaard continues smoothly, seeking out the judges, the opera singer in particular, all of whom are still on their feet, 'it is we who must give our bows and applause to you.'

Irmgaard bending low at the waist, the boys following suit. Yanni attempting to join in, not thinking it through. His Svetovid head toppling, bouncing from the stage into the fire-pit. A horrid moment for Yanni, fearing he's ruined the moment. Irmgaard saving him, beginning to clap loudly.

'Even Svetovid bows and applauds you!' Irmgaard calls, boys joining in with the clapping, and soon everyone in the entire chapel is doing the same, laughing, slapping each other's shoulders. Heraldo's mandolin, lilting away in the background, caught by the opera singer's acute ear and she starts singing again those last two verses, picking up the tempo, Heraldo easily keeping pace.

Flow fast, oh river Sava, flow quick and fast,
And Danube, never lose the power of your voice.

Every last person in the chapel joining in, mismatched tributaries pouring into the confluence of the whole, blood rising, feet stamping, hands clapping, become the beating heart of their anthem, their love for country, which is what this entire competition has been about.

By the time they're done singing Irmgaard has reached the chapel door, flings it open, her boys swirling about her like Sava's fast flowing waters.

'Onto the sledges and down the mountain!' she cries out. 'A feast awaits you down below!'

The folk in the chapel parting like the Red Sea to allow the judges through before pouring on behind them into the darkening afternoon. Judges swiftly guided onto waiting sledges, furs flung about shoulders and knees. Boys ready with their lighted brands, dogs panting to be gone, leashes tinkling with bells.

And then they're off.

Boys racing down the mountain at the fore, brands licking and flickering, lighting the way for the sleds coming on at their heels. Men behind them whooping and hollering, hie-ing up the dogs, running alongside, keeping them right. Women in the village below seeing the flickering line of lights slewing first one way and another as the cavalcade zig-zag haphazardly down the slopes of Suvid. Women taking bread from their ovens, stirring their various stews bubbling over their various fires, tipping them into warmed dishes, getting ready for the onslaught they know must come.

And up above, standing outside the chapel, are the three people who engineered this event and have elected not yet to leave.

Heraldo, Grettir and Irmgaard.

Snow falling all about them and on them.

Dry snow, large flaked, the kind that settles yet can be brushed off in a moment.

Someone else emerging from the chapel, taking his stance beside them.

'I apologise. Got a bit caught up. Hope I've not wrecked your chances.'

Irmgaard shaking her head as she turns towards Marko.

'Sorry be damned,' she says, smiling broadly. 'I think you've just won us our day.'

28

And Yet, And Yet

New day for the Pfiffmaklers, new plans. All decided in the huddle of Hulde's tent after Longhella and Diderik had departed. The mystery of the shipwreck grabbing them by the throat. *A certain amount of drama in it,* Longhella had said. And maybe a new play. Pfiffmaklers always latching onto local history, weaving its stories' threads through their own, and plenty here to work with: shipwreck and sabotage; a Royal Geographical Expedition, a Government Enquiry; sea-chests, filled with who knew what, lost below the waves.

Boys out the moment the Running Wolf had departed, badgering Jochen into showing them where he'd found his moon calendar. Spades at the ready, excavations begun. Jochen wryly amused, joining in, although not with the digging. Jochen instead walking slowly along the highest strandlines marked by wriggles of dried bladder wrack, fingers of kelp, the stones to which they'd calcified themselves. Ortwin keeping him company, finding digging hard work. Not enough air in his lungs to go at it for long.

'Do you think we'll find anything?' Ortwin asked. Jochen wanting to let him down lightly, for he didn't think they would.

'It's been years since that ship sunk,' he cautioned, 'and although I've never really looked I have to say I think it most unlikely.'

Ortwin nevertheless doggedly trailing up and down the strandline, kicking at the detritus with his boots; bending down occasionally, picking up a crab carapace, a cuttlebone, a mermaid's purse, a strange bony object with odd protuberances which Jochen identified as the skull of a dogfish.

'I modelled a lot of sea life when I was an apprentice,' he explained. 'Made them out of wax before my masters cast them in glass.'

Ortwin intrigued, asking a myriad questions, then dipping down, pulling up a dulled piece of metal.

'Look!' he exclaimed, puffing his cheeks in excitement, turning the object in his fingers, holding out to Jochen a tarnished lump of lead topped by a short neck through which a length of twine could be threaded. Jochen rubbing it gently on his sleeve to free it from sand and sludge.

'I'm sorry, Ortwin,' he said. 'It's only a cloth seal. They were attached to bolts of wool and linen and so forth to prove their provenance and quality. It's old, but I doubt is of significance.'

Ortwin undeterred. Eyes catching a second dim metallic edge.

'Another one!' he called out, the light of discovery housed inside Ortwin's young shell not be dimmed. Had the thing out with alacrity and, to Jochen's amusement, rubbed it on his sleeve exactly as Jochen had done with the first.

'This one's different,' Ortwin declared. 'It's got a bit of shine to one corner.'

Jochen smiling tolerantly, liking this scrap of a boy with his hollowed-out chest and endless stream of questions. Jochen's smile hovering at the edges of his lips as he inspected the object further, examined its rounded body, poked his fingernail into a slit down one of its sides.

'Well, well,' he said after a few moments, 'this might be something indeed.'

Delving into a pocket, bringing out the set of miniature tools used for making minor adjustments to his telescope. Sitting down on the edge of the dunes, rolling out the small pouch, selecting a flat-bladed screwdriver a few millimetres in diameter at the working end, a small blunt-edged punch, a tiny hammer the length of his finger.

'Here, Ortwin,' Jochen said. 'Hold it at top and bottom and side to side.'

'What are you going to do?' Ortwin's chest tightening in anticipation as Jochen set forth at his task.

'I'm going to do…this…'

Face creased in concentration, inserting the screwdriver's blade into the hair-thin aperture, tapping its end lightly with his hammer, moving from the centre to first one end and then the other, then back to the middle. Opening it just enough to take the end of the punch, which he cushioned with a pinch of moss from a nearby piece of wood.

'And next this…cup it gently now.'

Ortwin feeling the coolness of the metal, each gentle strike Jochen sends from his hammer.

'It's moving!' Ortwin exclaimed, the metal bending as Jochen tapped at it repeatedly, recreating the roundness flattened away by years of grinding salt, shifting tides, scrapes of sand and stone. Jochen meticulous, taking the object from Ortwin's fingers and having to again with blade, punch and hammer. Ortwin's eyes fixed on Jochen's slender fingers as he worked, stupefied when Jochen was finally finished, when Jochen removed his tools, polished the object vigorously with a sprinkle of sand held by the corner of his shirt, holding the object up, handing it to Ortwin.

'Shake it,' Jochen said and Ortwin did, a high sonorous rattling coming from inside.

'Oh my!' Ortwin exclaimed with unguarded joy, admiring the sound, the fact that Jochen had transformed a two dimensional object into one with shape, form and function.

'It's a Crotal Bell,' Jochen happily informed Ortwin. 'I saw one in Herrenburg. The church there has the most extensive collection of bells anywhere in the world so they told me, and I've no reason to disbelieve them.'

Ortwin hardly listening, too intent on scrutinizing the small pear-shaped object in his fingers.

'They've bells there a thousand years old,' Jochen went on, 'and more modern ones of course. And almost all are still working. And this one you've found, Ortwin, well. It's very like one they...'

'Ooh, and look. There's something here on the front.' Ortwin's young eyes catching what Jochen's had not. Ortwin repeating the scrubbing Jochen had started, taking the edge of his own shirt and a pinch of dried sand.

'It's like words, but sort of not,' was his imprecise opinion. Jochen re-approaching his pouch, taking out a thumb-nail magnifying glass.

'Interesting. Words, like you said. Maybe Persian. See these arabesques? Very typical of that language, particularly when used in decoration.'

Ortwin too interested to reply. Ortwin squinting, tracing the curves with his fingertip.

'Persian,' he repeated. 'I've never heard of it. What would it have been used for, this bell?'

Jochen pursed his lips, thinking back to Herrenburg.

'People hung them around the necks of animals or carts, still do in many places. Others are playthings for the young. But this one, I suspect, given the delicacy of the inscriptions, was more likely ritualistic. Lots of religious ceremonies use bells.'

'Is there anything you don't know?' Ortwin asked, awed by this man who'd built his house from a wrecked ship, could bring a scrap of metal back to life, who used words like *arabesque.*

Jochen laughing lightly, not something he often did. Last time, now he thought of it, being when Jansen had come tripping over to Jochen's around Yule-tide, pickled as a herring, shouting out insults he'd obviously been mulling over, too soused to get them out as he'd intended.

You're a pernickety pen-pushing pig… of a…of a prig. I've said it once, and I'll say it again. You're a spernickety pen-pusher! You and your Sput Spreko Smora. I'll Sput Spreko Smora you, oh yes I will!

At which point he'd stumbled, bashed into the billy's enclosure and been bitten full on the cheek by the goat who'd no love for Jochen, even less for his neighbour. Jochen standing in his doorway, ready to flatten Jansen if he came any closer, watching Jansen scrabbling about in the dirty snow, hands clutching at the fence, pulling himself up, barely able to stand.

You're as fucking barmy as your fucking master, Jansen had yelled, shaking impotent fists first at the goat and then at Jochen. *I'll spucking well get you both one day, you see if I don't! You spucking spernicky…spig…you spickling goaty goatster…*

Blood dripping from his cheek as he headed off home on hands and knees, managed to right himself for a few minutes before toppling again, got himself up by means of grabbing hold of the *Put Preko Mora* sign he'd been so liberal in despising, moving one hand gingerly above the other as if he were climbing some unfathomably tall tree to which he could see no end.

Jochen leaving him to it, closing his door, guffawing with such gusto he'd got a stitch in his side and had to lie down for a full ten minutes before the pain subsided. Humour perked up all over again the following day when he'd sought Jansen out, Jansen stumbling about his duties with a head thick and heavy as a thunderstorm, plainly having no memory of the incident at all.

'Want to know how you got that wound on your cheek?' Jochen had asked, overly cheerful. 'How you holed the knees of your trousers? Got those scrapes on your palms?'

Jansen grumbling, coughing, spitting up a gob of phlegm that landed right on his boot. Having great difficulty getting out a coherent sentence.

'Don't want no bloody nothing from the likes of you,' he'd muttered. 'You piggling piece of pig shit.'

Shades of his former invective vaguely retained somewhere inside his hungover head.

'Can enlighten you,' Jochen had gone on in gleeful tone. 'Got to ask the question if you want the answer.'

And got to look if you want to find.

Searching the strandline for maybe half an hour, and already they'd found two small objects. Stood to reason there might be more. Jochen never finding because he'd never looked. Recalling Longhella's questions from the previous night: *why aren't they scattered over the dunes like sandflies, and why has no one ever bothered to look?* Ortwin's finds might have been here a hundred years. Or maybe only thirteen. Chests tightly locked, plummeting to the sea floor, rest of the ship coming down upon them. Buried chests, subject to over a decade of shifting currents, tides, sands and erosion, maybe no longer so locked nor tight.

'Come on, Ortwin,' Jochen said. 'Show me what else you can find.'

§

Their play had been a storming success, they all knew.

'I think it's in the bag,' Grettir happily opined, rubbing his hands together as they turned from the snow, went back inside the chapel. Fire to be doused, backdrops disassembled, benches tidied and stacked, dishes and pots stowed to be taken back down. One bottle of wine remaining. Grettir uncorking it after their duties were done. Pouring it out for himself, Irmgaard and Heraldo. Marko outside, securing the rocks and ropes to keep the roof canvases in place for as long as they could. Marko adamant.

'I'm going to rebuild it,' he'd stated. 'Go at it brick by brick, beam by beam, tile by tile. Get it back to what it used to be. I don't care how long it takes.'

A fine sentiment nobody disapproved of. Admiring Marko for going into battle with the vandals of wind, snow and Bora, despite them having destroyed his previous handiwork.

Let him have at it, Grettir's unspoken verdict.

Gregor would have helped, if he was still alive, being Irmgaard's.

I knew I came here for a reason, was Heraldo's. *And here it is. Thus has Svetovid spoken.*

'A toast!' Grettir announced, the three of them sitting on the edge of the fire-pit, dangling their legs over its edge, savouring the last of the warmth soon be put out for good. Unless Marko saw fit to reignite it at some future point. Which would mean a god-awful task of shovelling away the ashes which had to be at least a foot deep. 'A toast to you, your boys, your play, and to the renovation of St Vid.'

'Seconded!' Heraldo exclaimed, holding his cup awkwardly with his splinted fingers.

'And to Heraldo,' Irmgaard added. 'We couldn't have done it without you.' Clinking her cup against his. 'Maybe you really were sent to us. And if we do win…'

'You will,' Grettir said with surety. 'You saw the look on the judges' faces.'

Irmgaard hopeful, although felt the need to hedge her bets.

'If we win,' she qualified, 'it's going to mean a lot for the village. There'll not only be the prize money but the notoriety coming with it. I can't thank you enough. Both of you… and Marko too.'

Marko coming in at that moment, blowing into his hands.

'Marko too, what?' he asked, closing the door behind him, seeing the disparity of three adults dangling their legs over the fire-pit with the gay abandon of children.

'We're toasting our success,' Grettir called out. 'Come, Marko. Take a cup of wine with us.'

Marko and Irmgaard exchanging a quick glance, a quick smile. Neither quite ready to fully believe they might actually have won, for who knew what other performances and marvels the judges had to deliberate about, how many more there were to come.

'You do know you were the last on their itinerary?' Grettir added casually as Marko joined them, took his cup, took a sip. The rich red warmth of the wine slipping down his gullet, the rich warm certainty colouring his cheeks.

'I happened to ask,' Grettir went on, 'as they were alighting their sledges. Asked, more specifically, the opera singer.' Holding up a finger to allay questions. 'I know, from my previous life as a civil engineer, how tenders go. Last in line always getting the advantage, earlier ones by then faded somewhat from memory. And she was very complimentary,' Grettir added. 'Told me this was unlike anything else they'd seen, and in a place unlike anywhere else they'd been. Took my hand,' Grettir added, a little wistfully, 'and shook it. Which has to mean something.'

Everyone thinking about that. Draining their cups, eager to get down below, see what was going on with the judges. If Grettir's optimism really had legs.

'All right then,' Irmgaard said, getting to her feet. 'Let's get off. They did leave us a sled?'

'They did,' Grettir replied. 'Just got to lash the dogs and we'll be off.'

Marko helping Grettir up, unaware that whilst he'd secured roof tarps and rocks his little talisman had come free from his neck, was now displayed across the background of his shirt in full view of anyone who was looking. And Grettir was looking. Could hardly not, being eye-level with it as Marko hauled him up.

'That's very unusual, that amulet,' Grettir commented. 'Where did you get it?'

Marko flustering, grabbing the pendant, shoving it back behind his shirt against his heart from where it should never have left.

'Bought it a while back,' he blustered. 'A charm to St Vitus. Come on, let's do as Irmgaard says. Let's get going.'

Which they did.

Heraldo, Grettir and Irmgaard slotted side by side into their sled, uncomfortably jammed, three where there should have been two. Marko standing at the rear on the running board, urging the dogs down the mountain.

Talisman safely tucked beneath his shirt, Marko believing all was well.

Heraldo and Irmgaard at first alarmed by the speed and then exhilarated, Marko so obviously in control, giving the dogs the orders they needed, taking every curve with grace and sure-footedness.

Grettir enthralled by the ride, the mastery with which it was being done. And yet and yet, Grettir uneasy. A snaggle he couldn't place as they negotiated the icy curves that would lead them to the village in record time.

29

Turning Stories Into Plays

'We're going where? We're doing what?' Longhella clicked her tongue in annoyance. 'This is so like you, Hulde. Why can't you leave other people's problems well alone?'

'It makes perfect sense,' Mergim weighed in. 'No point hitting the main centres of population before we're ready. And it will give Heraldo more time to catch us up.'

'Can't be soon enough,' Longhella grumbled, beginning to break down her tent.

'Jochen will make sure he knows where we're going,' Jericho added, thinking their new plan grand. Who wouldn't want to go on the trail of saboteurs and murderers?

'Jochen bloody splocken,' Longhella muttered, better with her words than Jansen would ever be. 'Don't see why we should be helping him at all.'

'Because he helped us?' Hulde asked in her habitually mild way. 'And will help us too in the long run. Give us a new piece of theatre, local and relevant, particularly to Odense.'

'And very dramatic,' Lupercal added, who couldn't get the shipwreck tale out of his head. Had dreamt of it the previous night, been there in it, experienced the unutterably terrifying speed of it. The panic, his face pale as a water lily lifted and sunk by the height and strength of the waves, clothes and boots dragging him down. Sea in his mouth, filling his lungs as he tried to call for help that would not come. Woke in a judder of panic, fingers gripping his bed roll as if it were a life-raft.

'And a grand part for you, Longhella.' Jericho's final spur to their plan of leaving Møns, going back to Falster and from there to Odense to seek out the enquirer who had spoken to both Jansen and the survivor, get Jochen some answers. 'Think of it,' Jericho threw out his hands. 'You could be the captain's wife. The solo you could do when you have the dreadful realisation the ship is going down.'

Ah yes, the trick now turned. Longhella running through the verses she could use and adapt.

'And I could be the captain,' Diderik enthused, seeing as well as the rest Longhella had been swayed, was slotting herself into the starring role.

'Let's not get ahead of ourselves,' Mergim advised. 'Staging a shipwreck isn't going to be easy. And we'll need a convincing back-story, which no one has yet provided.'

Hulde chewing her bottom lip, thinking on what Ortwin had found on the beach:

The cloth-seal and the Crotal bell.

Several coins inscribed with arabesque script Jochen determined to be Persian. Mergim narrowing it down to Turkish Arabic, having come across similar in Zadar, that great melding pot of civilisations on the edge of the Adriatic Sea.

And three toy soldiers Jochen was convinced had been made from melted-down musket balls.

'Came from the same mould,' he'd pointed out. 'See that small misalignment there at the joins? Sort of thing soldiers did before battle to busy their hands, take their minds off what might come. Hope they'd be alive afterwards to take them home to their sons.'

Ortwin looking at the little soldiers with new eyes, each barely the height of his middle finger, wondering if they missed their companions. No idea how big a musket ball was, but surely bigger than these three little men put together. Such sadness he saw in their skewed faces, their squared-away jackets, the sabres held in both hands.

Had to think these little men had never been allowed to return to their creator's home. Had instead ended up in a sea-chest at the bottom of the Baltic Sea, and then the sands of Nyord Bay, kicked back into some semblance of life and relevance by young Ortwin's boots.

Lupercal and Jericho had found nothing.

All they had to go on, as far as the ship-sinking went, being the moon-calendar, the miniature bell, the coins, and these three soldiers who, Ortwin was thinking, were perhaps not at the end of their particular war. Had more to tell, if only he'd the ears to listen. Thinking about it as they travelled away from Møns, Pfiffmaklers throwing ideas here and there about how they should present their new show. First idea coming from Lupercal and Jericho.

'It's got to be a scuttling. Captain has difficulty keeping up with the luxurious ways of his wife…'

'His beautiful wife,' Longhella adds. 'The most wonderful creature he has ever seen. He and his crew would do anything for her.'

Lupercal rolling his eyes.

Jericho furthering the tale.

'He knows his ship holds the contents of an expedition hosted by the Danish Government, and will therefore be insured so decides to take his boat down during the storm…'

'With the help of his lovelorn crew,' Longhella interrupts again.

More eye-rolling, a few smiles, although Longhella's additions are certainly making a more convincing, multi-layered tale.

'With his crew right behind him,' Jericho ploughs on. 'No regard for the few passengers, who have no idea what is going on.'

'Except the Expedition Leader,' Lupercal throws in, adding what he knows Longhella wants to hear. 'Who has also fallen for our leading lady. Who has suspicions but fails to act. Heroic song there for someone.'

'They're in sight of land,' Jericho continues. 'Believe, erroneously, they'll all be cast safely ashore.'

'But all goes wrong,' Lupercal chips in. 'Realise too late the storm has changed, the wind too strong, waves too high, currents misjudged.'

'A terrible tragedy ensues,' Jericho ends. 'Lots of songs there. Lots of special effects.'

Mergim nodding.

'Yes, boys. That could work. Morals there about greed and the allure of the unattainable.'

Sounding like he'd been on the circuit his whole life.

'I like it,' Longhella said decisively, before anyone else had a chance to speak. 'Although in my opinion the leading lady should survive. Borne up by the waves, bedraggled but still beautiful, cast languorously onto the sands. Survives, claims her reward, goes on to live a happy life without her dolt of a husband.'

'Maybe with the Expedition Leader who also survives?' Diderik, Longhella's own dolt of a husband, asked shyly. 'True love and all that?'

'Which rather casts aside the morals of the tale,' Mergim observed. 'Any other ideas?'

Looking at Hulde although it was young Ortwin who spoke up, his mind still on the soldiers.

'I think we could tie it in with another Andersen tale,' he said. 'The one about Holger the Dane.'

Loud sigh from Longhella, not liking where this was going. Holger so obviously a man who would happily stomp her into the ground, take over her starring role.

'Go on,' Mergim encouraged. 'Who is this Holger?'

'He's a Danish legend,' Ortwin answered. 'An ancient warrior who fought against the Saracens in his youth. He's supposed to lie sleeping and dreaming in Kronberg Castle until the Danes have need of him, when he will rise up to fight again.'

Jericho and Longhella speaking at the same moment, from opposing corners.

'Ooh now that's good.'

'Warriors? Really?'

'Point is,' Ortwin persists, 'an old woodcarver sculpts him for the figurehead of a ship...'

'Of course he does,' Longhella clipped wearily. 'There's always bloody woodcarvers in these tales, and I suppose this figurehead comes to life?'

Ortwin blushed, went manfully on.

'Not exactly. He finishes the figurehead off with the Danish coat of arms: lions and hearts. And when he looks into the hearts he sees them burning, flares of fire moving and dancing. And in the first of them he sees...'

'His blasted handiwork going up in flames?' Longhella suggested hopefully. 'Puts the kettle on, has a cup of tea and goes to bed?'

Ortwin smiled tightly.

'He sees a dark prison, and in it a beautiful princess...'

'Aha! Tell me more.'

'She's Eleanora Ulfeldt,' Ortwin explains. 'The most noble and stoic of Danish women. Daughter of a king, falsely accused of treachery, spends twenty-two years in a prison cell with only rats and lice for company...'

'Not sure about the lice,' Longhella commented, imagining her role. 'But rats?' Rubbing her hands together. 'Quite right. Always good eating when you've nothing else to hand. So, squalor and valour going hand in hand. Dies a tragic heroine?'

'Survives,' Ortwin disabused her. 'Spends her later years writing about other women who have undergone ordeals similar to her own.'

'Still a heroine, then,' Longhella murmurs, thinking how many stories there must be out there in the world of women who have suffered lifetimes of imprisonment in a myriad different gaols.

'All very interesting, Ortwin,' Mergim said, 'but what's this got to do with our play?'

'Ah,' Ortwin held up a finger, 'because that's only the first flame. The second takes him to a real ship called the *Dannebroge,* mid-battle during the Great Northern War against the Swedes. Cannons roaring, fire creeping up the deck after the ship is hit, soon to catch the store of gunpowder. This second flame binding to the heart of the ship's commander, Hvitfeldt. Hvitfeldt standing on the deck of his burning ship, knowing it will soon explode. Knowing he and all his men will die but, by doing so, because of the strategic position of their ship, the rest of the Danish fleet will stand a chance of escape. His body, and those of several of his men, later found on the beach of the Køge Bugt, which,' he stated with certainty, having not only read his grandfather's notes on Andersen's tales but also consulted the maps he had helpfully included, 'is not very far from Copenhagen and might be useful later on.'

'So how does that work with the princess? Was she on board too?' Longhella demanded.

'Well no,' Ortwin admitted. 'Not in the tale, which is all about the grand history of Denmark and its great...' was about to say men, swiftly changed his mind. '...men, and women.'

Mergim clearing his throat, seeing a way through.

'A mythic tale, then, and no reason we can't tinker with it. No reason we shouldn't have Eleanora on the ship as a ghostly presence, encouraging the captain to do what is right and best, even though it means his death.'

Hulde speaking up.

'I remember you reading me that story, Ortwin. The figurehead casts a giant shadow on the wall and ceiling of the workshop, seems to move like a living person because of the candle flickering in the breeze. Like Svetovid in the crypt of that church.'

Silence. All remembering that crypt too well.

The place where Ludmilla's body had rested after she'd been found.

'Love and strength,' Hulde went on quietly. 'That's what the woodcarver's visions made him see in the coat of arms. And he goes on to tell his grandson the heart of the tale, which is how strength comes in many forms. Points to his bookcase and tells the boy *There lies another. The power of the word.* Tells him of Tycho Brahe, the Danish astronomer, who used his strength not to chop people's flesh and bones into pieces, but to cut a road to the stars.'

Looking up into the morning, the clouds raked into tatters by the claws of the departing wolf, as if she could see the darkness beyond the light.

'*Put Preko Mora,* and *Put Ka Zvezdama,*' Mergim concluded. 'One Road Across the Seas, another to the Stars.'

30

Coming To Rest

In the village at the base of Suvid mountain all was in joyous up-roar, seeming to the bemused judges an unexpected adjunct to the performance in the chapel as they sat on hay-bales about the fire. Snow falling flat-flaked, large-bodied, ghostly moths about their shoulders, backdrop to this scene of boys tending a suckling pig, fat dripping from the spit onto bowls of potatoes, beetroot and turnips roasting below in the embers. Platters of cheese and bread handed round before the main feast begins. Local folk songs in the offing with fiddles and pipes, and a xylophone Marko had made for Yanni a few Christmases before.

Irmgaard and Grettir immediately joining in once disembarked.

Marko away with the dogs to his shed, where the others had already been penned. About to start oiling the sled's runners when he noticed Heraldo leaning on the door jamb like a broken stick.

'Can I help?' Heraldo asked. Marko's eyes sliding towards Heraldo's splinted fingers.

'Could get the dogs fed,' he replied, jutting his chin towards a trapdoor situated between the pens. Heraldo taking the several yards with easy stride, tugging up the ring of the trapdoor with two thumbs, gazing into a charnel house of body parts heaped in a haphazard pile.

'God's sake. What's down here?'

Flashbacks to a village not a million miles from here where Hulde had been found.

'Portions of meat,' Marko said. 'Hogs' and sheep's heads the women didn't want for brawn. Worst cuts of deer and boar.'

Marko standing, roughly ruffling the head of the nearest dog, glad to have them here, to feel a warm tongue licking his hand. Shed hadn't seemed right without them.

'It's all frozen,' he added. 'Dogs'll not mind. Good for their teeth.'

Would only have them for the night. Best feed them till they almost burst, use up what he could.

Heraldo hoiking up portions in cupped hands.

'Enough?' he asked.

'Enough,' Marko agreed. 'I'll go break the water in their troughs, then chuck one apiece to each. Wait until I'm clear. Don't want any one to lose a hand.'

Spoken lightly. Would never have happened with his own dogs. Couldn't be certain of these others.

'Can I ask you something?' Heraldo asked, lobbing in a portion here, another there, dogs ripping in, Marko back with his oiling cloths going at his sled. Marko knowing the importance of having tools and sled-runners cleaned tip to top. Looking over at Heraldo who had stopped at the last pen, leant himself against its wood, bad hands cribbed against his chest. Marko wondering why Heraldo had not gone off to join the festivities, which were in full swing. Could smell the pigling on its spit, hear Yanni and his friends singing, the vaguely eerie sound of the xylophone. Happy Yanni had gone to the trouble of trundling it out of the barn to entertain their new guests.

'You can,' Marko replied, rubbing mechanically at the running board, having moved on from the runners. Taking his time, was all for staying here, creeping back to his cottage, shutting out the rest. Thought in him maybe Heraldo was doing the same.

Heraldo staring at a dog gnawing the frozen shin-bone of a deer, fascinated by how it moved its claws, positioned the meat within them. Not many kinds of dog could do that, only intelligent ones with dextrous fingers. Foxhounds or beagles who would grip at the wire-cages they'd been put in, plainly figuring there was a way out at the top if only they could get there. Sat at the bottom for days, planning escape, until one went for it. Claws moving up and up the wire until she'd her head out, wriggling the rest of her through the small gap up top. Not long before the others followed.

A lot going on in Heraldo's head as he thought of those hounds.

'What do you know about Kragujevac?'

Marko taking a quick breath he found hard to let out, hand going to his chest, to his talisman, answering in quick staccato sentences.

'It's the heart of Serbia. Seat of our awakening. First capital after independence. Meaning roost of the hawks. The falcons they used to hunt with there. And the men who fought to set us free.'

Heraldo nodding. Knew a lot about the Serbian Wars for Independence, as did the rest of the Pfiffmaklers. Nothing like getting caught up in the aftermath of a revolution to have such history imprinted, never to be scoured out. Honing his question up a notch.

'It's the prison I want to know about.'

Marko letting out that breath. Hand falling away. For, oh thank God, it was nothing to do with him.

'The prison?' Marko asked softly, ignoring the cacophony going on outside this dusky shed filled with dogs and their noises, their warmth, the smell of their damp flanks. Remembering how feared he'd been that he'd be locked behind that prison's walls. 'Why would you want to know?'

Marko having no notion of any Pfiffmakler connection, of Mergim's previous incarceration.

'There's someone there I'd like to visit,' Heraldo explained. 'If visiting is allowed.'

Certainly Mergim had never had any.

No family left, no friends either.

Saying this to Heraldo after Ludmilla had gone missing. Telling Heraldo about his fellow prisoner, the mathematician. Trying to comfort Heraldo by explaining the Birthday Paradox, the notion of randomness as the mathematician had explained it to Mergim.

Every life is like a tree growing in a vast forest. Every decision made throws out a branch here, a twig or leaf there. Wind comes and wind goes. Rain falls or it does not. Lightning strikes, cleaves the bole right down its middle, burns out its core. Or it does not. The totality is out of our control.

Saying too what the mathematician had said the last while the two had been alone together before Mergim's release.

Told you about the wood, the trees, all that randomness. But there's times you can choose which leaf to let fall, which seed to re-lease. You'll never know what will become of it but, when you get that opportunity, if you get that opportunity, don't ignore it, Mergim. You're the only one of us might get such an opportunity again.

Mergim swiping tears from grizzled cheeks as he'd given this counsel. Heraldo staring back stony-eyed, stony-hearted. Angry at the glibness masquerading as advice. Walking away, leaving Mergim to his weeping and his worthless words.

Not so worthless later, same words indirectly leading Heraldo to St Vid.

Heraldo wanting to meet the man who had given them, if he was still alive. Couldn't be such a long shot. Mergim released early the previous year. So much happening in the Pfiffmakler world these last few months it seemed a century might have past. Surely not the case within the fortified walls of Kragujevac prison where time must creep slow as an ailing skin-scarred snake, belly-down over an alien landscape littered with grit and broken glass.

'How would you know anyone there?' Marko asked, perplexed, watching Heraldo from the corner of his eye, hands busying themselves hanging cloths over a small wooden horse to dry. Saw Heraldo take a deep breath, raise his eyes to the rafters, ease his head upon his neck. Marko totting up what he knew about Heraldo, which was next to nothing. On some kind of pilgrimage to St Vid, saving Yanni and his friends from being buried alive, thereby saving Marko himself, and their performance. A debt owed Marko doubted he could repay.

'It's too long a story.' Words dragged from Heraldo, as if he feared they wouldn't be safe out here in this wild world. 'Shouldn't you be with the others?'

Marko hauling another crate from the corner of the shed, closing the door previously ajar.

'I've time. Don't want to be in all that merriment, if I'm truthful. Not really my thing. Rather be with my…with the dogs.'

Heraldo relaxing. Companionship here in the darkness broken only by the few glimmers of light coming from the oil lamp on the ledge above Marko's head. Sitting on the crate Marko had provided. Saying what he'd wanted to say ever since Marko's rescue. Parallels with Ludmilla's way of going never far from his mind.

'What were you thinking out there, when you were trapped in the snow?'

Marko leaning back, resting his shoulders against the shed wall, less surprised he'd been asked than that no one had asked before. Not Yanni, not anyone. Marko lowering his head.

'Felt like a fool. Knew how badly I'd misjudged the situation. Thought of Einar Sokkason. *Things have taken a sharp turn for the worse, and in no small measure through my own contrivance.* Because it was my own contrivance. No one's fault but mine.'

Marko lifting himself from the shed wall, leaning forward. Putting elbows to knees.

'I was certain I was a goner. Absolutely certain. Already buried.'

Cleared his throat, rubbed fingers against thumbs. Some loss of sensation from mild frostbite. Lucky not to have lost the lot.

'I wanted to see the sky again. Managed to tether myself to one of the marking poles. Gave me direction. Began scraping away. Finally had my head clear, but all that digging lodged the rest of me in tighter.'

'Did you know what was happening?' Heraldo asked quietly. 'When you were caught, when you realised there was no escape. Was there any pain?'

Marko uncertain. Unutterable relief when he'd got his head out into the night, taking a suck of it that almost froze his lungs from the inside out. Had, for the few moments before the wind took hold, felt becalmed. Sharp memory of seeing the chapel devastated. Anguish to know Yanni was in there and nothing he could do about it. Vague memory of other lines from his uncle's book.

Heaven's Lord bless me. Let hover thine hawk-perched hand over me and mine.

Speaking slow and soft to Heraldo, eyes two bright glints in the dim light of the lamp.

'Only one way into life, my uncle used to tell me. A hundred, maybe a hundred thousand doors out. No one getting to choose the door they eventually go through. Thought that was mine, out there in the snow.'

Heraldo not letting it go.

'Did you see it opening, that door? Could you see anything beyond?'

Marko sighing.

'No unworldly revelations for me. Only how tired I was, how cold. The futility of the fight. Closed my eyes...'

Marko doing just that. Closing his eyes, lowering his head, breathing shallow.

'Prayed for a dreamless sleep,' Marko whispered. 'To take me from one life to the next, if such exists.'

A tumble of thoughts whirling in his head: of his uncle, the verses from the *Lay of the Towering Waves*, the man who had composed it. His prayer for safe passage from the Cape of Farewell in faraway Greenland where that Christian missionary had made his temporary home. The awful comparison to the prayers the men Marko had caused to drown had likely made, their own last doors gaping before them, sucking them in. How they must have kicked away from them, slammed their waterlogged heels against the jambs of those doors, willing them to close again, keep them on the right side of life. Might have confessed everything there and then, had not Heraldo spoken.

'My wife died in the snow. We couldn't find her in time.'

'I'm sorry.' Marko's lips moving of their own accord.

Silence for a while, the two sitting on their crates. Dogs quiet, sated, laying themselves down to sleep. Easy expectation of the morrow bringing more food, more excitement. Such uncomplicated lives.

Marko the one to speak first.

'I was too late, like you were.'

Giving a brief precis of how his own wife had died.

Heraldo responding by telling Marko of the crypt Ludmilla had been brought into, where Svetovid still ruled. The old words the pastor had given to guide her on.

Go swiftly, child, into this black night, and may our fires light your path onwards.

More fires out there in the village at the foot of Suvid.

'Will you do something for me?' Heraldo asked. 'When you've finished rebuilding St Vid, will you light a fire?'

For both our wives.

No need to say it out loud.

Taking from his backpack a small well-worn book. Handing it to Marko.

'And this, will you put it in the chapel?'

'*The History of Rügen Island*,' Marko read out loud, 'by Professor Otto Günther von Gruuthuse.'

'It's sort of our history too,' Heraldo explained. 'Hers and mine. It's about St Vid and the play your boys did. How ideas travel. How Svetovid came from where she died to here. Which is why I came, and it's here it belongs.'

A raucous shouting coming at them from outside, a cavalcade of hallooing and *well, what do you think about that?*

Marko hardly registering the noise, cradling the book between his hands. Ideas travelling, Heraldo had said, as too the Professor on the dig. The proof of it the reason for his expedition. A night for ghosts. Hearing his uncle's voice.

The word holy *means just that. Keeping whole what needs keeping whole. Like tree boles.* Always had to be trees, with his uncle. *Everything kept within its right bounds, without waste or baggage. Which is what makes life whole and holy.*

Heraldo standing up at the cacophony, opening the door a pinch, light-headed now he'd passed on the book, given it a fitting purpose. Waste and baggage shed. Having a sudden tremendous ache to see Hulde's face, hear her voice. Pushing the door open a little wider as if she might be out there on the edge of the circle. Listening intently as the cut-glass voice of the opera singer regaled the villagers with anecdotes of her high life in Vienna to claps, gasps of astonishment, merry laughter as she name-dropped shamelessly. Ending with a moving aria, slow-sung like folk music instead of artificial operatic drama.

Purcell's *Hush, no more, be silent all,* from his Fairy Queen. Gentle notes shimmering like clear ice skittering over the burns high up in the karst beyond St Vid. The moon rising huge and bright as Heraldo raised his eyes. Heraldo waiting, seeing its slow and easeful sail above the scratch of trees, the crenellations of the highest crags, taking its rightful place amongst the stars.

'It's time to go home, my love.' Words barely a whisper on his lips. 'Home to Hulde. Please forgive me.'

No one to hear him but Marko, holding the gift Heraldo had entrusted him to celebrate and commemorate the memory of his dead wife, and perhaps of Marko's too.

Marko's way as clear to him as was Heraldo's.

Heraldo's to go back to his Hulde.

Marko's to go up the mountain, do what he'd tasked himself to do: build up the chapel of St Vid whether they won this contest or no. Build it up, find a place in it for Heraldo's book where it could be seen and read. Reveal the history of Svetovid to the people who would come to visit.

Inadvertently reveal Othmar Voort's theories to the world.

31
Slips And Slime; Possible Crimes

Odense, named for Odin. A god of war, like Svetovid, who chose to sacrifice himself in his unquenchable thirst for knowledge. Struck himself in the side, bound himself to Yggdrasil, tree of life. Hung there for nine days and nine nights whilst Yggdrasil's wisdom seeped into his flesh from its wood.

Died because of it. And because of it was resurrected.

Unlike the men who resurrected Odense at the start of the 1800s, who laboured eleven years wielding picks and shovels, digging the canal—twenty-five feet deep, five miles long—bringing Odense to the sea and the sea to Odense. Turned from obscure bishopric, fluctuating seat of royal patronage, into a place of significance. Pilgrims flocking to the site where King Knut the Holy was felled by an Odin-like lance to his side before the altar of St Alban's priory.

Pfiffmaklers, knowing nothing of its resurrection, sailing up the canal into the heart of Odense which had recently been declared Denmark's second largest city. Pilings for the new water-works and gas-works going in, the glove factory booming. Still a pretty place. Lots of trees. Lots of merchants' houses overlooking the winding river going on as it always had, despite the rivalry of the canal. Maybe because of it. River left undisturbed by the boats and barges that might otherwise have plied its waters, clogged it bank to bank. Herons allowed to stand sentinel, kingfishers dartling to and from their burrows of bones, cranes wading in the shallows, storks heaping their untidy nests upon the crowns of nearby buildings from where their single-brooded nestlings peeped, swaying comically on large splayed feet.

Pfiffmaklers disembarking in a rambunctious ruffle on the edge of the harbour, dismayed to see a large board there advertising the latest show being put on at Odense Theatre, the first to be established outside of Copenhagen and running strong for more than fifty years.

'That's put a hole in it,' Longhella stated succinctly. 'Folk here not going to settle for crumbs when they've got the whole damn loaf every day of the year.'

Plans swiftly altered. Questions asked of the locals, answers gleaned and acted upon. Pfiffmaklers dragging their carts a few miles north to some outlying villages on the edge of Naesbyhovud Lake, the eastern part of which had been incorporated into the canal, the rest subsequently slowly draining away, its five islands subsumed back into marshland, which too would soon be desiccated.

Hulde and Ortwin left to seek out the Royal Geographical Society, locate the enquirer who'd hot-footed it to Møns within a week of the shipwreck. Society's headquarters easily found, nestled within the small heart of the town not so far from the theatre. Ortwin nervously tugging the bell-pull outside the huge and ancient door, rubbing clammy palms against his trousers. The door swinging open, a corvine man with a stark white collar enquiring what they wanted.

'Would it be possible to see Mr Christian Schumann?' Hulde asked politely. 'About the wrecking of the *Put Preko Mora*. We only need a few minutes of his time.'

The doorman neither prevaricating nor asking further information.

'If you mean Mr Schumacher, you're in luck. He's due off to Copenhagen tomorrow, but please…'

Motioning them in, leading them along a narrow corridor, rapping politely on one of its many doors.

'Visitors, Mr Schumacher. A few minutes only. Can you spare the time?'

Brief harrumph from within.

'To do with what?'

The doorman clearing his throat, looking at his visitors with a modicum of curiosity, a quick twist of his lips that plainly meant *don't fret, you're in.*

'The *Put Preko Mora*, sir.'

Hulde and Ortwin not slow to check the immediate change in circumstance at these words, hearing inside a man plainly rising to his feet, stepping quickly to the door, flinging it open. Regarding the hollow-chested boy and the pretty round-faced young woman with the manner of a bird eyeing a beetle, wondering if it would be toxic or a juicy morsel indeed.

'Come,' he said shortly. 'Introduce yourselves. State your business.'

Returning to his desk. Doorman swiftly darting in, positioning two chairs at its front.

'Hulde Pfiffmakler,' Hulde said, not about to be intimidated as had plainly been the intention, 'and Ortwin von Gruuthuse, grandson of Professor Otto Günther von Gruuthuse of Copenhagen.'

Ortwin blushed, had not expected this. The man behind the desk raising his eyebrows as the beetle squirmed. Academic circles small in Denmark, particularly in Copenhagen where everyone knew everyone else. Von Gruuthuse one of them, a linguist and gatherer of folk tales, intimate friend and collaborator with the great brothers Grimm, and a regular at the coffee houses where such men gathered, fugged wall to wall with grand chatter and tobacco smoke. His interest piqued, writ large upon his face despite his intention to remain inscrutable.

'We're here to ask about the wrecking of the *Put Preko Mora*,' Hulde forged on. 'We think we have information you do not already possess.'

Christian Schumacher's saggy jowls wobbling as he looked from one to the other, fixed his eyes on Ortwin.

'What could that possibly be? I was there on the doorstep not long after it happened. And you, you come here unbidden many years later professing to have learned something new?'

The sarcasm could not be missed. Ortwin leaning forward in his chair.

'We think there was a second person who made it off the ship, sir, apart from the one you spoke to. And we have discovered several small objects that may have come from whatever was on board.'

Schumacher narrowed his eyes. As far as he was concerned the entire hoard was long gone. Had always suspected treachery, that the wretched Othmar Voort had never loaded his expedition finds onto the ship, had somehow squirrelled them away to his Prussian overlords and got away with mass murder to cover it up. He'd never been able to prove it, but had made damn sure Othmar Voort never worked again, not in Denmark.

Besmirched his name, blackened his reputation, dogged him down those first few years to let Voort know exactly what was thought of him and what the Society believed he'd done. Had argued vociferously against the small pension the government nevertheless saw fit to apportion him. It had rankled back then that Voort had never left Danish soil, presumably in order to keep his tawdry little pension going, would probably have chortled and wallowed over his evening beer ever since to know he'd got away with everything, deceived the Society and the Government, made fools of them and of Christian Schumacher most of all. And by God it still rankled now. Schumacher not a man to give up on grudges, certainly not on the say so of these two gallimaufry intruders.

'If you've found anything from that expedition then it belongs to us, to the Society,' he spoke sternly, rapping a finger knuckle on the table to emphasize his point. 'And why in blazes would you think anyone else survived? I spoke personally to the man who saw the ship go down, and to the wretch who got dragged out of the water.'

Grinding his teeth. Unable to speak Othmar Voort's name out loud. Irritated when the young woman had the temerity to question the validity of his conclusions.

'Did you never find that strange?' Hulde asked. 'I mean that he only got out by the skin of his teeth?'

'I think he was a damnable fiend and a scoundrel to boot,' Schumacher growled, 'and unless you can prove otherwise, so I will continue to believe.'

Hulde keeping her eyes fixed on Schumacher's, which was damned unnerving. She'd hardly moved since she'd sat down, her demeanor as serene as it was serious and utterly beyond her years. Unlike her companion, who fluttered and fidgeted like a chaffinch tethered inside a crate catching sight of a crouched cat not far distant. Chaffinch Singing Contests all the rage when he'd first come to Odense fifteen odd years previously, as it was in other fashionable societies across Europe. Bets made on which birds would sing the loudest, make the most perfect *toll-loll-loll-chickweedo's*, umpires employed to count every full phrase during a fixed amount of time, shush any competitors who might be prompting their birds.

'You spoke to Jansen, the lighthouse keeper,' the too serene young woman stated. 'But you never spoke to his neighbour, as we have done. And he has much to say.'

Christian Schumacher twitched. His own crouched cat seen out of his own blinkered eye.

'And why should I have done that?' he argued. 'What would have been the point?'

The young von Gruuthuse grandson speaking up.

'Because he lives on the same stretch of sand Jansen does, on Nyord Bay, in sight of where the ship went down. Not that he saw it go down,' Ortwin added quickly. 'Dark night, storms and all. But later, the wreckage of the *Put Preko Mora* washed up on that beach.'

'Tell him about the morning after,' the girl put in, although kept her gaze firmly on Schumacher. *Like some goddamn seer,* he thought. *Like she knew he'd overlooked something. Made a mistake.* Which thought was ratified by what the lad said next.

'The morning after the storm Mr Steggle noticed a few oddities,' Ortwin went on, still fluttering, although not as much as Christian Schumacher's heart to hear the rest. 'Supplies pilfered, a handcart missing. Some oilskins abandoned on the sand. And then there's these...'

Pulling a small hand-kerchiefed parcel from his jerkin pocket, putting it on the desk, pushing it tentatively towards the large man with the scarily wobbly jowls that couldn't hide the nervous bobbing of the Adam's apple in his throat.

'What's this?' Christian Schumacher blustered, disliking challenge, disliking these two people come to his door to do precisely that.

Ortwin leaning forward, about to unwrap the handkerchief.

Schumacher slapping Ortwin's thin fingers away.

'They've got Turkish script on them, sir,' Ortwin murmured, withdrawing his hand peremptorily. 'We think they may have washed up from the ship.'

Schumacher regarding the folded handkerchief with trepidation.

Going at it slowly, taking away first one corner and then another until he had it open.

Three coins lying there on the blank linen field. He pushed at them, separated them. Could not deny the boy's assertion, for Turkish Arabic it was. He'd pushed and pummelled at Othmar Voort, once the man had returned to Denmark. Chivvied and cajoled him. Got him to give up details of every find he'd made on his expedition. The start of the folios Grettir had seen in Othmar's home. Othmar going at it systematically ever since. Schumacher doubting Othmar's veracity, despite the fact that Othmar had bombarded him with new pages of memories of all he'd found.

Schumacher believing it a smokescreen behind which Othmar Voort assiduously hid himself. Schumacher petitioning auction houses in Prussia, Germany and beyond for many years in the hope of finding Othmar out, of locating the missing hoard that should by rights be housed here in Odense from where Othmar's expedition had been assessed, approved, encouraged, most notably by

Christian Schumacher himself. The reason he'd been so dismayed when he'd heard of the shipwreck; the reason he'd gone to Møns with such swift alacrity, interviewed the lighthouse keeper who'd been the only witness. Apart from Othmar Voort himself.

The huge cache of finds Othmar Voort had later periodically written to him about meant to make Odense an important cultural hub for the whole of Denmark and beyond. Meant to make Christian Schumacher's name. And instead he'd been denied. Casually written off in this backwater that was not Copenhagen. Been left to stew here ever since. Othmar Voort's failure to supply the necessary being Christian Schumacher's personal undoing.

'This is nothing,' he said tightly, trying not to shout, shoving the coins back towards Ortwin. 'And what you have told me is nothing.'

How dare these people, these youngsters, come and tell him he'd misconstrued, missed a witness, made an error. It was unconscionable.

'We found other things,' Hulde began to say. 'A crotal bell and...'

'You've to leave.' Schumacher would not listen. Stood up. 'I've important business in Copenhagen tomorrow and I cannot be wasting my time on the likes of you.'

Hulde and Ortwin standing too. Not the outcome they'd hoped for. Hulde not yet done. Hulde scooping up coins and handkerchief.

'Can you at least tell us the name of the survivor you interviewed? Where he might reside?'

Christian Schumacher feeling a hot red rage seeping through his gullet. Felt no need to dissemble. Let these charlatans do what they would.

'His name is Othmar Voort. Lived in some backwater outside Sønderborg on Dybbøl Peninsula. Still there, far as I know.'

Knew it well. Othmar Voort still living out his days despite Schumacher's attempts to oust him. Had kept tabs on the traitor. Had even tried to skew the workings of the planned Dybbøl defenses against the enemy Prussians to get him turfed out of a land where he did not belong. Plans unaccountably frustrated by the civil engineer placed by the government to oversee the work, his word taken over Schumacher's, his expertise accepted, his alterations agreed to.

Which had frustrated and angered Schumacher all the more. Grettir bloody Wyssling. Another name he'd never forget, but he swore this was it. He was done with the whole affair. He would wash his hands of it. His business in Copenhagen the following day his latest attempt to get himself transferred back to the Society in the capital.

Suddenly aware his blood was thumping at the back of his head as he followed Hulde and Ortwin across the room to make sure they were leaving. Ortwin deferentially opening the door to allow the young woman on before him. Still some manners then, although Schumacher would certainly seek out Otto von Gruuthuse when he got over the water, seek him out, tick him off for allowing his grandson to grow up to be so slippery and sly as to march into the office of an important man like Christian Schumacher and accuse him of doing a half-arsed job back when the lad could barely have been out of the cradle. Incensed beyond reason when the lad had the temerity to turn and smile at him, thank him politely for his help.

Brief vision in his head of an Ichthyological Exhibition he'd been obliged to attend a few weeks previously boasting to have mounted on its walls all the fish of the waters in and around the Danish Isles, how his companion had been arrested by one particular exhibit and forced Schumacher to stop and take a proper look.

'The tench, *tinca tinca*,' he'd informed. 'Scales covered in an extraordinarily thick slime previously used for medicinal purposes. *Tenacious of life*,' he'd continued, leaning forward to read the notice, '*able to hibernate in Winter and aestivate in Summer and therefore to thrive in the tiniest of pools where no other fish can survive. Even live without water, for a short while at least.*'

Slippery, slimy and tenacious of life.

So exactly like the young, like these visitors sauntering in and having the temerity to challenge him. And so exactly like Othmar Voort, it had Christian Schumacher grinding his teeth as the slippery slimy offspring of Otto von Gruuthuse closed the door practically in Christian Schumacher's face.

32

And Oh Lord, What A Storm

The next morning Marko, Heraldo, Yanni and Grettir congregated about the table in Marko's home, Grettir telling them the judges were loving this trip, this extravaganza of conviviality. Eager to be taken direct to Kragujevac, where the Serbian Council resided. Had started their six month peregrination there, and there would their peregrinations end, borne by a hustling bustling line of dog-sleds, harness-bells ringing, village men bawling out their songs.

'And it's just where you wanted to be,' Grettir said to Heraldo. 'The start of your sojourn back to your family. And, about your visit to the prison…'

Yanni lifting his head.

'Why are you going to the prison?'

Marko's guts pulling themselves inward. Found himself thinking of that place with its gaunt walls, its high fences, its stinking moat, its hidden murderers and thieves.

Heraldo taking a sip of coffee.

'There's a man I'd like to visit there,' he explained. 'A friend of a friend.'

Grettir taking up the reins exuberantly, still a little drunk, if truth be told.

'Your best way in is bribery. A few decent bottles, some cured sausage and peppered ham. And before you protest,' holding up hand, 'it's all arranged.'

Producing a small sack from beneath the table.

'There's not a single person in this village doesn't know what you've done for them,' Grettir announced. 'This their thanks. And have to add,' Grettir went on, 'you've done me a favour. Without you bringing me here, without me meeting the judges, I'd never have learned another secret Kragujevac holds, besides its prison.'

Heraldo giving no immediate answer, too overcome with gratitude.

Marko compelled to fill the brief silence, a whispering chill inside him as of winds imprisoned in mountains.

'Which is?'

Grettir garrulous, going on excitedly.

'Their latest exhibition. Rather unusual, so the judges say. Thank you, Yanni.' Taking the plate of toast and eggs with relish. 'They've apparently had a crate of artefacts stored away in some basement for years. When the competition was declared some bright curator remembered its existence, brought it out. They've designed a special room in the Senate to exhibit them. Mmmm! Delicious! Marko, could you pass the salt?'

Marko sitting like he'd been turned to ice.

'Sounds exciting!' Yanni said. 'Know any more about it?'

Taking the salt-cellar, handing it to Grettir.

Grettir taking a few mouthfuls before enlightening Yanni. Marko knowing all too well.

'Archaeological specimens,' Grettir affirmed. 'From an expedition, ending with some very dramatic finds in Kosovo. Exactly as you had in your play, Yanni.'

Grettir pausing dramatically before repeating the words he'd intoned so impressively at the chapel.

'And from Varna, from the Black Sea, from Bulgaria, Svetovid trod his way to our southern coasts. Came, in 1389, to our Field of Blackbirds…'

Marko coughing, standing up so abruptly he almost toppled his chair.

'Apologies,' he muttered, exiting swiftly from the room, his breakfast untouched upon its plate. Yanni trying to excuse.

'He'll be worried about the dogs.'

'All the more for me!' Grettir was gleeful. 'May I?'

The plate passed over. No one liking waste.

Marko blundered towards the dog shed, gripping his keepsake through the fabric of his shirt.

Oh, so small a slip. And how great might be the consequences.

Pax Tibi Sanctus Vitus. Peace to you, Saint Vitus, my path and my way forward.

The words pounding syllable by syllable through his head.

No way of knowing if Grettir remembered his brief glimpse of Marko's amulet, nor if the exhibition would include the notebooks of Othmar Voort Marko had provided.

But certain it was that if they were put on display, and if Grettir thought to leaf through them—and Marko sure Grettir was the kind of man who would—he would undoubtedly recognise Othmar's drawing of the talisman Marko knew was there. Had leafed through the notebooks many times. Couldn't read a word of it, although remembered what Othmar had said of it on the dig.

One of a kind, never seen before nor since as far as I can ascertain. A talisman believed to have been forged by one of the Serbian leaders going into battle in 1389 against the Ottomans. The quality of silver supports this theory, as does the casting, the manner of the lettering, the type of engraving…

One of a kind.

Grettir never going to believe Marko had fortuitously picked up a copy in the market place, as Marko had said. Not given those several words he'd picked out from Irmgaard's and Grettir's conversation when they were holed up in the fire-pit, after Marko had been rescued from the snow.

Shipwreck. Survived. Othmar. 1839.

Wouldn't take long for Grettir to join the dots.

Those previously feared walls of Kragujevac prison rearing up from the snow as if they had always been there waiting for him, the stink of its noisome waters in Marko's nose as he got the dogs into their harnesses, hands shaking to think on the quandary for which he could see no solution. The bells jangling harsh and loud, reminding Marko how slowly the tocsins sounded at funerals and executions, of which Kragujevac had seen its fair share.

Kragujevac, with all its thieves and murderers, its murderers and thieves.

Marko shivering with the knowledge that he was both.

§

The leeches lipped their way up the Tempest Prognosticator, ringing the bell not once but twice. Othmar oblivious to the fact it was not the prognosticator's bell being pealed, instead the one hanging dolefully unused by his door.

Hulde, outside, ringing it again. Knew someone was in there, had seen him through the window hunched like a heron in a Winter field.

'We should go,' Ortwin advised. 'He obviously doesn't want to be disturbed.'

Hulde answering by pulling the bell cord a fourth time.

'He will, once he knows what we've to say.'

They'd not come all this way to be ignored. Longhella chewing her ears off when they'd got back from Christian Schumacher's office.

'So we're off again? To another dratted island?'

Adjusting her opinion when Hulde suggested it only needed she and Ortwin to go visit the survivor.

'Not likely, my girl,' Longhella taking over. And, now they were here, Hulde glad she had.

'Hey!' Longhella called out in her most strident voice. 'Mr Othmar Voort!'

Rapping her knuckles against the window. Othmar, hunkered down at his desk looking through his list of suspects for the hundredth time, finally taking note. Standing up in irritation, flinging open his door.

'You're not welcome. I don't know who you are but you can…'

Longhella as annoyed as he. Longhella spilling into his abode, pushing past him, telling him what was what.

'So you're Othmar Voort.' Sighing deeply as she looked about her, as if incredibly disappointed by what she saw. 'And you spend your time doing what? Doing all this?' A hand waved with easy abandon above his desk. 'Want to know what I think?'

Othmar did not. Did not want this woman in his house, nor the other two waifs who trailed by him on her skirt tails.

'Sorry,' Hulde apologised, as Longhella went on in full flow.

'We think you've been living under a delusion,' she stated starkly. 'We think someone else sunk your *Put Preko Mora* and left you with the blame. We've spoken to Christian Schumacher, who seems to me to be a more ignorant man than you.'

If that's possible, she muttered under her breath.

Longhella magnificent.

Longhella spilling out onto the table the crotal bell, soldiers, and coins.

'Seen any of these before? Ever thought to follow anything up?' Longhella barbative and bellicose. 'Of course not. Got accused by the slug Schumacher and hid yourself away in this hole. Never did anything further. Never bothered to find out you weren't the only one got off that wreck. Pfft,' she added dismissively, through pursed and pretty lips. 'What a waste.'

Othmar standing for a few moments on the threshold of his home, shocked by the intrusion and the words. Taking a few steps towards the desk on which Longhella had thrown her wares, putting out long fingers, touching them one by one.

'But…how…where did you find these?'

Hulde more solicitous, pulling a chair behind Othmar so he could sit, which Othmar did. Slowly, heavily. Fingertips playing over the small objects as if they were the tousled heads of long lost sons.

'You found them…'

'On the sands of Nyord Bay,' Longhella informed. 'Like you might have done, if you'd ever taken the time to look.'

'Nyord Bay,' Othmar repeated very quietly. 'I don't know where that is.'

Longhella clicking her tongue, started flicking quickly through Othmar's folios.

'And yet here they are. Here,' another flick, 'and here and here. Did it never occur to you to go take a gander where everything might have ended up?'

Othmar blushing beetroot red from temples to neck because no, it never had. Not once in all these years. He'd allowed Christian Schumacher's vindictive vendetta to beat him down, make him hide away. Brief release in his correspondence with Grettir Wyssling, the latest of which had made him re-evaluate the circumstances of his survival, his memories and folios, write out all he could recall from the notebooks lost to him.

Had regretted terribly the loss of the artefacts he'd collected, yet never had he tried to figure out where they might have washed ashore, or if they ever had. He knew they'd been in the cargo holds, despite Christian Schumacher's bombastic accusations that he'd loaded only chests of straw, spirited the actual chests of finds away to Prussia by unknown means. Had never stood up for himself, argued his corner, how impossible it would have been for one man to organise such a spectacular vanishing act on the tumultuous quays of Trieste which teemed with activity, day and night.

'Let's all take a seat,' Hulde advised. 'Ortwin, get some water on the boil.'

Ortwin quick to the kitchen space, finding it scattered over with dead mugs, grime-smeared plates, a keeled-over heel of bread so dried out it was of no interest to even a mouse. Finding a jug of stale water, with which he returned. Hulde shoving a handful of thick branches from the near empty basket into the burner in the nick of time. Nothing in it except embers and the charred corpse of a single log on the brink of extinction. Hulde casting her eyes over Othmar Voort, noting how unkempt he was. Clothes creased and crumpled, obviously inhabited for days on end. Unruly stubble on cheeks and chin, skin sallow. This not a man at peace with himself, and not only because of their coming.

Something had jarred him, she understood, and very recently.

Longhella's initial whirlwind had blown itself out as quick as it had come. Had latched instead onto Othmar's list of names lying in full view. Saw the under-linings, the crossings-out, the question marks. Grasped the nature of it immediately.

'So you've not been completely idle then,' she said, turning the list around to show Hulde. 'Narrow your suspects down much?'

Othmar sluggish. Could not comprehend why these people were in his house, at his desk.

'Let's start at the beginning,' Hulde advised. 'I expect Mr Voort has questions.'

The leeches reaching the lip of the Tempest Prognosticator at that very moment, setting its tinny little bell ringing.

'A storm,' Othmar said quietly. 'It's telling us a storm is on its way.'

And oh Lord, what a storm.

33

Frost There And Cold, Horrors Untold.

They flew on towards Kragujevac, dogs swift and certain, halting when they were adjacent to the Lepenica River. Everyone dismounting from their sleds, stretching their legs. A small while to wait, for their ingress into Kragujevac was to be magnificent and memorable, arriving as the setting sun spread long, gilded shadows from every tree, every building. The cavalcade to look like a bonny necklace strung along the track by the Lepenica which would be shining silver with its plates of shifting ice as they galloped for the gates.

Scouts sent ahead on swift horseback to alert both Senate and townsfolk the judges were returning, making their eventual entrance triumphal. The retinue sweeping through the city gates with jingling bells and loud songs kept up by the men, the melodious soprano of the opera singer. Everyone waving at the gathering throngs who sprinkled their way with armfuls of dried flowers and crinkling beech leaves shining like copper and gold on the snow.

A happy laughing gang of children clearing their path, leading them into the square above which the Senate members were seated grandly on their balconies, eager to hear how the Judges' travels had gone, for they'd been infuriatingly tight-lipped about what they'd witnessed, no hints of where their sympathies lay.

Heraldo, red-nosed and ruddy-cheeked from the travelling, laughing to realise this delivery of the judges was a performance unto itself.

Pfiffmaklers all, in that moment.

Couldn't have orchestrated a grander way of setting himself for home and proper Pfiffmaklers. The entirety of Kragujevac having emptied themselves from homes and workplaces, swarming around them, shaking hands, kissing cheeks, leading judges and village-folk off to the Senate building where they were ushered into the huge banqueting hall. Only half a day's notice, yet the tables were thronged with comfits and candies, platters and pots of savouries streaming in from every quarter.

Grettir and Heraldo still in the square saying their goodbyes, Grettir giving Heraldo an awkward hug.

'Thank you,' he said, sniffing back a few tears. 'It's been an honour. If you'd not come to my door this whole grand adventure would have passed me by, and I've loved it. Every minute.'

Heraldo smiling, shaking his head.

'Hmm. Almost buried by an avalanche, Svetovid and St Vid. I suppose it's not your everyday.'

Grettir laughing, wiping his eyes, placing a hand on Heraldo's shoulder.

'Indeed not. Nor the pleasure of taking part in a real live performance, meeting a famous opera singer and more new friends in the village than I can count.'

Bowing formally.

'Thank you, Heraldo Pfiffmakler. And may St Vid guide you on your way, bring you the peace you've been seeking. And try not to get locked up in that blessed prison.'

No one to overhear this brief exchange except Marko, hidden in the shadows, seeing to the dogs, securing them and the sleds.

Only Marko to be struck by those restrained words of parting:

May St Vid guide you on your way, bring you the peace you've been seeking.

If he'd been hoping Grettir Wyssling had forgotten that tantalising glimpse of his talisman, he was sorely and certainly disabused of that hope now.

Oh so small a slip, so small a glimpse.

Frost there, and cold, along with horrors untold, as Marko's uncle's Norse Atlantic Saga had it.

Othmar Voort's predicted storm about to blow Marko off his feet.

§

Prisoner 1397 was contemplating coincidence, as he often did. A Professor of Mathematics and Statistics in his life previous to Kragujevac. *Coincidence As A Concept* his first class of each semester, explaining to blockheaded students how what presented as fantastical was nothing more than mathematics playing itself out. How out of the thousands of chance meetings, dreams, occurrences, inevitably one or two here and there could be interpreted as significant, even supernaturally ordained. The person you idly chatted to in a queue turning out to be the daughter of a neighbour from another town, another country, you'd lived in thirty years previously; the ring you buy for your fiancé in Dubrovnik revealed to be the very same ring plundered from her grandmother during some long ago war.

Significant, astounding. Statistically explicable.

His allocated number, 1397, a case in point. Consisting of two primes, 13 and 97; 1, 3, 9 and 7 added together equalling 20, a tetrahedral number, product of a squared prime. Basis of vigesimal systems of counting—ten fingers, ten toes—used by Aztecs, Mayans, and many extant Asian countries. Linguistically traceable in European languages too, as he'd told his students on numerous occasions.

French, Danish and Albanian all use multiples of tens and twenties. Quatre-vingts, tresindstyve, trikratdwisti. 80, 60, 80 respectively.

The number 1397 assigned him by chance when he'd entered Kragujevac Prison to begin his incarceration within its walls.

His life made up of coincidences he'd tried many times to rationalise.

If he hadn't been three nights without sleep because of the great breakthrough he believed had to be put down there and then before it eluded him; if he hadn't finally nodded off in his chair; if he hadn't left his desk scattered over with what was important and what was not; if his wife hadn't been similarly sleepless because of his constant nagging she see to him because of the importance of his work and her trying to quell the frequent screeching of their young son…

If, if, if.

None of it mattered. He'd killed her good and proper, and that was an end to it. An end to her, an end to his career, an end to his life as he knew it. The latter perhaps the only just and true thing to come out of the whole appalling affair. Fingering the burns on his hand he'd caused when the regret had become too great. Remembering Mergim bandaging him up, his solicitousness, his kindness. How later, on the eve of Mergim's release, he'd passed over his letter to Mergim in the faint hope it would offer some apology to his son for the terrible way 1397 had murdered his mother with such abject, undeserved cruelty.

Closed his eyes.

Saw it all again.

The needless shitty waste of it.

The stain of coffee from the cup she'd brought him besmirching the cover of the paper he'd laboured over three days and nights to get exactly right. Not a thought for her. How she'd been doing a goodful act for him when she too was at her wit's end. One minute bringing him his coffee at the exact time he'd specified, next minute head-down in her husband's piss-pail, his rageful ink-stained fingers holding her under.

'Thirteen ninety-seven,' a voice boomed out. 'Get yourself kitted and ready to be taken to the visitor room in five minutes.'

1397 could not have been more surprised. Possibilities tumbling through his head in spectacular succession; fractions and algebraic formulas amalgamating and disbanding. Ultimate conclusion irrationally fixed upon: here his significant moment out of all the many thousands that might have presented.

It's Mergim. He's come to give me news of my son!

Shivers going through him as he pulled on his thin outdoor boots, his threadbare coat.

Jolts of anticipation, jubilance and trepidation juddering through his body as he was led across the snow-filled yard. The little circle of the guard's bobbing light picking out irrelevant details: the handle of a shovel poking from a snowdrift; a scrap of dark fur and two pink paws where a mole lay half-buried on its back, having picked the wrong moment to surface instead of staying warm within its earthbound burrows; the way the moonlight made colours seem other than during the day.

Heart pounding as he ducked into the visitors' room: a dark place set with crudely hewn benches and tables made by the prisoners; the barred cast-iron lattice of the opposing door blockaded by another guard, the glint of keys jangling at his belt.

Unsteady beat of blood in ears and throat as he was shackled to the table. Common knowledge murderers weren't to be trusted, having nothing to lose. Brief memory of the balladeering poet who'd chosen to go out into a snowy night and die rather than spend another moment inside the walls of Kragujevac. Three years back, maybe. Couldn't be sure. Time here having no markers, not like on the outside.

Couldn't help but think of the mark that had brought him here: the circular spill of coffee besmirching the cover of his breakthrough paper that would never be presented to his colleagues. His *Statistical Analyses of the Demographic Data of the Shifting of Ideologies through Geographic Spaces and Cultures* taken into evidence, presented at his trial. Was now presumably mouldering unread and unseen in the storehouses beneath the courthouse where he'd been convicted. Could see every last page of it strewn out across his long-gone desk. Its carefully constructed algebraic equations neatly scripted and arranged like the delicate two-pronged tracks of deer running steadily across an otherwise untouched field of snow.

Snap out of it, he told himself. *That's finished. Nothing here but Mergim, who is going to give me news of my son. Nothing more important than that.*

Quickly lifting his head as the guard took up his keys, found the right one, put it into the lock of the latticed door and had it turned. Eyes fixed on the iron bars as the guard shifted to one side and swung it open.

Confusion for 1397, who would have sworn on the death of his wife, on the head of his orphaned son, that he'd never clapped eyes on his visitor, a gaunt young man with splinted fingers. No vigesimal counting system for him.

'My name is Heraldo Pfiffmakler. I've news of your friend Mergim...'

§

Grettir Wyssling dallied before joining the villagers in the Senate, deeply moved by his parting from Heraldo, that he might have, in some small way, been a part of Heraldo's healing, his returning to his family. Brushing snow from a bench, sitting himself down. Began composing in his head his next letter to Othmar Voort.

How odd, your survival, he'd written not long back, and how much odder what had so recently occurred. His life enriched beyond compare by the fortuitous arrival of Heraldo at the door of his insignificant museum, and so many adventures to tell to his friend.

You must come visit! See the chapel, and the exhibition the Senate are putting on which has, I'm told, some finds from your very own

Field of Blackbirds which is not so far away. Given your expertise we might even be able to engineer permission for you to do another dig!

Not to mention his astonishingly coincidental meeting with Irmgaard Prögen, Othmar's lost love—about which 1397 might have had words—imagining Othmar in his Irmgaard-strewn study opening the letter Grettir was writing in his head. The joy it would bring him, and the joy Grettir would have in leading Othmar around the Senate's exhibition if he could inveigle him here.

Grettir ceasing abruptly as another thought intruded. That niggling he'd had on the journey down from St Vid's. The brief glimpse of Marko's amulet; the words he'd spoken to Heraldo that had come unbidden to his lips about St Vitus. An echo there, something he'd seen in Othmar's folios.

Thought never getting to its end.

Letter never to be written.

Grettir one moment sitting on his bench, the next prostrate in the snow with blood in his mouth. Couldn't grasp what was happening, the thumping in his head, the significance of the whispered words punctuating each crack of his skull as it was bashed into the snow.

I'm sorry…I never…wanted it to come to this.

Marko howling his anguish into the night once the deed was done, once he'd pulverised Grettir Wyssling's skull into a bloody spatter of brain and bone spilled into the snow by the running board he'd untied from one of the sleds. Only weapon to hand. Only way to halt his own demise. No one to hear him except the dogs who belonged to others and whose howls answered his own. No one to hear those howls except Yanni, who was on his way back from the Senate Building to encourage his father to come join the celebrations.

Only Yanni to see his father kneeling in the snow beside the batteration of Grettir Wyssling, tears pouring down Marko's cheeks, freezing in his beard.

Only Yanni to take the bloodied board from Marko's hands, flinging it to one side, youth and jubilance draining away as he fought to find reason for his father's actions.

Only Yanni to put his hands about Marko's chin, lever him up, ask *Why have you done this?*

Yanni piling snow over the wreckage of Grettir Wyssling, unable to look on it, while Marko heaved from his heart everything that had come to weigh him down, weaved its way back into his life since Heraldo and Grettir's arrival. The scattering of a few overheard words bringing back all he'd previously buried. How it had started with his own few words of outrage: *Those you should not touch!* All that had come because of those words: the theft, the sinking of the ship, his escape, his assisted flight back home. Gregor's help in it, and Irmgaard's innocence. The downfall of Othmar Voort, about which he'd known nothing until Grettir put all in place; about Grettir glimpsing his talisman, how the moment Grettir clapped eyes on the Senate's exhibits Marko's guilt would burst into the world, bury him alive for a second time. Grettir the one to inter him instead of rescue him this time around.

Yanni's turn to take a terrible decision.

The walls of Kragujevac Prison visible on the other side of the Lepenica, high and dark, formidable, unassailable. Yanni knowing that if his father ended up inside those walls he would never get out. Yanni knowing Heraldo Pfiffmakler was in there at this very moment to visit his unnamed friend of a friend. Yanni dithering on that pinhead philosophers espouse might house a thousand angels.

Yanni jostling the possible outcomes as they would not be jostling in the head of Grettir Wyssling, a man he'd liked and without whom the performance at St Vid would never have gone the way it had. Judges and feasting not far away. Night watchmen sure to patrol this square at some point. Yanni breathing quickly, pushing away the fluttering wings of conscientious angels, retrieving the murderous running board, scrubbing it clean with handfuls of snow which went ochre with the scrubbing and had to be buried in their turn.

Yanni scooping them up, placing them beside the bench, beside Grettir Wyssling's snuffed-out body, and more snow heaped over the wretched corpse to hide it completely. Youth and jubilance gone from Yanni, shame filling the void, pouring in on him from every side. Had lost one parent, couldn't contemplate the other being torn from him. Wasn't certain he could ever speak again to Marko or look him in the eye, yet pity and loss urged him to save his father if he could.

Before the performance at St Vid he'd no notion how strong the love for one's country could be, nor for its past, nor the atavistic reverence in which both could be held. And no wonder Marko had been the one to stand up and sing *Oh Beautiful Country*, given all he'd perpetrated in its name.

Decision and determination coming to the fore. Survival at its core: of Yanni and his village, the abundance the performance at St Vid might bring to their doors. Unable to tolerate it being wasted, thrown away by this one misjudged act. His cup of anger overflowing, despising his father for forcing his hand. Rage cold and fierce enough he might have pummelled his father as his father had pummelled Grettir, except right then Yanni was given a sign, a way forward, the snow colder and fiercer than his rage as it began to flurry and fall, covering the tumult of tracks and footprints, blood and body, brain and bone.

Yanni hurriedly prodding his father.

'Get to the dogs. Take a single sled and head back to the village. Now! Do it now!'

Marko sluggish, obeying in slow motion.

'Christ's sake, man. Get a move on!' Yanni's voice harsh and insistent. 'And when people ask, tell them you had a sudden fear of the snow, of the cold, couldn't stand to wait any longer.'

Easily understandable, given Marko's recent encoffinment.

Marko doing as told.

Marko heading off into the snow. One look behind him, seeing Yanni releasing the dogs, slapping them away before dragging off another sled, leading it deliberately from the square in the opposite direction Marko was going. Yanni abandoning it a few hundred yards yonder, before curling back through the trees hemming the farther edges of the square, re-joining the main thoroughfare, steeling his heart, wrapping a cage about his grief and anguish as he returned to feast and frivolity, false smile fixed on his face, false laughter upon his lips.

New play in the offing, new plot to spin, new lines to regurgitate to his audience.

Sick within to have to spill them out with such feigned abandonment.

No sign of father in the square. An artful shrug of his shoulders. *Then again, it's started snowing heavily. He's probably taken shelter somewhere nearby.*

Grettir? No. Not there either. Must have decided to go with Heraldo to the prison.

He'd wait an hour, maybe two, depending how long the celebrations seemed to be going on, before suggesting someone should go check on the dogs, on the sleds, on his father, given the snow. Pandemonium then ensuing to discover the dogs gone, sleds abandoned.

Yanni on hand to suggest robbery if no one was coming up with the idea all on their own, an idea bolstered by the discovery of that single sled dragged away and abandoned, presumed to be too heavy to drag through the newly fallen snow. Obvious implication being, when Grettir was finally found, that he'd been in the square mid-theft and attempted heroic intervention, cut down because of it.

Oh Marko. What have you done to your only son?

All Marko could think on as he steered his dogs homeward.

I've made him complicit in my sins. I've given him Hrolf's nightmares, as he gave his to Styrbjorn. Marko muttering the words from his uncle's saga over and over.

I see the evil that will fall on both our heads, a grim fate from the sea bringing dread.

Frost there and cold, horrors untold.

Spilled signs I see, about the man who will be killed.

Remorse flowing through Marko as the dark waters of the Lepenica pushed lethargically beneath their upper floes of ice. Marko hearing the groans and creaks of those floes as they bashed against one another between their banks, forging their fettered way towards the sea. Marko's grim fate to understand that he and Yanni would henceforth bash and bump against one another exactly so, only interactions being creak and groan, groan and creak. Everything between them spoiled and rotten, frost and cold. Horrors untold.

Couldn't bear it.

Could feel Grettir's accusatory blood rising from the running board on which he stood. Felt it hot and vengeful in his feet, his legs, racing its way up his body into his heart.

'God help me, St Vid, guide my path,' he whispered, then hollered at the dogs, turned the sled around and set himself back on the track towards Kragujevac.

34

Destroying The Music Of The Spheres

Prisoner 1397 doesn't move as Heraldo announces himself.

'I've come to thank you,' the young man says, funnelling himself onto the bench. 'Without you, Mergim would never have found us.'

1397 stirs. He's heard of the Pfiffmaklers, of course. A name to conjure with. Quite literally, in the German, people who whistled up performances; employed cunning trickery to impress their audiences.

'It was your letter,' Heraldo confided, settling on his uncomfortable seat. 'The one he delivered to your son. If it hadn't been for that…'

If, if, if.

The letter to his son.

Heraldo stopping as the colour leeched visibly from the mathematician's face, skin the same sickly pallor as the goat-glue they used to prime their canvases. The little nibblings and parsings of muzzles, feet and sinews added to the clippings of skin the tanneries had no use of; steeped, reduced to a viscous liquid into which they dipped their brushes and lathered across their linens to tighten the unsteady threads, or dried into cubes for later use when they'd last for years and years.

'Years and years I've been in here.'

1397's voice thin and chapped. The squeaky-door vocalisations that mole might have made having burrowed through the snow to realise its mistake. Same sounds made by the threadbare cat his wife had doted on. Fur chewed from flanks and legs, yowling like it was made entire of creaky hinges.

'Here you go, you little bag of nothing.' His wife throwing scraps from their back door. 'And don't you come looking for more.'

Which of course it had.

Every day for years and years. Cat purring like rusty cogs around his wife's skirts every time she went into the yard to scratch it's scrawny head, its raspy white-furred tongue licking her fingers.

1397 repulsed by the mere thought of that tongue. Had to swallow down a retch.

Heraldo leaning forward to catch the mathematician's words, seeing how skinny he was, shoulders knuckled beneath his thin coat, neck scrawny as a bolted cabbage stalk bulging with several boils, sparsely bristled chin blotched and pointed as if finished off with rough sandpaper.

'It's been hard for you,' Heraldo tried, when the mathematician offered nothing more, eyes glancing over the crude stonework encrusted with lichen, the rusty iron of the gate-work, the enormity of the locks, the unsmooth plane of the table. 1397's hands trembling on its surface, fingertips swollen, rimmed with torn cuticles encircled by rips and scabs.

A further series of creaks as the man gave a sarcastic laugh, drew back his lips revealing skewed teeth blackened at their roots, stranded in gums pale as salted driftwood.

'You don't know what hard is, 'till you've been here a couple of decades,' he said bleakly. 'Only myself to blame.'

No self-pity for 1397, merely a statement of fact. Hard in any prison, harder in Kragujevac than most given the tall thick walls made of hand-hewn karst. A harsh kind of stone, trapping cold air during winter, draughts funnelling through its many tunnels dripping with moisture or crackling themselves over with frost. Stifling in summer, sucking in the heat, imbuing its inhabitants with the nauseating odours rising from the moat, platoons of flies feeding on rotten excrement, the waste tipped from the prison's chutes into water thick and brown as the borscht the prisoners made from beets and potatoes well past their best. Dull sludge forced between their lips easing the passage of dense black bread flattened into pans licked with rancid lard.

'He'd be twenty-two or three, my son,' 1397 told Heraldo. 'I often wonder what became of him.'

Heraldo frowned.

'Has he never visited?'

Had been meaning to talk of trees and leaves, opportunities, randomness. How, had this man's letter to his son not brought Mergim to Osijek Mergim might never have tracked the Pfiffmaklers down. The mathematician grimacing. Heraldo wincing at the sight of those bad teeth. How agonising they must be.

'He never came,' said 1397. No hope in those words, and no wonder. The boy barely weaned when put into the care of his grandparents. Father murdering mother a millstone tied about his ankles, wilfully cast aside when he came of age. Mergim appearing out of nowhere the previous year, handing over the mathematician's *apologia*. Grandparents likely dead, grandson maybe married, settled into a trade.

'Was my boy still alive?' 1397 asked.

Heraldo uncomfortable, for Mergim had never specified. Never a thought in Heraldo what had become of the son, it seeming irrelevant. And now callous.

'Said he had a smallholding outside Osijek. Found no one in. Tacked your letter to the door and left.'

To find us. Was enthused, had found word.

Heraldo dismayed Mergim had been so keen to find them, to find Hulde, he hadn't done more. Hadn't hung around to meet the mathematician's son, talk to him, explain how important it was to his father for his son to receive his letter.

The mathematician wilting; a bunch of thinning spinach doused in boiling water, grey from being left in too long.

'I'm sorry,' Heraldo said. 'Yours was the last letter Mergim delivered…'

'And he was keen to be on his way,' the spinach went on for him. No inflection to his voice. A logical deduction 1397 could not deny Mergim. He'd done what had been asked of him. What more should there have been? He was out of Kragujevac and had a life to pursue in the form of these Pfiffmaklers. One of whom was sitting right across from him.

'Tell me then, of Mergim.'

No point dwelling. His son must have known his whole life 1397 was in Kragujevac and had never tried to contact him. 1397's letter the last strand of hope, of reconciliation. A vain hope. Letter delivered and ignored.

His son wanting nothing to do with him.

1397 surprised when his visitor smiled, placed his elbows on the table and leaned forward, plainly unafraid 1397 might lunge forward, lock Heraldo's head in his shackles and do him in before the burly guard could intervene. Burly guard not paying the slightest attention. Burly guard sitting on his chair, feet propped on a stool, snoozing. Hard days and nights in Kragujevac, not only for the inmates. Grettir Wyssling's offerings having effect. A little too much of the good stuff knocking the man off his best.

'Mergim is doing well,' Heraldo informed eagerly. 'At the moment he's Father of our Fair, and that's something. He didn't want it, but he earned it. Has become a man of honour. Helped us when he didn't need to. Saved Hulde. I don't know if he talked about her.'

The mathematician nodded.

'He did. He told me everything. Only the once. Enough for me to know he wasn't like the rest of us.'

Heraldo relieved. Hadn't relished reciting that intricate saga. Heraldo tapping his working fingertips upon the wood.

'We've a huge amount to thank him for,' Heraldo said, wanting to jettison the sadness, heighten the joy. Leave this man heart-gladdened by his visit in this dank undercroft. Gave 1397 a quick precis of his pilgrimage, the excitements at St Vid, near disasters, eventual rescues and successes, thrilling rides on dog-sleds. Heraldo pointing out that if 1397 had been looking out across the Lepenica not long back he'd have seen them coming, the gay bobbing of lights as they swept into town.

Heraldo assuming they were nearing the end of their encounter. Anticipated a swift, awkward shaking of hands, given splints and shackles, before he made his departure.

Not how it went.

1397 a man deep as a well. Seeing mathematical constructs in the simplest of actions. Had all manner of probability theories racing through his head. Pascal's Triangle to the fore. A misnomer, given how long it had been known and understood before Pascal. A simple construct, an illusionist's parlour game any intelligent child could master, or maybe any Pfiffmakler. A deck of cards laid out, a person invited to take one from here, one from there. Gist being that if you understood the logic behind the triangle you can always predict which is the hidden card lying at the apex.

And at this particular apex was 1397.

His letter leading Mergim to the Pfiffmaklers, and ultimately to Heraldo coming here to find 1397. The only contact with the outside world he'd had since his incarceration.

'So many different ways of dying,' he whispered. *So many hundredth doors.* 1397 schooled in philosophy, as were all mathematicians. Logic at the heart of both.

Heraldo getting jittery. Wanting to be gone. Felt on the brink of happiness now he'd spilled out his story, made his decision to return.

'Hippasus,' 1397 announced. 'Do you know him?'

Falling into lecture mode. Heraldo the only pupil near to hand. The only pupil he would ever have again. Neglecting to see Heraldo trying to pull away.

'Lots of the ancient Greek philosophers died in implausibly strange ways,' he continued, words coming easy, the script seen before him. 'Chrysippus from a severe paroxysm of laughter caused by watching his donkey trying to eat a fig.'

Casting a glance at Heraldo, whose brows were creased, fingers fiddling. No matter. Students always did the same at this point.

'Empedocles,' he went on, 'leaping into the crater of a volcano. Socrates forced into suicide by hemlock. Heraclitus covering himself in scalding dung in an ill-advised attempt at curing his dropsy. All thinking men, by their very definition as philosophers. Lovers of knowledge. As am I.'

Pausing. Swallowing. Rubbing his lips together to bring some moisture to them. Back in lecture halls. Back in better times.

'Which brings me to Hippasus who believed, as did many of his contemporaries, that the visible world, especially the movements of the heavens, were reflective of the underlying order of the universe. Everything ruled by mathematical constants, a harmony of ratios. And like you, he was concerned with music.'

Heraldo having a twitch of interest.

'The music of the spheres?' he guessed.

'Quite so,' his lecturer agreed. 'And Hippasus did more than think, wanted physical demonstration instead of mere intellectualising. Cut metal discs of differing thicknesses, filled ewers with differing amounts of liquids. Compared their sounds when struck.'

'I've done that,' Heraldo interjected, 'with jars of water. Partially empty to almost full. Called it my water harmonica. Thought I'd discovered something new.'

The professor telling him otherwise.

'This an experiment performed two thousand years before you were born.'

1397 lifting a lip at the young man's consternation.

'The dependence of musical interval on numerical ratio, was how Hippasus put it,' he explained. 'A man not content with accepting all he'd been taught, without external validation.'

Finding his way, not sure what he was trying to say. Years of bad diet and worse alcohol making the progression harder than it should have been. Urge in him to pursue his own external validation in the form of the first visitor he'd ever had in Kragujevac.

'Hippasus imbued with the study of geometry, as were all in his philosophical stable.'

Ah, now I have it!

1397 leaning forward, ordering the thoughts swirling in his head.

'Specifically the geometry of isosceles triangles,' *thank you Pascal,* 'those with uneven sides. His dreadful discovery being that there are certain numbers which do not cohere to the norm, are not perfect, cannot be rationalised, go on forever. Numbers you can scratch your head about but never get to the end of. Like Pi, or the square root of two.'

Blundering as a man will do through a maze, certain the centre is just around the corner.

'And if numbers themselves could be irrational, unable to be the sum of two integers, then the whole Pythagorean conception of the universe must be laid on wrong foundations. The universe losing its perfect music, for if numbers can be irrational then so too must be the universe.'

Letting out a sigh. Couldn't quite banish the fog from his brain. Running Wolf finding new avenues to explore.

'Outcome being his friends bringing about his murder. Taken out to sea by his fellow philosophers on a fishing trip, thrown overboard. Left to drown.'

Heraldo quiet, awaiting the revelation he assumed must come.

1397 providing it.

'Murdered because his fellow philosophers couldn't contemplate their perfect world order not being as it seemed. Couldn't contemplate a slight discord to their music, couldn't see how imperfection might make it more perfect instead of less. And yet surely, surely, they as thinkers, as lovers of knowledge, should have interrogated his proofs, gone over them. Found them worthy.'

1397 not feeling worthy. His own perfect world order destroyed by a coffee stain. No Hippasus he. No friends sent to drown him, had instead drowned his wife for a reason that was no reason at all. Lost the thread. Forgot where he'd been heading.

'Ignore me,' he excused. 'I'm rambling. I'm taking up too much of your time. Haven't spoken to anyone like this in a while.'

Giving a sheepish grin, made more sheepish by the baring of his long bad teeth.

Heraldo lifting his head, for by this circuitous route he'd been led to the centre of his own maze.

'No,' he said, 'I understand.'

Irrational numbers in the form of various parties, including Mergim, introduced into the Pfiffmaklers' world, whose progression no one could have foreseen. Wind comes and wind goes. Rain falls or it does not. Lightning strikes, cleaves the bole right down its middle and burns out its core. Or it does not.

'The totality,' Heraldo cited, 'is out of our control.'

1397 unaware the quote was his. More than a little drunk when he'd said those same words to Mergim.

'What starts as one thing,' Heraldo concluded, 'ends as another. A metallic harmonica leading indirectly to the destruction of a universal certainty. Hippasus murdered because of it.'

And my Ludmilla.

1397 not sure Heraldo's interpretation was what he'd actually meant. Glad anyway to have given this young man something meaningful. Feeling lighter, as if his life had had a purpose after all. Mergim's Hulde, the ancient Hippasus, and now this young Heraldo, shining like beacons strewn from past to present. He stretched his crooked back, inadvertently clinking the chains securing him to the table which caused the guard to come out of his snooze, twitch himself awake.

'Time's up,' he slurred, stumbling to his feet. No idea how long he'd been asleep, feeling an urgent need to empty his bladder.

'Is there anything I can do for you?' Heraldo asked, now his visit was truly almost at its end. 1397 hesitating, taking a sheaf of papers from inside his jacket, shoving it across the table towards Heraldo.

'Only this,' he said. 'It's the outline of my thesis. I started it when Mergim left. Thought he might visit, take it with him. Thought it might...'

Reinstate him.

Make his life of worth.

Leave something behind of value when I'm gone.

'The original went as witness to my case. I've put back together as much as I can.'

Pages thin as the papery bracts cusped about the base of gorse flowers, edges pitted, chewed by mice and wood-mites, surfaces scratched over with scrawls and equations resembling the complex patterns of fritillary flowers. Inks varying in colour from sepia to deep ochre concocted from lichens, boiled-up onion skins, ash, coal tar, wood-pitch scraped from inside ovens and burners.

'Choosing to let fall your leaf,' Heraldo said, expecting a smile from 1397. None forthcoming. No memory in 1397 of those words so well chosen. Heraldo changing tack. 'Is there someone I need to take it to?'

Fingertips hovering over the pages. All gobbledegook to him. He knew engineering and mechanics. Nothing like this.

1397 had no answer.

The guard yawning loudly, fussing over his bunch of keys to find the ones needed.

'No contraband,' he recited without enthusiasm. 'No passing over of goods.'

Not that he cared. All he wanted was his bed. Turned his back on the prisoner and his visitor, Heraldo taking the opportunity to tuck the papers into a pocket.

'Do with them as you see fit,' 1397 answered as the guard took him roughly by the elbow, shook the shackles until the lock came into view.

'Back to your hole, mister.'

And back to his hole went 1397.

Last sight of Heraldo Pfiffmakler being Heraldo raising a hand, touching it to the side of his head in salute.

'Thank you, again and again. We are beholden to you.'

1397 lying down that night on his cot, whispering those words once, twice, a thousand times.

Thank you, again and again.

A shriving for 1397, a blessing given him by a man he'd previously known about only due to Mergim's telling. Heraldo Pfiffmakler. Putative father to the girl Hulde who, because of Mergim, because of 1397, because of the logic of Pascal's Triangle, was still walking this earth.

Time to sleep easy for 1397 that night.

And tomorrow would see him, pincers in hand wrenching every last one of those bad teeth from his bad gums. A short period of agony followed by peace.

Penance truly done.

Inheritance handed out into the world in the form of his thesis in Heraldo's pocket.

Mergim alive and thriving, as was the unknown Hulde so beloved. As had been his son. As had been his wife.

1397 deciding this was it. Time to turn his face to the wall and breath out his last. Had in his head the words of Purcell's Fairy Queen once sung by an opera singer come all the way from Vienna to Osijek.

Hush. No more. Be silent all.

Sweet repose has closed her eyes, soft as feathered snow does fall.

Softly, softly, steal from hence. No noise disturb her sleeping sense.

Hush. No more. Be silent all.

Hush and silence all prisoner 1397 craved. Reduced his rations day by day, month by month, small as they were. Was almost at his end, when he received the most extraordinary letter.

His messenger, Heraldo, doing more than 1397 could ever have anticipated.

Thank you, again and again. We are beholden.

1397 as beholden to Heraldo as Heraldo had been to him.

Opening that letter, reading those few introductory words:

My name is Othmar Voort…

35

Pilgrimage And Penance

Tea had been made. Thin, tasting of tin, brewed from dust scraped from the bottom of the near empty caddy. Othmar not inclined to apologise. Not touching his cup. Stung into life by Longhella's little speech. Hulde right. He had questions. Like who were these people, and what were they doing here? Why the interest in him or the *Put Preko Mora*? And where in God's name was Nyord Bay where they'd apparently uncovered part of the hoard of finds from The Field of Blackbirds?

Answers given in swift succession.

We're the Pfiffmaklers.

We met a man named Jochen Steggle who made his house from the remnants of your shipwreck.

Who told us there were bore-holes in some of the staves from the cargo holds.

Which is why we looked on Nyord Bay, for where the ship came aground so might have other things.

We spoke to his neighbour Jansen, who saw the ship go down.

And he told us about Christian Schumacher, who told us about you.

And so we are here.

'I still don't understand exactly why,' Othmar said.

'Because,' Longhella replied, oozing sarcasm, 'our dear little Hulde believes you've been wrongly done by. And,' she added, with the nonchalance of a true fair's person, 'we thought we might make a theatre of it. Spread word of your innocence far and wide.'

Ortwin choking on his tea.

'You want,' Othmar said slowly, 'to make an entertainment of me?'

Hulde quick to the fore.

'We want to see right done, find the real saboteur. And, if we do, tell as many people about it as we can. Clear your name.'

Set me free. Othmar Voort couldn't stop the words running through his head.

'So, Mr Othmar Voort,' Longhella's turn again, 'who do you suspect? You obviously suspect someone.'

Nails flicking over Othmar's list.

Othmar leaning back in his chair. Pondering that same question since he'd received his last letter from Grettir Wyssling. Othmar surveying his guests, his interlopers. Nothing short of miraculous they'd come to his door when they had. Vague recollection of a paper he'd read years before: *Coincidence as a Concept,* by some Serbian professor he couldn't recall the name of. Gist being coincidences happen all the time and are rarely as coincidental as they seem. Thinking maybe this was an exception to the rule, despite the rigorous logic that professor had provided to prove the opposite.

'I do,' he therefore said, in answer to Longhella's question. 'I have no proof, but I have narrowed it down. I believe it to have been a conspiracy between my assistants…'

A withering look from Longhella.

'A conspiracy, is it? Oh dear Lord.'

Othmar battling on.

'Two men from the Royal Archaeological Society chosen by Schumacher…'

'Well that makes sense,' Longhella interrupted. 'I'm sure he'd have approved of them sabotaging his career.'

Shushed by Hulde, who encouraged Othmar to go on.

'Including a merchant from Odense, who'd given considerable contributions for the expedition. They were writing a travelogue, I'm sure of it.'

'And wanted to end it with a bang? Oh please.' Longhella could see holes from here to Sunday in this plot.

Hulde more practical.

'If so, only one of them made it to shore. Like we said before. Is there anyone else in the mix? A single individual, perhaps?'

A tic developing in Othmar's left eye. Going back to a previous suspect.

Those you should not touch.

Clear as yesterday in his mind that man's self-righteous anger, the way he had stood on the lip of the dig and accused. Sun behind him, face shadowed, no clarity of features. One man. Surely made more sense. His accusation against two men of standing seeming as outlandish as Longhella had supposed.

'There is someone,' he stammered. 'I've no record of his name, only a face, and rather a sketchy at that. One of the Serbian workers. Look here.'

He slipped the ledger from beneath Longhella's fingers, turned a few pages to reveal a portrait that was insubstantial at best.

Longhella rightly dismissive.

'His own mother couldn't make him out from that.'

Othmar colouring.

'Well no. He was only a labourer, and there were so many of them coming and going all along our route.'

'Little ants, doing your bidding,' Longhella tutted.

'That's unfair,' Hulde put in. 'There must have been a great many. No one would remember them all.'

Othmar belittled by the girl's defence of him, needing to speak on his own behalf.

'Hundreds,' he said sharply. 'Nor can I see how he could have ended up on our ship.'

'And who was on your ship? Out of your work force, I mean.' Hulde asked.

Othmar on firmer ground, returning to his list, running his fingers down the names.

'My three direct assistants. And all the students, mostly from Danish universities, others from Germany and France.'

A diverse work-force, whose names he'd struggled to remember. Magnussen, Hermann, Peder, Otto, a couple of Hans, at least one Knud. Fairly certain there'd been a Ludwig, a Frederik. The French lad Louis who, of all of them, had worked the hardest. A shy lad, the left side of his face stained with a large purple birthmark. Another of Louis's compatriots who might have been Pierre, and another he was more sure of being François.

'No women then?' Longhella asked pointedly. 'Not a single one?'

Othmar drew in his chin at such a ludicrous question.

'Women? Why would we need women? It was an expedition, not a picnic.'

Longhella straightened her back, waved a lazy hand about her.

'So who is this here, you've plastered over your walls?'

His portraits of Irmgaard not going unnoticed.

Othmar flustering.

'She's no one,' he snapped. 'At least no one you need be interested in.'

'Let's get back to your list,' Hulde tactfully intervened. 'Looks like there's about thirty five people coming back to Denmark with you.'

Othmar lowered his head. Cleaned the bottom of his glasses with his fingers. No need for Hulde to say how likely it was all were dead. Young and old. Students and would-be professor-conspirators. My God, the letters he'd received via the Society from their families. Vituperative, vengeful and vile. Another sickening blow of fate he'd had to endure. All those words of calumny pouring into his life like March flies clustered about his buckthorn hedge, about his head. All their dangling legs. Their curses and condemnations, the threats of revenge. Weeks and months looking over his shoulder, days spent trembling at every shadow, every person spied on the horizon. Every night expecting to be bludgeoned to death in his bed by an avenging relative. All of them blaming him for the demise of their sons. Not to mention Christian Schumacher carrying out a personal vendetta, trying to get him turfed out of his home. Would have succeeded, had it not been for Grettir Wyssling.

'This other person,' Hulde went on, when Othmar Voort made no reply, looked to be collapsing in on himself and needed shaking out of it. 'The Serbian worker. Why are you so certain he couldn't have been on the ship?'

Othmar took off his glasses, laid them down on his list.

'How could he be? He was a casual labourer, a local. Employed for barely a month. The ship booked before the expedition started. Only passengers on board being from the expedition. I simply don't know where to go from here.'

Hulde biting her upper lip. Life so black and white for men like Othmar Voort, who never properly registered those they considered below them. People like the Pfiffmaklers. Maybe appreciated, maybe not. Seen briefly, forgotten the moment they stepped out of view. Hulde waiting for Longhella to say the obvious, which was not long in coming.

'Let me summarise,' Longhella stated, drumming her fingers on the table. Othmar irritated. Longhella not letting up. 'You now suspect a particular man whose name you don't recall, and you don't recall his name because he was a lowly worker.'

The drumming of Longhella's fingers really getting on Othmar's nerves. Othmar prickling uncomfortably, as if he'd been thrown into a bed of nettles.

Longhella not helping.

'And you've no idea how such a man could have got onto the *Put Preko Mora*. Its passage reserved specifically for you and the members of your expedition.'

Othmar chancing a glance at Longhella's handsome face. Wishing he hadn't. Such disparagement there, and despisement. Saw the set of her chin. Saw Irmgaard.

'That is so,' he agreed, words clipped and short.

Focussed on his own thin fingers splayed uselessly across the table. Presentiment of another downfall coming his way.

'And it never occurred to you,' Longhella persisted, slowing her words, suspending her drumming. 'It never occurred to you, Mr Othmar Voort, not for a single second...'

And here it came, Longhella milking the moment as she always did. Hulde admiring the carefully judged hiatus.

'...that such a man, a casual labourer, a local, might not have been able to simply sign on as a member of the crew? Nothing apparently to do with you or your expedition? Merely a man who asked for work and got it?'

Othmar could say nothing. Othmar, who'd pursued lines of logic all his life, who had presumed himself to have created further lines with his expedition where none other had gone, proved worthless and wanting. An explanation so self-evident a child of five might have worked it out had he ever asked one instead of puzzling over the problem for years without satisfactory solution. Othmar's blood thumping in his ears, ticking in his temples, pressing itself against the backs of his eyes.

'And there we have it, children,' Longhella pronounced triumphantly. 'A possible who, a probable how. All we need from you, Mr Not-So-Very-Clever-Clogs, is the why. Unless you'd like us to ruminate for a few minutes and work it out for ourselves?'

'Goddammit!' Othmar exclaimed, slamming his fist onto the table. His recriminations reserved for himself. It was pitiful. He was pitiful. And pathetic. Already the entertainment these people wanted to make of his life, could see the laughter poised on that strident woman's lips. Breathed out long and low to quell his anger.

'Do you have any idea?' Hulde asked quietly, wanting to halt this man's obvious distress.

Othmar thinking back to his unknown man, his no one.

'It must have been the bones.' Voice a notch above a whisper.

Seeing them laid out in their pit, nose to tail, heads to feet. The damaged femurs and arm bones, the scapulae and tibias, the slashes and gashes caused by sabre strikes and swords. The skulls, the jaw bones. The little soldiers made from cannonballs, the real soldiers those cannonballs had blown limb from limb.

Those you should not touch.

§

Othmar's unknown man, his no one, was standing outside the walls of Kragujevac prison when Heraldo retreated across the moat. Hard to make him out, given the paucity of evening light, the falling snow, as Heraldo approached.

'Marko! What are you doing here? Why aren't you at the Senate with the others?'

Marko shuffled his feet, fighting to get out the lies which, now he was saying them out loud, didn't seem so outlandish, had a ring of truth.

'I've been thinking about what you told me, about how you lost your Ludmilla. How I lost my wife.'

Marko adding a few details not previously divulged, to do with guilt, getting there too late, the parallels to Heraldo's experience.

'And when you told me why you came all this way to find St Vid as a sort of…I don't know. Your pilgrimage and penance. It got me thinking, perhaps I should do the same myself.'

Marko forging onwards.

'I went close to Denmark once, when I was young.' Wouldn't do to mention the how or why. 'Thought maybe I should go back. Do as you did, in reverse order as it were…'

'Pilgrimage and penance,' Heraldo echoed.

'Pilgrimage and penance,' Marko repeated. 'Would you object to a companion? I'm aware I might be a burden. I've nothing to offer…'

Heraldo smiled into the gloaming. Heraldo liking company, liking Marko.

No objections from him. One small detail to be cleared up.

'What about Yanni?' he asked. 'What does he think about this?'

Glad to see the back of me, after what I've done.

Glad never to have to look me in the face again.

They'll all think I'm dead, the robbers doing away with me as they did Grettir Wyssling. Chucked my body into the Lepenica, slotted me under the ice, never to be found.

'Did your Hulde chide you?' Marko asked quietly. 'Did she not understand your reasons for going?'

No, and yes.

Hulde doing exactly as Marko had surmised.

Heraldo seeing the two sides of the equation as 1397 might have done.

Heraldo leaving and Heraldo returning, and now Marko doing the same.

'Yanni knows why I must do this,' Marko added, desperate to be gone. Desperate not to bring his own shame and guilt down on Yanni and their village, to besmirch the winning of the competition, should they win, make it less than it was. Make it vile and worthless. Snatched away at the very hour of triumph.

Heraldo looking at Marko, the sturdy set of his shoulders, the pallor of his face that hadn't left him since his near burial in the snow when his hundredth door had been yawning before him as it had done for Ludmilla and, unlike Ludmilla, Marko saved.

Grettir Wyssling there for Marko, as Heraldo had not been for Ludmilla. Grettir putting his engineering knowledge to use, ramming boards into the snow to keep it back. Excavating a hole no one other than himself would have known how to do. Grettir Wyssling the one man at St Vid able to pull closed Marko's hundredth door before he tumbled through it.

Heraldo, primed by Mergim's mathematician, seeing a rightness here. A path onwards. Rescuing one soul as he'd been rescued by his pilgrimage, as Grettir had rescued Marko. Heraldo's turn to take the baton.

'Well then, my friend,' he said exuberantly. 'If Yanni's glad then so am I. The days and nights we'll have together! And I'll be able to introduce you to my family once our travels are done.'

§

The two setting off forthwith. It might be dark, yet young was the night. And after his talk with the mathematician Heraldo was keen to be gone from Kragujevac. Slough off the smell of that wretched place with clean snow-laden air. Tracks out of town well-travelled, easily followed. No worry in him where they would stop to eat and sleep. They would stop where they would stop, bivouac in a barn, nestle themselves into a hayrick, take cover beneath an abandoned wagon. Find outlying villages where Heraldo would offer entertainment, would sing, play his mandolin.

If someone gave them a bed for the night, a gulp of soup, a step of bread, then all would be fine. If not, it would also be fine.

And so begins their journey out of Kragujevac, out of Serbia.

Pilgrimage and penance for Heraldo done. Home and Hulde on his mind.

Pilgrimage and penance, for Marko, only just begun.

36

Phantoms, Arise And Take Form!

Jochen Steggle heard fast approaching footsteps, Jansen's harsh voice calling out.

'Steggle! Get your bloody self out here. Someone's coming!'

'Heaven help me,' Jochen whispered, wiping his hands on his apron, giving his latest full-body phantom a last polite stroke to his waxen hair. This particular creation at its end.

'It'll be the transporters,' he called out to Jansen. 'I told you they were due.'

Jansen cursing, kicking at the ground with his feet.

'It's not the buggering transporters,' Jansen yelled back. 'They've no cart. It's a man on his own two feet. If you've brought the buggering taxmen to our doors I'll have you skinned alive!'

Jochen loosened the fists he'd unconsciously bunched. Jansen might not have been able to carry out his threat but Jochen was up to the task. Had skinned plenty of animals during his apprenticeship. Jansen wouldn't be a problem.

'Then go see what he wants,' he shouted out. 'Maybe he's come to sling you into the jail in which you belong!'

An unfair comment. Jansen might by annoying, but went out of his way not to be aggravating to the authorities he was so feared of. The reason he'd come to Jochen's door, cursing and shouting.

'Get yourself home,' Jochen therefore added. 'I'll deal with it.'

A short silence while Jansen took this in.

'He's at the pastures. He's not going to stop.'

'Get gone, Jansen,' Jochen repeated, opening his door. Seeing the trepidation on Jansen's raddled face. 'I'll come tell you what it's all about later.'

Jansen giving a short nod, which was all the thanks Jochen would get, and legged it lopsidedly to the bay from where he could cut back to his home.

The man came on, drew level with the sign announcing the name of Jochen Steggle's home. Jochen seeing him pause, thinking it must be the transporters after all. A new crew who'd not been here before, wanting to verify they were in the right place before dragging their cart all the way down the track.

'Hello,' Jochen called. 'Can I help you?'

The man, in a creased and crumpled suit, speaking as he crossed the yard, taking off his hat.

'Are you Mr Jochen Steggle?' Jochen tipping his head to indicate it was so. 'Then I'm very pleased to meet you. You've already helped me more than you know.'

Jochen none the wiser, leading his visitor on.

Pfiffmaklers at the heart of this he intuited, goose-bumps rising on his skin.

Quick reflex of revulsion as Othmar saw the corpse laid out on the table. Jochen explaining hurriedly it was no recently demised relative or random murder victim, rather a teaching aid created out of wax.

'I thought you were one of the transporters,' he said. 'They're due any day. They'll be taking him over to Odense and from there to Copenhagen. He'll be well travelled by the time he hits the dissection slab.'

This introduction inviting some general exchange about Jochen's work as courtesy demanded, until Jochen cut it short. Curious who this man was and why he'd come. Othmar, glad the genialities were over, did not shilly-shally.

'It's your house. It's you.'

An excursion not taken lightly. First time he'd exited the narrow environs of his homestead since his disgrace and expulsion from society. Pension drawn by arrangement with his bank, exchanged for rations delivered to his door along with any remaining cash.

Had taken some drumming up of nerve to leave, don his neglected togs. Frightening, those several miles of walking to the nearest port, boarding a boat to take him over to Møns. Irrational fear that the moment he deserted his demesne Christian Schumacher would be there with a demolition crew. Paranoia, he understood. Christian Schumacher long consigned to the past, most likely never giving him a second thought.

If only he knew.

Blast of sea air doing him good. Same creeping nausea, which unaccountably disappeared an hour in. Allowed him some pleasure in the travelling.

'I had an unusual set of guests a while back,' Othmar explained, 'by the name of Pfiffmakler, with whom I gather you are acquainted. My name,' Othmar added slowly, 'is Othmar Voort. I was considered the only survivor, until they talked to you.'

Jochen awed by how swiftly the Pfiffmaklers had not only acted on his theory of a second man coming ashore, but had found the original survivor. Much to talk about, much to discuss.

Jochen explaining about the boreholes he'd found in the wood.

'It really was sabotage then,' Othmar said.

'I believe so,' Jochen agreed. 'And not by you.' Which was a burden off Othmar's shoulders. 'There's something I'd like to show you.'

Jochen fetching the object from its shelf.

'The Pfiffmakler girl, Hulde, deduced it was a moon calendar. I confess it had bemused me for years.'

No need to ask if Othmar recognised it. Othmar taking it reverentially, running his fingers along the incised lines.

'I dug this up near Skopje in Macedonia. Came originally, I believe, from, the Danubian Basin in Bulgaria. Late Neolithic. Five, maybe six thousand years old.' His voice low and hoarse. 'It was our first major find. I can't…it's hard to express how…just to see it again.'

Crotal bell, soldiers from cannon balls, coins from the reign of Murad II, and now this calendar. Much to thank the Pfiffmaklers for. Could hardly bear to think he would have turned them from his door had they not been so insistent.

'You found this out in the bay?' he asked Jochen.

'I did. Very near the place I dug out the keel.'

'And why was that?' Othmar looked over, seeing his companion properly for the first time: a man in his late forties, skilled at his chosen occupation. 'Why come here? Why not set up shop in Copenhagen?'

'I'd had enough of cities,' Jochen answered. 'Hated the noise, the stench, the constant interruptions. I need silence for my craft. So after my apprenticeship in Dresden with Leopold Blaschka…'

An audible gasp from Othmar Voort.

'*The* Leopold Blaschka? An artist of the first order. His son even better.'

Jochen nodding.

'His father a good master, as I well know. And kind. Leopold giving me a signed contract, if only I could find a suitable place of work. Found this plot of land. Nothing here except a corrugated shack barely big enough for bed and board.'

Allowing himself a wry smile. Hadn't known then of his near neighbour Jansen, who'd been actively skewing away every possible neighbour for years. Jansen the single reason the land had been cheap enough for Jochen to afford.

'I'd no clear plan,' he explained. 'Had the land, permission to access the forest to source wood for building. But the logistics involved, the chopping and hewing, the transportation, I'd not considered them at all. And then I looked anew at the *Put Preko Mora* already stranded in the sands, saw what I could do with it. Hard work, but doable. And so your wreck became my home, my work space. Without it I suspect I would never have been able to support my livelihood here. It was a godsend.'

Othmar looking about him at this extraordinary home in which this man did such extraordinary work. All built from the timbers of the ship that had wrecked Othmar's life.

'There's someone you must meet,' Jochen said. 'Stay. I'll not be long.'

Setting out a glass, a bottle of wine. Othmar nodding dumbly. Othmar, during Jochen's brief absence, wandering about the workshop, studying the bottles containing Jochen's reference phantoms standing neatly on their shelves. Admiring the precision and skill gone into their making, the neatness and brevity of their summarising labels. How alike this visual display was to his own folios. Othmar returning to the table, regarding the moon calendar. The first viable proof of his Grand Theory hemmed inside its fragile form.

'Give over, you fucking arse!'

Othmar almost knocking the moon calendar off the table with the shock of the interruption. Frisson shivering through his bones to have almost destroyed six thousand years of history. Jochen opening the door, Jansen tumbling in before him. Jochen regretting his decision to bring Jansen here, Jansen already three sheets to the wind. But done was done.

'This is my neighbour, Jansen,' Jochen announced, coming in on Jansen's heels, cupping his hand about Jansen's elbow, trying to steer him to a chair.

'Get yer bleeding hands off me,' Jansen wriggling, throwing Jochen off. Managing to locate a chair, wobble himself onto it. 'And yous is the man,' focussing ineffectually on Othmar, 'what got offa the wreck. Well, if it ain't a miracle I dunno what is. Went down like a stone, it did…'

Jansen reciting his narrative of the shipwreck, as Jochen had intended. Slurred but word perfect, so often had it been told.

Waterlilies and stones.

As if God Himself had punched that ship from one existence into the next.

Too much for Othmar Voort, who wept quietly to hear his tragedy so vividly and dispassionately described.

Too much for Jochen Steggle, who booted Jansen out before he could get his feet too comfortably under the table.

'I was just getting into it!' Jansen protested, as Jochen practically hauled him out by his collar. 'C'mon, my mate Steggle. We can yaw a bit more, us three…'

Jochen unforgiving. No need for a man like Jansen to further blot the landscape of Othmar Voort's plight. Jansen's unpartisan and visceral retelling of Othmar's ordeal obviously shaking him. Bolstering the belief his escape had been the merest of flukes.

'You're such a pissing shit!' was Jansen's parting conclusion on the matter. 'Spending your time pissing at the pissing moon.'

Jansen stumbling over words and feet, flailing impotent fists, for if anyone had a right to talk to this newcomer it was he. Chewing sour lemons didn't cover the half of his bitterness. Deciding to take revenge, let go the billy from his paddock. Succeeded only in getting bitten on the behind as he struggled with the heavy plank keeping the animal in. Jansen cursing as another billy-mission was aborted, another pair of trousers ruined.

'I apologise for Jansen,' Jochen said, as he heard a short screech, made a correct deduction about what Jansen was attempting to do and what had instead been done. Othmar waving a hand.

'Please. There's no need. I needed to hear what he had to say. I always knew the way the ship went down was wrong. He's confirmed it, for which I'm grateful.'

Grateful too to Grettir, who had caused him to rethink everything about that night. The only lifeline he'd had all these bad years. Flicker of concern to realise he'd not heard from Grettir for a month or more, which was unusual. One of Othmar's few pleasures to hear about Grettir's travels in the hills, the progress of the models made for his Wind Museum. A breath of fresh air in the stuffy house Grettir had singlehandedly saved.

'Grateful too to the Pfiffmaklers, I think,' Jochen added. 'On both our counts. And, as you say, grateful once more to Jansen. He was the one goaded me into attending the performance they gave on the cliffs. If not for that I would never have known of them nor, consequentially, of you.'

Companionship for these two men, one ejected unwillingly from society, another choosing his own retreat from it. Jochen taking Othmar, with his telescope, down to the sands to stare at the pissing moon. Othmar, lying on his back gazing up at the stars, reminded of doing the same during the expedition when he'd lain on other sands, other soils, in other countries, slotting ideas around in his head. Sorting through the details of his finds, fitting them into the grand thesis he'd never written.

The moon calendar a prime example of how civilisations had moved north to south instead of the opposite, as most archaeologists assumed to be the case. From the Greeks and Romans all must come. God forbid they might be wrong. Othmar always convinced they were. His expedition meant to prove it. His expedition come to a crashing halt, along with his career, in this very place. Nyord Bay. And now, thirteen years later, Nyord Bay where the redress might begin.

The leeches in his prognosticator might die while he was away. So be it. There were always more leeches, bred by the million all over Scandinavia, imported to every corner of Europe by extravagant means and vessels. He didn't consider them medicinal miracle-workers, but let others believe what they would.

His belief now was this: because of Jochen Steggle and the Pfiffmaklers he might yet be exonerated.

Six weeks since he'd received Grettir's letter in which the oddity of his survival had been mooted.

Six weeks since Heraldo had led Marko away from Kragujevac.

Six weeks since Grettir had been discovered, carried away to the village and up the mountain, buried in the grounds of St Vid chapel where everyone knew he had earned his place.

Six weeks since Marko had been declared dead and gone, murdered by the same thieves presumed to have murdered Grettir Wyssling. Nothing to bury of him, at St Vid or otherwise. A moving encomium given by Irmgaard nonetheless, which had Yanni blushing and turning away.

Several months since the Pfiffmaklers had removed themselves from Rügen to the Danish Isles, a few more weeks since they'd departed the home of Othmar Voort. Leeches in his leechorium ringing the tiny bell several times after Othmar had left for Nyord Bay.

Storms a-coming, those blood-sucking miracle-workers insisted, as they'd insisted before. *Storms a-coming.*

37

New Entertainments, New Arrivals

Pfiffmaklers back on Falster, on the island's tip at Gedser, airing their new theatrics. Playing it safe, sticking to the margins, wanting to plane off any rough edges before shifting into Odense where Mergim and Ortwin—working more miraculously than Othmar's leeches—had bargained their way into a spot on the stage of the theatre there. Ortwin's grandfather's name proving its worth. Pfiffmaklers crumbs no more. Soon to be a slice of the main loaf.

Mechanics of the performance engineered by Lupercal, Jericho and Hulde, who had painted yards and yards of canvas into service. All carefully wound onto their rollers, all scenes expressed—under Hulde's direction—in the style Heraldo might have done. Mood and evocation preferred over realism. Jansen's telling influential of this direction, which would have marvelled him had he known.

Father of the Fair standing straight-backed and imposing on the dais of the stage.

Moon waned and waxed, back to full.

High spring tide, waves thrashing against chalk cliffs on both sides of the isthmus. Eerie shuffles and shoofs as pebbles shift upon their stony beaches, others stumbling up above before rushing headlong down scree lines to the shore below.

We will tell you tales, Mergim announces, *of your land, of your history. Of not one shipwreck but two. Of Holger and Eleanora. Of war and sacrifice.*

Broad sweeps of colour, dark black hue of night. Flashes of white as the captain hollers into the wind, orders down the sails, orders down the anchor and the passengers to their berths. Soft singing of shanties as his men go about their work, defiant in the face of the storm that has not yet done its worst.

Swirling curlicues of surf and brine, bright splashes of lightning, deep undercurrent of waves getting higher, climbing like cliffs made of running wolves. Pinpricks of luminescence from stars, moon and lighthouses; tall white cliffs of Møns, so like Gedser's own, dipping here and there, up and down: Spire and Speaker, Queen's Seat, Castle Gables. Deep rumbles of thunder coming from the wings thrumming through the audience's bones, making them feel they are out there on this ship, in this storm. Makes them shudder, disturbs them as comes another façade of roaring waves, a distant and then deafening dirge, a building crescendo of desperate cries as the ship tilts over, spills its human cargo onto an unpredictable tide, detritus piling high upon higher waves, all maelstrom and chaos.

A great expedition, Mergim informs, *undergone to bring back to Danish soil thousands of artefacts dug up from the Black Sea to Montenegro, from Albania to Kosovo, from the Field of Blackbirds.*

Gedser folk leaning forward, memories tugged as they hear the name of the splintered boards tossed about on the storm-struck sea. *Put Preko Mora.* No time to slot them into place, for a tumultuous battle overtakes the scene. Becomes that same Field of Blackbirds.

Mergim reciting the tendrils of treachery binding the two narratives together, underpinning them like for like.

That first ship wrecked by the hand of a saboteur.

The Battle of Kosovo with its heroes and betrayers.

A dizzying collage rolling out before them: a fight savage and brutal, hand to hand, swords and sabres. Blood thick and visceral on the canvas, appearing to seep from canvas to stage as dark-clad youths enact a small violent corner of the action.

A quest to save the soul of Serbia! Mergim roars out. *Remembered from that day to this, as you remember your own Great Northern Wars.*

Another ship appears: the *Dannebroge,* its name writ large.

Cannons roaring, fire creeping up the deck once the *Dannebroge* is hit, soon to catch its store of gunpowder, as everyone knows. Shudders in the audience. Mergim pleating the stories together.

Remember the legend of Holger the Dane, as retold by your very own Hans Christian Andersen. Bring to mind his woodworker's workshop, the figurehead he creates which shoots flames into Eleanora's prison and binds to the heart of Hvitfeldt, the Dannebroge's commander.

Longhella taking to the stage, become Eleanora Ulfeldt in her tiny dirty cell; Eleanora stitching, lamenting the bad vicissitudes of fate perpetrated by the hand of her husband leading to her long years of enjailment. Eleanora next transported—ethereal, ephemeral, seemingly transparent in her ghostly mode—onto the *Dannebroge* to remind Hvitfeldt what he must do: sacrifice himself, his ship, his crew, in order to save the Danish fleet. Souls stirring as Longhella sings out her pleas, drives her song through the darkness of the night.

Your ship is done for, my brave Hvitfeldt. A bad hand you've been dealt.

Your men could be saved, as could you, if you threw yourself into the Baltic blue.

Yet I implore you, do otherwise! Open instead your eyes and arise!

Upfurl every sail, bellow yourself into the wind. Do sin to those who have sinned

Against you. Against every Dane! Go for gain!

Do right, Hvitfeldt. Do not let your courage melt.

Make the Dannebroge *the fatal dart driven into your enemy's heart.*

Audience on a knife edge, knowing of the self-sacrifice of the *Dannebroge,* of Hvitfeldt, of Eleanora, the most noble of Danish women.

Three narratives seamlessly sewn together by Pfiffmakler machinations, songs and music, yards of painted canvas drawn from one side of the stage to the other.

Grand finale waiting in the wings. Pfiffmaklers not disappointing.

Hans Andersen advises us to cut a road to the stars, not by the sword but by the word. For words, my friends, are the most powerful tools in the world. Here your great warrior Holger, and here too Eleanora.

Gravestones, stately sepulchres.

Both sleeping, as they sleep in the hearts of every man, woman and child in Denmark. Waiting, should they be needed.

Woodworker back in his workshop, figurehead on the canvas backdrop towering behind him dashing out its flames, flickering in the candlelight, in the sparks thrown up from the fire-pits. Woodworker bending down to his grandson, whispering in his ear, although everyone in the audience hears those whispers, feels them working through them, winding through their minds, their hearts.

You must not fear, my dear. For if they're needed, when they're needed, Holger and Eleanora will open their eyes.

As they do: Diderik and Longhella, stately and luminous, rising up as did Svetovid in the chapel of St Vid; Holger and Eleanora giving a descanted version of the Danish National Anthem. Pfiffmaklers knowing National Anthems always a good way to go out on a high. Diderik and Longhella loud and lovely, alto and baritone, Hulde's lute doing them proud.

There is a lovely land, with spreading beech trees, near salty eastern shores.

Hills and valleys gently fall in our beloved Denmark, our Freya's hall.

Here, in ancient days, armoured giants stayed between their bloody frays

Of fighting foes hand to hand, face to face.

Here now, in stony barrows, they await like arrows

Primed and wise. Until, until...

Huge upsurge of the music. Lute replaced by crashing cymbals, insistent drumming.

Flashes as of lighthouses scanning stormy seas. The white cliffs of Møns, or of Gedser, luminous behind the stage. An out-rolling of bodies on the surf of a long white beach. And then calm again.

A single zithered note as Holger and Eleanora join hands. Last yard of backdrop pulled into place behind them: ship high, vaulting on its waves. Waterlilies scattered all around it. Holger and Eleanora chanting beneath the moon.

Until you need us to arise, when we will open our eyes, raise our harried cries.

Narration of their tripartite tale almost complete.

Mergim taking to the stage, booming out a challenge. One argued about, Hulde winning out. 'No better place,' she'd said, 'than here.'

And we need you, people of Gedser, to open your eyes and arise! All of you who remember the wrecking of the Put Preko Mora *thirteen years ago. For know this: all was not as it seemed. The sole survivor branded a saboteur. What was not told you, what we have recently discovered, is that he was not the only one who made it off that ship.*

Puzzlement pulsing through the audience like one of the waves out there in the darkness.

Ask yourselves, Ladies and Gentlemen, who was that other who stole onto the shores of Nyord Bay? And who the most likely saboteur. The man who was very nearly swept away by the currents, dragged out of the sea half alive, or the other who crept from Møns like a thief

in the night, who did not raise the alarm, nor see fit to shout out to
the world: For God's sake, send out boats, send out lines and ropes!
Save those who might yet be saved!

Murmuring in the audience, for this was news indeed.

Keenly remembered were the twelve long miles of flat Falster beach after many of the bodies from the *Put Preko Mora* had washed ashore. Thought at first to be seals, before here and there were spied bright flashes of colour: a gaudy necktie, a splash of green from a fine satin jacket, the red-and-white stripes of a cook's apron. Gedser folk going to investigate. Dismayed by what they'd found. People strewn like uprooted weeds over the beach's white sand, and many of them so young. All brought up and placed side by side. Twenty-three bodies, nameless at the time. Twenty-three bodies later claimed and mourned, once the fate of the *Put Preko Mora* became general knowledge.

Families of the dead returning over the years to the white sands of Falster to sit and grieve, especially the families of the youngest. Students, they remembered. Students on the archaeological expedition the Pfiffmaklers had begun their performance with. Folk coming all the way from France, from Germany, from other parts of Denmark. Folk of Falster quietly welcoming, bringing nosegays of flowers, platters of food, to those families stranded by their grief upon Falster's sands.

Recalling the investigator Christian Schumacher, an important man from Odense, who came to their doors, documented the numbers of the dead, the names that might be matched with particulars of the bodies. Sketches made of clothes and faces, where faces still remained. Which was not the case for all. Some hammered into non-existence by flotsam and jetsam, others scoured away by rocks, or had eyes and flesh nibbled away by fish and crabs.

Everything itemised that could be: pocket watches, signet rings, chains about necks, bracelets about wrists, that large port wine stain on one of the younger students' left brow and cheek. A boy who'd come from France, they'd later learned. A boy named Louis, who'd been so entranced by the possibilities of the expedition he'd put on hold his marriage to the girl he'd been engaged to since he was fifteen.

Every death noted and notarised.

Everyone informed by Christian Schumacher this had not been a natural disaster, instead a calculated calumny. A sabotage perpetrated by the one man who had survived.

Pfiffmaklers puncturing that certainty.

Pfiffmaklers telling them Christian Schumacher had been wrong.

Folk of Gedser outraged. Shouts coming up from the audience.

Who was this other man? Why have we never heard of him? What in God's name really happened?

§

Christian Schumacher, at this moment in Copenhagen, having no idea what might be about to ensue because of it.

Pfiffmaklers leaving Falster, making their way to the banks of the river outside Odense, communally evaluating the success of their new entertainment, how much they could slot into their upcoming performance at the theatre in town. A single hour allotted during which they could go with the new, stir things up, or stick to comets and dying children.

Everyone, bar Longhella, keen to go with the new.

'We could really kick up the wrong kind of storm,' Longhella argued.

Hulde flipping a couple of flatbreads in her pan.

'We can't let everyone go on believing Othmar to be the villain when he isn't.'

Loud exhalation of breath from Longhella.

'Why would they care? I mean, really...'

Retaliation arrested as Hulde broke in.

'Look,' she murmured, pointing west where the sun, moments before, had sunk away below the horizon in an orange glory. A man appearing from behind a blinkered stand of apple trees, taking calm and measured steps towards them.

Hulde's hands going to her mouth.

'Oh my,' she whispered.

Longhella leaping to her feet, knife in hand, ready for what would come.

Not at all ready when Hulde lifted herself and began running forward, for she was in no doubt. Heraldo. It was Heraldo. He'd found them. He'd really found them.

Mergim leaving messages at every church in every village they'd passed through, as agreed before Heraldo had left. It finally paying dividends.

Heraldo home.

Hulde running and running, holding out her arms, holding them out until Heraldo, for it was he, had her closed and tight.

'Home!' exclaimed Heraldo, wrapping Hulde up. 'I'm finally home, and I've so much to tell you, oh so much to tell.'

38

Hopes And Harnesses

Jochen and Othmar were in fine fettle. Jochen readying spades and rakes, a small picnic to take down to the sands where Othmar was about to reprise his dig, for if the Pfiffmaklers had found several of his lost artefacts merely by kicking their boots about the strandline it stood to reason there had to be more. Jochen in full agreement, eager to help, point out the place where the keel had been stranded, where'd he'd chanced upon the moon calendar; the further spots where Ortwin had discovered coins, crotal bell and cannonball soldiers.

Both eager too to seek out the Pfiffmaklers, if they were still in the vicinity. Making plans.

'We know they went to Odense where they met Christian Schumacher,' Jochen said, 'and from there to you.'

'And from me back to Falster,' Othmar replied, 'and from there to Odense at some point, they implied.'

To perfect their show of me, their entertainment.

Recalled the woman flicking her skirts as they'd left his door, left him stepping out from the tatterdemalion shadow he'd lived under before their visit. Longhella, hands on hips, performing a small dance. Presumably an evocation of the play they were planning. A jolt to Othmar, for it was so like the pose of the terracotta figurine he'd found at Tjerrtorja in Kosovo. A specimen of the Vinca culture. A somewhat genderless figure he'd nevertheless christened the Goddess On The Throne, given what he knew about the Vinca's cult of the Great Mother of the Earth.

Another loss that might be swilling about on the bottom of the Baltic, maybe used by kelp to bolster their roots, or scraped away by water snails and urchins. Or waiting to be disinterred by the spades he was itching to put to use.

Conversation interrupted by a sharp knock on Jochen's door.

Transporters here.

A weight off Jochen's mind, couldn't have left until they'd come. His phantom too valuable, too delicate. Overseeing the packing, checking the bed of straw and heather in the coffin-like crate, the laying in of the waxed linen, the laying out of the phantom in its shroud.

'I imagine the Pfiffmaklers much admired your handiwork,' Othmar commented as Jochen fussed, packed dried moss about the phantom's sides, beneath its head, cradling it as best he could.

'Pfiffmaklers is it,' one of the transporters answered, leaning back again the desk, banned from this delicate operation. 'Them as are doing a spot at the theatre?'

Couldn't mistake that name. As exotic and provocative as the bill of fare plastered on one of the billboards outside the theatre, which this man passed every morning on his way to work.

Battles! Shipwrecks! And a mystery to be solved!

Othmar jerked to attention. Jochen too intent on his work to pay the comment any mind.

'The Pfiffmaklers?' he asked the man. 'Where? What theatre?'

The man pulling out a voluminous handkerchief, blowing his nose.

'Odense, of course. Oldest theatre in Denmark, after Copenhagen.'

Proud of his town being the second most cultured place in the land.

'When are they performing?' Othmar persisted. 'Is it soon?'

The man sniffed, clamped his septum with finger and thumb to stop a sneeze. Felt about in his pocket for his little casket of snuff. Tortoise shell, plain and functional. Othmar remembering other examples found on his expedition. How the Ottomans had tried to ban tobacco after the English introduced it to Turkey. No great success until, in 1633 a man fell asleep in his boat near the shores of Cibali in Istanbul. Lit tobacco stick falling with him, fire ignited, leaping from boat to boat and from boats to shore.

Twenty thousand houses destroyed.

Fifty thousand people left homeless.

Strict ban ensuing.

Coffee houses abandoned. People stinking of tobacco arrested and executed. Twenty thousand of them, mirroring the number of homes lost, if the accounts of the time could be believed. Bans and executions making little impact in the long run. Tobacco a trade with monied legs, both in Turkey and the Balkans. Their excellent qualities from those regions soon famed around the world. Plantations and production employing thousands upon thousands, including those who made boxes in which snuff could be kept. Like this simple little piece of tortoiseshell.

'Ooh now, let me see.' Flipping open the lid with a practiced flick of his thumbnail. 'Got the opera on just the now. Some starcrossed lover shit. Don't care for it meself. Been putting the wife off, but she'll not have it. Gonna have to take her when I get back.'

The transporter letting out a sigh, placing a pinch of snuff on his thumb joint, snorted it up.

'Medicinal,' the man explained, banging at his chest. 'Got weak lungs.'

Not a great trait for a transporter, one might have thought.

'The Pfiffmaklers?' Othmar prompted. Transporter obliging, after wiping his nose on his handkerchief following a short cannonade of satisfying sneezes.

'Back end of next week, if I recall rightly. Couple of performances Wednesday and Thursday, followed by the Big One at the weekend.'

Bitter begrudgement there. Theatre a saved-up-for treat, looked forward to, affordable mid-week when the smaller fry were on, place packed like straw in a bail. Main shows reserved for Fridays and Saturdays when commoners like himself and the wife were not welcome. Burly men at the doors beating away the undesirables.

Othmar, not privy to the transporter's inner seethings, excited.

Back end of next week, meaning lots of digging time if Jochen would agree to his presence for so long.

Jochen agreeing.

Days to be spent scouring the sands with spades and rakes.

Nights dallied through in quiet contemplation at the telescope or of any finds they'd made. And make finds they did.

Part of a terracotta ritual vessel and one of three inscribed tablets originally found in Gradeshnitsa on the way from the Black Sea to Albania. *From the same Vinca culture as the Goddess On The Throne.*

The backbone of a silver fibulae brooch. *With a bukranion—a stylised ox-head. From Vladinya, Bulgaria. Probably early fourth century BC.*

Several bronze elements from a horse-trapping, including a three-dimensional head, the hair a network of polygons covered with incised lines, a squared aperture at the neckline through which a bridle-leather could be passed. *The base piece, with the roaring face of a lion in relief, broken away. Found near Orizovo.*

Several more coins akin to those Ortwin had found.

Two lengths of triple chain, twisted gold, holding a coin from the reign of Caracalla set about with eight precious stones. *AD198- -17.*

Small silver salt-cellar, a statuette of a seated child holding a dog in his arms. *Possibly of Greek influence, given the style of the hair.*

Bronze figurine of Apollo on horseback, all their legs broken away. *Hollow, now filled with Nyord sand. Greek inscription still extant on belly of horse.*

Two rings, one from the Pleven district, another from Brestnitsa. *Incised spirals still extant. Stones missing.*

One of four ritual spoons, hammered from a single piece of copper alloy, designed to sit the one inside the other. This the smallest. *Undoubtedly Iron Age. Incredibly rare. A handful of examples from England, one outlier from France.* This one a startlement, found near the twin lakes of Ohrid and Prespa which are linked by mysterious underground rivers. An ancient trading nexus near the Via Egnati, an old Roman road.

An enigmatic place entrancing Othmar. Hundreds of thousands of migratory birds on their waters during the winter month they'd spent there. Remembered Louis, the French boy, scribbling frantically in his journal those he could identify: various species of herons, geese, swans and grebes, cormorants, crakes and coots, warblers and waders, pelicans and pipits. Louis's journal as lost as Othmar's. Or maybe washed up with his body on the beaches of Falster, pages blanked, drawings and notes washed clean.

Sharp memory of the letter from Louis's parents. The only one sent him amongst the many to not condemn him, had instead thanked Othmar for providing their son with the richest experience of his short life. How joyous Louis's missives had been, how gladly received back home to hear how happy he was, how they knew from Louis what a good and dedicated man Othmar was. Knowing, because of it, he could never have done what he'd been accused of. Othmar weeping as he'd read those words of endorsement.

One lone voice in the wilderness.

'Well, well,' Jochen said, leaning back in his chair, stretching his back. 'Off to Odense tomorrow. Do you think we've found enough?'

Othmar nodding. Grateful they'd found anything.

'I do. We had fifty-one crates all in all.' Eleven more than had been bargained for on the Trieste ship, captain cajoled into taking the extra. 'And what we've found so far has come from five separate crates.'

Both men regarding the treasures laid out on Jochen's workbench, vacated of its cadaver. So much more to be discovered, if only divers could be brought in. Men trained to hold their breath for three or four minutes. Not so deep out there, time enough to snatch up more from the sea-bed into baskets before the need to resurface. If Othmar could persuade the Danish authorities it was worth the challenge and expense. If these artefacts brought up from the sand were proof enough it needed to be done.

Jochen stood up.

'Got to do a last check on the livestock,' he said. 'Make sure the billy hasn't murdered all the rest.'

'About that,' Othmar replied, eyes lingering on the bronze pieces from the horse-trapping, the figurine of Apollo minus all its legs. 'My thinking is he'd not be so foul-tempered if he expended his energy in other ways.'

'I can hardly let him run loose,' was Jochen's opinion. 'He'd be off in a second, in the vegetable plot in two, and no getting him out of it until he has the lot destroyed.'

Othmar smiled, dashed out a quick sketch.

'So we put him to work. Turn his perverseness into productivity. We used goats to pull carts, when I was a boy. The stronger the better, and the strongest ones always the most wilful.'

Jochen let out a chuckle.

'This one's wilful, all right. It's bitten through Jansen's britches on several occasions, and me more times than I can count.'

'They're the best kind,' Othmar holding up his sketch. 'Trick is to get them harnessed and blinkered, the only way they can go being forward so the more they protest the more they pull. I can get it rigged in no time, if you've suitable materials.'

Jochen had. Off to the shed—the original lean-to Jochen lived in before he'd thought to make use of the *Put Preko Mora*. All the old stuff still in it, including an ancient leather harness hanging on a hook.

'Brass-work needs a bit of attention,' Othmar said. 'But with a load of saddle soap to flex the leather and a bit of restitching, this is going to do just fine.'

§

Come the morning, come the billy.

Billy mad as hell as the two attempted to manhandle him into the harness.

'You've got a real mad one there,' Othmar panted with the exertion, and still no result. 'Think we need a third man.'

Jochen's stomach souring, for only one third man he knew.

39

The Third Man

Pfiffmaklers pitched on the banks of the river, which meandered in gentle curves through Odense; a long meadow behind them, and behind it a pretty orchard giving them privacy from the buildings marking the farthest edge of town. Heraldo's return prompting a Pfiffmakler pageant: boys to the river to net as many fish as they could, Longhella murderous with her bow and arrows. Several ducks soon on the spit above the fire, fish sizzling on the griddle pan.

Hulde curving into Heraldo's side, soaking up his presence as the flatbreads did the juices of both fish and fowl as each were served in succession. The company presenting some of their new songs, performing abbreviated versions of Dying Child and Comet, eager to impress Heraldo with all they'd done. Heraldo in turn spilling out stories of his journey, where he'd been, whom he'd met, how he'd found them. Capped off with when he'd finally reached St Vid.

Restoration and destruction. Destruction and restoration.

His fingers healed, a little stiff, yet able to conjure tunes on his miniature mandolin as he sang songs composed on his journey homeward of snowstorms, wind museums, Bora, avalanche and rescue. Filling the intervals with spoken detail, the names of those most involved: of Grettir Wyssling, Irmgaard Prögen, Yanni, Marko, the opera singer.

'It was a great adventure,' he said, echoing Grettir Wyssling's last words to him. 'And one I'm glad I've done.'

'Not so glad as we are to have you home,' Hulde said, giving Heraldo another hug to add to the hundred she'd already given him.

'Meaning we can at last oust the Father of the Fair who should never have been given the title,' chipped in Longhella, although raised a tumbler in Mergim's direction, for it had to be admitted he'd not done badly. Mergim accepting the salutation. Offering one of his own.

'The king is dead. Long live the king!'

Relieved his reign was done. More pressure he'd never been under.

His toast taken up by the others, eager to endorse how well Mergim had handled the duty given him.

'I've one more surprise,' Heraldo said, draining his cup. 'I brought someone back with me from St Vid.'

Who? Where?

Questions fired at him from all sides.

Where indeed?

Marko, on the very edge of Mecklenburg, insisting Heraldo re-join his family on his own.

'As it happens,' Marko said, 'there's a place near here I need to go. Where Irmgaard came from. They sent us letters, did Irmgaard and

Gregor, about their life there. About all the village folk. It was like we knew them, had grown up with them, and we correspond still.'

A tradition carried on down the years. A strange intergenerational community of two far flung villages whose disparate lives were integral to their own, despite never having met. Their letters a library of sorts, where other lives could be dipped into and experienced without direct involvement; weep over tragedies, laugh over small misfortunes, celebrate their great days. Marko curious about that other village, although would not declare himself, would present merely as a traveller passing through.

Heraldo nodding, understanding.

§

'And take news of them back home?'

Marko dithering. No home left for him. Best for everyone, particularly Yanni, if they believed Marko dead and gone. Marko trying to raise a smile.

'Will follow you on in a few days, follow the same clues.'

Pfiffmaklers leaving word at every village they passed through.

Heraldo more enervated the closer they'd come to Mecklenburg, to Rügen, desperate to find his family. Marko desperate to get away from his. This wandering with Heraldo so unusual, so peculiar. Clearing Marko's mind on certain points—namely that he would never return to his homeland—clouding it on others, like what he was going to do with his life from here on in.

Make me a coffin and put me overboard, let me find my own way home.

Pfiffmaklers the pieces of wood to bring him to shore, keep him afloat until he grounded himself once more.

Would maybe then write to Yanni. Let him know how all had turned out.

Heraldo enthusiastic, jubilant, shaking Marko's hand.

'Find us sooner rather than later. They're not going to believe me if I don't have your corroboration!'

§

'How cursed annoying,' Longhella tutted. 'You build this Marko up with all your stories, and now can't produce him. It's like a magic trick without the final reveal.'

Hulde more forgiving.

'It merely prolongs the mystery. And now Marko gets to meet all the people Irmgaard knew, all those villagers Marko has only known on paper. It's rather romantic.'

Longhella rolling her eyes.

'You'd find romance turning up a stone, finding a pile of wood-lice there. *Ooh look.*' She pointed dramatically. '*There's Mr and Mrs Slater and all their silly slatey children going about their business.* It doesn't cut it for me.'

Heraldo smiled indulgently. So good to be back to find everyone as he'd left them. Longhella sparring as always, a stickleback with its spines permanently erected, whom he would have no other way. Glancing at Diderik, who was scratching the side of his mouth, inner thoughts writ large upon his face considering his own sudden romance with Longhella.

Mr and Mrs Slater, with all their little children.

And more little Pfiffmakler children would be no bad thing. Heraldo doubting he'd have any of his own. Thinking back to Yanni and the letters his villagers had exchanged with Irmgaard's own. Remembering another letter. Remembering the mathematician. Regarding Mergim, solid and certain within their circle, relaxed, at ease. The Father of the Fair he'd usurped by his return, yet no rancour in it. More like relief. A great debt he owed this man, and more respect than Mergim would ever believe he deserved.

'I forgot to say,' Heraldo said. 'On my way back I upturned a different stone. I went to the prison before I left Kragujevac.'

Mergim almost dropped his cup, looked up sharply. Saw Heraldo looking directly at him.

'I met with your mathematician, Mergim,' Heraldo explained. 'He's all you said he would be. And gave me this.'

Taking out of his backpack the mathematician's cobbled-together manuscript amidst a clamour of questions from the wider family, who'd no idea what Heraldo was talking about. Mergim ignoring them as he took the papers Heraldo was thrusting at him.

'What is it?' he asked, looking with consternation as he flipped through the pages, at all the formulas and workings out he couldn't understand. Recognising nonetheless the mathematician's writing. 'And why did he give it to you?'

Hulde coming to his rescue. Hulde the only other person, apart from Heraldo, who Mergim had ever told about the mathematician.

'I think he means you to do him right by it,' Hulde said. 'Get it out there. Get it studied.'

She couldn't understand the mathematics, but saw from the title what others hadn't. Hulde looking down the years, seeing the grand scheme laid out before her, making connections. Saw moon calendars and coins. Saw parallels with someone else's work.

'Othmar Voort,' she said. 'We've to get it to Othmar Voort.'

40

Night Shirts And Slippers

Othmar heard Jansen's carping as he and Jochen approached.

'The fucking billy! You can fucking well fuck off. I ain't going near that devil ever again.'

Othmar intervening.

'There's good money in it, if you'll help.'

Jansen's reaction immediate, turning, sauntering towards Othmar.

'Money is it?' Jansen replied 'Well why didn't you say? Always glad to help out a neighbour when he asks.'

Jochen, a step behind Othmar, furious. Red in face and cheek.

Nevertheless having to admit that without Jansen's help the harnessing of the billy would be impossible. And, once harnessed, Othmar hitched up the cart, began loading their bags onto it.

Jansen immediately suspicious.

'Where are you going? What are you doing?' he demanded.

Othmar, missing Jochen's warning signals, answering lightly.

'We're off to Odense to meet the Pfiffmaklers again.'

Jansen narrowing his eyes.

'And when do I get me gelt? Now, is it?'

Othmar prevaricating.

'Well no. I'll need to get to my bank. Hadn't foreseen this trip. Jochen will bring...'

'Jochen will not,' Jansen declared hotly. 'You'll be in my sight until I have it in me hands. Until then, where you go so go I.'

Jochen sighing loudly.

'God's sake, Jansen. You know you can trust me.'

'About as much as I trust that fucking billy.'

Said fucking billy choosing that moment to let out a volley of ear-splitting screams, setting all their teeth on edge.

'We've no time for this,' Jochen said. 'We've to get going.'

'Fine with me,' Jansen retorted, ''cept I'm coming with.'

'You've nothing packed...'

'Don't need nothing.'

'What about the animals? Who'll feed them?'

'We'll send a boy from Borre. Your mate's deep pockets, so he says.'

Othmar shaking his head.

'All right then. It's decided. We'll all go.' Holding up a hand to ward off Jochen's remonstrations. 'Your neighbour is only looking after his own.'

Jochen sucking air in over his set-on-edge teeth, placated by Othmar's arm upon his own.

The trio setting off, Jochen and Othmar either side of the trap, ropes in hand, keeping the billy straight. Jansen taking up the rear, keeping up a stream of invective.

'It always go like this, folk taking advantage. Folk who thinks themselves better, which is a joke and a half. Folk who've been digging sand up all bloody week. Don't know what gives them the right to think they can do a man like me out of what's rightfully owed him. But not today, sirs. Oh no, not today. Today Jansen's going to get what's coming to him, that's a fact…'

Jochen and Othmar dearly wishing they could give to Jansen what he had coming and, half an hour in, wishing they had another trap, another set of ropes. Billy not so aggravating as their unanticipated companion. Billy performing remarkably well, settling into step, pulling onwards. Letting out a blood curdling scream on occasion, for which they could not blame him. Might have done the same themselves, had not Jansen eventually quietened once they'd left Borre.

Jansen regretting his rash course of action.

I should go back.

Had never been off the island in all his years.

What, and let bloody Jochen Steggle take the upper hand?

Might well have turned tail had not Jochen bloody Steggle been directly in front of him, marching on with purpose beside his new best mate.

Should at least have brought a few flagons of the home-made.

Unwilling to admit how queasy he was to be so far from home. Started at every shadow, jumped at every creak of the refurbished harness keeping the billy within its bounds. Felt an odd kinship with it, both as obstinate and obdurate as each other, which gave him comfort.

If he can do it, then so will I.

And so they did. Only two days of travelling and they were done.

Billy given into the care of an ostler on the edge of town. Jansen lingering, not wanting to be parted. Horrified by how many people were abroad, pushing and shoving at every turn. Himself pushed on by Jochen and Othmar who were excited, exhilarated, as they approached the theatre in the heart of town, arriving in the nick of time.

'They're on tonight! Any minute now!' Jochen declared. 'I've got to get tickets, tell them we're here.'

Jochen and Othmar surging up the steps leaving Jansen adrift and panicked, shoved to one side by the gay crowds following on their heels. Jansen leaning against the corner of the theatre, tears leaking from his eyes, as he heard the show inside begin.

'Welcome, Ladies and Gentlemen! We're here to tell you tales!'

Dying Child ensuing, which Jansen found oddly soothing. Something of home. Streets deserted, a few light-men setting their brands to the oil lamps. A yawning theatre-hand gathering in the billboards displaying the Pfiffmakler wares.

A man Jansen didn't notice taking the steps into the theatre a moment before the Dying Child was embraced by his angels and the Pfiffmaklers moved up a notch.

Shipwrecks! And a real live mystery, Ladies and Gentlemen.

§

Marko is threaded by a tutting usher to an empty seat. Marko settling, having no idea what is about to come.

Performance already begun, backdrops heaved into place.

Broad sweeps of colour, dark black hue of night. Flashes of white as the captain hollers into the wind, orders down sails and anchor, the passengers to their berths. Soft singing of shanties as his men go about their work, defiant in the face of the storm that has not yet done its worst.

Othmar shivering as the birches long-johned in ice had in his letter to Grettir Wyssling.

Swirling curlicues of surf and brine, bright splashes of lightning, deep undercurrent of waves climbing like cliffs made of running wolves. Pinpricks of luminescence from stars, moon and lighthouses… deep rumbles of thunder thrumming through the audience's bones, making them feel they are out there on that ship, in that storm.

Othmar's stomach lurching.

Marko stirring, hand going to his talisman.

Christian Schumacher, for he is there, glancing at his time-piece, wondering how long until all is over. Sighing because the star-crossed lover shit he too hates is still to come. A tragedy by

Adam Gottlob Oehlenschläger, author of Denmark's recently adopted National Anthem, given the Grand Cross of the Order of the Dannebroge by the King himself. Because of which, when the performance moves on to the *Dannebroge*, people start to murmur.

Cannons roaring, fire creeping up the deck once the *Dannebroge* is hit, soon to catch its store of gunpowder, as everyone knows. Shudders in the audience as Mergim explicates.

Our first ship wrecked by a saboteur, sinking an archaeological expedition which ended in the Field of Blackbirds.

The Battle of Kosovo with its heroes and betrayers.

The legend of Holger the Dane, as retold by your very own Hans Christian Andersen. Bring to mind his woodworker's workshop...

Othmar holding his breath as the play continues apace.

Marko starting to sweat.

Christian Schumacher scratching his beard, not grasping the implications of what he is being told.

The rest of the audience on a knife edge, as they had been in Gedser, knowing of the sinking of the *Put Preko Mora,* the self-sacrifice of the *Dannebroge,* of Hvitfeldt and Eleanora.

Three narratives seamlessly sewn together by Pfiffmakler machinations.

Grand finale waiting in the wings.

Mergim not disappointing.

Your Hans Andersen advises us to cut a road to the stars, not by the sword but by words...

Next come Holger and Eleanora...

The woodworker whispering in his grandson's ear...

Oehlenschläger's National Anthem. No joining in this time, Diderik and Longhella allowed to sing it by themselves.

There is a lovely land...

All carrying on as had been rehearsed on Gedser.

Mergim lastly calling out to his audience, begging them to right a wrong.

And you, people of Odense, must open your eyes and arise as Holger and Eleanora will surely do in time of need! All who remember the wrecking of the Put Preko Mora *thirteen years ago. For know this: all was not as it seemed. The man branded a saboteur was not the sole survivor!*

Othmar's head buzzing, as were his nearest neighbours who recalled the scandal of the *Put Preko Mora*. The shame it had laid at their doors.

Marko gripping the arms of his seat as he had gripped the rope tethering him to his barrel. Heart hammering. Couldn't comprehend how or why the Pfiffmaklers were doing this.

Christian Schumacher puckering his brows, trying to contain his rage. These people publicly accusing him, if not naming him, right at the moment he'd been reaccepted into the Society in Copenhagen.

Pfiffmaklers not done.

Jochen having managed to speak to them immediately before the performance, listing what they'd found in the sand.

Mergim standing tall, calling out into the auditorium.

So who was that other who stole onto the shores of Nyord Bay? And who the most likely saboteur?

Shouts coming up from the audience, as they had in Gedser.

A gambit long discussed by the Pfiffmaklers before this final performance.

'They'll drum us out of town,' was Longhella's opinion. 'But what the hell. We've been paid. Might as well go out with a bang.'

'We're doing a righteous thing,' was Hulde's take.

'Mr Schumacher's going to roast us alive,' Ortwin added, glumly.

Heraldo steering them into calmer waters.

'It could be our making here in Denmark. No one is going to remember an insignificant travelling fair, but this is something else entirely.'

And something else it was. Othmar and Jochen turning up out of the blue bolstering their bold decision.

And the man so wrongly accused, Mergim booms, accompanied by Heraldo's thunder-box, *is right here in this audience this very night! Please, Professor. Join us on stage.*

Othmar suddenly grabbed by the elbow, Lupercal leaning down, whispering in his ear.

'Come on, sir. Just do as Mergim directs.'

Othmar getting stood on wobbly legs, allowing Lupercal to lead him on.

Othmar steered through the seats, accompanied by a repeated chant from Longhella and Hulde:

Make way, make way, we are here to right a wrong this day.

The aisle a glittering cascade of emerald flashes as Jericho scampers on before them, he and his brother helping Othmar up the steps and onto the stage.

'Here he is!' Mergim throws out his arms in welcome. 'Our Expedition Leader, Mr Professor Othmar Voort!'

Jochen getting to his feet, clapping loudly. Others following suit, whooping, caught up in the moment. Othmar, completely at sea, as he had been before, wondering what would become of him. Othmar gazing out into the crowds, fingers going to his collar, eyes flitting back and forth, glimpsing faces here, others there.

Another roll of thunder, a flash of lightening, the crowd quieting. Jochen and the others sitting back down in their seats, agog, wondering what would come next, which was Mergim catching hold of Othmar's shoulders, pushing him forward.

'Thirteen years this man has suffered,' Mergim tells his audience, his voice seemingly soft and sonorous yet fills the anticipatory silence the auditorium has fallen into. 'Thirteen years of being shamed and accused. Thirteen years, Ladies and Gentlemen, since this man was supposed, singlehandedly, to have spirited away fifty-one crates of archaeological finds from one of the busiest ports in the world, from Trieste, over the course of a single night.'

Mergim shakes his head.

'How is that possible?'

Murmuration sweeping through the crowds as they realise it wasn't.

'And how,' Mergim hammers home the nail, 'could it be, despite the verdict of the Accident Investigator, that thirteen years after the shipwreck, after all those crates had supposedly been taken directly from Trieste to Prussia, that nineteen separate artefacts—Nineteen! All documented from that very same expedition!—have recently been dug up from the sands of Nyord Bay, where the *Put Preko Mora* laid down its bones?'

Jochen's quick briefing swiftly changing the end scenario.

'Who then, is our saboteur? This man, this Professor, who has given his life to the study of archaeology, or that other shadowy survivor who crept away from Nyord Bay? Answer me that!'

Uproar in the audience. Outrage. The logic so obvious none could fault it. Men once again getting to their feet, women tangling in their skirts as they attempt to do the same.

Christian Schumacher, fearing recognition as that same investigator, trying to remove himself, tripping over his nearest neighbours in his attempt.

Pfiffmaklers about to send out their last lines concerning justice, Eleanora and Holger, of the Danish spirit, the heroism of the *Dannebroge,* sent off swerve by Othmar Voort who has singled out a face from his stance, his glance, from the stage.

Those you should not touch.

'It was you!' Othmar Voort accused, pointing a finger. Couldn't fathom how the man could be here, in this theatre in Odense, but would swear on his life it was so.

Christian Schumacher unfortunate to be in the line of that pointing finger, already stumbling, marking himself out. Odense not large, people knowing others of their rank, particularly those who regularly attended the theatre.

'It's Schumacher!' the shout went up. 'He was the investigator. I remember it! And he's trying to get away!'

Pfiffmaklers, discombobulated by the turn of events, gathering centre stage.

'Not him,' Othmar whispered. 'Not Schumacher. I mean *him.*'

Hulde following the pointing finger, picking out a whey-faced man in his early thirties hemmed in on either side by enthusiastic young men kicking back their seats. Theatre never so exciting as this. A riot in the making. Hulde recognising the unnamed worker Othmar had sketched from the Field of Blackbirds.

'There!' Othmar exclaimed.

'Four rows in,' Hulde added, 'two seats from the right-hand aisle.'

Heraldo taking his place by Hulde's side.

'But that's Marko,' he remonstrated. 'The man I brought back with me from St Vid.'

Longhella coming up beside them, elbowing her way between them.

'God's sake,' she said. 'What the hell is going on?'

'Othmar recognises that man in the audience,' Hulde explained. 'The one who most likely sunk the ship.'

'It's Marko,' Heraldo repeated. 'How can that be?'

Longhella pushing herself forward.

'Who cares? Let's get to him before he...'

'He's getting away!' Othmar yelled, Marko having shot to his feet as if a hot iron had been put to his soles. Began struggling against the throng of men who were surrounding Christian Schumacher, pinioning the investigator's arms behind his back.

'We've got him!' they called with enthusiastic merriment. 'Come on, lads.'

Dragging Schumacher with them, bundling him up the steps onto the stage.

Jochen uncertain behind them, seeing Longhella dodging the newcomers, dragging Heraldo with her, taking a leap off the boards in a bright flurry of orange skirts, landing with the elegance of a cat. Heraldo not so graceful, rolling off his feet. Jochen quickly to him, steadying him.

'That man,' Heraldo said, getting his breath. 'We've to stop him.'

Jochen pulling Heraldo on, Longhella already on the trail, high-tailing it up the aisle, Marko several yards ahead. Marko panting, gripping so hard at his talisman it came away in his hand. St Vid still guiding his way. No one between himself and the exit. Every-one surging forward to the new unscripted drama happening all around them, eyes concentrated on the young men of Odense and their captive now spot-lit on the stage.

Marko swerving, pushing away the curtain hiding the door, getting through. Getting away. Running past the ticket man who was blinking sleepily, blurry thoughts in his head that something had occurred, although no idea what.

Marko taking the steps outside two by two, no notion where he was going, what he was going to do. Longhella fast behind him, at the top of the steps as he gained the base. Seeing the fleeing man turn his face indecisively left and right. Seeing too what Hulde had. Same profile as in Othmar's drawings. Swift admiration for Othmar's accuracy, then Longhella was bounding down the steps behind him.

'Hie!' she shouted. 'Stop!'

Marko making a random choice, turning to the right where dark alleys snaked away at every turn from the main thoroughfare. Spools of light from the oil lamps. Shadows deep and dark between them. Had to be a chance.

St Vid, guide me. Lead me on my right path.

Right path brought to a sudden end by a leg thrust quickly across his path, left cheek hitting the cobbles with a crack, air going from his lungs, thin shadow materialising above him, bright flash of orange in the corner of Marko's eye as Longhella bore down upon him. Heavy weight on his back as she sat and straddled him. Body relaxing. No point fighting. Wrists grabbed. Sounds of running feet, of heavy breathing, as several others appeared on scene. Marko surveying with his one open eye the boots surrounding him on all sides. Volley of words heard, if hardly understood. Head pounding.

'Oh well done, Longhella.'

Quick light voice refuting the congratulation.

'It wasn't me. It was Jansen here.'

Vague recognition of the lilt in that voice. The singing. *In Freya's hall…*

Lines from his uncle's Saga coming to mind.

The gods I'll not blaspheme, but Freya a bitch I'll deem.

The bitch incarnate sitting upon his back.

Always had life been this way. Christians against heathens, Ottomans against Serbs, St Vid against the rest of the world. Always struggles. Always fights. Lines drawn, lines crossed. This his Field of Blackbirds. His battle done. Marko letting go. Fingers loosening.

Hulde plucking the talisman from his open palm.

'This was in Othmar's drawings.'

'More proof, if we needed it,' Longhella summarised. Jansen handing her a length of filthy string from his filthy pocket in case it was needed.

Othmar arriving as Hulde read out loud the words on Marko's trinket.

'Pax Tibi Sanctus Vitus, Semitam Meam Subibant.'

Othmar, by reflex, reciting his notes .

Peace to you, Saint Vitus, my path and my way forward.

'Didn't get this little specimen very far,' Longhella commented tartly.

Heraldo, bad fingers tingling, did not agree.

'Got him all the way here. I don't understand any of this.'

Heraldo not alone. Pfiffmaklers used to the extraordinary, if nothing like this. Mergim speaking up. Mathematician to the fore.

'Rain falls, or it does not. The totality is out of our control.'

Longhella clicking her tongue.

'We don't need your spouty nonsense, Mr No-Longer-Father-of-the-Fair. What's needed is explanation. Does anyone know what the beggaration is going on?'

Wise words cutting their way to the stars. Or to the ears of the small corps of men charged with enforcing the law in Odense, soon arriving at the theatre on high alert expecting the place to be going up in flames, or a small riot at the very least. It had happened before. Plays having a way of igniting passions. Hadn't anticipated one of the eminent men of town being hustled down the steps of the theatre by a gang of belligerent young men all talking over one another. Nor the secondary plot of Pfiffmaklers surrounding a prostrate man, apparently having taken him captive. Nor the embarrassingly coarse curses pouring from Christian Schumacher's lips as he tried to shake himself free.

All above their pay-grade.

It might be almost ten o'clock at night but they were damned if they were going to sort it by themselves. Off to the courthouse with the lot of them, magistrate's door pounded upon until he opened up, dressed rather comically in night-gown and slippers. Odense's entertaining nightlife not for him, preferring to spend his evenings listening to handsome young law students reading to him the works of Homer as he sat in his comfortable chair by the fire, glass of good Flemish wine in his hand.

Courthouse filled to the brim, as had been his erstwhile glass, as he tried to get to grips with all the garbling. Homer so much simpler. Heroes' adventures guided by the convenient intervention of various gods to help the plot along. No gods present to aid him, sift through all that was being shouted at him by one party or another. Pfiffmaklers this, Pfiffmaklers that, shipwrecks and saboteurs. Christian Schumacher apparently at the heart of it. A weaselly man he'd never liked. And someone called Othmar Voort, whose name he vaguely remembered, if not the context of his hearing it. All a bit of a blur, if he was honest. Perhaps a little too much good Flemish wine.

Magistrate calling time, announcing his decision like any decent Homeric god might have done.

'Put the accused into the prison cells. Everyone else go home. We'll reconvene in the morning. Eleven sharp.'

Giving him time for a decent sleep, a long well-deserved breakfast.

Far too late to be dealing with the likes of this, to be standing at his lectern in the court room in night-shirt and slippers.

In night-shirt and slippers, for heaven's sake! What was the world coming to?

41
Rivers Rolling On

The river rolled on.

Kingfishers slept in their bone-lined burrows, cranes in their rickety-rackety nests ratcheted onto chimneys and gables, coots and moorhens secure on their rafts. Magistrate in his bed. Soft white shapes amongst the reeds: swans in moonlight, heads tucked beneath warm wings.

Pfiffmaklers picking over the events of the evening as they ate late plates of shredded duck, garlic-and-pepper pancakes. Jochen, Jansen, and Othmar with them. The latter the talk of the town, young men leaving the courthouse blood-high, recongregating in taverns and coffee houses to hash out all they'd taken part in. Biggest news in Odense for a long while, and would remain so for several months. Christian Schumacher soon to be publicly humiliated. Thrown out of the Society. Disowned. No pretty pension for him.

Pfiffmaklers weaving together the two ends of the story, one side from Denmark, the other from Heraldo and St Vid's. Pfiffmaklers enlightening their guests about the relevance of Svetovid, Rügen Island, the reason for Heraldo's journey. Heraldo telling them of his fortuitous meeting with Grettir Wyssling because of his Wind Museum, and of Irmgaard Prögen, Yanni and Marko. Othmar swallowing at the mention of Irmgaard, covering his excitement by telling them of his own coincidental association with Grettir; Mergim, seeing the animation in Othmar Voort, bringing up the mathematician again, taking out his thesis, handing it to Othmar. Othmar reading the title page:

Statistical Analyses of the Demographic Data of the Shifting of Ideologies through Geographic Spaces and Cultures, by Zoran Ralić. Same Serbian professor, whose name he couldn't previously recall, who'd produced *Coincidence as a Concept.*

And *Coincidence as a Concept* so blindingly relevant right here, right now, Othmar found the words blurring, eyes filling with tears.

For here, in the manuscript Prisoner 1397 had entrusted to Heraldo, were all the mathematical proofs needed to endorse his own thesis of the transmigration of civilisations from north to east and south which, unlike 1397, he had never written. Had given up on following his disgrace.

Such a waste. One Othmar would not tolerate. Would get his theories down on paper the moment he got home, include references to the work of Zoran Ralić, get the two papers published side by side. Would write to 1397, confer with him, collaborate, and together they would prove each other's work beyond reasonable doubt. Prisoner and ex-disgraced ex-saboteur. What a team they would make! A literary sensation. Too enrapt in this yet-to-come future to hear the finer points of the tale the Pfiffmaklers were still mulling over.

'You can talk to me all you want about statistics and coincidences,' Longhella as usual slicing through the guff. 'I get the stuff about Kosovo, the Field of Blackbirds, the expedition, the local workers. Blah, blah, blah. But why in heaven would this Marko leave his life and son, come all the way here with Heraldo?'

A puzzle and a half. Pfiffmaklers stumped, calling it a night. Tent accommodation reorganised to provide room for their guests.

Othmar, spark out from the wondrous events of the evening, dreaming of the glories that would come, the letter he would write to Irmgaard.

Jochen turning on his side, thinking how odd life could be. How like his phantoms. Peel away one part of a body, or a life, and there's always another layer beneath.

Jansen quiet the whole evening, too disturbed by being away from home, being hemmed about by strangers, having to huddle up with Jochen and Othmar who grunted, snored and wheezed. Jansen creeping out of his tent two restless hours in. Going down to the river, towards the white glimpses of swans in the reeds. Alarmed to see someone there already, knees hunched up beneath her skirts, unclad toes burrowing into the soft mud of the bank. Longhella turning, patting the grass beside her. Jansen, obeying the unspoken command, sitting down uncomfortably. Longhella opening with a statement, and a question.

'You, Jansen, are your own man. But you do know you're a bit of a shit?'

Jansen's mouth drying.

Longhella sighing. Letting up. Refreshing for someone other than Mergim or Hulde to find her.

'What pushes you on each day?' she asked. 'What makes you so angry with life you can't help but be angry with everyone else?'

Jansen flinching, thinking on Jochen's billy who was hopefully bucking at every kindness given him by the ostler as he'd always done back home. Jansen having a bit of a revelation. Back home the only place he ever wanted to be. Bitter to the bone, as was the bucking billy, through no fault of his own. Built that way. Looking up into the star-strewn night, horribly aware of the small swathe of orange skirts an arm-stretch from his knee.

'I like being alone, is all.' Soft words, deep convictions. 'Never needed company. Never wanted it.'

A sentiment never previously formulated. Longhella breathing deeply beside him.

'You're a real running wolf then. On your own, away from the pack.' Stretching her neck, white as the swans. 'Something rather admirable in that,' she added, giving a short nod in his direction. 'Honest, even.'

Admirable and honest. Two qualities never associated with Jansen. Jochen would have laughed so hard he'd have knocked his head off his shoulders.

'I saw her, my sister,' Longhella added quietly, 'back in Nyord, when the Running Wolf came down. Saw her clear as I see you now.'

Which couldn't have been that clear, Jansen thought but did not say, given how dark it was. Only the flickers of the dimming fire, glinting reflections on the back of the river. Jansen not sure who Longhella's sister was, not really keeping up with the conversation back in the camp. All those twists and turns. A jumbled mumble of words about events having nothing to do with him.

'Why do you think that is?' Longhella asked, perhaps not specifically of him, although he felt compelled to answer.

'Fog like that makes folk see things that ain't really there,' he offered blandly, wishing he had the strength to stand and walk away. Cold dew creeping through his trousers. Chapped buttock-crack in the offing because of it. Jansen starting as a shadow loomed over them out of nowhere.

Mergim, large and imposing, speaking soft words. His voice so different to how it had been on stage Jansen couldn't reconcile it. Made his skin crawl, how these Pfiffmaklers could be first one thing and next another. Jansen might be bitter and angry, a man who would cut his nose off to spite his face, or cut his face off to spite his nose , but at least he was consistent.

Levering himself up.

'Gotta get back to me tent,' he said. 'Get started for home in the morning.'

Couldn't come quick enough for him.

Catching the brief exchange between Mergim and Longhella.

'Come on, my dear. You know she's not out here. And now Heraldo's back…'

Soft rustling of skirts. Mergim helping Longhella to her feet.

'But I did see her, Mergim, in the Running Wolf. I really did.'

Jansen believing her.

Running Wolf always playing tricks, as he'd told her.

Jansen seeing waterlilies that same night, drifting on the waves of mist as they'd rolled in. The faces of men and boys he'd never previously thought of as real people, merely a story he'd told over and over to anyone who would listen. Spooked him rotten. And would spook him rotten over the years because ever after, every time the Running Wolf crept over the sands of Nyord Bay, he would glimpse in the corner of his eye not only those faces but a conjuring of Longhella's missing sister. Always ghostly, ethereal, there all the same.

Orange skirts, twisted braids of chestnut hair.

Neck stretched and white as a swan's.

Jansen never telling anyone about it.

Jansen branded honest and admirable by Longhella, which characteristics he silently gloried in every day.

A real running wolf.

Best thing anyone had ever said of him.

42

And Now, The Ending

The solution to the puzzle of Marko's travelling revealed the following morning when the Pfiffmaklers arrived at the courthouse at the appointed hour. Magistrate in appropriate regalia, slippers tucked under his bed, nightgown beneath his pillow. Magistrate calling for silence as the townsfolk of Odense crowded in. Courthouse another theatre as far as they were concerned, this particular performance promising heartbreak and tragedy far more meaningful than any tale of star-crossed lovers, shit or otherwise.

Magistrate startled when he'd arrived to learn a full confession had been made, Marko having spent the night in his cell with paper and ink at his request. Unable to sleep for many reasons, including Christian Schumacher's incessant blubbing punctuated by protestations of his innocence. How he needed to be set free immediately.

Christian Schumacher to be dealt with later.

Marko the main event. Magistrate reading out Marko's stark account of how and why he'd sunk the *Put Preko Mora,* how he'd planned and executed his escape. Magistrate reaching the end of Marko's summation, reading the lines as well as any actor upon the stage, replacing some of the cruder phrasing—Marko's Danish poor, smatterings from the dig and later from Gregor and Irmgaard - with lawyer-speak more appropriate.

I cannot undo anything I have done. I believed, back then, I was performing a service to my country, preserving our very precious history. I confess I never considered the ramifications caused by my actions, nor the very many lives I caused to be lost, nor the families thereby diminished, the individuals who have suffered because of them.

No mention of the friend who'd helped him. Never giving Gregor Simiĉ up.

Shockwaves rippling through the audience during this recitation, more so when the Magistrate reached the latter part of Marko's confession, slipping an unexpected frisson into the plot. Marko giving an abbreviated version of how he had also murdered one Grettir Wyssling, fearing imminent discovery as the perpetrator of the shipwreck. Running board and blood. Snow and silence. Another plan of escape, this time improvised. No mention of Yanni's hand in any of it.

A horrible shock for Othmar Voort to learn so brutally why he'd not heard from his friend.

A sigh of understanding from Heraldo and the Pfiffmaklers.

'I see no reason to dissemble. This confession has been fully and freely given, confirmed by the guilty party who freely and fully gave it.'

Quick glance at Marko in the dock, who stood with head lowered. Was not about to dispute it, thank God. Magistrate able to go on. Straightening his back, which had been rather sore the past few weeks so took a bit of an effort. But needs must. This was going to be one of the most important cases he was ever going to oversee.

'Therefore, barring any other diversions, and following up several small details to confirm the prisoner's guilt, and time to contact the families of the deceased, sentence will be given four weeks hence.'

No one doubting what that sentence would be.

You couldn't go around murdering a ship-load of men and another with a running-board and expect to get away other than by having your neck hauled high in a noose.

Yet another performance the folk of Odense could look forward to.

Not so the Pfiffmaklers, who'd seen their fair share of justice served.

Moved on before they could witness another.

Heraldo, the only Pfiffmakler to have known Marko, visiting him the day before they left Odense. Marko pushing back to Heraldo *The History of Rügen Island.*

'Do you want me to pass a letter on to Yanni?'

Marko shaking his head. Had thought about this long and hard.

'I don't want him to know. Better for him to think I've gone on to another life.'

Heraldo frowning.

'He'll likely find out. The Magistrate will be obliged to write to the authorities in Kragujevac, inform them of the provenance of their new exhibits.'

Marko hadn't thought of this, several scenarios rushing through his head.

They'll not advertise it. It might reflect badly on them.

Of course they'll advertise it. Such a story would draw in audiences from across the region.

God, they might even seek Yanni out. I've got to warn him. What if he has a fit of conscience and tells them the truth? They might charge him with being an accomplice.

'It's also probable,' Heraldo added, 'that the Society underwriting the expedition costs will demand the return of all those artefacts.'

Could be a diplomatic bloodbath, was his opinion when Othmar told him this.

And that they really were going to send divers into Nyord Bay, see what was salvageable.

Not to mention the insurance. Christian Schumacher's investigation concluding the cargo holds had been empty when the *Put Preko Mora* sank, meaning payment to the ship's owner had been minimal. Not so now.

Political inferences too. Denmark still at loggerheads with Prussia. And now the saboteur scenario of Othmar favouring Prussia over Denmark had been blown out of the water it was only going to get worse. Ramifications about to roll over the land like a Running Wolf, teeth bared, claws out, fur bristling.

All because an insignificant casual labourer on a dig had called a halt.

Blackbirds rising from their field flying far and wide.

Marko feeling their dark wings gathering over him, extinguishing any remaining light.

Agreeing Heraldo should tell Yanni all, and how much his father loved him and, most importantly, to say nothing about Yanni's involvement in the aftermath of Grettir's death. Yanni not to be besmirched.

A lot of weeping about to ensue.

From Marko, because had not Grettir been at St Vid to save him Marko would not have been alive to end Grettir's Wyssling's life.

From the families of the lost, once informed of what had really happened to the *Put Preko Mora*.

From Prisoner 1397, when he got his letter from Othmar Voort advocating collaboration, promising publication of the thesis Professor Zoran Ralić had believed would never see the light of day.

No weeping for Othmar Voort. Blackbirds singing sweetly in his heart as he penned his letter to his lost love, whose snippet of hair might one day be recovered from the sands of Nyord Bay.

§

To my Irmgaard, my one and only love.

It's been so long and so much has happened. I know Heraldo has written and explained everything. It has taken me a while to pluck up the courage to write to you. To tell you I have always loved you, and always will. It was my calling set us apart, and for that I can only blame myself. But since you are now widowed and my name cleared, I write to you as the same man you knew so very many years ago. I ask simply, my darling, for your hand. I can give you a good life here in Denmark, take you away from the foreign land you were exported to through no fault of your own. We can be happy, my darling. We deserve to be, after all we've been through. I enclose a most treasured find, the one that from my expedition I most regretted losing, in the hope our way forward will be together.

With all my love,

Your Othmar.

No blackbirds singing sweetly in Irmgaard's ears as she read those words, neither any weeping.

The foreign land she'd been exported to through no fault of her own...

Since you're now widowed and my own name cleared...

We deserve to be happy after all we've been through...

What an absolute arse. And such arrogance!

She scrumpled the letter up, threw it into the nearest bin.

The talisman she kept. A good addition to the new chapel of St Vid she, Yanni, and the villagers, with the money from the contest, were rebuilding. A chapel museum, which would become a very fine attraction within a very short space of time, teaching its visitors the history of St Vid and its origins. Of Svetovid, of Rügen Island, of the Pfiffmaklers' connections to both.

Not shied away from was Marko and the shipwreck, whose tale was also told as both testament and warning of Serbia's history, of all the ties that bound it to its unfolding future. Included too was the very present danger and lived experiences of the Black Bora that had almost destroyed the chapel and those in it, which section of the exhibits included all the models retrieved from Grettir's Wind Museum alongside Heraldo's written recitation of the legend of the Bora as told to him by Grettir himself.

St Vid become a memorial, a must-go-to place for the Grand Young Men who travelled across Europe in the latter half of the 1800s.

A Grand Opening highlighted by the opera singer who returned to the village many times, became a great friend to Irmgaard Prögen. Opera singer singing, on the opening night, the national anthem of Serbia, Running Wolves unintentionally in the mix.

What is the fog hiding? I can hear our people's awful screams.

Who is it who prays for death? The free or the downtrodden?

Flow fast, oh river Sava, flow quick and fast,
And Danube, never lose the power of your voice...
Our fallen heroes have been put into their graves and still we will
love our homeland
While we have hearts that beat.

§

Hearts beating in Odense, as the crowds were readying themselves to witness the execution of the mass-murderer Marko Poplovič.

Hearts beating, several months later, the night St Vid's doors were opened.

Hearts beating too in the Pfiffmakler encampment about the same time.

Longhella swearing and cursing, belly full, waters broken.

'Get this little shit out of me!'

Little shit duly brought out, screaming like her mother, eight and a half hours later by Hulde, designated midwife.

Longhella swearing and cursing the whole night through.

Longhella exhausted, yet finding strength enough to swat Diderik across the face.

'We're not doing this again, not ever.'

Not even Longhella able to change the future. Longhella the survivor of three more pregnancies, providing four healthy additions to the Pfiffmakler clan. Pfiffmaklers continuing to traverse boundary lines, islands and countries several times over. And once, a decade after leaving Denmark, returning to Serbia, to the village below Suvid Mountain.

Pfiffmaklers fêted and feasted.

Heraldo whisked away, taken to Marko's old cottage where lived Yanni and his wife—the ladybird girl in her blue dress, grown now, confident and freckle-faced—and their three young children. Irmgaard with them, proxy parent to Yanni after Marko disappeared from his life.

'Oh, it's so good to see you!' Irmgaard exclaimed, taking Heraldo by both hands, leading him in. 'Fingers healed well, by all accounts. Your music as beautiful as always.'

The two sitting side by side, warming their toes by the stove. Yanni and his family discreetly giving them space, pretending to be bustling about preparing food and beds, children elbowing each other as they fought for space to put their ears to the door. Irmgaard, perspicacious as ever, calling out to their would-be eavesdroppers.

'I know you're there, my little darlings. But this is a private conversation. Go see to the dogs, or get yourselves trampled beneath your parents' feet, or go outside to meet the other Pfiffmaklers.'

Heraldo smiling warmly.

'You haven't changed, nor should you.'

Irmgaard patting his hand.

'I might be a little long in the tooth, but I still have bite. So tell me, my dear, what has been going on these past few years?'

A decade hardly a few years, although it had gone swiftly enough for both. Heraldo outlining his own trials and triumphs, Irmgaard doing the same. Best part being how happy they'd both become.

'It's been a real joy,' Irmgaard told him, 'building up the chapel, making it all it has become.'

'You've done well,' Heraldo praised. 'We hear about it all over Europe. People wanting to come here in droves.'

Irmgaard nodding.

'They do. And we couldn't have done any of it without you.'

Heraldo blushing in the dim light of the room.

'No need to be coy,' Irmgaard chided. 'You told me once you felt you'd been sent here. I admit that at the time I thought it nonsense. Yet now, looking back. Well. It seems I may have been wrong.'

The two of them quiet for as they contemplated this admission.

Heraldo, since his meeting with Mergim's mathematician, having come to the opposite conclusion. That 1397, Professor Zoran Ralić, had been right to posit his theory of *Coincidence as a Con-*

cept. Heraldo's experience of life seeming to be exactly that. If this, if that. One road taken, another not. For who knew which fork in the road would lead you to where.

One fork in the road taken the following morning, branching off the main track to Kragujevac leading them away from the village and up the mountain. Pfiffmaklers ceremoniously poured into sleds from Yanni's sheds, dogs slotted into harnesses. Villagers hie-ing up the animals, procession starting up the slopes, over the snow, path flattened and waymarked to ease their passage. And up they went, around boulders and curves, up and up and up. Heraldo seeing the copse of trees, the topmost edges of the chapel as they rounded the last bend.

'Oh my,' Heraldo whispered, the rebuild of St Vid so much better than he had imagined.

'Come,' said Irmgaard, linking her arm through his. 'I've things to show you.'

A tremendous fandangle coming from behind them as one of the sleds overturned, youngest Pfiffmaklers spilled out into the snow.

'Your work?' Heraldo asked, giving Irmgaard's arm a squeeze, knowing how unlikely such an occurrence was given his previous experiences here on this very mountain. Suspecting conspiracy.

'All mine,' Irmgaard agreed. 'This is for you and me alone.'

The two going into the chapel. Irmgaard pointing out Ortwin's grandfather's history of Rügen on a lectern, alongside a narration of the Pfiffmaklers' involvement there and the further accounts of Othmar's expedition, the shipwreck, the chapel's connection to both. And to the reconstructed totem of Svetovid; the large panels displaying an illustrated version of Grettir's mythology of the Bora; Grettir's artefacts and dioramas.

Heraldo lingering over each and all.

'You've done us proud,' Heraldo congratulated. 'You've made this place something…really special.'

Irmgaard steering him on.

'There's these last,' she said. 'I hope you'll approve.'

Taking him to the first of two memorial plaques she and Yanni had integrated into the chapel walls.

'For Grettir Wyssling,' Heraldo read. 'Founder of the Wind Museum, who did so much to ensure this chapel stayed alive.'

Having to wipe his eyes.

'That's a great credit to him,' he got out. 'He'd be pleased.'

Off to the second plaque. Irmgaard nervous.

'We can change it.' Speaking quickly. 'We didn't know exactly...'

Heraldo putting his fingers to the plaque, running their tips over the words as he had them read.

For Ludmilla Pfiffmakler, beloved and lost. This her legacy, for without her the resurrection of our chapel would never have happened. And for Heraldo, her husband, who brought us all home.

'I didn't bring Marko home,' Heraldo murmured.

Irmgaard tutted.

'For which we thank you, after what he did.'

Her heart still smarting over that egregious injustice. Had imagined spending pleasant evenings with Grettir, chatting over a modest meal, talking about the latest news, his models, how the rebuild of St Vid was going. He'd never have replaced Gregor, but was ten times the man Othmar blasted Voort would ever be.

'Happy with it?' Irmgaard asked. Heraldo nodding.

And happy too were the mob of Pfiffmakler children bursting into the chapel, followed by a merry scrum of villagers brushing snow off boots and gloves. *Ten minutes,* Irmgaard had dictated. *More if you can manage it.* Which they had.

'Try not to break anything!' came Longhella's strident call. 'Or if you do, make sure you scoop up all the pieces so your father can put them back together in his own kack-handed way.'

Kack-handed father putting an arm around his wife's waist, calling out.

'A compliment from your mother, children. Which means celebrations and cakes!'

'You're such an idiot,' Longhella said, pushing away his hand, snatching it back into her own a moment later.

Hulde coming on behind, making straight for Heraldo and Irmgaard, eyes going to the plaque, skimming the words. Brimming up, tears falling.

'That's beautiful and apt, Irmgaard. Thank you.'

Planting a kiss on Irmgaard's cheek.

'It was our pleasure. And I'm glad you're here, my dear. There's something else I want to show you both, when we get back to the village.'

§

The three of them, later that night, gathered about Irmgaard's table.

Irmgaard placing a well-worn book on the cloth between them.

The copy of Marko's uncle's North Atlantic Sagas.

Heraldo leaning forward.

'I've heard of them, when we were in Denmark. The Vikings sailing off to discover Iceland and Greenland.'

He flicked through the pages, saw sentences underlined, extensive notes in the margins.

'Lots of shipwrecks in here, I'd wager.'

Irmgaard smiling, Heraldo going straight to the heart of the matter.

'A great many,' she agreed. 'Lots of feuding, bloodshed, feats of survival against the odds. But there's something more. Go to the bookmark.'

Heraldo obeying, Hulde speaking for them both.

'The Story of Einar Sokkason.'

'One of the lesser known sagas,' Irmgaard informed, 'according to the person who compiled this book. What happens is a band of Greenland Vikings, led by a man named Sigurd, are exploring the hunting and fishing opportunities near where they have settled. They come across a large merchant's vessel cracked in the ice, bottom badly broken. Near it there's a great hall of the type the Vikings liked to build and, as they approach, they see an axe lodged in a block of wood. Next to it a corpse. They suspect he was chopping wood when he was murdered by marauders. Suspicion confirmed when they find another corpse beside another abandoned axe. *Servants,* they deduce, *for the merchants in the hall.* Deducing too that the merchants in the hall must be dead too, so they swing open the doors and retreat, let the stench of the dead be cleansed by fresh air before they enter.'

'Sensible,' Heraldo commented.

'Indeed,' Irmgaard agreed. 'They go in the following morning. Find the merchants expired as expected, and find also the very valuable cargo of artefacts and coins they had been transporting.'

'Artefacts and coins,' Hulde echoed, no notion where Irmgaard was leading them.

'They're good Christian converts, Sigurd and his men,' Irmgaard adds, 'so they boil the flesh off the corpses, gather up their bones...'

'Jochen would approve,' Hulde says, smiling at Heraldo.

'It makes me feel a little queasy,' Heraldo answers.

'But practical,' Irmgaard carries on her tale. 'Because now they can give them proper burial. Take the artefacts and coins, donating most to the Bishop at Gardar to be used *for the good of the souls of the dead.* Take a little for themselves for their trouble, as was the Greenlandish law of find and recovery.'

Hulde swallowing a small sip of wine.

'When was this?' she asks. 'When did all this happen?'

Irmgaard tipping her head, not the first to wonder why this young woman had such an interest in dates and times. Irmgaard doing her homework, had reread this book several times, absorbed its conclusions.

'The first people on Iceland seem to have been Irish monks who got there in the last years of the eighth century, although lord knows why.' Monks going anywhere and everywhere, usually only staying in places where they could browbeat the natives into their own preferred versions of religion. Not so Iceland, where there were no natives to be found.

'The Vikings,' she went on, 'have their first recorded circumnavigation of Iceland around 860. Greenland sighted by others not long after, blown off course.'

'So long ago,' Hulde murmurs. 'That's about fifty of my lifetimes. Almost exactly a thousand years ago.'

Irmgaard looking over at Heraldo.

'It never seems so long,' he says, as he'd said before, 'when Hulde puts it like that.'

Irmgaard shifting her gaze from Heraldo to Hulde, who was staring at the pages of the book, at the woodcuts made by Olaus Magnus in his *Historia* of 1555 about those earlier events. Irmgaard resisting the urge to translate her own life lengths into the lacuna lying between then and now.

'What's of most interest,' she says, clearing her throat, 'is what happened next. Back in Norway, where the merchant ship had sailed from, the kinsmen of those who perished got wind of it and the treasures. Saw the return of those treasures as their rightful inheritance. Got refused. Ozur and the other relations of the dead merchants getting very angry. And so,' she flips over a page, Hulde and Heraldo seeing a heavily underlined passage, a crude woodcut of the ensuing action, 'they took revenge. The bishop's ship was in harbour. Ozur and his men taking their axes to it, slashing holes into the strakes along the lengths of each side. Ruined it. Causing it to sink where it stood.'

Heraldo leaning back in his chair, Hulde letting out a long breath.

Here the explanation they'd been seeking. The how, the why. The germ of the idea. The *throw my coffin overboard*.

Marko, master carpenter taught by another master, his uncle, who had steeped his nephew in the lore and history of the North Atlantic sagas. Another nephew, Ozur, who believed the artefacts and coins of his ancestors rightly belonged to him and his. Holes hammered into the planks of the ship belonging to his perceived enemy. No axes needed latterly. Merely a bit and brace in the hands of the right man, in the hands of Marko, reader of the sagas, who had taken Ozur's claim as his own. Done as Ozur had done. Sunk a ship to save what he believed should not fall into the wrong hands.

Life and death of little consequence in the early settlements of Iceland and Greenland.

A precarious living.

Not unlike that of the peregrinatious Pfiffmaklers, who returned often to the village below St Vid, talking with Irmgaard and Yanni, performing their plays for the incoming sightseers whose numbers grew with every ongoing year.

This the way of the Pfiffmaklers.

A way that has done them well, for which I could not be more glad.

Hulde the one to tie everything up that last evening with Irmgaard.

'What do you really think about Marko?' she asked. Irmgaard pausing. Had thought on this over many a long evening. Would very much liked to have passed those long evenings with Grettir Wyssling. Still bitter Marko had taken so much from her, and from Yanni. Yanni having finally confessed his part in the proceedings, about which she swore Yanni must never mention again. Lips sealed, as Marko's had been about her husband Gregor.

'I think he tried to do right,' she said, 'but in doing so he did the worst wrong he could do.'

'I think he knew that, at the end,' Heraldo put in.

Enough for Hulde, for Irmgaard, and them all.

§

Only one man having a score to settle.

Jansen, about to remove himself from the Pfiffmakler encampment, learning that Jochen had not the slightest intention of removing the billy from the ostler's care.

Jansen incandescent.

'You'll get that fucking billy home if I have to break both your arms,' was Jansen's take.

'You and whose army?' was Jochen's reply. Jochen walking away. Whistling, like he'd not a care in the world.

Jansen approaching the ostler, passing over his last coins before being allowed to lead the billy away.

An entire bloody week to get back to Nyord. An entire bloody week of walking with that blasted billy biting and bucking in his harness at every turn.

Jansen couldn't have been happier.

Two belligerent buggers, cursing and kicking their way through life—admirable and honest, as Longhella had posited—going home.

As Heraldo had finally done.

Which is so often the best place in the world, wherever home happens to be.

Dedicated to Lynore Blackbeard, a woman I liked and admired. An artist not well done by in this world, who took her own Hundredth Door by her own choice in December 2018, as did my godfather Tony Sumner in 2024. In his mid-nineties when he'd had enough. Stopped eating, planned his end, dedicated his body to science.

At his asking I contributed to his Service of Celebration:

In the immortal words of *The Sound of Music* and of Dylan Thomas:

So long, farewell,
Auf Wiedersehn, good bye.
Go gently, Tony, into that dark night.

The title is derived from John Webster, *The Duchess of Malfi*.
I know death hath ten thousand several doors
For men to take their exits; and 'tis found
They go on such strange geometrical hinges,
You may open them both ways: any way, for heaven sake.

I've tinkered a little with the geography of Møns, Nyord, Borre and Magleby.

The Man Who Couldn't Get Warm is an old ballad. I have a version of it by the Seven Dials Band.

'On the first sounds made by animals': taken from *The Collins Field Guide to Wildlife Sounds* by Geoff Sample, HarperCollins 2006.

Niels Petersen, 1791–1862: *Guide to Northern Archaeology; in English, 1848.*

Gwyn Jones: *The Norse Atlantic Saga, 2nd ed.* OUP 1986
Hafgerðingadrápa, The Lay of the Towering Waves. Only four lines still extant, as stated.

Transit of Venus: nearest occurrence, given Jochen's looking out for it, was 1882.

Zvijezda: a guess on my part, because I can't find any actual references to Suvid other than that it's in the Dinaric Alps, and this name seems like a cognate.

The Goddess on the Throne: discovered in the 1950s; a symbol adopted by Kosovo, on display at their National Museum.